"HAVE I EVER TAKEN ANYTHING THAT YOU WEREN'T WILLING TO GIVE?"

"Yes," Blair screamed. "You are holding me against my will; you kidnapped me. But that wasn't bad enough—"

"Go on, Mrs. Teile. I'm breathless to hear the rest of this," Craig declared coldly.

"There is no rest," Blair denied too late.

"Oh, there is a rest, and if you're suddenly finding that the cat's got your rapier tongue, I'll finish for you," Craig interrupted. "You're hating me because you did trust me. Because you came to me. And you opened yourself to me. And now you think I've betrayed your trust, but you're wrong. And let's bear in mind that you came to my tent; I didn't drag you out of yours. And let's also be honest here. You asked for something. I merely gave it to you."

"You really are loathsome!" Blair raged furiously. More than any time before in her life she wanted to strike out and hurt, to cause pain as violent as the one that lay inside her.

"No," Craig retorted. "No, I'm not loathsome, nor am I even remotely so to you. But if by loathsome and traitorous you refer to the fact that I did eagerly accept you and take all that you offered—love, beauty, trust—then I do plead guilty. I wanted you from the moment I saw you, and if you became mine, and realized that you were a passionate, desirable, sensual creature, more a woman than you ever knew, don't ask me to apologize. We were two human beings touching, Blair."

<u>BOOK YOUR PLACE ON OUR WEBSITE AND MAKE THE READING CONNECTION!</u>

We've created a customized website just for our very special readers, where you can get the inside scoop on everything that's going on with Zebra, Pinnacle and Kensington books.

When you come online, you'll have the exciting opportunity to:

- View covers of upcoming books
- Read sample chapters
- Learn about our future publishing schedule (listed by publication month *and author*)
- Find out when your favorite authors will be visiting a city near you
- Search for and order backlist books from our online catalog
- Check out author bios and background information
- Send e-mail to your favorite authors
- Meet the Kensington staff online
- Join us in weekly chats with authors, readers and other guests
- Get writing guidelines
- AND MUCH MORE!

Visit our website at
http://www.zebrabooks.com

TEMPESTUOUS EDEN

Heather Graham

Zebra Books
Kensington Publishing Corp.
http://www.zebrabooks.com

ZEBRA BOOKS are published by

Kensington Publishing Corp.
850 Third Avenue
New York, NY 10022

First Zebra Printing: June, 1999
10 9 8 7 6 5 4 3 2 1

Printed in the United States of America

For Jason, Shayne, and Derek, and for our own little "princess," Bryee-Annon.
And for the very special people who have made it all possible, generously supplying faith, vision, time, and patience.
Anne, Mary Ellen, and Lydia—a true *paragon of patience!*
Thank you all so very, very much.

PROLOGUE

MEMO
From: Taylor
To: G.M.

Chief—

As per latest assignment, I have one main question.
WHY?

Taylor

MEMO
From: G.M.
To: Taylor

Taylor—

I have one main answer.
CLASSIFIED!

Your orders are concise. Stick with Huntington's daughter; keep her safe; keep her in the dark; move when told.

G.M.

MEMO
From: Taylor
To: G.M.

Sir:

Please! I have faced bullets in Londonderry, bombs in the Mideast, and dysentery in Africa. Don't do this to me. I am no good at baby-sitting Washington aristocracy.

Taylor

P.S. Couldn't you send me back to bullets, bombs, or dysentery?

MEMO
From: G.M.
To: Taylor

Taylor—

Sorry. No!
The powers that be have elected *you.* Think of it as a vacation. For you—a piece of cake.

G.M.

MEMO
From: Taylor
To: G.M.

Chief—

I have never been big on pastry. Why not send John Denner? This is much more his line.

                                                    Taylor

MEMO
From: G.M.
To: Taylor

Taylor—

Haven't you heard? "Real men *don't* eat quiche!" The higher echelon have spoken. My hands are tied. I repeat— consider it a vacation!

                                                    Sorry,
                                                    G.M.

MEMO
From: Taylor
To: G.M.

Dear Sir!

Harboring some do-gooder socialite is not my idea of a vacation. Withstanding "CLASSIFIED," can't she be told to get her cute butt out of Central America?

                                                    Taylor

MEMO
From: G.M.
To: Taylor

Taylor—

The woman you have been assigned to protect is hardly a child. But that is inconsequential. Answer is classified.

G.M.

P.S. If you are worried about ennui, relax. I hear our socialite is an independent wildcat who can make bombs and bullets and jungle hells seem tame.

MEMO
From: Taylor
To: G.M.

Chief—

Thanks.
Hail Caesar.
We who are about to die salute you.

Taylor

MEMO
From: G.M.
To: Taylor

Taylor—

Ha ha! Meeting with Huntington is scheduled for tomorrow at nine sharp. Don't be late.

G.M.

A man stood at the window of the sparse but elegant office. He was well past any definition of youth, yet his posture was straight, that of a young man despite the cap of white hair upon his head. His face, though weathered by time and the harried life he had chosen to lead, carried an expression of kindly dignity that could best be described as patrician, although he would have laughed with his rare, wry humor to even hear himself so termed. For he possessed another character trait rare for a man of his power—humility.

In four decades of service, Andrew Huntington had seen everything that was to be seen, yet his heart had never hardened.

He turned from the window to stare down at his desk. Manila folders covered parts of the newspaper clipping he gazed upon, but his eyes could still assimilate most of the story. The rest he knew by heart. And he knew it to be false, though by no fault of the reporter.

... seems to have simmered down. With the new government fully in power, the guerrilla activity has been mini-
mal, both near the capital and in the outlying areas. This
poverty-stricken and wartorn country appears to be making the first steps toward recovery, receiving the aid of
the U.S., other allied nations, and international relief organizations. Roberto Estevez, new head of Foreign Rela-
tions, announced yesterday: "The peace we have long
fought for is now within our grasp. . . ."

Andrew Huntington was not a man prone to unreasonable anger, but as a violent sweep of his hand sent the paper and the folders to the floor, his low curse described exactly what he thought of the contents of the clipping. From the instant he'd seen the article a few days ago, he had realized that it was time to get some gears moving. Sure, the guerrillas were quiet. And they would stay quiet as long as their intended prize was taken far from their reach.

Classified! he thought with pained anger. How he was coming to hate the word. The word that had ruled over so much of his life.

The time to take advantage of his position and the friends that he had in high places had come. The result: this morning's meeting with the visitor who now waited just outside his office door.

At the sharp rap on his door, Huntington bid his guest enter. He looked up as the younger man entered his office, and for a moment allowed himself the luxury of nostalgia. There had been a time when his own physique had been riddled with steellike muscles, when his face had been a basilisk of inner relentless power. A time when his own gaze had been direct, piercing. A time, many years ago.

But the temperance of age had come to him now, and his power lay in his wits. And it was now a time to use those wits for the one person who still gave his life true meaning.

But he also needed this man—this younger man with the physical strength—this practical stranger he had researched to the *n*th degree. He had watched his career with interest for years. An unassuming man of loyalty and principle, sometimes embarrassingly blunt, but straightforward in a way that made him completely trustworthy.

"Thank you for coming."

Andrew Huntington's visitor remained standing, hands clasped behind his back. He inclined his head briefly, his piercing yellow eyes set high and wide above a severe, hawklike nose, giving away nothing. And still, the older man stifled a smile. He knew how odious Craig Taylor was finding this assignment. But in all his years Huntington had never made a single request for himself.

Now he wanted a favor.

He wanted the best there was.

"Will you sit, please?"

Craig Taylor complied, crossing long, sinewed legs negligently and reaching into the breast pocket of a quiet but impeccably tailored navy suit. He lit a cigarette with clean, broad hands, inhaled and exhaled, returning a cool scrutiny all the while.

Huntington gave way to the smile tugging at his lips. This stranger didn't know what he was up against, and yet he was perfect for the job. Despite his polite and restrained manner, he exuded a force of determination. There was a touch of ruthlessness to him, but that was necessary too.

The older man leaned back in his seat behind the massive mahogany desk. "I think you have the details; I just thought that we should meet before you left. I also wanted to give you my personal thanks."

Craig Taylor finally smiled, but it was a rueful movement, full, sensual lips pulling back to bare a row of hard white teeth. "I won't lie to you, sir, I'm not happy about this."

"But you'll do your best." It was a statement, not a question.

"Yes." A little bitterly. "You will have my best effort."

Huntington grimaced. "You, sir, will need your best effort."

The younger man merely shrugged, and the white-haired Huntington hid another grin. Craig Taylor didn't know what he was up against.

"Sir"—an arm that should have belonged to a prize fighter leaned against the mahogany—"this could get very sticky. Possibly very dangerous. I don't understand. Why can't you just demand—"

"Please." Huntington waved a hand in the air and closed his eyes painfully. "I can't 'demand.' My daughter is almost thirty. She is mature, intelligent, and responsible," he said in a mutter, slightly bitter now himself, "but we're back to 'classified.' I can't explain further to you—orders on this one are coming straight from the Oval Office. Suffice it to say I have reason to believe we're past the point where she could leave by conventional means." His eyes clouded in a moment of unguarded fear. "Far worse things could happen. If she believes you're a terrorist, she'll survive. She has spirit."

"But, sir." Craig Taylor suffered a moment of discomfort. "She is most certainly going to fight me—"

"And, if and when we reach that point, you will employ *any* means necessary to keep her safe. Give me one month. Just one month. Our boys should have things under control by then."

"Any means, sir?"

Huntington paused and almost shuddered at the look in the hard, blazing cat eyes. He straightened with a sigh, but he nodded. He had been around a long, long time. Scrapes and bruises healed, so did anger cool and pride regain its strength.

Only life could not be redeemed.

"Any means," Andrew Huntington echoed softly. "Just keep her safe. Keep her safe, and if it comes to it, get her out."

Huntington barely recognized the Craig Taylor that sat beside him in an official limousine the next morning. He hadn't realized that the tawny hair, administered to sharply by a comb the previous morning, was quite so long, nor that a night's growth of beard could make his severely chiseled features appear so rugged and craggy. His business suit had been exchanged for worn jeans and a blue work shirt. Scuffed hiking boots adorned his feet.

Perfect. No hint to his identity, no way to tie him in.

"The picture I promised you." Huntington stuffed a Polaroid three-by-five into the younger man's hands. For a second his leathered features contorted. "She's all I've got."

"Yes, sir." Yellow-gold eyes swept the picture.

Princess, the young man thought. His term for her seemed correct. Emerald green eyes gazed out at him imperiously, a light in their sea depths hinting at the amusement that tinged the corners of beautiful, wide lips. The hair that flowed to her mid-back was a lustrous auburn, picking up highlights from the sun even in a picture. Her brows were delicate arches, high above the seascape eyes.

Her finely sculpted face was that of her father. More refined, more delicate, yet equally hinting of a cool, collected determination.

Terrific, he thought dryly. *I'm to play baby-sitter to a Park Avenue model.*

"Sir—" Craig began as the car came to an abrupt halt.

Suddenly looking very old, Huntington shook his head sadly with a knowing grin. "I doubt if things could be different without the 'classified' ratings. She hasn't much faith . . . you see, her husband was under protection when he was killed. And remember, she considers herself anonymous in relationship with me."

The younger man nodded emotionlessly. "Good-bye then, sir."

"Good-bye and good luck."

Craig Taylor tossed his duffel bag over his shoulder and strode toward the waiting plane.

Andrew Huntington smiled wanly as he heard the faint echo of his companion's single expletive.

How concise; he felt that way himself.

But it had to be.

CHAPTER ONE

It was a steamy, miserable day; perspiration was dripping stinging salt through her brows into her eyes. Blair Morgan impatiently swiped the back of her hand across her forehead. She
paused in her soup-ladling efforts to squeeze her eyes shut,
wryly thinking that the heat here today wasn't much worse
than on any tennis court in Acapulco or St. Martin. In all
honesty, she much preferred this place to those luxurious play-
grounds. Then, without warning, she felt the most absurd, unex-
plainable longing for home. Not D.C. per se, but the manor in
Maryland that was really home. The proud Georgian house
with its rolling acres of cool, blue-green landscape . . .

She blinked, and met a pair of small, deeply beseeching
brown eyes. God, she thought fleetingly, what a beautiful kid.
Then she snapped out of her trance to smile encouragingly and
serve him a bowl of soup.

"*Gracias, señora,*" the child whispered, silently adding,
angela de dios. Angel of God. She was beautiful, this *norteamericana,* with eyes like the greenest pasture and hair that flamed

like a brooding sunset, deep and rich. To the children she was kindness itself, but Miguelito also knew she was capable of being an avenging angel, like some of those out of the Old Testament in the Bible they studied with the padre at the chapel. He had seen her flame into action against the official-looking men who sometimes came in their big jeeps to inspect the compound.

"*De nada,* Miguelito, *de nada.*" She smiled, but she seemed distant, and Miguelito clutched his crust of bread and his soup bowl and moved away.

Blair continued ladling, wondering idly if her right arm would grow larger than her left with a massive muscle like the jai alai players she had met years ago in the Basque country of Spain. No, she told herself, glad to find a source of inner amusement, ladling soup was not comparable to jai alai.

Finally the waifs of the recently devastated village were all fed. Blair lifted her floppy straw hat from her head and waved it in the still air as she pulled back the neckline of her short-sleeved khaki shirt, the saturated material clinging to her body.

It was times like these that made having grown up filthy rich a pity. The only time she had actually ever perspired as a girl had been on purpose—to acquire a perfect tan. And when the sun bore down too heavily, she would simply roll into the shimmering water of the cool, crystal-clear pool.

Well, she wasn't a girl any longer, she told herself staunchly. Those days were gone forever. She was here in this war-ravaged country because she chose to be. Life had been good for her, but when it had fallen apart, she had decided to try and return some of the good.

The useful activity had kept her from growing bitter, from following a spin of society that might have resulted in only superfluous affairs to combat the loneliness of her first loss. And she was needed here. No one cast those you-can't-be-serious looks at her—looks which she had been schooled to tolerate whenever she had attempted to do something solid.

She winced, squinting her eyes into the sun. Analytically she supposed it was possible to understand such attitudes. She, the daughter of a wealthy man, had married a wealthy man. Even a master's in psychology did little to get it across to anyone that she was an intelligent human being, capable of manual labor. Thank God for Kate! Kate, who had believed she could do much more than preside over diplomatic teas with efficiency. Kate, who had helped her make her dear but possessive father realize that what she needed after the tragedy was an outlet for her energy and grief.

As she thought of her friend, Blair glanced up to see the slight, redheaded young woman walking over to her, waving a straw hat in the heat as she was. Blair laughed at her approach and called dryly, "I think you look as sticky as I feel."

Wrinkling her nose again, Kate cupped a bowl of the thin soup and stuck a finger in the tepid liquid to taste it. "I can tell you something that might make you feel a little better."

"What's that?"

"There's a beautiful little stream not a half a mile away." Kate sighed happily. Pleasures such as bathing were a luxury and not to be taken lightly.

"Wonderful! Are the males of our crew being gentlemen tonight and allowing us first dibs?"

She was teasing. Their crew consisted of six—three women and three men who were always gentlemen. Thomas Hardy was a dedicated doctor who was barely aware of his own wife, the cheerful matron who was the third female, Dolly. She claimed that staying with the Hunger Crew was the only way to see her own husband, but she was a motherly sort who couldn't be torn away from needy children. Harry Canton was a thin, studious fellow in his early twenties who blushed when a foul word was heard. Juan Vasquez, their native navigator, was a grandfather several times over and an educated man with a gracious Latin flair. He kept the women knowing they were feminine with a teasing charm he complained of being too old to fully vent upon them. He reminded Blair of a swarthy version of her own father.

"We get first dibs," Kate said cheerfully. "But Tom wants to see you in the med tent first. Seems we have a reporter coming in tomorrow, and he wants to warn you to make a disappearing act."

Blair groaned. The Hunger Crew was an apolitical organization, although it was supported by several governments. Every time a reporter came in, it was apparent he hoped to trap someone into voicing a political opinion—sure to twitch official noses. But it was worse than that for Blair. She used her mother's maiden name on official registrations, but if she was seen, her notoriety followed her. Few knew of her father, but even fewer failed to connect her face with that in the newsreels of Senator Teile's untimely and tragic death. The Hunger Crew accepted her anonymity; a reporter seeking a story did not.

"See Tom," Kate said. "I'll wait for you in the stream."

Blair strode quickly across the small compound to slip into the doctor's tent. As usual, when he wasn't busy patching up wounds or injecting antibiotics, his thin face was pressed into a book while he stroked his graying beard. Blair called his name twice to get his attention. He looked up absently, then slammed the book shut. "Blair," he smiled. "Come in. Sit."

She did, realizing as she perched on a hard, fold-up chair just how tired she was. "What's up?"

He scratched his head and vaguely grinned. She saw that he was unusually puzzled and serious. "Kate told you about the reporter?"

"Yes. Is there a problem?"

"No, no, the usual stuff. I really wanted to talk to you about something else."

"Oh?"

"Were you thinking of going home, Blair?"

Blair frowned, now puzzled herself. "Well, yes, but not now. I signed up for two years. That's some months off. Why?"

"We're being sent two new recruits," the doctor said, shaking his head slightly.

"That's wonderful!" Blair exclaimed. "You've been requesting extra help—"

"Yes, but never expecting to get it." He rose from his seat on his bunk and began to pace the hard earth floor. "I was just wondering . . ." He shrugged and looked directly at her. "Do you know something I don't?"

Blair shook her head. Tom Hardy never mentioned the family connections she wished to keep hidden, so she felt she owed him an honest answer. "I'm sure nothing big is up," she answered truthfully. "I just got a letter the other day." She smiled ruefully. "And I guarantee you, Dad would have given me dire warnings if there was a possibility of danger. No"— she shook her head again—"the elected government is now firmly in power. There hasn't been a report of guerrilla action in almost a month."

"Ah, well." He sat again, scratching his brow. "Maybe they've just begun to appreciate us a little!"

"That's probably it," Blair agreed, rising with a sheepish grin. "Now, if you don't mind—"

He waved a hand to her, picking up his book. "Get on out, Blair. Enjoy your swim."

She did. The stream was beautiful. Sheltered by a riot of multicolored foliage, it was a natural haven, running from the slope of a cliff with a bubbling noise that sounded delightfully like laughter. There was even a little place beneath sculpted rocks where the stream flowed off to form a small waterfall.

Kate was briskly drying herself when Blair appeared with soap in hand. "You won't believe this," she warned Blair, "but that water is actually cold."

"Good!" Blair laughed. She couldn't really remember what cold was, but the sensation, when her warm flesh hit the water, was marvelous. Goose bumps now rose on her skin, but she happily ignored them and swam leisurely to the waterfall, twisting her face to receive the cascade. She barely acknowledged Kate's wave and call of "I'm going back."

Nor did she notice that the foliage to the left of the foaming pool fluttered slightly without benefit of a breeze.

It would have never occurred to her on that late Sunday afternoon that she was being watched.

He stood in the bushes, motionlessly, his breath a whisper that joined the air, vital yellow eyes the only sign of life within him.

It was her. She didn't resemble the picture much at the moment, with her hair a sleek wet mane down her back, but her fine features were unmistakable. And, of course, she had been clothed in the picture. A muscle twitched in his jaw; he didn't like the role of voyeur. Yet he couldn't suppress a purely male, purely human appreciation. The photograph had given him no clue that her form was as fine as her face—healthy, tanned, with a wiry strength apparent in long slender arms, longer, shapely legs. Her breasts were high and firm; the narrow expanse of her waist and rounded curve of her hips inviting, just right for a man's hand.

Heat suffused through him that had nothing to do with the humid day, and he had to call on reserves of training to keep himself from wiping a new layer of sweat from his jaw. *Princess,* he reminded himself, efficiently quenching the ache in his loins with the reminder that he despised being where he was, and that it was the fault of her and her little tilted-nose defiance. . . .

Still, she did create a scene of surrealistic beauty, her form exquisite as she lingered in the cool, clear water, laughing with a melodious sound harmonious to the rush of the stream. Her legs were folded beneath her as she perched upon a boulder beneath the fall and lifted her arms high as if in supplication, stretching with an intoxicating arch of her supple back.

Damn. It was pathetic to be wishing himself back in the

Middle East. This assignment could just be the trigger to an early retirement. . . .

Eventually she left the stream and he was able to backtrack to his own small encampment. He ate a desultory meal without tasting it, and tried without success to make his lean body comfortable in a sleeping bag.

Despite the insect nets, he was eaten alive by mosquitos. When he finally slept, he had forgotten all haunting images of the woman in the stream.

He was too busy cursing her.

Craig Taylor drove his jeep into the complex of the Hunger Crew unit just as the pink streaks of dawn began to take on a yellow hue. Already there was a bustle of activity; scores of natives were lined up to receive portions of gruel from a massive iron pot.

His eyes quickly scanned the scene, but he didn't see Blair Morgan. A slim redhead was spooning up the sticky stuff that looked to be some type of porridge; a young man barely out of his teens was doling out milk to children; a middle-aged woman seemed to be dispensing fruit.

As the ignition of his jeep sputtered out, Craig saw a frazzled bearded fellow rushing out to meet him with an eager smile upon his face. And once again he silently railed against the powers that be for putting him in this position. The man was ecstatic over the extra help he thought he was receiving.

"Welcome! Welcome!" The bearded man extended a hand. "I'm Tom Hardy, in charge of this chaos."

"Craig. Craig Taylor," Craig returned, responding to the surprisingly strong and enthusiastic handshake. He grabbed his duffel bag and leaped agilely over the side of the jeep, twisting his features into a facsimile of a light-hearted grin. "Where do I start?"

"I like that exuberance." The doctor laughed, assessing the

new man. Odd, he didn't look the type to be here. In spite of his shaggy haircut and casual attire, something about his striking yellow eyes denoted authority. And he was built like steel piping. This was no young idealist out to save the known world. Oh, well, he decided philosophically, people all had their reasons for joining the outlands. He didn't ask a lot of questions; in his area he could judge a man or woman for themselves and for the fruits of their labor.

And as he thought of "fruits of labor" his smile increased to a degree that split his shaggy beard. It was going to be nice to have an intelligent and brawny man around. Especially with the supply wagon due in.

"For now," the doctor said, not at all ashamed to hide his elation, "you can meet the others. Later ... well, I'll have some heavy work for you. Unloading. Hope you won't mind being put into action."

"Not at all," Craig said, issuing his lie with remorse. "That's what I'm here for." Hell, he'd be happy as a lark to get anything done for the trusting doctor. The man was just as much a pawn as he. More so. Hardy didn't have the benefit of knowing.

"Come on along and meet the crew," Tom invited. "And I'll get you moved in."

Blair heard the arrival of the jeep and assumed that the reporter was arriving. It was time to make herself scarce.

Pulling her sunhat low over her forehead, she quietly disappeared into a trail behind the tents, becoming immediately swallowed up by the brush. She didn't need to push far into the jungle, nor did she care to. A little clearing within hearing distance of the compound afforded her shade from the heat and a smooth flat rock to call a chair. She settled down with a handbook to edible jungle foliage, determined to wait it out.

Blair quickly set aside her book, however, when she heard the arrival of a second jeep. Curiosity overrode caution and she tiptoed back through the sheltering trees.

The second jeep had brought the reporter—she knew it

instantly. The man alighting did not belong in the tropics. He was dressed in jeans all right, but designer jeans. She could see a multitude of labels even from her distance. He wore a tailored shirt, the long sleeves rolled to his elbow. A pencil was perched behind his ear; his stance was a swagger.

A budding Cronkite, Blair thought dryly. Her life hadn't left her overly fond of reporters. Some were responsible professionals, but she had also met those devoid of sensitivity or a sense of responsibility about getting the facts straight.

Blair listened idly while Dr. Hardy droned on in bored, clipped tones, bluntly refusing to give an opinion on anything that involved the politics of this remote, ravaged country, no matter how the young Cronkite persisted. The interview didn't last long; Dr. Hardy knew his place in life; he knew what he wanted, what he was doing. No reporter was going to twist anything out of him except the mundane truth—the Hunger Crew had one purpose, and one purpose only: to bring relief to the civil victims of disaster.

The young reporter was obviously discouraged. Dr. Hardy turned away even before the man had climbed into the jeep. Ready to take the short walk back, Blair suddenly froze instead. Apparently the man had spotted her hair through the trees. Instinct was pulling him out of the jeep again, and in her direction.

Blinding, bitter memories of the press kept her feet still when she should have been moving. The reporter didn't know who she was yet, but if he came any closer . . .

Her feet had almost begun to move when immobility assailed her again, this time from surprise.

"Where do you think you're going?" A deep voice leaped out at the reporter, spinning him in his tracks.

Blair glanced swiftly from the reporter to the unknown man issuing the curt demand. He was another stranger, a man to fit the voice, so tall that his tawny head would brush the peak of their tents. He wasn't looking at her, but at the bothersome visitor, his yellow stare a tangible thing that fixed the reporter where he stood. There was a definitive aura of danger to the tall, tawny man, an essence of quiet power that seemed to radiate throughout the compound. Blair could well understand the reporter's hesitance to take another step.

Suddenly the stranger looked her way and she met his eyes. A slight smile of understanding twitched the corners of his lips and then he turned his attention back to the reporter, who was saying he'd like to interview a few more members of the crew, particularly the woman disappearing into the jungle.

Blair listened while the stranger stated firmly that the woman had no desire to be interviewed. There had been something in those topaz eyes that had met her briefly, an empathy that went beyond the timely protection he offered. He was a man she knew instantly that she was going to like, and yet also . . . fear. His entire bearing was too openly masculine, assured, imposing. His eyes were too knowing.

She wasn't sure what was being said anymore, but the stranger gave the reporter a wicked grin, one that didn't touch his piercing eyes. Blair held back a chuckle as she saw the cool, swaggering reporter—not so cool or swaggering anymore—duck by his brawny adversary and hightail it back to his jeep. The vehicle roared into quick action, coughing and sputtering, ripped into gear, and skidded off into the direction from whence it had come.

Yellow eyes flicked at her briefly through the trees and once more met hers. Bemused and compelled, Blair smiled back and began to make her short return trip through the foliage.

She came to him in the compound and for a moment they both stared at each other, smiling over the reporter's hasty exit.

"Ms. Morgan," the man said with an easy grin.

For some reason, they both broke into laughter at the same time. Blair offered her hand to him, surprised at the little constriction that circled her heart.

He wasn't the handsomest man she had ever come across—

his features were far too severe—but he was certainly the most striking. His unusual eyes seemed to exude a fiery power; she was sure no one who had seen his gaze could have ever forgotten it.

"I'm at the disadvantage," Blair told him, wryly feeling the unintended double entendre. She was a medium five foot five; the man stood a good head above her. "You know who I am, but"—she grinned bluntly—"but who are you?"

"Craig Taylor." He smiled in return. "I was to introduce myself, but I stumbled into your little predicament. I'm one of the new recruits."

"Oh," Blair murmured, shielding puzzled eyes with thick lashes that matched the dark flame of her hair. Like Dr. Hardy, she was thinking that the man simply didn't fit, although, unlike the reporter, he did know how to dress for a mucky jungle. His jeans were worn, but made of heavy duty, work-weight denim. His shirt was breathable cotton, a standard blue work shirt. Peeking at the ragged hem of his jeans, she saw a commendable pair of sturdy boots.

"Do I fit the bill?" he asked dryly.

Blair flushed, and her eyes flew back to his, which were flashing a golden amusement. She had definitely been caught in the act of assessment. "Yes," she mumbled hastily, then grimaced. "No. Actually," she told him bluntly, "you look like a cross between Tom Selleck and a leftover from the Haight-Ashbury days."

He laughed easily. "I think I'm supposed to thank you for the first, and as to the second—leftover—huh!"

"Craig!"

The call came from the doctor's med tent before Blair could respond.

"I think I'm being paged. I'll see you later and you can give me proper thanks." He grinned with a devastating charm that made his devilish features beguiling. "I did save you from the one fate worse than death—a reporter!"

Suddenly feeling a little on the defensive, and abruptly aware that the man could be dangerous in a way she hadn't previously suspected, Blair crossed her arms over her chest and unconsciously adjusted her casual stance to a straighter, more dignified one. "I appreciated your timely arrival." She frowned. "But I was fully capable of handling the situation myself."

"So I've been told."

Did she detect a subtle shadowing in those yellow eyes? A dry bitterness in his tone? No, he was still smiling easily.

"Okay," he joked, "I exaggerated. Will I see you at dinner?"

"Around here," she replied ruefully, "there really isn't a tremendous choice."

"We all eat together, huh?"

"More or less."

Craig rubbed a firm chin hinting of stubble as if he were in deep contemplation. "Save me a seat—or ground space—beside you."

Blair smiled, relaxing her guard slightly at the earnestness of his appeal. And admittedly he was intriguingly attractive. She couldn't deny that her heart fluttered more quickly in his imposing presence, or that her breathing quickened by more than a pace. It had been a long time since she had been so touched by a man, if she had ever experienced such an instant reaction. If she were as smart as she felt herself to be, she would steer clear of him immediately. If this little encounter was stirring long-dormant senses . . .

But it would be impossible to really steer clear of anyone in the unit, or so she argued. And despite her fairy-tale marriage and the shattering tragedy, she didn't consider herself an emotional cripple. He was a fascinating man. She would like to get to know him.

"Sure," she murmured, the nonchalance of her comment marred slightly by the warm tint that rose to her cheeks again. "I'll save you a place."

"Thanks," he grinned, pausing in a lithe movement to add, "and if you tell me what Blair Morgan is doing in this godforsaken place, I'll tell you why Craig Taylor is here."

"Well," Blair hedged, "we'll see."

"Yes, we will, won't we?"

Searing yellow eyes held hers an instant longer, then he waved nonchalantly and his tawny-headed height and breadth strolled away with leisurely assurance.

Blair stared after him for a moment, pondering her unease. She was terribly attracted to him, alarmingly so. But despite his easy banter, she sensed a tension in him, a powerful energy that simply didn't jell.

He was clearly an intelligent man; his eyes absorbed everything they pierced. But he was also starkly physical, a man of action.

What was he doing in the jungle? Would the stories she received tonight be any more honest than the ones she would tell?

It was obvious he knew she was Ray Teile's widow. Why else shield her from a reporter? But he didn't look like a reporter looking for a scoop himself. Was he showing her a special interest?

Perhaps he knew of her father?

The night should, at least, she decided, prove interesting.

CHAPTER TWO

That night, though Blair did make good on her promise, Craig did not join the group for dinner until most everyone had finished. Odd, Blair thought, for his first night with the crew. But perhaps his work during the day had tired him out. Then there was the change in climate to contend with; the steamy rain forest heat was capable of sapping the strength from even the fittest specimen. *Even* from Craig Taylor, she thought, smiling to herself. How many nights had she returned to her tent after a long hot day, too exhausted to eat or even talk? Too bone weary to do anything but sleep.

Though he did sit down beside her, favoring her with a special smile in greeting, Craig talked and joked easily with everyone. He seemed totally relaxed in their company, as if he had been with the crew for months instead of merely hours. He was charming them, Blair noted, just as he had charmed her earlier in the day.

Instead of joining the others at the fireside after the meal was cleared, Craig was the first to say good night and return to his tent. Blair had expected ... Well, what had she really expected? She stretched out wearily on her cot and stared up at the low canvas ceiling of her tent, her eyes just becoming adjusted to the dark. Had she expected to be singled out by this man? To be joined at the fireside and maneuvered into a private conversation? Yes, she had to admit that she'd expected the evening to go that way. Now that it hadn't happened at all like that, she didn't know whether she felt relieved or disappointed.

Blair found that his behavior toward her that first night was to set the pattern for the following days. Though she did catch sight of him as they both moved around the complex on their assigned duties, they didn't have a chance to speak at all, except during dinner. From the little she observed of him at work, she did have to admit that whatever his reason for joining their crew, he did it wholeheartedly. The unloading of the vehicles usually took two workers the majority of the week to complete. Craig Taylor was managing nicely by himself in what would be the same amount of time, or less.

On those nights when she did speak to him at dinner, or at the fireside afterward, he certainly wasn't standoffish, yet Blair sensed nothing more in his feelings toward her than friendly interest. He certainly showed her no more attention than he showed to any other member of the crew. He had yet to make good on his promise to explain why he joined the crew. But she decided not to pursue it. Inexplicably drawn to this man, Blair was still aware of some instinctual suspicion or even fear that his disturbing presence aroused in her. He was right in every way; yet, she did not trust him.

On Friday afternoon he had stripped off his shirt, and in passing him Blair had surprisingly shared her father's impression—the man should have been a prize fighter.

Perhaps not. He was excessively tall, six-three or six-four, if her estimation was correct, but not quite heavy enough for a fighter. His muscles, rippling golden beneath a merciless sun, were not massive or unwieldly, but rather tight coils of sleek, enduring iron. His abdomen was as tight as a drum. His shoulders were broad, but narrowed to his waistline like a triangle. His chest was thickly tangled with tawny hair that burnished and glistened in the rays of the sun, and when he glanced at her to give her a quick smile, she caught sight of his yellow eyes again. She smiled in return, but her unease tingled her flesh. The smile softened features that could best be described as severe, rugged, and craggy, but those features, coupled with the compelling eyes and startlingly powerful physique, suddenly gave her the impression that she was facing a lion, supreme in his own might, lord of his territory. He moved with assured, controlled tension, yet she felt he contained a leashed force that could explode upon the unwary at any time, and God help that unfortunate prey. A lion, stalking his victims playfully until the pounce.

"Stop ogling, Blair," someone whispered in her ear. "It's rather impolite . . ."

Blair spun around guiltily at the tap on her shoulder. Kate was staring at her with a mischievous smile. "I wasn't ogling," Blair protested dryly. "I was wondering what the hell he's doing here."

"Okay," Kate laughed. "You wonder, *I'll* ogle!"

"Seriously Kate—"

"Oh, Blair, don't look a gift horse in the mouth."

Blair raised speculative brows in an arch of wisdom. "What about a Trojan horse? He just doesn't look as if he belongs here."

Kate laughed ruefully and gave her friend a wry assessment. "And you do?" Devoid of makeup, her dark flame hair in a knot, her slender figure covered in well-worn jeans and a plain brown work shirt, Blair was still strikingly lovely and still exuded an air of breeding and regal poise.

"Oh, brother!" Blair murmured in defeat. She couldn't really explain her feelings to herself; it would be impossible to get them through to Kate. She waved briefly as she headed toward the med tent. "See you later. I have a whole pack of trusting little souls awaiting my tender touch with a needle."

Kate sniffed, calling, "Lucky you. I'm on lice squad."

Laughing, Blair hurried back. She had been staring—ogling, wondering, speculating, whatever!—longer than she had meant to. The tent was filled with scared little faces, all watching her with wide brown soulful eyes that proclaimed her the wolf and they the lambs for slaughter.

She paused for a second at the tent flap, filled with anger and steeling herself for the task. It was the children who were always hurt, she thought. Generals waged self-righteous campaigns, shouting the valiant triumph of victory. The children lost their homes, their parents, their limbs. Sometimes they lost their lives.

Blair didn't give a damn what set of guerrillas claimed power. She lived in the political arena all her life and learned the sad truth that the best man didn't necessarily win, nor even the most powerful.

It was the most eloquent speaker who usually took the prize.

Not that there weren't good men in that arena. Her father, personal bias aside, was one of the finest men alive. He had served with and under many fine statesmen.

But character and principle weren't always enough to keep the wheels of political machinery running smoothly. Those in power, even when possessed of high principles, had to look at the whole, and they often had to turn their backs on suffering.

They couldn't allow themselves to take a good look at the things she had seen.

Blair gave herself a little shake. Philosophizing was getting nothing done. She lined her charges up and spoke soothingly to the children as she prepared inoculations, making a game of the shots. After a quick swipe with a cottonball soaked in alcohol on each little arm she drew a happy face, swabbing in eyes and a mouth with sunny yellow marks, which were actually a disinfectant.

The nose, she explained, was the lightning quick and expert injection she gave. Each child left the tent not quite sure of what had happened, but much closer to laughter than tears.

She was unaware as she worked that a pair of leonine eyes peered into the tent at one point, observing.

Dr. Hardy, however, did come upon Craig. "Quite an amazing woman, our Blair, don't you think?" he inquired of the newcomer. He smiled with what he thought was sound perception. "But watch out for her, Taylor. I think God made redheads with fire in their hair to warn of the fire within."

Craig laughed at the dire warning. "I'll watch out, Doc." His expression sobered and he continued with a tone of apology the doctor couldn't understand. "She is amazing. Really good at what she does. Not one of those kids has let out a squeal."

"I taught her everything she knows," the doctor said proudly, his furred lips then twisting in a sheepish grin. "Not that teaching was much effort. She picked it all up within two weeks—including the language. Which isn't surprising—" The doctor clamped his jaw shut. It wasn't surprising that this woman had such a high intelligence quotient and a facility with languages—not when you knew who her father was. But that was confidential information, and he had almost baldly handed it over to this stranger.

He sighed with relief when it appeared that Craig Taylor wasn't going to press him. He stroked his beard and reached for the tent flap. "Guess I'd better get back to work," he said absently. "How's the unloading going?"

"Done."

"Done?" Tom shook his head as if a magician had just waved a wand. "Damn, Taylor, I'm sure going to like having you around."

"Yeah, thanks."

It appeared that the sandy-haired giant winced, and Tom

frowned in a moment of perplexity. Then he shrugged. This was not the type of man who needed to be patted on the back. Actually, few who stuck it out in the corps did.

The man with the piercing yellow eyes slipped a serene smile back into his features. "Looks like they're struggling with that fire over there." He pointed to the clearing where Kate, his wife, Dolly, and young Harry Canton were indeed having problems starting the dinner fire beneath the huge black kettle which would furnish a nourishing stew that night. "I guess I'd better run over and lend a hand." With a rueful wave he strode toward the gathering.

Dr. Hardy went on into the tent, still shaking his grizzled head. Blair was drawing her last happy face on a little brown arm. "Annnnnnnd . . . pop! There goes his nose!" she said in barely accented Spanish, grinning cheerfully. The youngster looked from Blair to his arm, confused as to whether he had been hurt or not. It had been so quick. He laughed at the smiling *señora*.

"All done," Blair told him. "Go on now, there will be dinner at the big pot soon." As the child scampered out of the tent with a broad smile, Blair turned tiredly to the doctor. "That's the lot of them. Anything else on the roster for me?"

"Nope." Dr. Hardy shook his head with a pleased grin. "Our new man put us way ahead of schedule."

Blair rose from her seat on the cot and stretched with a slight frown. 'What do you think of him?" she asked.

"I think I'm in love," Dr. Hardy replied quickly with a rare quirk of humor "They've finally sent me a man."

"But why?" Blair mused, tapping her chin reflectively with a forefinger.

"I don't really care," he said bluntly. "He's here, and he's a goddamned work horse." Patting Blair's back, he added, "Be careful not to chase him away with your questions, huh? I've seen that devious gleam in those eyes, and you're up to no good. Give the guy a break; he might be looking for a little privacy just like you are. I don't let anyone give you the third degree; now, don't you do it to him.''

Her emerald eyes could appear very innocent when she wished. ''I'm not going to chase away Hercules on you! He's already offered to tell me why he was here.''

''Well, then you'll have your answer.''

Still not satisfied, Blair murmured, ''Why me?''

The doctor chuckled as he began to clear up various medical paraphernalia. ''If you don't know the answer to that one, young lady, we have had you in the brush too long.''

''You think he's attracted to me?'' Blair frowned.

''I know he's attracted to you, and''—with a friendly gesture he tugged on the neat knot of her hair—''so do you. And I think you're attracted to him, otherwise you'd leave the poor fellow alone.''

''He is attractive,'' Blair allowed, taking no offense. ''But don't you see—he's *too* attractive.''

''Maybe that's because you see too few strong healthy men your own age,'' he suggested, scowling as he realized he had a stone in his boot.

Blair shook her head with renewed exasperation and grasped his elbow to steady him as he pulled off his boot to remove the offending pebble. ''I wasn't born in the wilderness, Tom. This guy isn't like other men. Not even like attractive other men. And I'm not saying that to pretend I don't find him . . . arresting . . .''

''Sexy,'' the doctor interjected, refitting his boot.

''All right, I'll grant you the semantics.'' Blair gave in with a slight twinge of pink reaching her cheeks. ''But he's more than sexy. He's confident, powerful. A man like that knows where he's going in life. This type of life could offer him no challenge.'' The doctor wasn't replying, and Blair finally grew frustrated trying to get her point across. There really weren't words to describe what she felt. It wasn't that she believed Craig Taylor incapable of giving. In fact, she believed he would give generously of his time, strength, and talent. But this just wasn't what she thought would be his choice for an outlet.

"Oh, never mind," she sighed, releasing his arm as he regained his own balance. "I'm heading for the stream."

"Have a nice bath." He waved her on, his mind already moving on to other subjects, if she had really ever had his attention in the first place.

In her small private tent she collected her soap and a towel and rummaged through her clothing. The good doctor was right about one thing—she was extremely attracted to Craig, and she wasn't sure whether she liked the feeling or not. In a way it was wonderfully exciting; it seemed like forever since her senses had been touched in the least by a man. It was also nerve-racking. She had made a sound point herself, which her friend had totally ignored. *Craig Taylor was no ordinary man.* In a field of thousands, he alone would stand out, exuding power, exuding vibrancy, exuding quick and perceptive intelligence with topaz eyes.

Blair realized a little ruefully that she was rummaging through her clothing so thoroughly because she was determined to find her most attractive "brush" outfit. Craig *was* a wild stimulation that she couldn't deny, and she was automatically responding as a female.

Merely sound tactics, she assured herself. If she was entering a battle of wiles with this man, the better her tactics and ammunition, the better her chances of emerging the victor. She wasn't a politician's daughter for nothing.

Her hands suddenly went clammy and she sank to her sheet-covered cot. Her marriage—which she had entered into with the natural enthusiasm of any young bride—had gone from happiness to tragic misery so fast that it had taken up to now, and the presence of Craig Taylor, for Blair to realize that she had never been this affected by a man before. She had socialized a bit after Ray's death, and indifferently accepted good-night kisses, but had never been stirred as she had by the sound of

Craig's voice and the sight of his lean body and magnetic eyes. She had never even been so stirred by Ray Teile. . . .

He was just a man, she told herself sternly.

He wasn't just a man.

But stirred or not, she wasn't a naive innocent herself. She was an experienced widow. She wasn't sure why she was going to battle with Craig, but she was. They were skirting each other carefully now; the depths of their diplomatic war would have to surface later.

Impatient with herself, she stood purposefully and grabbed soap, towel, and clothing—the best she had with her, a tailored blue cotton shirt and her least worn out pair of jeans—and hurried out of her tent across the compound.

Kate was still busy ladling out food. Unable to resist, Blair caught her friend's eye. "I'll be waiting for you at the stream!"

Kate rewarded her with a good-humored grimace.

The sound of the water was soothing, as was the wild and colorful beauty of the foliage and the small jagged cliffs that bordered the stream. Blair could almost feel the water against her skin as she approached the embankment—and stopped short.

Someone had reached the stream ahead of her.

A pile of dirty clothing lay in a neatly bundled ball beneath the outstretched arm of a sturdy oak. Upon the branch rested a clean pair of blue jeans and a tan cotton shirt similar to her own.

Craig.

She didn't see him in the water, but she knew it was he without even recognizing the dirty clothing. Her senses sent out an alarm that warned her it was he. Slight shivers began to play havoc, rising from the base of her spine to spread to every limb. Her mind was working entirely on its own, imagining his golden torso emerging from the water in glistening masculinity, his hips, as sturdy and trim as the oak.

Oh, Lord! she chastised herself, backing away from the stream with self-annoyance. She had been in the brush too long.

No, it wasn't that. He was unique.

And it wasn't her imagination anymore. His sandy head, darkened by the water, emerged, his hawk-rugged features, then the broad, matted torso gleaming bronze from the shimmering stream just as she had imagined.

Yellow, impaling eyes caught hers. A slow grin crept into sensuously full lips. "Coming in?" he called.

Blair shook her head, but she ceased backing away. If he had already seen her, she wasn't going to run like an adolescent.

"When you come out, Mr. Taylor, I'll go in," she called. "I guess we forgot to tell you the protocol. Ladies get first dibs on bathing facilities."

"Sorry," he shouted in return, staying in the water respectably to his waistline. Still, the thick brush of sandy hair that covered his chest thinned as it approached his navel, and continued, presumably extending in a narrow line until it thickened again in parts concealed by the water. Blair found with irritation that she was having difficulty maintaining eye level contact— hers wanted to follow that enticingly suggestive line of damp, coarse curls. He walked closer to the shore and for a second Blair feared he would walk boldly out.

But he didn't. He had simply come close enough for them to carry on an audible conversation without shouting at each other over the bubbling of the stream and the roar of the cascade.

"I couldn't find anything else to do," he explained, folding his arms over his chest as an engaging smile curled his lips. "I wandered around until I found this place, then ran back for my clean clothes."

Blair smiled, dimly aware that the danger in his eyes was only masked by his boyish grin. "That's all right," she told him, "you don't need to apologize. We should have told you."

He cocked his head suddenly and laughed. "I think you may

eventually be glad I accidentally broke protocol. I made another discovery that I'll bet you haven't yet.''

''Oh?'' His eyes, Blair realized, were not, of course, really yellow at all. They were hazel—lime green with golden brown stars shooting from the irises like crystal in a marble. ''What's your discovery?''

''Un-unh.'' He shook his head ruefully. ''My discovery can't be explained. You have to see it for yourself, and since you don't want to join me . . .'' He lifted his hands with a parody of sad regret.

''That's a hell of a line if I've ever heard one,'' Blair said, smiling dryly,

''I'm crushed!''

''The hell you are.'' Nothing, she was sure, would ever crush him.

He raised both brows and shrugged. ''One day,'' he promised lightly, ''I will show you my glorious secret and you'll regret that scorning distrust. But for the moment''—his brows rose even higher and he inclined his head toward his clothing— ''why don't you turn around so that I don't insult your virtue further.''

Blair took a few steps past the tree and turned, nonchalantly crossing her arms over her chest. She was trembling and praying her demeanor would keep him from noticing. There had been times after Ray's death when she had considered escaping to anywhere with anyone, just to convince herself that she was still normal, capable of a feminine passion that could bring pleasure.

But wisdom had tempered that frivolity. She would never prove anything, and possibly harm herself further, by attempting an affair without emotion or true desire.

Now, suddenly, out of the clear blue, when she didn't want the attraction, it was so strong that it was a fevered desire.

Even the emotion was there. She didn't trust the yellow-eyed enigma of a man, but, inherently, she liked him. She sensed him with each nerve end as he left the water; she felt his powerful but supple movements resonate throughout her entire body. . . .

"Can I borrow your towel? I won't soak it too badly, I promise."

"Please, go right ahead." A statesman's daughter could keep her voice level.

It was an excruciating eternity, but he finally quipped, "I'm decent."

Blair hadn't known she was holding her breath until she let it out. She turned to find him watching her with open speculation as he reached into his pocket to produce cigarettes and a lighter.

"Smoke?"

"Yes, thanks." She accepted a cigarette, noting with approval that her fingers were steady. Their eyes met, very close, as she leaned toward him to accept a light. Smoke plumed into the air, yet still they held, assessing each other, which for a minute neither attempted to hide.

"American," Blair said with appreciation, studying the cigarette.

Craig chuckled. "Yes, I brought a few other American goodies with me for the entire crew."

"Oh?" Blair said. By mutual agreement they sank to sit casually on the grassy embankment. "What are you, independently wealthy?" Dr. Hardy would have her neck for that one.

Taylor wasn't offended. "Not independently, I'm afraid. I inherited a nice little trust fund." So far he wasn't lying. He had purchased everything he brought himself, and also made a sizable contribution to the main offices of the organization. But he could hardly pat himself on the back for that; he did have money, inherited money, that he could take a lifetime to spend. "What about yourself?"

He didn't have to ask the question; he knew everything academic that there was to know about Blair, not only the date of her birth, but the exact minute and even her mother's hospital room number. But all the dossiers in the world couldn't really give him an answer to just what this fiery, independent, and determined woman was *herself*.

Blair inhaled deeply on the cigarette and shrugged, thinking out her reply carefully. "Guilty of the same, I'm afraid. I grew up in the lap of luxury."

"And you've repudiated it all?" A smile touched his lips.

"No," she grinned dryly in return. "I have nothing against responsible wealth. I never wanted to throw it all away. I think a lot of good can be done with money channeled correctly, and, as the saying goes, it takes money to make money." She laughed a little in admission. "Besides, I'm extremely fond of good plumbing systems, lobster Newburg, and, when available, silk sheets."

"Then what are you doing here?" Craig demanded.

"I said 'I'm fond of,' not 'I can't live without,' " Blair reminded him. Damn! She was doing all the talking. Time to reverse the questions as he had.

"What about you?"

He shrugged, inhaling deeply. "I ran away from home once twenty years ago, but ran back for dinner." His eyes were alight with amusement. "You appreciate the silk sheets and the lobster Newburg a whole lot more when you've been away. I did a stint in 'Nam, saw a bit of Europe and the Middle East, and also learned that you could live without what you're fond of." That also was basically truth.

Yet they really hadn't told each other a thing.

Craig crushed out his cigarette and hopped lithely to his feet, once more reminding her of something leonine. "I'd better leave you to your bath," he said with a grin, walking cheerily away.

Round one was over.

Blair rose slowly in his wake, unbuttoning her shirt as she watched his broad back disappear through the brush-strewn trail. Her betraying fingers began to quiver, and she fumbled with her clothing. *Damn, what is with me?* she groaned to herself.

The more she talked to him, the more she saw him, the more she wanted him. And she didn't really think he'd be averse to the idea—the problem was in letting him know . . .

She jumped into the stream.

The cool deliciousness of the water soothed the heat of her flesh, which wasn't only from the sun today. She chuckled dryly as she imagined herself being deadly honest with Craig. *Excuse me, Mr. Taylor, I feel I should tell you first that I don't trust you as far as I could spit nails, but I think I'd like to go to bed with you. I say* think, *you see, because I'm just slightly terrified. You see, I had everything once . . . and I lost it and I'm scared and would you mind being very gentle, and very tolerant?*

"Hey! How's the water?"

Kate interrupted those shockingly lascivious thoughts as she approached the stream, unabashedly shedding sweat-soaked clothing while still on the trail.

"Nice and cool, Kate," Blair replied.

Unfortunately it wasn't quite cool enough.

Craig Taylor had promised to provide a "special treat" for Friday's dinner, and he had certainly come through. The wine was French, and there were several bottles of it, somehow smuggled through in his duffel bags.

It wouldn't last long. But it did provide them with one night of real feasting.

Happy chattering and ribald compliments cheered his effort on as Craig loosened the first cork and Blair knew she had never attended an affair of state that offered such honest-to-God pleasure and amiable camaraderie. The illusion of luxury was more glittering than a hundred-tiered chandelier.

"All we need are the silk sheets!" she laughed to him as she handed him her tin cup to acquire her portion of wine. He glanced at her, and she realized the possible implication of her statement. She hoped the heat of the fire hid that of her face, and her lashes dropped quickly, rich crescents of deepest auburn against her cheeks. Yet before she shielded her vision, she caught something in his remarkable lion eyes that hadn't been there before, that bore no resemblance to danger, query, or lust. . . .

It had been tenderness, but a tenderness touched by a wincing pain.

And it had disappeared completely, as if it had never been, by the time she steadied her cup and looked back up.

Craig filled his own cup with wine and helped himself to a plate of stew, the crew's fare for that night.

"Let's take our dinner over by that oak," he suggested, balancing his plate and tin of wine as he indicated a heavily dipping tree that offered semiseclusion and privacy.

Blair found herself mutely nodding, and preceding his indicated lead.

The light of the fire was some distance from them as they took their seats on the ground, erecting a wall of partial darkness between them and the others who laughed and chatted nearer the tents of the compound.

Craig clinked his mug to hers, and the tin gave off a sharp rap. "To those of us who can admit we prefer silk sheets," he toasted. "And by the way, when do you plan to return to yours?"

"A few more months," Blair replied, digging immediately into a portion of stew composed mainly of vegetables and native potatolike roots. One of the benefits of the Hunger Crew was the impossibility of getting fat while being a member. "I signed up for two years. I'll go back when my stint is over—and when my replacement arrives."

"Anybody waiting for you to come home?" Craig asked nonchalantly.

"No," she murmured, concentrating on her food. "Well, yes. My father."

"Other than a parent," he said softly. "I know that you're a widow, but it's been a while. Is there a friend, a lover—"

"No," Blair interrupted him quickly. "No one like that."

Craig said nothing, continuing to chew. He knew his questions were too personal; they might be painful. He was treading in dangerous waters, pushing, maybe too far. He didn't know why he had voiced the questions in the first place, except, as a man, he'd wanted to hear answers from her own lips. They couldn't expect him to always *think* like a damned machine.

"Your turn."

"Pardon?" He glanced from his food to Blair to find her openly meeting his eyes.

"Your turn," she repeated blandly. "Have you anyone waiting for you. A wife . . . a lover . . . ?"

"No. I've always traveled a great deal. I've never thought it fair to impose myself on a wife."

Blair saw him suddenly stiffen; his keen yellow gaze went instantly alert and scanned the foliage near them as he quietly set down his plate.

"Wha—" she began in puzzlement.

He touched a finger to her lips and indicated the dark brush behind them, then hopped to his feet silently, the leonine agility never more visible and chilling as he moved without a sound. He took a few steps, and his arm lashed out through the trees.

He pulled forward a trembling Miguelito. "My God, boy! What are you doing sneaking up on people through the trees?" Craig demanded, giving Blair a surprise as he spoke in Spanish far superior in accent to hers.

The boy stood shaking, terrified of the towering man. His eyes turned to Blair, pathetically seeking mercy. Blair glanced from the boy to the man, shaking her head just slightly and hunching her shoulders. She gave her full attention to the child, speaking with reassurance. "No one is going to hurt you, Miguelito. You startled us, you frightened us by crawling around. You should be home in the village with your mother. Why are you out here?''

The simple story came out in broken bits and pieces. Miguelito had smelled the food. The enticing aroma had been too much for his young discipline, and he had doubled back to the camp as if pulled by a string.

''Oh, hell!'' Craig muttered. ''Is that it?''

''What were you expecting?'' Blair asked him, her arm protectively and defensively around the boy.

Craig merely shook his head, dismissing the subject. He stooped down for his plate and offered the untouched stew to the little boy. ''Enjoy it, Miguelito, but don't tell your *compadres,* huh? There isn't any more tonight where this came from.''

Blair was feeling a pang for having wolfed down her own meal so quickly that she'd had nothing to offer the boy. She was still feeling tingles race down her spine from having watched Craig. She hadn't heard a thing from the trees—the natives could run through the countryside as quiet as mice— but Craig had been so instantly alert and prepared that it was more chilling than the thought of being secretly observed.

He had been in 'Nam, he had told her. He most certainly had learned the intricacies of jungle defense there.

And it was hard to be suspicious of a man who had just turned his own meal over to a hungry waif.

''What are you going to eat?'' she asked Craig in quiet English.

He shrugged indifferently. The keen light of danger had left his eyes; a subtle mask of amusement replaced it. ''I eventually get to go back to the lobster Newburg. Miguelito doesn't.''

Yes, but not tonight, Blair thought with a touch of admiring respect. Craig had done the work of a bulldozer during the day. With his physique, there could be little doubt that the kindly act of giving away his food would cause him some serious hunger pangs during the night.

The child ate voraciously, and when he finished, the look he gave Craig was nothing short of adoring. *"Muchas gracias, señor,"* he said shyly. *"Muchas gracias."*

"De nada, de nada," Craig returned a little impatiently. "Now get on home little Miguel, *pronto!* No more crawling in these bushes; it could be dangerous."

The little boy disappeared into the darkness, heading like a fleet-footed deer for the village. Craig and Blair both took their seats beneath the tree again, a little less easily than originally. Blair heard herself in an echo of the question Doc had thrown to her the day before.

"Do you know something I don't? Is it dangerous here?"

"No," Craig assured her, his yellow eyes blankly innocent. "Last I heard, the new government is fully in power." That was true, there was no danger to the Hunger Crew. There probably was no danger to Blair. But he had been assigned her protection, and his instincts were highly sharpened. Years in turbulent areas had left him able to detect the lightest change in a breeze, the lifting of a single leaf. "I just worry about kids out alone after dark," he said with a shrug.

"He really shouldn't be out," Blair murmured. "But I'm glad you gave him the stew. These kids get so little."

That bland, innocent look was back in his face. The boy next door. No, not the boy next door. He was still too overwhelming for that. His yellow eyes still perceived too much.

And being next to him was too disturbing.

"How about more wine?" he queried with an idle grin. "We do have a few extra bottles, I believe." He slipped her dented tin cup from her fingers with a gallant flourish. "Allow me, madam."

He left her to join the others at the fire and refill their wine "glasses." As she watched him she heard an easy bantering; he had enchanted the entire crew. And why not? she asked herself dully. He would have been a rare find in a populated, civilized world. Out here he was nothing short of a miracle.

Bright, powerful, generous, uncomplaining, unshirking. Keen wit. Polite, courteous, and friendly. Breathtaking to look at.

Was there really such a man as Craig Taylor?

Oh, yes, he did exist. He was very real, coming back to her with bright, appreciative, sparkling eyes. Ruggedly, tautly, excitingly handsome in the simple tan shirt and tight jeans. He transferred the cups so that he held both in one hand and extended the other to her.

"How about a walk in the moonlight?"

Blair glanced skeptically at the sky, where a sliver-thin crescent made a feeble effort at illumination.

"All right." He chuckled at her doubt. "How about a walk beneath the stars?"

There were a few dotting the heavens.

"I don't know," she said, rising even as she demurred. "Should big kids be out after dark?"

"Only with me," he replied suavely with a slight lift of a brow. "I'll bet the stream is beautiful at night. . . ."

They did walk, they did talk, they did meander down to the stream and sit upon the bank where they had been earlier. The little jungle haven seemed like a paradise at night, the hibiscus emanating a soft red glow, the grass a smooth, cloudlike carpet, the waterfall rushing gently into a pool that caught that slender moon and glistened beneath it like a diamond-studded sea.

Blair found herself forgetting where she was, who she was. She even forgot to wonder who *he* was . . . it was easy. They discussed books, music, movies. Food. Nothing highly personal, nothing controversial. And as they talked it was very natural that his arm came around her. She didn't protest the movement, and in time it was very natural that she began to touch his fingers, idly running her own along them.

She had never felt more natural with a man, more comfortable, more secure. And still so excitingly stimulated. She loved being exactly where she was, harbored in his shoulder, leaning against his strength, idly talking, and inhaling his deliciously masculine scent. So drugging, so potent.

In time he stood and helped her up beside him. "I guess we'd better 'walk beneath the stars' back," he said regretfully, his tone husky and slightly strained. He didn't move the support of his arm, but he made no attempt to kiss her, and she was strangely disappointed. She was sure he had wanted to, and yet held back with that leashed control.

Blair nodded mutely.

The fire had died low when they returned, glowing only faintly in pale yellows and oranges. It was early; the rest of the crew had turned into their tents for the night.

Craig walked Blair to hers, pausing at the flap. His golden eyes seemed to bore into hers, more magnetic and compelling than any fire of heaven or earth. There were mixed emotions naked in them for a moment; the desire she admitted she desperately wanted to see, and that strain and regret she had earlier puzzled over in his voice.

She moistened her lips, unaware that her own yearning for something as yet unfulfilled was beautifully visible in her face. Craig felt that he really saw emeralds, shimmering like the sea, returning his gaze. Her hair was a rich wave of deep flame cascading down her back as she tilted her head to his; her lips were moist, pink, slightly parted, and enchantingly inviting.

A groan rose from the core of his body, sending shudders through him. The sound came out as a rasp of desire. Damn, he thought again, he wasn't a machine . . . a goddamned computer.

His lips fell hungrily to hers. They were fierce, they were tender, they demanded, they conquered. His tongue deeply invaded the mouth that parted sweetly to his assault, grazed over pearl white teeth. He inhaled her clean, fragrant scent, inducing him as nothing ever had before.

It was the first time in his life he had lost control in any way.

But he had lost it. Her lips were clinging moistly to his.

They had been tentative at first, not offended, but shy. Now her mouth was like a flower, intoxicated by the full bloom brought by the sun. As if she had been a sheltered maiden, she seemed to take, and learn, and then give with a beauty that saturated his senses. His arms held her, and she was so soft, so pliant, so wonderfully, wonderfully feminine, warm, and receptive.

A moan tremored in Blair's throat. She wasn't aware that she issued the sound; she was barely aware of anything, barely conscious.

His touch was everything she had imagined and more. The sensations he sent through her with his sensuously demanding mouth were driving her blissfully mad. Her body quivered against his hardness, her limbs turned to mercury. He gave her the proof of her womanhood with each parry of his tongue, each stroke of his hands, thrilling her to a wild, reckless abandon. Belatedly she realized that what she had needed all along was the right man, and that her emotions had been touched as well as her flesh.

His fingers tangled into her hair, their touch strong and possessing. She wanted to stay where she was forever. His heat was permeating her body, seeming to fuse it to his own as his heady kiss burned her as no fire ever could.

Too late, too late she realized she had offered the kiss, and taken, taken so thirstily and wondrously all the raw and masculine enticement he had to give.

But having given away a piece of her heart in return, she could deny him nothing. . . .

His lips pulled away, but he drew her closely to him, holding her as they regained their breaths and the beating of their hearts slowly subsided.

He was in control again. His mind had harnessed the desires of his body, but his body was busy viciously hating his mind.

Hell, he was definitely quitting after this one.

Blair slowly surfaced back to her senses as he held her. He *was* an unusual man, she decided wryly, because he could have had whatever he wished. Or did he sense her fear beneath the boiling excitement he created in her blood?

His arms released her as his hands gently cupped her chin.

"Good night, Blair," he said softly.

And turning, stuffed his hands into his pockets, clamped into fists of frustration as he walked past the dying fire toward his own tent, across from and almost separated from the compound.

Blair watched him go with a catch in her throat, foolishly accepting the fact that she was falling a little in love with this man, who by his own admission had no room in his life for involvement.

But it was so wonderful to feel. Even wonderful to love when that love could bring only pain.

He had probably left her, knowing that he could offer her nothing permanent. She was sure, innately sure, that he had wanted her as desperately as she had wanted him.

Still she wanted him, even for a night, even for an hour.

Even though she still didn't trust him as far as she could spit nails.

Shaking, quivering, trembling, Blair ducked into her tent. Her hands remained unsteady as she undressed and slipped into a long cotton gown. She could still hear the erratic pounding of her heart as she lay in her bunk, staring at her green canvas ceiling.

Craig had a way of beguiling her into trust. He was with the Hunger Crew now; she would be seeing him day in and day out.

She wanted him, yes. But what scared her, what kept her trembling in the night, was the very real possibility that she just might get him.

*   *   *

Craig Taylor returned to his tent, but whereas he should have been catching a few hours of sleep, he, like Blair, stared unseeing up at green canvas.

He had never wanted a woman more in his life, and he was painfully aware that this time the wanting went far beyond the instant chemical attraction.

Chemical . . . it was electrifying.

A force like nothing he had ever come across.

But that force was part of it, too, being beguiled, bewitched . . . whatever. It was the sea depth of her eyes, the silky softness of her voice, her casual pride, devotion, caring, intelligence . . .

Whoa now, he warned himself, aware that he was shaking in the cool night breeze. Five days had passed. Five lousy days. How was he going to handle the time to come when in a night . . .

No amount of training could have spared him the misery he felt that night, all the more devastating because it was the first time he had ever been caught in such a spell.

A spell he refused to put a name to.

The hours passed. And the appointed time came. Like a wraith, as sleek and silent as a cat in the night, Craig left the compound. He was neither seen nor heard as he moved through the jungle.

He reached a clearing. It was midnight. It appeared as if heat lightning streaked the foliage. . . . But it wasn't lightning. It was a code Craig flashed more quickly than most eyes could see by powerful beams from clearing to hilltop.

HAVE ARRIVED . . . STOP . . . LOOKS GOOD . . . STOP

The reply was instant.

HOLD POSITION UNTIL ALERTED . . . STOP.

The jungle cat returned in the night, unseen.

CHAPTER THREE

Blair experienced an unsettling twinge of panic with the coming of the morning. With the often painful wisdom of hindsight, she was acutely aware of her own behavior.

Granted, there was something between them. And granted, the feeling was wonderful.

But she had all but thrown herself into his arms. It would have been impossible for him not to realize that he had held her easily in the palm of his hand. He had been the one to control, the one to practice restraint. What was he thinking of her? she wondered. The thought of facing him in the light of day suddenly drained her of all color. And yet the thought of seeing him again was also the burning focus of her day.

She cocked an eyebrow at herself in the mirror that was a tiny square cast at a slant beside her cot. "Really, Blair," she asked herself wryly, "just what do you want?"

The answer was still beyond her reach, and she shook her head disgustedly. "It doesn't really matter, does it? I have to get moving one way or another!"

But it was something to suddenly find oneself devastatingly attracted to a man one still didn't trust.

Facing Craig proved to be easy. He was the first person she saw that morning. Shirtless—bare bronzed muscles worked within a torso that certainly wouldn't allow for an inch to be pinched—he was attempting to shave just outside his tent. His mirror, the regulation size of Blair's, rested precariously in the indentation of a pole set up for just such a purpose.

His smile, beneath patches of lather, was instant as he saw her. Instant and warmly sincere. The simple gesture seemed to speak volumes, saying all the right things. Yes, there was something between them. His expression was not one of denial, but rather of acceptance. His golden gaze seemed to sweep away the morning chill.

She didn't feel awkward at all.

"Good morning," he told her with a grimace. Indicating lightly with the hand that held the razor, he continued. "I used to be good at this. My hands seem a bit shaky this morning."

Blair chuckled softly. "You don't look like the shaky type."

"I'm not," he agreed. "Not usually."

It was going to be nice, Blair suddenly realized. Perhaps he sensed her reservations, or maybe he was just as confused by the feeling as she. But he had never really drawn away from her; he had just held back. A few words honestly spoken without awkwardness or embarrassment, a simple look that passed between them and she suddenly seemed to have answers. Both wanting, they would take a little time. An easy road to discovery.

Replying to his honesty, Blair murmured, "I'd offer to help, but I'd probably do more damage than good. I'm a bit shaky myself."

He laughed; they looked at each other a moment longer. Blair felt as if his mere glance was a caress.

"I guess we're the first up," she murmured. "I'll go get the coffee started."

Craig grinned. "I beat you to it—it should be perked by now. Bring me a cup, will you?"

"Sure." Blair grinned back and turned for the mess tent. It was amazing what he could do to her, she thought, lips twisting with her inner dreams.

She had always enjoyed her work with the Hunger Crew— the camaraderie of her coworkers, the interplay with different peoples, the sense of self-value she had been able to achieve. But it had taken till now, and the coming of Craig Taylor, to make her realize that not even her work had been able to give her back an important aspect of her being that she had lost with Ray Teile's death. She realized it now, because suddenly she had regained what she had lost—a spark of enthusiasm with which to greet the day and each little task. This morning she could see the crispness in the air, smell the delicious aroma of the brewing coffee, hear each tiny little sound that was a part of the jungle life, part of the compound life.

Her senses had opened to a new dimension of joy.

"Well, Mr. Taylor," she murmured to herself as she poured two cups of coffee, "I still don't trust you . . ." A flash vision of him standing before his mirror—taut waist narrowing with intriguing precision to the waistband of the jeans that hugged the powerfully muscled thighs—filled her eyes even as she closed them. "But I'm glad of your being."

She brought him his coffee.

That morning Craig seemed to have set a pace for the days that followed. He had no qualms about spending the majority of their free time together, and yet he continued to hold back.

The relationship was a comfortable one. The intense nervousness Blair had been feeling began to dissipate as she realized surely that he wasn't going to demand anything she wasn't entirely ready to give. And in that aspect he perhaps knew her better than she knew herself.

She was afraid. She felt it inevitable that they would eventually come together in a sheer explosion of physical senses, and though she accepted, no, yearned for, that inevitability, the growing relationship between them was taking away the raw edges of that fear.

He is seducing my trust, she thought wryly one day. It was still there, that thought in the back of her mind that something just wasn't right, the pieces just didn't fit. But her sharp, intuitive suspicions dulled as she watched him work daily, a never-tiring powerhouse of energy. It was impossible to believe that he was less than sincere in any of his efforts.

The children of the village at first had seemed to share her awe and nervous fear of this golden-giant of a man, yet they now flocked around him. He didn't return their apparent affection with emotional or physical displays, but with a quiet concern, occasionally whittling little toys for them before sending them on their way. His word, Blair noted quickly, however, was law. He never spoke without being instantly obeyed.

She was meditatively watching him late one afternoon two weeks after his arrival, from the shelter of the med tent when Dr. Hardy came upon her, startling her with a chuckled demand.

"Are you still spying on that man?" he queried bluntly. His bushy brows were raised with teasing affection. "I would have thought myself that things were kind of fine between the two of you. I haven't seen a night pass yet that the two of you weren't deep in some kind of conversation!"

Blair flushed slightly. "I'm not spying on him, Tom. I'm just watching him."

"Constantly," the doctor remarked shrewdly. He chuckled again. "But I guess that's only fair; he constantly watches you."

"He does?" Blair was startled. She hadn't realized that Craig was returning her surreptitious scrutinies.

He acknowledged her query with a broad grin. "I told you from the beginning that he was attracted, and I'm sure you know it as well as I by now. And if I'm not mistaken, I'm sure as hell willing to bet his feelings are reciprocated."

Blair didn't protest his statement, but she frowned. "But why does he watch me?" she wondered aloud. Her eyes met the doctor's squarely. "Doesn't that seem a little suspicious to you?"

"Oh, Blair!" he chuckled. "I can't believe you're still trying to fathom the secret life of Taylor! No, it isn't suspicious that he watches you. He's a healthy man. I'd say it was only normal. And why would I think it suspicious that he watches you any more than I would think it suspicious that *you* are always watching him?"

Grudgingly admitting that Tom had a point, Blair grimaced and said nothing.

"Taylor has been like a gift from heaven," he told her flatly. "If I get to keep him for just a few months, I'll be happy. He's had us actually caught up for an entire week." Tom shook his head with the wonder of such an event actually happening. "I don't much care if the man is hiding something; I know what he's giving me."

Blair shrugged "I guess you're right."

"You still distrust him?"

"No, not too much of the time anyway," Blair admitted.

"But occasionally?"

"Yeah," Blair agreed. "Occasionally."

"Women!" he snorted with tolerance. "You've spent hours with him; you know him better than any of us. What do you talk about most of the time?"

"Oh," Blair said vaguely, "all sorts of things." She took the liberty of reaching into the doctor's shirt pocket for his package of cigarettes, handed him one and took one for herself, lighting both with a weak plastic lighter before continuing. "Craig has traveled a great deal. We discuss countries, customs. Art, music." She hesitated, the frown furrowing back into her brow.

"What?"

"His Spanish is awfully good, don't you think?"

"So what? We all speak Spanish! It's not difficult to pick up when that's what you hear all day!"

"No, but he came here speaking that well."

Dr. Hardy sighed and lowered himself wearily to his cot. "Blair, I spoke Spanish long before I came here. Taylor happens to have a knack for languages. Some people do. You do yourself . . ."

"What do you mean, languages? Just how many languages does he speak?"

Cornered, the doctor shrugged. "Only five fluently."

"Only five!"

Again her companion shrugged. "I happen to know because we needed a quick translation of a letter from a German correspondent the other day. Taylor spent some time in Germany. He picks up languages quickly. I never mentioned it to you because I know how your mind works."

"Well, I had been losing my mistrust," Blair admitted dryly, "but I think it's making a comeback."

"Because a guy who looks like Hercules happens to be bright?"

"Ah! We're back to square one! I can't explain what I feel."

"I can tell you what you are feeling, young lady," the doctor said sternly. "Something very normal, and you should go with it instead of fighting it. You like Taylor, you really like him. And it's scaring the pants off you, so you're looking for ways out, for protection. You don't need protection, Blair. You need to let go and take a chance."

Blair chewed her lip silently for a moment. Was Doc right? Was she hiding behind these imagined suspicions because she had decided that caring meant hurting? "Doc," she said softly, "I have been going with it. You're the one who noticed that I spend all my free time with him."

"Yeah." Tom smiled sagely. "I guess I am." He stood and crushed his cigarette butt into a nightstand ashtray. "Anyway, you studied psychology in college. You should be able to read your own mind. Although I don't think we need Freud to decipher this situation!'' Laughing, he tousled her hair. ''Anyway, I suggest you go take your bath before the males in this crew start getting restless. Kate left some time ago, and it has been a scorcher today! Don't deprive an old geezer like me a cooldown too long!''

Blair chatted idly with Kate as they relished their leisure time in the cool water. Kate, as usual, began to feel the chill of the water first. ''I never understand this!'' she moaned, crawling from the water and wrapping her towel around her shoulders, teeth chattering. ''First, I'm so hot I could die! Now I'm dying for a cup of coffee to warm up!''

Blair chuckled. ''Go on back. I'll be right behind you.''

Kate looked momentarily unhappy. ''I always hate leaving you alone.''

''For goodness' sake,'' Blair demanded. ''I'm fine! No one is around for miles except at the compound. Go on!''

Kate smiled. ''I guess I will.'' Her eyes flashed mischievously. ''Since all I have to return to for a warm-up is coffee, I guess I'll go for the coffee.''

''And what does that mean?'' Blair demanded laughing.

''I just wish Taylor wanted to warm me up!''

''Kate!'' Blair protested with a frown. ''Craig is just a friend, but he's certainly your friend too.''

''That's the problem.'' Kate sighed. ''He wants to be my friend, period. He wants to be a whole lot more to you!''

Blair shrugged. She and Kate were too close for her to attempt ridiculous denials. ''I don't know,'' she murmured, suddenly grave. ''With a man like Craig, I think it might be best to be a friend and friend only. He will travel on, you know.'' Her gaze to her friend was slightly wistful. She had inadvertently made another point to herself. Craig would move on. By his own admission his lifestyle wasn't geared to permanent attachments.

Was that why she looked to find fault with him? She had known love, and love had meant excruciating loss. Was she afraid that the combustion she felt inevitable between herself and Craig would leave her dependent, needing him, when she was sure that though he cared, he would still be gone?

No . . . she told herself. She knew what she was up against, knew that a physical involvement was not a commitment, but still accepted that she did need to experience that loving again even if it may be only physical and not eternal. She might never meet another Craig Taylor again, and she might go through life with her heart never freed from the past to allow her to live again.

"Don't underestimate yourself," Kate advised with a bluish smile. Blair, still standing waist-deep in the water but impervious to its chill, suddenly realized her friend was shivering.

"I don't underestimate anything!" Blair returned, chuckling and dropping her gravity. "Would you please go back? I can't stand you turning blue like that right in front me. I'm coming right now, okay?" To prove her point she crawled to the bank and grabbed her towel.

"I'm gone," Kate replied, zipping up her jeans. "I'll bring a cup of coffee to your tent."

"Thanks," Blair called after her retreating form. She ruffled her towel strenuously through her hair, drying the long auburn locks as best as she could. Then, as she shifted her towel to rub the rough cloth over her shoulders, she paused.

She hadn't heard anything; she hadn't seen anything. But she had the sudden uncanny feeling that she was being watched. Pulling the towel around her, she made an alert instant survey of the surrounding foliage.

There was nothing there. Only grass, brush, and trees, occasionally rustled by a whisper of the faint breeze. All that gazed upon her were the brilliant leaves of croton bushes and the heavy green of grass and trees that was a never-ending part of the environs.

The only sounds were those of the rushing water and the faint, barely audible movement of the air.

Shaking herself impatiently, Blair dried off quickly and started slipping into her clothing. Jeans zipped, blouse halfway buttoned, she paused again, peering around her.

Again there was nothing to see, nothing to hear.

But she knew the feeling. It was an extra sense that most people did acquire at one time or another—a sense that was almost a certainty, warning that eyes were watching them. . . .

"What is it with me lately," she murmured impatiently to herself. Perhaps her imagination was simply working overtime. She was suspicious of every action of Craig's, she was imagining herself being watched. Annoyed with herself and her lack of rational thinking, she quickly finished buttoning up, slung her towel over her shoulder, and followed Kate's path back toward the compound. Her thoughts turned back to the fact that poor Doc would be waiting for her all-clear before heading down to the stream for his own bath.

But she was being watched, and not by a happy observer.

Craig was part of the whispered rustle of the brush again— a voyeur in pain. It had been bad the first day he had come upon her, but nothing compared to the misery he felt now. He knew the woman now, he longed for the total person—the mind, spirit, and essence of her—not merely her tantalizing body.

He spent his entire time frozen in the foliage with his every muscle taut, his mouth a grim line.

Too much of this will drive me over the brink, he thought bitterly. God! And the woman couldn't possibly imagine that her every movement was a study in fluid grace, that her simplest motion was a lesson in sensuality. He tried to close his eyes each day as she rose like a Venus from the water, drops cascading down the tanned silk of her flawless skin, sometimes hovering with enticement upon a rose nipple, then falling like crystal prisms. But closing his eyes didn't help. Her form was ingrained upon the lids—beautiful full breasts, firm above the slender midriff, hand-spandable waist, and slimly shadowed hips. Shadowed, wonderful, mysterious . . . beguiling.

She didn't know the torture her daily bath inflicted.

But he had to follow her to the stream, just as he had to watch her constantly.

Usually it was easy. They worked closely in the compound, and once he knew her itinerary for the day, his "baby-sitting," as he had once termed it, was a breeze. The vacation the chief had promised. And it hardly bothered him to watch her as she worked. He enjoyed it. He felt he came to know her more each day by watching as well as talking during the evenings. He loved to see the concerned, serious knit to her brow when confronted with a problem, the smile slash her face with infinite warmth and beauty when she worked with the children.

Actually he loved watching her at the stream, but that was part of his misery. He cared too much for her to spy on her unawares; he wanted to see her so, free and easy in the water, but he wanted her to know that he was there. He wanted her revelry to be with him, for him.

It could be so, he told himself, then gritted his teeth harder. She was Huntington's daughter; he was on an assignment. And for the first time in his life he couldn't grasp pleasure for the easy sake of pleasure. He didn't dare define what he was feeling, but it was there.

And he could control himself, so he would. He wouldn't repeat the mistake he had made the very first day—that of allowing himself to be seduced out of control by the sweet trust that she seemed so willing to give him.

And so he was doomed to unhappy voyeurism. She had to be watched at the stream. If there were to be an attempt at abduction, this would be the perfect time and place. She was often alone here, far from the others, far from the compound.

Taking a deep breath, Craig followed her back through the quickly falling darkness to the compound. Right at the outskirts he changed his pattern, appearing to come from the opposite direction. He managed to reach the fire with her simultaneously.

"Hi," he greeted both her and Kate, but his eyes were for Blair. He made no attempt to hide his admiration, but he was glad she didn't know the extent of that admiration.

Blair smiled, wondering how he could show so much with his extraordinary eyes while still showing absolutely nothing.

"Coffee?" Kate was the one to return his friendly greeting.

"Surely, thank you." Craig accepted a steaming tin from her and ruffled her hair. Blair was surprised at the jealousy the meaningless companionable little gesture created within her. Not a spiteful jealousy—Kate was her friend and dead honest. It was a peculiar spurt of envy; she didn't receive enough of Craig's touch herself to feel generosity with his bestowing it on another.

The moment was over quickly. Craig turned back to Blair. "May I presume on dinner this evening, Ms. Morgan?"

Blair shrugged but she couldn't conceal her wry smile. "We can all presume on dinner this evening, Mr. Taylor!" she advised him.

"I think that's my cue to exit!" Kate said with a smile. "Two at the old cooking pot are company, three are a crowd!"

"Kate!" Blair and Craig both protested at once. "Don't be silly," Blair continued. "We're eating mush out of a pot! Not dining at the Four Seasons!"

"I don't think it really matters does it?" Kate asked in her usual straightforward manner. "Besides I have to find Dolly. She wants to instruct me in a new vaccine before dinner. Enjoy the mush."

Blair watched Kate walk away with dismay. Was it so terribly obvious that she and Craig enjoyed each other's company alone? Or as alone as it was possible to be in the compound. It was true that the group all ate together, but as if by anonymous decision Craig and Blair were discreetly left to their own devices. It was strangely similar at times to being prime patrons of an elegant restaurant. Although they didn't have the intimacy of a candlelit table in the corner, they did have the intimacy of the jungle's shadowy darkness and the filtered light of the fire's amber glow.

"May I?" Craig requested with a formal inclination of his head and gesture toward the "mush" pot. Blair shrugged with a smile and followed him. He prepared her a plate of watery stew with great care, a wry smile on his sensuous mouth.

Blair was silent until they were seated beneath the tree that they had both inwardly claimed as their spot. Then she went for a straight answer to the question that had been plaguing her since she had spoken with the doctor.

"I hear you speak five languages fluently. That's quite a talent. How did you come to be so proficient?" She stared straight into his eyes, alert to any inflection they might carry.

His eyes carried nothing; they returned her level stare. "I like languages," he said with a rueful smile. "They come easy to me."

"But five!"

He shrugged. "No great feat really. I grew up in southern California, so I picked up Spanish from the Mexican kids in the neighborhood. I had an Italian grandmother, and if you have Spanish down, Italian is easy. A lot of differences are only in accents." He smiled again. "I spent two years in Germany with the military, so I didn't really learn the language, I absorbed it."

"Go on," Blair prompted, determined. "With English in there, you're only on four."

Craig hesitated for a fraction of a second, a hesitation missed if one happened to blink, which Blair did. She was suspicious and he knew it, but at the moment, training was serving him well. She had no idea what a strain it was to keep his easy grin plastered to his face.

"French," he announced aloud. He was versed in a smattering of the language, but it wasn't one he would call fluent.

However, knowing that she quizzed him with a pegging instinct, he couldn't calmly announce that his fifth language was Russian. There hadn't been any Russian kids in southern California.

"Oh?"

She wanted an explanation for the French. Now he was sorry that he had helped Tom Hardy with the letter, but at the time the man had been so perplexed, wondering if they were about to be saddled with a German correspondent, that Craig had seen no problem with helping the doctor out of his difficulty. Guilt over his role with an operation as responsible as the Hunger Crew often nagged Craig; he tried to justify his existence within the compound whenever possible.

"I traveled a lot," Craig said simply. "You know that. I just liked French, so I took it as a language elective in school. Hopping in and out of France with a pack on my back, it was easy to improve on the books."

It was amazing, Blair thought, that a man with such hard, severe features could have a smile that dazzled and held one spellbound. As had been happening all the time they had spent together, her reservations began to dissipate beneath the warm glow of that smile. He laughed now, moving closer to her, his face just inches from her own, his breath caressing her skin. "I guess I'm just an aging hippie. I wanted to spend my life wandering the globe, and I had the money to do it. So I did."

"That's nice," Blair murmured. The reasons for her third degree were quickly slipping from her mind, as if she held a rope that spun crazily and ripped from her fingers without leverage to stop. When he moved toward her like that, she didn't worry about a future, she didn't worry about the past of the man. She was struck by immediacy, wanting only to feel the thrill of his full lips against hers again, feeling a warm desire burn from deep within her and spread, a desire to complete what he had curtailed a week ago, an impulse to forget all else and throw herself at him, demanding to know why he held back, demanding that he assuage her fears that he didn't want her as she wanted him.

He was caught just as she was. The spinner of spells, spellbound. Alone, they were still within vision of the rest of the crew, but it seemed of minor importance. Her lips were slightly parted so near his, moist, inviting. He knew their feel if he were to move. He knew the sweetness that her mouth would offer. A whisper away . . . just a whisper . . .

He had the power, Blair thought vaguely, the power to make her breath quicken from a mile, to race her blood, to shatter her entire frame with trembling. Indeed, still not touching, he had the power to move the elements. The fire danced, the stars seemed to tremble, even the earth began to move.

"Damn!"

Suddenly Craig's arms were around her, but it wasn't with tenderness or desire gone crazy. The earth was moving, and Craig Taylor was not the perpetrator of the action.

"Quake!"

She heard the word shouted from the fire. Then she was rolling in Craig's arms, and the earth beneath them was trembling violently. They rolled and rolled, even as her mind spun, and then she knew why. The tree they sat beneath, their tree, was careening downward, crashing to the ground not a foot away.

Voices were screaming in the night. Pandemonium set in. Explosive fear pounded into Blair's mind. There had been tremors before, many since she had first set foot in Central America, but nothing like this. The rumble went on and on, the sound of the brush falling throughout the jungle was that of a cacophony of drums.

Beneath her she could feel the parched earth cracking.

But above her she could feel Craig. His body covered hers, his broad hands laced over her head, sheltering her. There was tension in him. Along with the vibrations all around her she could feel his heart galloping along with her own, strangely giving a sense of security against all odds.

Tents jiggled and collapsed, and the rumble went on. In the heavens the stars jerked dizzily, like images displayed out of sync on a movie screen. The rumble rose to a roar.

And then ceased as abruptly as it had begun.

"Are you all right?"

Craig's face, strained, harsh in the darkness, hovered over hers, the pressure of his cradling fingers on her head intense.

"Fine . . ." She gasped, and then he was on his feet, drawing her up, gripping her hand and racing to the compound center.

There he released her hand. The authoritive power in him was unleashed. He was in control, his voice, calm, firm, was commanding the crew into action with swift assurance while also checking for injuries.

Thankfully, bruises, scratches, and fear were the only physical results among the assembly. It hadn't been a quake after all, Craig announced, but a very healthy tremor.

And they weren't a group of easily panicked people. The quick note of control in Craig's voice had them instantly in reciprocated calm. They were moving with brisk efficiency to pick up the damage.

But it was still Craig giving the orders.

"Juan, Kate, get into the village with the first-aid kits. Dolly, get set for any severely wounded. Blair—" His eyes lit upon her.

"I'll go with Juan and Kate," she volunteered in interruption. "I know the children the best—"

"No!" His command, even for the situation, was startling. The yellow of his eyes had never seemed more brilliant, more like a dangerous blaze that could sweep out of control. Then the fire was hidden so quickly that it might not have been. His voice softened. "You need to be here, Blair, with Tom in the med tent. If any of the kids come in hurt . . ."

Blair wasn't given a chance to agree to or to refute his

command. His voice went on for a second with further, all-encompassing instructions, and then, like a football huddle, they broke, all running off in separate directions to carry out their assignments.

Into a night that seemed to go on forever.

First on order for those remaining in the compound was the reconstruction of the tents. Craig, as usual, had matters well in hand. He asked for assistance to reorganize the med tent first so that Doc and Blair could get going with preparations. The rest of the reconstruction he could handle himself. Working alongside him briskly as the med tent was restored was the last Blair was to see of him at close quarters for quite some time.

The night and the days that followed were insane. The devastating action of the earth had been only a tremor, but in the village the destruction had been great. Flimsy walls had fallen; many had been left homeless.

But thankfully, no casualities had occurred. Blair treated a multitude of cuts and bruises, wincing each time an injury was so severe that stitches had to be sewn into young flesh, but the worst injury that had befallen anyone was a set of broken toes on a young lad, snapped by a falling shelf. Dr. Hardy was able to patch him up fine. The tremor had been far more violent farther north, near the base of a long-dormant volcano. Any extra help received in the country would not come their way; it too would go to the north.

It took them two and a half days of almost round-the-clock work to get back on even footing. And then, when things were caught up, they were disoriented.

It was always hard to understand the resiliency of the people. One day their homes had been in shambles—the earth itself had heaped ravishment upon what the war had left them. But they merely picked up the pieces as they had so many times before. They accepted help, they said thank you with sincere appreciation, and then they forgot and went on.

It was nightfall of their third day of whirlwind confusion when Juan returned from the village with news that the last hut had been rebuilt.

And Blair's last little patient had been released that afternoon. New supplies had arrived; all were stocked away.

It was incredible to suddenly have nothing to do. Nothing but go back to their usual schedule that was once so grueling, now so easy. Three hours a day for leisure now seemed like a fabulous vacation.

"It's as if it never was," Blair told Tom with disbelief, shoving back a lock of damp hair as they finished up in the med tent at almost five o'clock. She glanced past the raised tent flap, knowing she would see Craig at work lifting, hauling, or building in the compound. He was always close. She was never without the warm feeling of his presence, his energy, close to her. Yet he might as well have been miles away for all the chance they had to talk.

She caught sight of him carrying food cartons, still tirelessly busy. Frowning, she turned back to Doc. "I don't know what to do with myself," she told him lamely.

"Take a bath," he advised with a chuckle as he surveyed her wilted form. "And hurry! I want to get down there myself."

Kate, Blair discovered, had already been to the stream and was happily reclined before the fire with a book, cigarette, and cup of coffee. Loathe to disturb her, Blair hurried along on her own, enjoying the water, but still bathing quickly. With the emergency over, she was finding time to think, and thinking reminded her of the day she had been so sure she had been watched.

Funny though, all through the days of recovery from the tremor she had had that same uncanny feeling. But, then, Doc had told her that Craig watched her. Silly, he had been too busy to watch her. All his strength and wit had been working at top capacity, focused on the task of rebuilding and restoring order.

And yet he had always been close. He had appeared almost as if by magic each time something was needed.

But it would also be silly for Craig to watch her by the stream. Why watch covertly what could be yours if you said the word?

But then again, she wondered dryly, why did he never say the word? Or had he been about to? She didn't know. At least natural catastrophe had kept her from her reeling heart and mind for the last few days. But now they were back to square one. And she was finding herself overwhelmed by a sudden shyness. The man, the enigma were overpowering. She was at a loss.

Brooding, she headed back only to have her mental dilemma halted immediately by the appearance of the very enigma she pondered.

Craig was waiting for her on the path.

"Hello."

"Hi," she returned with a guilty smile. Did he know that she was plagued by thoughts of him constantly? That the last days, watching his caring, watching his competence had increased the feeling she hedged in her heart, drawn her even more irrevocably into his web?

"We finally have a night," he told her.

"Yes."

"I'd like to share it."

"So would I," she committed softly. He took her hand, and they returned to the compound together.

Craig was calling the tune, Blair realized, but she was glad of it. Their relationship had taken a turn again. She was still inexplicably wary, and he still sensed it.

But the time of hands off, of building friendship had come to an end. They were back to the simple but stark attraction of that very first evening.

He was touching her again. They brought their meals to the stream that night, and after they ate, they sat, Blair cradled into the tender strength of his shoulder. They spoke little; they were content to be in each other's company.

Yet he still held his distance. He did not demand the kiss she was dying to give, and she was more keenly aware of the powerful longing he leashed within his taut frame.

He returned her to her tent untouched, but the fire that blazed in his eyes was a pained one, filled with emotions she couldn't begin to understand. There was regret in eyes she saw as a clear, warm ache of longing. A need that nearly took over for a moment as he caressed the back of her neck with both hands and stared into a sea of emerald green. His lips brushed hers like a feather, and then he was gone, walking past the fire, toward his own tent.

"Craig . . ." The call voiced in her own mind didn't quite become sound. She kept watching him move away, misery welling in her heart.

And then she knew that he still sensed her terrible fear. The fear she never acknowledged in rational thought, the fear of pain that had been left her in legacy of Ray Teile's death.

There might be more to it than that—she didn't know. But suddenly she did know that she couldn't spend another night without him.

She couldn't spend any more time in long, deliberating thought. It simply didn't matter.

Filled with pain and need and a longing for the joy that only he could open to her, she felt her feet begin to move across the compound. Feelings moved her now, slowly at first, then with mindless determination, along the inevitable path she had been destined to follow since that very first day.

She needed Craig Taylor.

And she was very frightened that she loved him.

None of it mattered now—nothing.

Except that she be with him.

CHAPTER FOUR

Craig felt as if he had been tied into slow, tortuous knots, but because he was agitated, he made himself behave *normally*— whatever that was. He turned the flame of his kerosene burner very low and began to shed his clothing meticulously, placing his boots right to left beneath the cot on the hard earth floor, rolling his socks, neatly folding his shirt, jeans, and briefs.

Everything was in easy reach, but nothing was indispensable. In his line you never knew when you were leaving.

Naked, he stretched his length onto the cot and punched his pillow into a headrest. He crooked an elbow against the canvas wall and placed one hand behind his head; with the other he lit a cigarette from the packing case beside the cot that served as a makeshift dresser.

Inhaling slowly, he stared unseeing up at the angled, army surplus green that was his roof. This whole thing could be classified only as stupid, he thought, bitterness mingled with regret. He had expected a princess, a spoiled little girl.

He had found a woman. Both feet firmly on the ground,

intelligent, possessed of humor, character, wit, and a soundly reasoning mind. For the life of him, he couldn't begin to understand why the old man refused to discuss the situation with her. *Classified,* he reminded himself wryly.

Craig sighed deeply with a long exhalation of smoke. He was going to try one more time: In three hours he was due to send a communication, and an idea had taken formation in his mind. If those damn eggheads would only listen. But it was the old man, and even higher echelon personnel, who would make the decisions. And now that he knew what Huntington had at stake, he couldn't really blame him. Too bad he couldn't communicate his own seething emotions through Morse code. *Don't worry, sir. There's no way in heaven or hell I'd let anything happen to her. Sounds a little crazy, I know. I've only been around seventeen days, but I think I've fallen in love with your daughter. I say think, of course, because I've never really had time to find out just what love is. But I've never met such a woman, sir. She makes me shake, sir. Me, sir—can you imagine me shaking?*

The guys in Special Services would love relaying that one, he thought with a brief and dry laugh.

But there was something about Blair. She made him think about a home he could come to every night, sipping wine and discussing their days before a fire, waking up together, seeing her beautiful, bright face each morning, creating a family, a haven.

"Your machine is faulty," he told the powers that be in an unheard whisper through the night air. "Wrong man for the assignment."

He had thought that all along, at first with annoyance, now with something akin to pain. This woman whom he was falling in love with was going to hate him when she discovered what was going on. And it hurt like hell.

If he could only tell her. But what if the old man were right? Too much was riding high. The welfare of too many people.

Especially hers. Better to have her hate him and know that she was safe . . .

When she first entered the tent he thought he was hallucinating, that he had been thinking about her so much she had appeared in his mind's eye.

She stood hesitantly just inside the tent flap, her slender form straight, very proud. In the glow of the kerosene flame her hair was like a rich, dark wildfire in the night, framing the lovely contours of her face. Her eyes, mercurial green emeralds, swept his form briefly, registering his naked state, but unblinking. Her lips were slightly parted, still moist from his hungry kiss.

Blair stood motionless, watching him from the doorway. She saw little reaction. His eyes went blank for a second, his cigarette froze in midair, the smoke caught in his lungs, but then he was looking at her with a calm, unspoken query, his yellow eyes alert, the smoke released normally. He made no attempt to cover his body, so bronzed and tautly strong and perfect against the stark white of the bleached sheets, and so there was one involuntary reaction to her presence that she couldn't help but notice.

Blair flushed slightly, but didn't flinch or move. What must he think of her? she wondered a little desperately, coming so blatantly to his tent in the middle of the night. Could he possibly understand how special he had been to her? How he had already opened undreamed of doors?

She was starting to tremble; she shouldn't have come. She was never going to be able to carry off the role of aggressor. Good Lord, what if he didn't want her? He was always holding back . . . always able to leave her.

He did want her, she could see that.

"Blair," he said softly, the slightest tone of perplexity in his voice. "What are you doing here?"

She closed her eyes to gather her strength as she moved into the tent and allowed the flap to fall shut behind her. She couldn't quite stare into his golden eyes with bravado, so she kept hers lowered even as she opened them. Her first attempt at speech didn't make it. Her second was faint but audible and steady.

"I'd like to be with you tonight."

He froze again, for more than a second. This just wasn't fair. He could painstakingly control himself, but not both of them. The machinery was faulty as all hell, and what had been aching with warmth suddenly throbbed with a raging heat.

He should cover himself, he thought almost absently. For what? He'd look more like a tent than the damned tent did.

Employ any means, the old man had said.

But somehow he didn't think this was exactly what Huntington had in mind.

"Craig?" Her voice was soft, it was tremulous, it was throatily sexy, it sounded just a shade unsure, just a shade frightened. Such a strong character, suddenly so vulnerable, seeking reassurance from him.

The hell with the old man.

"Come here, Blair," he said, moving slightly to allow her room on the cot.

Blair was suddenly paralyzed. It had been so easy to imagine going through with it all in the security of his arms with his warmth rampaging through her. But he wasn't holding her now, and then there had been no thought, just natural, elemental action and reaction. Now she was thinking, he was thinking. It was all there in those yellow eyes, a tenderness that belied their rugged intensity, an understanding that even now offered her an out if she chose to take it.

She didn't want an out, she wanted to be here. Her legs began to woodenly take her to him, but her eyes remained downcast. Her knees buckled beneath her just as she reached the cot, and luckily she sank to it with some grace.

"Blair," he asked quietly. "Are you sure?"

She nodded, her throat having gone parchment dry. Her hands were on her lap, folded, wanting to touch, unable to touch.

What was it? Craig wondered, his thoughts no longer for anything but the exquisite, beautiful woman beside him, so close, not touching, but filling his senses with wonder. She wanted him, but she held back; she had boldly come to him, but now she quivered like a pine beneath the onslaught of a winter wind.

He had known desire before, and many women of different lands in different ports, but never anything as shattering as this. A desire that almost drove him mad, still tempered by the overwhelming need to be tender, to protect.

She was so beautiful. So breathtakingly beautiful. Her skin so fine, her eyes shimmering seas of green crystal barely visible beneath the concealing fans of flame.

Craig slowly lifted his fingers to graze lightly the velvet softness of her cheek. "Talk to me, Blair," he said soothingly.

Her lashes finally fluttered open, and he was met with the full force of shining green. "Will you make love to me, Craig?" The first word was faintly underlined. She actually doubted that he would.

"Good God, Blair, of course I will," he swore, his voice solemn and yet touched with a wondering amusement that was still unerringly gentle. He sensed the pain in her, the loss, the fear. He was instantly sure she had loved no man but Teile before, and that the memories of beauty were blotted by tragedy. "Talk to me about it," he whispered gently.

She shook her head, and he saw that she held back tears. "Just love me, Craig. Please, love me."

She was lost to the initiative, needing guidance. His fingers moved to the buttons of her blouse and he willed them to be steady, sensing she also needed absolute confidence on his part.

Difficult when you were shaking inside like a green boy.

His fingers were reverent as he undressed her, but confident or not, he couldn't control the indrawn gasps of air that came as he revealed all to his touch and sight that had only mesmerized him by distance before.

He wasn't particularly fastidious. Her shirt, the first to go, landed on the dirt floor. Her bra—a lacy concession to femininity in the jungle—shortly came to rest on top of it. He resisted the temptation to immediately set his lips to taste the rose-colored peaks upon the firm crests of her high, creamy breasts until he had slipped her khaki jeans off and the lace panties down the length of shapely, supple legs. She swallowed convulsively several times, but now her eyes never left his, and her graceful movements were all to his assistance.

Still she quivered, but still longing shimmered in the eyes that held him captive, eyes that were innately sensuous as well as tremulous.

He reached out fingers that were gentle as feather tips, controlled, tender, and slowly traced the high line of her cheekbones, down the white column of her throat, over breasts that rose and fell temptingly with the increase of her breathing. His fingers hovered over her navel, then plunged downward again, grazing her abdomen, her hips, her thighs. He felt her quivering increase, her senses beginning to rage as his lightness teased flesh so close to the core of her feminine sexuality.

But it had to be right, perfectly right between them. He drew her into his arms, savoring the feel of her breasts crushed to the hair-rough flesh of his chest, her long legs tangling with his, but still determined to hold back until understanding could intensify the pleasure for them both. He brushed against her, and he heard her moan, but although he did nothing to hide the near fever pitch of his need, neither did he yet let that need force him to impervious abandon.

"You came here to me," he murmured, his eyes locking with hers, "but you're afraid of me."

"Yes." Wide, honest eyes made no denial.

"Why?"

Her lashes wavered slightly, but she met his eyes again. "Because you're real. You affect me in a way . . ." she murmured. "I couldn't keep from coming to you, and . . ."

Her voice trailed away, but he could supply the ending himself. He did, aloud. "And there's been no one else since your husband died. Is that right, Blair?"

She nodded weakly, her lids once more lowered.

"Don't be afraid, Blair." He assuaged her fears, fingers threading through her hair and seducing as they comforted, massaging gently against the nape of her neck. "I'm frightened too. Can't you feel me tremble? I want to please you as you please me, as everything about you pleases me." So many times he had watched her, wanting her so badly. And now she was here. Nothing on earth or the earth itself could take her away from him now. Her eyes, steady on his with tremulous pride, were also filled with a guileless innocence. More beautiful, more touching than anything he had ever seen. He still held back. "You should talk to me, Blair."

She shook her head. "Not now, please, not now. If you want me, please, just love me." She buried her head in his neck.

Craig didn't need a second invitation; he couldn't have held back any longer anyway.

He pushed her down to the pillow as his eyes caressed her. Commanding, but so gentle, so tender.

"I want you, Blair," he said huskily. "I want you more than I have wanted anything or anyone."

She smiled and her eyes closed briefly with gratification, but when she reached to draw him down to her, he firmly caught her arms. "There will be no holding back between us," he told her softly. "I want all of you."

Pain had left her afraid for so long, but his assurance was now melting away her fears and the pain that had been so deeply rooted in her heart. He was still larger than life, and yet his intuition was also larger than life.

Again she thought this man, now possessing her with a complete and unabashed thoroughness, this determined man who would always demand all, did indeed know her better than she knew herself. Where she sought now to hide from his eyes, he forced her to meet them, to turn over her heart and soul and give free vent to the pleasure he brought. He thrilled her senses, drawing molten patterns over her flesh with an irresistibly persuasive touch, accepting her fear, her inexpertise, and guiding her along with him in a slow sensuality she had never imagined possible. Though she had wanted him before, she was slowly coming to a point of crazed, passionate abandon. And he kept watching her, watching his own fingers work their magic on her flesh, his breath growing ragged as a nipple hardened to a peak at his touch and Blair moaned aloud.

He ran his hands slowly over both breasts and followed a trail down her midriff and around her hips, curving his touch inward to tantalize her upper thighs. Then he groaned himself, yellow eyes now a golden inferno, and leaned over to take her lips in full demand, hungrily taking, seeking, searching. Abruptly he broke, whispered feverishly, and cradled her face as he whispered what she craved to hear.

He told her how lovely she was, extolling each of her virtues. Skin that was satin, touched by moondrops. Eyes that were emerald seas. Breasts that were firm rose-tipped pillows of divinity. Hips that were a perfect curvature, taunting, beguiling, haunting a man in his dreams.

Funny, he had never thought of himself as poetic, yet with her the words came in a stream. They were from his heart; they were voiced with a passion that now held his loins in explosive, radiating desire.

As Craig's lips followed his flowering descriptions of her anatomy Blair was seized by a new fit of trembling. A wonderful trembling, sweet, tortured, and splendid.

He commanded, and yet he also teased. Her past was swept from her mind. All she could think of was the magnificent, strong man who lay beside her in godlike bronze, whisking her away from earth to some plateau of heaven with a touch amazingly gentle for a man of his size and power. And then suddenly he wasn't gentle. He was demanding, his lips and teeth tugging with rough magic against her nipples, his hands assertively roaming, cradling her hips, parting her thighs, discovering the essence of her own fire, stroking, probing, driving her wild. His tongue found tender flesh, seared it, branded it, possessing her in a way she had never known, a possession that was irrevocable. . . .

Her fear was gone. He had known when to be gentle, when to be rough, when to seduce, when to take. His patience was infinitely rewarded as a creature of wild and fiery passion took shape in his arms. Blair writhed beneath his administrations, returning the intimate abandon he gave her. She touched him, and his gratified groans of approval rang as a sweet symphony to her ears. He no longer cajoled or asked that she give, but demanded, and she surrendered to each of his new demands, learning the potency of her own arousal. Nerves throughout her flesh, her raging bloodstream, her fingertips, took on new sensitivity, straining for the feel of him. His back rippled beneath her touch, his tempo became fervent. His yellow eyes consumed her in their golden fire as his body also set hers aflame.

The first velvet thrust of his entry filled her with a shattering wonder. She had never known two beings could fuse together so completely, so harmoniously, so beautifully. She clung to him, allowing her mind to savor the delicious delirium he brought while trusting in all the innate sensuality he had brought forth to respond. Her nails dug tiny half moons into the bronze of his shoulders, but neither of them noticed. They soared toward a rhythmic undulation of locked hips and limbs that steadily increased in wild, pagan need until it burst into a moment of climax so volatile that it was both sheer earthly pleasure and something glorifyingly of the heavens.

They clung together in a savoring aftermath, Blair ingraining each second of the splendor in her memory, Craig aware that she needed time to assimilate all that she had given and received. It was really a first for her.

But it was a first for him, too, and it took holding his—yes, she was his—flame-haired beauty in his arms in this almost ungodly satiation to realize that he had never made love. He had had sex, lots and lots of sex, and he had cared sometimes, but he had never known the true meaning of making love. He braced himself above her, loathe to leave her, and cupped her face between his hands. Her eyes were more beautiful than ever, heavy, dreamily clouded, sensual in the aftermath of passion.

"You," he told her simply, brushing the tip of her nose with a kiss, "are unbelievably lovely."

Her lips turned into a half-shy, half-knowing smile, and her eyes held his with a grave sincerity. She stroked his cheek with fingertips; no words were necessary between them.

He felt humbled by her; she silently thanking him when he had received so much. He kissed her forehead, and once more, her lips, savoring them now with passion momentarily spent, caressing very tenderly. Then he adjusted his weight, leaning beside her on an elbow as he watched her curiously, drawing absent patterns on her flesh that now comforted beguilingly.

"I want you to talk to me now, Blair," he told her with gentle command. "I can sense it in you—something that needs to come out."

She returned his scrutiny with dismay. "I . . . I can't talk to you," she murmured.

"Don't you see, Blair. Whatever was the past has to be cleared up. You find happiness with me, but I want more than the physical. I can sense that something is or was wrong . . . you were so hesitant, so unsure, and you are so perfect, so breathtaking." He fell silent for moment, and then his voice took on a graveled edge. "Did Teile hurt you or abuse you in some way?"

"Oh, no!" Blair gasped. "It just may seem trivial . . ."

"No, sweetheart," he assured her, seeming to understand something with a breath of relief. "Nothing that has anything to do with the way you think or feel could ever be trivial to me. And Blair—'' It was hard to bring up the name of the late Senator Teile now. But even though he had received her and fully given passion, Craig still wanted much more than that from Blair.

He was a fool, he knew. The more he had, the more he would lose.

But he was a man addicted. He could deny himself nothing now, no matter what the eventual consequences.

''Blair,'' he repeated, honesty and the need to fully understand her forcing him to take the gamble of bringing up her deceased husband's name. ''Teile was not a trivial man. Nothing about your relationship to him could have possibly been trivial.''

It was his constant, perceptive understanding that did her in. Perhaps she had always wanted to talk, but there had been no one she could talk to. Her father would have lovingly listened, but she would have increased the burden of pain he already carried for her. Kate would have been there, but she might not have understood.

Nor would Blair ever have been able to have spoken to another lover had she ever taken one. No one else could have possibly had the assurance and self-esteem to comprehend without insult or resentment her words of loss and agony for another man.

Craig did know her—the woman Blair. But he did not know the girl she had left behind, daughter of one famed man, widow of another. But she could talk to him, and it suddenly seemed imperative that she do so. Even if she didn't trust his existence, she did trust his heart. He would never betray her confidence. Next to her, propped on his elbow, legs still entwined with hers, he waited, hazel eyes warm now, colored with patience.

She closed her eyes tightly for a moment and swallowed, and then swallowed again, hoping she didn't sound ridiculous. Then she spoke. ''I suppose this is absurd,'' she murmured. ''Other women have lost their husbands.''

"Not absurd," Craig corrected gently. "And few women have lost a husband like Ray Teile in such a manner. Talk to me, Blair. I want to listen, I want to hear about Ray."

Her words at first were in a strained whisper, but Craig's hands were lulling, his heat soothing. The strain left her voice; her words continued in a toneless flow. On and on. And it was good to talk. The raw edges began to heal.

She had married Senator Ray Teile right after acquiring her master's in psychology. It was a sensational Washington wedding, hosted by the nation's capital. A marriage thought perfect, made in heaven, by everyone.

And Blair was happy. Ray Teile was a good man, God, what a good man. His campaigns were shockingly clean; he never found it necessary to throw dirt at an opponent. His platforms spoke for themselves, he practiced what he preached, he stood steadfast for his principles.

Craig listened to her without blinking. He felt some of her gut pain—he had been an admirer of Teile himself—tough, rough, but smiling and renowned. Surely a fine hopeful presidential candidate in his later years—which he was never to reach. A slender blond man, his bearing spoke of principle and determination, his face a halo of ideals to be dreamed and then achieved.

The honeymoon proved to be somewhat of a surprise—but a surprise that endeared Blair even more to her new husband. A handsome man—the "golden boy" of politics—Ray Teile had always been thought to be something of a playboy.

Not so, Blair discovered. He shyly, but with dignity, informed her he was almost as new at loving as she.

So together they had found themselves, special friends especially close with the secrets they discovered and cherished alone, like two giddy teenagers off on a voyage.

If their sexual relationship hadn't been wildly passionate or exotic, Craig learned, it was tender. And their life together was wonderful; they were friends, they loved the excitement of working together, they loved the same type of relaxation, they loved their home, they both looked forward to starting a family.

Craig sensed all the things she was feeling as she spoke, emotions that didn't need to be outlined clearly. They were universal emotions. She felt guilt that she was alive and able to love again while halfway knowing that that was what she must do. She was also afraid; Teile had been a kind and gentle man, a man she had married. Now she was facing an unknown after years of easy comfort and then abstinence.

Craig knew how hard this all was for Blair; he knew how she was trusting him, and it touched his already plummeting heart to fully realize that she had come to him out of instinct and instinct alone.

Trusting, caring.

He didn't mind hearing about Ray Teile, the real man. Craig could never begrudge the past, and her memories, good and painful, so badly needed this purging.

And so he listened, learning more about Teile, more about Blair.

The senator the world had seen had not been the real man.

No one ever knew that Senator Teile deplored football, disliking the brutality of the game. They never knew that he delighted in flowers, in birds, and soft music.

It was really an amazingly gentle man who became an American dream. But hell, Craig thought, he could understand the image. So many equated manliness to machismo.

And Teile had been good. Really good. Craig could hear it in every word his widow uttered, in her grief as she described him. She had loved him for all that he really was.

And then she had lost him.

Ray Teile had been shot dead by a sniper while on a goodwill tour, surrounded by highly trained secret service agents helplessly unable to do a thing when the first surprise bullet found its mark straight into the senator's heart.

And Blair stood by, watching as his life blood flowed surely from his body to the pavement.

Craig suddenly realized that she had stopped speaking. Her eyes were still closed and he kissed them lovingly.

"Blair," he said softly, and her eyes opened to him. "Teile was a very fine person, and it's very natural that you still grieve for him. But don't be afraid of loving again. You are alive, and you have so much to give."

Blair shuddered slightly. She had brought it all back, but it didn't seem to hurt so bad, and it didn't seem at all wrong that she was lying in this man's arms after talking about Ray.

She turned to him, smiling slightly as she traced a finger along the angle of his cheek. "Thank you for listening," she murmured. "I don't think I live in the past, it's just . . ."

"Hush." He pressed a finger to her lips. "Don't apologize to me, I wanted to listen." He held her close, his breath gentle on her forehead. "I wanted all of you, Blair."

Time passed as they held together, locked in a contented wonderment. Blair thought how strange it was the two men she had loved in her life could be so very different, so very special, so unique.

And then she realized that she was admitting to herself that she loved Craig.

Shifting against him, she brushed his chest with a kiss, then pressed her lips tightly to his shoulder. He moved to hold her again, but she shook her head and pulled back, rising from the ridiculously tiny cot that had become a bed of clouds for them both.

"Where are you going?" he demanded huskily.

"To my tent," she returned softly, watching his gaze narrow upon her. A mischievous grin curled her lips. "I'm not worried about my reputation, Mr. Taylor, or what anyone might think. I just don't think I could possibly share something as special as this night has been."

He wanted to stop her—more than anything in the world he

wanted to stop her. He wanted her with him through the night; he wanted to awake with her face beside his.

His muscles constricted, his jaw hardened. Reason held him back. In less than an hour he had to send a communication.

But reason didn't help him any as he watched her silently dress with her effortless, unconscious grace. And suddenly he was up beside her. "Tonight," he whispered, fingers tensing into her shoulders, "tonight I'll let you leave. But there will come a time . . ."

What was he saying? he groaned inwardly. Their time would be so limited—time when she would want to be his at any rate.

He released her abruptly. "I'm sorry, Blair." He turned his back on her.

Blair was silent for several seconds, watching the powerful breadth of his back.

"There will come a time," she whispered. Then with a rustle of air, she was gone.

She wasn't sleeping when he moved in the night, the wraith cat again, slipping through the jungle.

But she might not have heard a cannon. Her mind was full, her body sated. Distrust was not among her emotions.

She was savoring the feeling of fulfillment, of at long last knowing a complete peace of mind and body.

When she slept she missed his form beside her, but she slept a complete, total, and exhausted rest, a smile curving her lips.

They had both been right. A time was coming when she would stay, stay until he no longer wanted her with him.

Whatever the future brought with her wandering man, she would take whatever he gave and gladly bear the consequences.

CHAPTER FIVE

By morning's light Blair had forgotten that she had ever mistrusted Craig. The night had worked sheer magic upon her, and she was sure she could face anything that came. Maybe Kate had been right—perhaps she did underestimate her powers and Craig could possibly be the type to settle down in one place with one woman.

But if he wasn't, it didn't matter. For the time that they had, she intended to selfishly take whatever she could. She would never regret what she was able to have, even if she might never have such an experience again. She was gambling dangerously, having found a man such as Craig. She might never seek out another, knowing she wouldn't find such a perfect chemistry again. She was willing to gamble—she would never, never look back with regret.

She was anxious to see him, anxious for a few minutes to talk alone, just to share a secret smile, just to tell him with a look how wonderful she was feeling. But circumstances were against her. The compound was a bevy of confusion and activity even as she lifted her tent flap. A cacophony of excited Spanish rose to her ears; her first sight was that of dozens of native strangers milling around in confusion. Catching sight of the harried Dr. Hardy, Blair bolted after him.

"What's going on?

He stopped his headlong flight and blinked at her. "Oh, Blair—thank God you're up. These people have come from the north. The tremor wiped out their little village. We've got to get oriented here quickly with this many refugees. Get some food going with Dolly, will you? I've got to get Taylor. I need the man. We're going to need some quick makeshift housing."

Tom kept on talking, but he was already on his way again. With a sigh Blair made her way through the confusion, a practiced, soothing smile on her face while she inwardly groaned. They were in for another set of incredibly rough days. She would be lucky just to catch sight of Craig.

Berating herself for a fool even as she set to work with Dolly, Blair wondered why she had deemed it important to leave Craig last night. She had wanted to hug the experience to herself, she knew, to cherish it and ingrain it deeply in her mind. To decide how to handle her needs and desires and emotions and the real world that existed outside of his arms.

But now that all seemed so silly. She had cost them precious moments that could never be recaptured; the joy of holding tight with tender comfort, of waking together in the light of dawn.

She could only hope that he understood, and pray that things would be well between them.

It was long past nightfall when the activity in the compound died down. The victim now of high anxiety, Blair sought out Craig with her eyes. Just moments ago she had seen him bundling a young matron and child into a blanket so that they might bed down for the night, but now, suddenly, she couldn't see him.

He couldn't be far, she told herself . . .

Fighting an absurd urge to cry, Blair poured herself a cup of coffee and moved to the cooking fire, where the tired crew was gathering. She stood staring into the fire, mesmerized by the flame, thinking how like fire Craig's eyes could be and wondering desperately if she hadn't already ruined things with her reticence and fear.

And then she felt him behind her long before his hands actually came to rest upon her shoulders. "Craig . . ." She turned, and her eyes, wide and unguarded, told him everything that could be said. He kissed her, oblivious to the others, and his smile carried all the warmth and caring she could have desired. "Bad day," he said ruefully, "and I'm afraid we're in for some others. Tired?"

Blair nodded, not caring that she was tired.

"I'll walk you to your tent," he murmured, his eyes dazzling and his voice husky as he lowered his head to her ear and added, "We're being doubled up, you know. Kate's in with you, Juan's in with me."

Blair chuckled at his mournful tone. "Are you advising me against any nocturnal excursions?"

"I certainly am," he said sternly. "I'm fond of old Juan, but if he caught a glimpse of that delightful body I consider my own—hope that isn't too macho a statement—I think I'd make those dark Latin eyes of his a bit darker!"

Blair chuckled softly as they stopped before her tent. She stood on tiptoe and wound her arms around his neck, delighting in his height and breadth as she pulled his head down to hers and kissed him, slowly, savoringly. Feeling the heat grow from her action, she stepped back. "Coming from you," she said huskily, "I don't mind macho statements."

He grinned with the arch of a brow. "Good." He took the initiative then and pulled her back into his arms. "This will only be a few days," he said, his voice a deep, thrilling velvet. "Just a few days . . ."

But the few days stretched to a week—one that Blair often

considered pure torture. *It's because I know what I'm missing!* Blair thought wryly as she stayed awake nights staring at the canvas even though she was bone weary. And yet, even the torture was nice. She felt vaguely as if she were being courted— a bit backward, maybe, but courted nevertheless. Craig walked her to her tent every night and each night they shared a kiss. Each night they both knew they wanted so much more.

Blair wasn't enduring half the torture that plagued Craig. Slipping out of the tent for his midnight communications now that Juan was in the tent was tricky, and yet not impossible. That was actually the least of his problems. He was behaving madly, carrying on with Blair when he, unlike she, was fully aware that time was of the essence, and that in a matter of days, everything could crash in on their heads.

Yet he couldn't stay away from her. Couldn't help but pray that they would have just one more chance together before . . .

Before she hated him. Not knowing what was going on and not able to tell her anything, even about himself, she was surely going to think the worst. He was asking for trouble. He would have been a hell of a lot better off if this had been a simple little baby-sitting stunt for a wayward socialite.

None of it mattered. He was committed to the end. If there was an explosion . . . then be it. He couldn't willfully change things. So this was being in love, he thought miserably. What a hell of a damned time for it to happen to me. . . .

The tight schedule of the new-refugee confusion was just beginning to wind down when the second new recruit the doctor had been promised appeared.

He came in a jeep, like Craig, carrying gifts from the States. His name was Brad Shearer. He was a dark-haired Texan, a smiling country boy close in age to Blair. Instantly likeable. An enthusiastic Dr. Hardy turned him over to Blair to introduce to the others.

Blair found Kate and Craig together at the cook pot. "Kate, Craig—Brad Shearer.".

"Hey, west Texas!" Kate smiled warmly. "Glad to meet you." Blair suppressed a smile at the unabashed sincerity of Kate's comment. But then her smile began to fade with a trace of unease, the first she had felt in quite some time. She was almost sure she had detected a flicker of recognition in the man's eyes when she introduced him to Craig.

The second was over too quickly. "Nice to have you, Brad," Craig said easily, extending his hand to the other man, his nonchalant grin in place.

And then Brad was shaking his hand, his greeting cordial, but his eyes turning back to Kate.

The two women had some time at the stream that evening. The majority of the influx of refugees had moved back to the north with supplies, their cuts and bruises patched. Things were once again normal.

"What do you think of him?" Kate asked enthusiastically.

"Who, Brad?"

"Who else?" Kate demanded with exasperation.

"He seems nice," Blair responded warily. "Kate—did you notice anything funny today?"

"I haven't noticed anything *funny* in a long time," Kate replied dryly. "What do you mean?"

"I could have sworn Brad recognized Craig and then both of them acted as if they had never met."

"Oh, Blair," Kate wailed. "I thought you'd gotten over all of this!" Her eyes narrowed shrewdly. "I think you read too much."

"Kate!" Blair chastised with a chuckle.

"Really, some women have no appreciation for the finer things in life," she sighed. "Unlike myself of course," she hastily added.

Blair went pensively silent. She did have Craig Taylor and suddenly she wanted him desperately. Her suspicions began to melt from her mind as a warmth flooded through her. Tonight things would be back to normal. And she could be with him again. Tonight she wouldn't leave; she would find out just how content she could be waking beside the man she could now admit she loved.

She was so engrossed in anticipation that she gave no thought to the eerie feeling of being watched that so often plagued her.

Craig had only brief moments away from prying ears to spend with Brad Shearer. Brad was from a different office, but still, his appearance, like his own, could only mean trouble.

"What's going on," he demanded, a broad smile on his face as he and Brad apparently exchanged a casual conversation over the bottles of Budweiser Brad had brought.

"I don't know, Taylor, I don't know a damned thing. I didn't know I'd find you here. All I'm supposed to do is keep an eye on these people." Brad's face was plastered with the same negligent grin. Just two old back-home boys shooting the breeze. His voice lowered gravely, but his face remained passive. "That Morgan girl is Teile's widow and Huntington's daughter, right?"

"Yeah."

"And she's your assignment? Damn, man, I don't envy you that one." He sighed softly. "Hope I didn't give you away; it would help a lot if they let us in on what we were doing."

"Yeah," Craig agreed again, feeling his stomach tense. At the beginning he had been sure the old man was being overly protective. Now he felt a strange fear creeping along his spine. He was sure beyond a certainty that things were going badly, that he would indeed be racing the woman out of the jungle.

The woman who was now coming toward him from her

tent with Kate, smiling, laughing with that beautiful melodious sound that never failed to thrill him.

The woman with whom he had made the severe and deadly mistake of falling in love.

"The Rams looked good this year," he said automatically to Brad as the women approached. "But I'd put my money on either the Jets or the Forty-niners."

"I don't know," Brad argued cordially. "The Jets have a quarterback out with a busted kneecap."

Craig moved to pull Blair against his chest and slip his arms around her waist, hugging her back to his body. "What do you think, Blair?" he asked, nuzzling the top of her head and inhaling the sweet fragrance of her freshly washed hair.

Blair smiled, content in his casual hold that left no doubt as to the relationship forming between them. "Steelers," she volunteered off-handedly, accepting a sip of Craig's beer and returning the can. "It's getting late," she remarked then softly. "Can I interest you all in the dinner Brad brought? Steaks! Dolly is already by the fire getting things started."

The crew ate together, and Blair felt the anticipation and lulling sensation she had begun to experience earlier enveloping her. She was happy to be with Craig, enjoying the pleasant meal.

But she was anxious for time to pass.

And when it did, and when the crew dispersed, she took the initiative, following Craig to his tent with no pretense of going to her own.

With the tent flap down, he pulled her instantly into his arms. Their embrace was long and sweet, and then Blair extracted herself from it. "Juan is gone?" she questioned with an arched brow.

"Ummm . . ." Craig returned, standing back slightly with his arms crossed.

"Well, then . . ." Blair shrugged with a secret smile, loving his return—a compressed smile in the shadows of darkness. He watched her with that smile, a brow raised.

Nonchalantly she began to unbutton her shirt. His gaze darkened and narrowed, passion bringing golden brown highlights to his encompassing gaze. Hesitant suddenly, Blair felt herself begin to quiver again. But he had demanded that there be no holding back between them. Her movements still shaky, she kept going, slipping from shirt and jeans, then from bra and panties.

Again Craig felt humbled by her. She was so very beautiful, so exquisite, coming to him freely, shedding her clothing with that strange innocence that was also intoxicatingly lithe and sensual. The pale glow of the fire outside the tent caressed her shape with warm amber shadows, displaying firm breasts and haunting angles with an uncanny loveliness.

She stood before him, long lashes barely shimmering over eyes that were a combination of shyness and wanton boldness. He met that gaze, smiling encouragement as he cast his own clothing aside, unaware of the perfection of his own muscled physique in the ethereal glow. "Come to me, Blair," he murmured, and she did so.

He took her to the cot with reverence. His needs were strong. He had to have her instantly, but still he made love with tenderness, treating her with a tender fragility that belied the raging torrent of passion within him. They had some time tonight, he thought. He could make love to her over and over. He held her tightly, wincing. They had time, but not forever. A communication was due, and all hell could break loose.

But still, he did have hours. Hours to exhaust her, hours to leave her heavy with sleep.

Afterward, just when he was sure she had fallen asleep, she stirred in his arms. "Craig?"

"Ummm?"

"Do you remember the day you got here?"

"Explicitly," he breathed with many meanings.

"Do you remember you told me you made a discovery at the stream?" she queried softly.

"Yes?"

"Well, what was it?"

He laughed. "I wasn't just giving you a line that day, beauty. You still have to see it for yourself. Maybe tomorrow. We'll go for a swim before dinner."

"Why tomorrow, Craig?" she asked with a devilish glint in her eyes. "Why not now?"

"Now?" he queried. His mind ticked away while he hoped he had kept the dismay out of his voice. "It's late. We do need to sleep sometime."

"Oh, Craig," Blair murmured, shifting over his chest. "At the moment I'm anything but sleepy!"

There was time, he judged. As long as he left her sleeping . . . and the stream just might have that effect. Seventy-five minutes, he thought, glancing covertly at the luminous dial of his watch. He had a lot of "exhausting" to do in that time.

He came to his feet lithely, the lion, the decision made. He laughed and pulled a startled Blair up with him, the impenetrable keen shade of fathomless gold in his eyes. "The stream it shall be."

Blair nuzzled against his chest. "Thank you, Craig," she murmured, "for humoring me."

He grinned with a devilish recklessness. "To humor you, gorgeous, is sheer ecstasy for me." He released himself from her entanglement briefly to rummage through his footlocker for towels, and then caught her hand. "Let's go."

"Like this?" Blair demanded incredulously.

He twisted his lips in a teasing smile. "Do you suggest we go swimming clothed?" Duty or no, he didn't think he could bear to allow her to cover the beautiful sheen of her miraculously curved body at the moment.

"Well, no, but—" Blair's eyes sparkled as she left her word hanging.

"I'm sure the complex is sound asleep," Craig assured her. "But just in case . . ." He made an elaborate gesture of carefully wrapping a towel around her, taking time to tuck the flap in between her breasts. He wrapped his own towel over his lower torso. "Decent enough?"

"Not decent at all!" Blair chuckled. "But just fine."

Craig collected their scattered clothing and held out his hand. "We can come back dressed, just in case it's close to daylight."

"Deal," Blair murmured, momentarily overcome by shyness. She was a little shocked that this was herself, not actually seducing a man, but coming to him to be seduced, and then asking that their nights go on and on as if she were a honeymooner. But she didn't feel a speck of shame; she felt wonderful. Until tonight she had only been able to tell herself she wasn't an emotional cripple. Now she knew it for fact. She had learned from Craig that she was warm, sensual, and very much a woman. The new power was an intoxication in her mind that swept away caution and logic.

Craig paused long enough to grab a huge flashlight, and they moved into the night, fingers entwined as they ran across the compound with lightfooted stealth, holding laughter until they reached the trail to the stream. It was not a silent night—the sounds of the crickets and other creatures of the dark rang in a cheerful harmony that filled the air with vibrant life.

But then life itself had never been so vibrant to Blair.

She gasped as Craig suddenly dropped all that he carried, jerked away her towel, and pelted the remaining steps into the water with her in his arms. Silver droplets rained around them at impact, and their mutual laughter slashed joyously through the misty light of the crescent moon.

"Damn! It's freezing!" Blair chuckled, not minding at all the rush of the stream over her flesh.

"How can you say that with my arms around you," Craig teased, nibbling softly at her earlobe.

"It is difficult," Blair admitted as the warmth of his breath seared into her system, combatting the chill on her skin. Other words hovered on her lips, words she couldn't say. Did she really love him, or was he just a wildfire that came at night, illuminating darkness? A power that could never be captured or held.

Golden eyes glared down into hers, full of tenderness, full of mischief. "Want to see the great 'discovery?' "

"Of course," Blair murmured, suspicious of the devilish cast to his eyes.

Her suspicion was well grounded. He released her suddenly and she sank into the stream, devoid of his warmth. Slicing cleanly back to the surface, she found him swimming for the waterfall. His bronze arm, caught in the glow of starlight, beckoned to her. "This way!"

His "discovery" was a natural waterslide, sheared smooth upon the cliff by the countless years of nature sculpting her own play yards with water. Hesitant at first, Blair quickly discovered that the rock was as smooth as glass, and gentle to her skin.

She also discovered Craig to be a whirlwind of tireless energy. They enjoyed the crystal haven of the stream, teased in it, loved in it, until she was breathless, scintillated, and almost exhausted—almost.

She found new reserves of strength when he carried her back to the embankment, the bright teasing light in his eyes gone, replaced by something darkly hungry and primitive.

He made love to her again, no longer treating her like fragile glass, but demanding all that she could give. Ever so slightly rough, he taught her another new world of wonders, taking her with a fierce need that neared a pagan barbarism, amazing her still further with the rapture of eliciting pleasure while receiving, and thus creating that unique, wildly burning magic. She came to know his glistened body as her own, tasting, touching, totally uninhibited in the swirling vortex that captured them both by the stream, lovers as innately a part of nature as the rushing water that cascaded around them, singing a primitive duet to match their passion.

At long last they lay beautifully spent, cooling in the night air, a tangle of arms and legs and torsos in the soft carpet of grass. There were no words between them once the whispers of thirst and need had hushed with the coming of euphoria; they simply accepted the gift of ecstasy with a mutual peace in their souls. Blair vaguely knew that words had to come to lovers, that there would still be a reality of life. But not now; now was a time to hold, to cherish, to luxuriate in the male strength beside her, still radiating warmth and the masculine power that demanded capitulation even as it surrendered itself.

She was exhausted as she had never been before, her spirit as satiated as her body. He had created a heaven she knew she could not replace, and yet she was aware that even such a unique physical relationship—based even on instinctive friendship and respect, as it was—did not equate to undying devotion.

And yet what she had was enough. It could grow, nurtured by the very factors that brought them together. Yet if Craig were the unharnessable and untamable, mysterious cat of the night that she had first suspected, she could still never begrudge him this rare wonder of love.

Her lashes grew heavier and heavier against her cheeks. The soft grass provided a comforting mattress; Craig's body provided all the warmth she could ask. Within minutes she was sleeping deeply, freed forever from the haunting of her past.

Blair wasn't sure what awoke her, she had been so thoroughly, soundly asleep. She blinked, slightly disoriented, until she realized she was cold. She gained focus, knowing immediately where she was, but frowning as she stretched languorously for Craig, only to discover that she was alone.

She scrambled to her feet and glanced around the embankment. The light was very dim, almost nonexistent, but she quickly saw that the bundle of his clothing was gone.

He wouldn't have left her sleeping naked alone on the embankment, would he? No, she was sure of that. He might leave by the light of dawn, but he was not the type of man to leave a woman vulnerable.

Not that she was frightened. She wasn't far from the compound, and she had learned her way around the wilderness in her time with the crew She was, however, perplexed, and suddenly very cold. It also seemed as if a million eyes might be on her. For the first time during the night, her naked state made her nervous.

She moved quickly for the bundle of her own clothing and hastily began to dress herself, fumbling with hooks, snaps, and zippers. She was halfway through buttoning her blouse when she noticed the flashes of light coming through the foliage.

Her fingers stopped all movement as she realized that some sort of message was being sent. The sporadic bursts of illumination were dots and dashes. Morse code. She wasn't her father's daughter for nothing. But neither was she great on deciphering the code.

Her eyes riveted to the spot on the grass where the flashlight had haphazardly fallen earlier. It was gone! Her heart began to sink slowly, as if it truly dropped inch by painful inch to her feet.

Craig.

Her body stiffened; all thought of softness and love dissolved into a bitter gall that burned her stomach with the searing acid of betrayal. And just as quickly, she blocked out the agony of betrayal with a shaking rage and the firm determination to decode his message and call his charade.

Messages. He was being answered from some far distant hill. But from where she was, in the valley of the stream, she could make out nothing clearly. She had to find where Craig was.

Two years with the Hunger Crew had also taught her to move through the night with the agility of the natives, and with the light to guide her she stole almost silently through the brush. The trail led uphill to a clearing in the dense brush. Perched on his knee, shooting his flashes of light into the night sky, was Craig.

Blair flattened herself to the ground, trusting in the shelter of a wild banana plant. The flashes began to make sense.

. . . NECESSARY THIS WAY? STOP

The night sky went dark again as his words were received. It stayed dark for several moments, as if it were being transferred on to another point.

Then the answer came back, and Blair's heart now seemed to catch in her throat.

YES . . . TONIGHT IMPERATIVE . . . GET HER OUT . . . STOP

The sky again went dark.

She should have been frightened, but she wasn't. She was furious and humiliated and hurt, as if her heart had literally been ripped from her body.

God, what a fool! She had given him more of her soul than she had ever deemed possible, divulged secrets to him that she had thought to forever harbor. Given him herself.

Suddenly she began to burn within, thinking of the way she had come to him, teased him, loved him, lain beside him in intimate abandon. Not even an hour ago. And all the while he had been planning this . . . this . . . whatever it was. Plot. She had meant nothing to him; she had been as completely deceived as a raving lunatic.

Shocked into immobility, it began to seep through to her that she needed to get away from him. She was the center of some type of plot. GET HER OUT. She was a raving lunatic to be sitting so close, a sitting duck. Oh, Lord! Who the hell was he? Someone out for a ransom? Or worse? Someone who knew of her father's importance?

Quietly, barely daring to breathe, she inched to her knees, to her feet. She would go straight to Dr. Hardy and the others. Together they would confront Mr. Craig Taylor.

A flash of light streaked through the night again straight into her face. She threw an arm instinctively above her eyes to shield them from the sudden flare. The light left her face and became softer, clearly illuminating the space between herself and the yellow-eyed stranger who now watched her.

They stared at each other as countless seconds ticked by in what seemed to be an eternity. There was no tenderness in the leonine eyes now; they were rigidly unfathomable, denoting all those qualities she had once sensed. Power. Steely determination. A grim ruthlessness.

He didn't move. He didn't try to invent an explanation. He sighed, and there was a shade of regret and sadness to his voice.

"I'm sorry you had to see that."

She stood as still as he, her shoulders squared, her head high. She spoke in a grating, contemptuous rasp, aware more than ever of the striking intelligence and unwavering strength in his hawklike, angular features.

"Who are you?"

He shrugged with a brief inclination of broad shoulders. "My name is Craig Taylor. I have only one name, I don't need an alias, which is more than can be said for you."

Blair swallowed, but didn't flinch. She realized now that he knew who her father was.

"You can understand why I don't use my real surname," she said coldly. "It keeps me away from creatures like you."

Did he flinch? She wasn't sure.

"I really am sorry, Blair. I wish you hadn't woken up."

"Why?" she charged, straining to fight hysteria. "You are

evidently planning to abduct me." With acid sarcasm she added, "I'm sure I would have noticed at the time."

"I didn't mean it to be this way."

"Oh? What way could it have been? Were you going to ask me nicely if you could kidnap me?" Her voice was rising shrilly. That was it. She needed to scream. Could anyone hear her this far?

"I would have taken you away trusting me—"

"Trusting you?" The words were a scream. Trust him!

The yellow eyes held hers. Steady, firm, still ruthless, but still holding that sad regret. "Blair, I'm not going to hurt you."

She started to laugh. Oh, God! If only he had hurt her. If only he could do something to make this betrayal easier.

"Who in the hell are you?" she shrieked. "Who are you working for? What government? Are you a torch-waving fanatic? Or a simple mercenary?"

He took a step toward her. "No, Blair. I—"

"Don't!" She put up a hand as if it could ward him off. "Don't come near me, you despicable creature. You bastard." She clipped off her expletives like chips of ice.

Craig's forbidding jawline took on a hardened twist. "I'm asking you to trust me, Blair."

Her answer was quick. "You have to be kidding."

"This isn't what you think."

"Then who the hell are you."

"I'm not at liberty to say."

She smiled, slowly, bitterly, the action never reaching her eyes. "You and your kind are the dregs of society, and you're asking me to trust you?"

Something snapped inside Craig, an explosive fury at everyone involved, including himself. He inwardly railed at the old man for having gotten him into this fiasco, himself for having broken the first rule and become personally involved, and her for her blatant condemnation. Christ, she wasn't giving him an inch. *Princess.* He had to start thinking of her as that spoiled little bitch who had created this mess in the first place, a do-gooder socialite who needed a good kick in the—

Who was labeling him everything she could think of in her certainly expansive vocabulary.

She was speaking, her voice full of loathing, but he blocked out the words. She thought he was some kind of terrorist.

Damn it! Let her think it! After all they had shared, she couldn't offer him an iota of trust.

He leaped forward, the lion pouncing, his fingers digging into her shoulders. "Stop it!" He shook her, quelling her to silence, but drawing no fear. "You can stop right now, Mrs. Teile. You're right, madam, I'm the goddamned dregs of society, but you're coming with me, and you're stuck with me."

"The hell I am!" Blair hissed, wondering immediately after if she was a complete fool. He towered over her, his eyes impaled her, biceps strained against the fabric of his shirt and his grip an iron vise. And God, even now, even when she knew she was used, her blood began to race at the nearness of him. No! She tilted back her head and gathered breath for a scream.

"Don't!" His word ripped the air. "You little idiot, I don't want to hurt you!"

Her mouth opened, but no sound came. She was never really sure what happened; his knuckles connected with her jaw, but she felt no pain. All she had was a memory of his voice, strangely tender again.

"I'm sorry, Blair. God, babe, you really don't know how sorry."

The entire world was equally as strange as she slipped into a blackness ridiculously laced with tranquility.

INTERLUDE

In the small clearing, Craig Taylor caught the woman's slender body as it crumpled in his arms. He laid her gently in the grass, then tenderly touched the spot where his fist had connected with flesh.

A breeze suddenly sprung up; the foliage around them rustled and whispered in the darkness. The sound of the crickets could be heard—in the distance if one listened, the pleasant trickle that was the sound of the stream.

Anger sliced through Craig with a jolt. Sometimes he was absolutely sure that the high brass sat on their brains. They had better have a damn good explanation for this one, he thought grimly. He had been right in the first place. Bombs in the Middle East would have been easier than the task of dragging an unwilling prisoner through the jungle.

Your own fault, old boy, he chastised himself harshly. Rule number one: Never fall in love with gorgeous, brave women about to be abducted and smuggled out of the country. Never,

never, never make love to them. Never become the victim of the victim even when she is an enchantress.

Tense with anger, furious with himself, he jerked to his feet.

There was another flash of heat lightning disturbing the lush environ of the jungle—a final communication from Craig.

ON OUR WAY . . . STOP

The darkness of the night descended.

Craig hefted the inert bundle into his arms. He became a wraith of that darkness, moving in to move out.

In his tent he set Blair down, careful not to look at her face. He had to get moving and he didn't remember how just hours ago they had shared the cot.

His hands trembled for an instant and he made them stop. He had to give her a sedative; he needed clear sailing for the hours to come. A great distance needed to be covered.

Almost impervious to pain himself, he winced as the needle pressed into her flesh. She released a soft whimper. No sound on earth had ever reached his ears with such reproach. He glanced quickly at her face, and then away. The soft skin, the waves of auburn hair that curled in luscious mounds of disarray around the fine, proud profile—for now he just couldn't look at her. In drugged sleep her beauty was wistful, ethereal. It reminded him achingly of the trust she had given him, the trust that he, like a fool, had encouraged.

Tomorrow, he thought wryly, he would be facing more than wistful beauty; he would be in for one of the definite dangers the chief had guaranteed him—this woman's wrath.

Though his thoughts plagued him, he moved mechanically, gathering the essentials. Seconds later he had her secured over his shoulder. Moving with all senses keenly alert, he sought out the jeep in the rear of the compound. A fifth sense warned him that someone was near; he tensed and stood perfectly still, trying to pinpoint the source of disturbance.

A soft whistle sounded and he breathed again, relaxing and proceeding.

Brad Shearer, almost invisible in black jeans and black T-shirt, awaited him at the jeep.

"I had a feeling you'd be moving out," Brad said softly. "In a hurry. I stashed you a few extra provisions in the back of the jeep."

"Thanks," Craig returned briefly, depositing Blair in the passenger seat. She slumped instantly to the side. Brad responded automatically, adjusting her fallen head to a position of comfort. The gesture caused a constriction that clamped Craig's throat.

"She's a stunning woman," Brad commented idly, pushing back a tendril of drooping auburn hair.

"Yeah," Craig returned abruptly, hopping into the driver's seat. "I'm popping it out of gear," he told Brad. "Give me a push, will you? I don't want to run the engine yet."

"Sure." Shearer pitched his weight against the vehicle. The jeep began to roll; both men heaved it along, Craig half in the vehicle, half out.

"Good luck."

"Thanks."

The distance between the rolling vehicle and the compound increased quickly. Out of earshot at last, Craig spurred the engine into action.

They were on the road.

Back at the compound Brad Shearer slipped into his tent. He smiled wryly. Craig Taylor—he had always been a little in awe of the man; he wasn't considered quite human within the ranks of the special forces, a cat with nine lives and the ability to always land feet first. Just the power in the man's damned golden gaze could quell trouble before it began.

But now he seemed to be in a slightly different predicament. If guerrillas were at large—which Brad could only assume to be the case although everything about this one was classified info—he had no doubt that Craig Taylor would make every right move. But that would be the least of Craig Taylor's problems.

Brad had watched his comrade that night. It was normal to befriend the woman since he was guarding her, but there was more there than friendship. And Washington was full of rumors of Huntington's daughter. Charming, pleasant, lovely, intelligent—but a demon caught by the tail if crossed.

Shearer was glad he wasn't going to be around when that one blew. He chuckled softly as he stretched his length into his cot. There was some kind of saying, wasn't there?

'Twas beauty killed the beast.

Craig's thoughts were running along similar lines as he moved the jeep through jungle trails. He was alert to anything out of the norm in the landscape he traversed, but his instincts were such that his scanning of the terrain was an automatic thing, as much a part of his being as breathing. He was, unfortunately, quite able to think.

Theoretically tonight would be the worst. He would have to take constant care. Once they cleared land, he should be on easy street, maintaining direction, waiting for the allotted time to pass and the final destination to be reached.

Tonight he was flirting with the possibility of guerrilla snipers. But then again, tonight just might be the best of it. At least his hostage was out of it. Tomorrow she was sure to be pitching fits that would strain both man and professional training to the *n*th degree.

Blair's drooping form suddenly moved again; her head careened to his lap, spilling a wealth of auburn silk over his knees. She moaned slightly, and shifted, casting a slender hand limply against his thigh and beneath her cheek.

Clenching his teeth so tightly that his jaw ached, Craig drove on. So trusting . . .

Despite better judgment, she had always come to him. He was painfully aware that she had said things to him that she had shared with no one, things she had kept inside, things which in giving spoke eloquently of her heart.

He should have stopped it, never have allowed it to grow. No, he couldn't have stopped it, he had been an addict of a drug more potent than any other.

But now it was time to pay the piper. He would never forget her eyes when she saw him in the clearing—the scorn, the horror, the contempt, the scathing rage that altered their gleaming brilliance to glacial emeralds. She thought he was a terrorist, of course. But if she cared for him, she should have had some faith.

He was wounded, and so he reverted to anger again. He also doubted that she was going to feel much better in the eventuality that safety was reached and that she was told the truth of her abduction and his true vocation. Because a certain truth would still be there to her—he had sought her out with a specific plan.

He quirked his lips in a grim, mirthless smile. Why was he worrying about eventualities now anyway? He was going to have to deal with the coming days. And he might as well determine to harden right now; it was going to be a battle of wills from here on and no matter what the hell he was thinking, he had to be the consistent victor. A mask must be worn that couldn't be allowed to slip.

The hum of the wheels, the grind of the engine, and the ceaseless reiteration of his own thoughts followed Craig through the jungle. Hours passed. Still Blair slept on. And then the first lap of the journey was accomplished without incident; a rendezvous point was reached. But there was no one to meet them as Craig drove the jeep into the foliage that banked the river. Steeling himself, he shifted his leg and rested Blair's head against the empty seat. Moving just a few feet, he found what he sought.

A boat. Of sorts.

Barco de vela—a sailboat to the natives. One that would blend right in with any other native vessel traveling the river—chipped, cracked, peeling—the furled sails a dingy, tattered gray.

The vessel rested against a dilapidated dock. Catching the lead line, Craig hopped aboard, senses once more alert. He wasn't expecting trouble at this point, but . . .

It looked like an old wooden crate, Craig judged, but it would move. It was fixed with a motor, one of the best available he was sure. "Well, this is it," he murmured to himself. "A castle to house my princess."

He didn't take time to check supplies or the galley that adjoined the sleeping quarters in the one-room cabin. He wanted to get away under cover of darkness.

He returned to the jeep, collected Blair, and lifted her onto his shoulder, desperately trying to raise a clinical barrier. With his free hand he stooped for his duffel bag and the "CARE" package that Brad had supplied.

In the morning, he knew, the jeep would be gone, as if it had never been. Someone else, who had no knowledge of its recent passengers, would simply be assigned to pick it up.

Activity in the jungle would be unchanged. The crickets would keep chirping, snakes would slither along the branches of the trees, birds would call. Life would go on.

Craig carried Blair down to the cabin and laid her on the wide single bed that fit against the starboard side. He kept his eyes from her face, but quickly removed her boots to offer her a modicum of comfort. The sun should be high in the sky before she awakened, he thought. Time enough for him to start their water journey, hopefully time for him to catch a little sleep.

Craig released the lines. Like a ghost ship, the dilapidated *barco de vela* moved into the river current under power of the motor that was designed to wheeze like a sick sea serpent despite its technical wizardry.

Road to river; river to coast. Their journey had begun.

In time Craig felt he had gone sufficient distance to cast anchor near the shoreline and catch a little sleep. Securing the boat, he slipped down the splintering ladder to the cabin.

His princess slept on, her face sweetly at peace.

Sighing, Craig laid his length beside her, noticing gratefully that the Agency had decided clean sheets would not be a give-away. He pulled a blanket of rough native wool over the woman, folded his hands behind his head, and tried to sleep.

The effort was ludicrous. He would be better off on the planks than here beside her, when all natural instincts decreed that he should reach out and touch her, curl her soft frame into his. . . .

But he couldn't do that. Not when he knew she would loathe the touch she had once surrendered all to, not when she was unaware, a victim of his sedative.

And so he stared up at a new ceiling—one of ragged, peeling planking. He listened to the soft sound of her even breathing, felt her slightest stir, her warmth so close to his.

Time ticked by. In her sleep she shifted. She inched closer to him, her body naturally gravitating to his heat—following a natural urge against which her mind would rebel.

Craig tensed every muscle. Then with a long exhalation of breath he cast an arm around her and hugged her to his chest. She adjusted again accordingly, fitting snugly into his muscled length.

He would be up long before she, Craig knew. He couldn't deny himself this night. And yet, as he finally dozed, he knew his hostage would deplore the intimate scene if she knew of its existence.

But he also knew that he was far more her hostage than she was his.

CHAPTER SIX

Waking for Blair was a slow process. She became aware of things little by little—a dullness in her head, the sensation of floating in space, no, not floating, rocking. There was something soft beneath her . . .

Still swirling in a nether world, she felt the foggy return of memory grow stronger.

Craig Taylor. He had struck her, taken her . . . where? Her eyes flew open as she automatically tested her jaw. It worked just fine, and she didn't feel a hint of pain.

Wonderful. She had been knocked out by an expert!

Her eyes refused to focus at first, and then she realized she was staring up at rough planking—knotted boards, with very little left of a one-time coat of varnish.

The rocking sensation continued as she desperately tried to collect her scattered thoughts and raging anxiety. *Don't panic!* she warned herself fervently, forcing herself to remain still and shadow her eyes as she surveyed her surroundings. Her fingers quietly clutched the softness beneath her. Sheets, a mattress.

She was lying on a bed. A monotonous, light slapping sound registered in her ears. A boat. She was lying on a mattress in some kind of a boat.

No other sounds came, just that of the continuous slapping. Slowly, carefully, she lifted her head.

"Some kind" of a boat had been right. She had seen a great deal of the rustic while in Central America, but even for rustic the cabin was a masterpiece of squalor. The single room was galley and sleeping quarters, comprised of the bed she lay in, a round table that obligingly peeled along with the wall it was bolted to, a drab cloth-covered booth that was attached to the port side and encircled it, and a set of tarnished metal workings that were sink, stove, and galley storage.

A single door was aft. A head? she wondered, asking herself disdainfully why she was worrying about bathroom facilities under the circumstances.

The light of day was streaming through to her from a porthole beside the bed and also from a square piece of hatch that sat foreward above a rickety wooden ladder. Blair stared at the opening, at the blue sky she could see through it, for quite some time, her mind working anxiously away.

She would not panic. She would face facts, even though the facts were rising like another blow in the face to cripple her with physical pain. Traitor! Craig Taylor was a traitor. He had come to her, beguiled her, won her trust . . .

With this as his intention. Blood flooded her face with fury and humiliation, increasing a nauseated, spinning sensation. Suppressing a moan, she wondered what he had done to her. No permanent damage, she decided quickly. She was certainly in one piece.

Oh, dear God, no! She had been harmed. The agony of his betrayal was like a thousand wounds. She had been such a fool! She had instinctively suspected him from the beginning, but she had wanted to believe the best; she had wanted him, and so she had capitulated like an easy teenager against all the wisdom of her maturity.

She had fallen in love with a man who had taken her confidences and done nothing more than used her, amused himself at her expense when all the while he had been planning . . . what?

She blinked fiercely, trying to rid herself of the fog that persisted in shadowing her mind like cobwebs. *Stop it!* she warned herself. She had to forget the last three weeks. Damn! Would God that she could! Mortified anger assailed her as she remembered the way she had instigated intimacies between them, intimacies that went beyond any she had previously known. Her insides crawled as she remembered pressing her body to his, tasting, touching, crying out, beseeching him to make her his.

Her flesh could remember his touch; her loins seemed to constrict as her mouth went dry and her skin burned.

Revolted, she told herself, she should be revolted. But the memory of his lips upon her, his seeking hands bestowing pleasure even as they raided every secret of her femininity, was not revolting even in the fierceness of her anger. She could hate him now with the gut-piercing pain of his betrayal, but she still couldn't force the lie upon herself that he was repulsive to her.

Stop! she railed to herself again. *Stop!* Whatever, it was the past. She had been used, mentally and physically seduced by a wolf in sheep's clothing. Now she had to put it all behind her, all the time that she had learned to truly live again.

She was Andrew Huntington's daughter. Her chin rose up, pride winning out. She was a soundly reasoning, intelligent, mature woman. She had to find out what was going on, what Craig Taylor's plan was. A shiver suddenly riddled her body with the full import of her situation. She was a prisoner, a hostage. For what devious means she didn't know. She didn't know what or who Craig Taylor represented. Obviously he

knew about her father. Was she a pawn in a play for power?
Or merely the victim of greed, her kidnapping nothing more
than financial?

But Craig had money! she reasoned. Or did he? He had told
her he came from an affluent family, but was that just another
filament in a carefully woven web of deceit?

Lord, she didn't even know if she was still being held by
Craig. Her eyes once more rested upon the hatch that looked
out to the sky. She would have to go up.

A quaking of fear riddled through her again. What was the
game? Was her life to be forfeit if things didn't go as planned?
No, she soothed herself, she hadn't been physically harmed.
Knocked unconscious, yes, but not permanently injured in any
way. Her still grieving heart plunged over her emotions. She
couldn't believe that Craig would hurt her. He had lain beside
her, taken her, possessed her.

"Stop!" This time she wailed her fervent plea to herself
aloud in a pathetic whisper. This type of thinking was going
to get her nowhere and she would need all her courage, all her
assumption of cool hauteur to climb up the rickety, splintering
steps and face whoever piloted the craft she was upon.

Sliding her legs over the bunk, Blair moaned softly as she
clutched her head, spinning anew with the sudden effort. She
sat, clenching her teeth while the motion died down. She stood
very slowly, pushing up on the bed for support while her mind
ceased its reeling. Between the inexplicable dizziness and the
lazy sway of the boat, she had to wait several seconds before
assuring herself that blackness was not going to overwhelm
her again.

Finally secure in her growing strength, Blair let go of the
bed and carefully approached the steps. *You are a hostage,* she
reminded herself. *Make no stupid moves, but keep your eyes
and ears alert.*

What was correct hostage etiquette? she wondered, fighting

hysteria. Name, rank, and serial number. *Keep your dignity,*
she begged herself, *you will get out of this.*

Pride, dignity, and the hate born of betrayal would sustain
her, allow her to meet whoever lurked above with aloof and
cutting precision. She set foot on the first of the ladder rungs,
unaware that within her subconscious she was praying that
Craig was still her captor and that he hadn't turned her over
to another, perhaps even more loathsome . . .

He had known that she would come up eventually. What
other course did she have? From the tiller he watched as she
stepped into the sunlight, shielding her eyes from the sudden
spurt of brilliance with the involuntary action of casting an arm
upward. He was certain that her gaze had rested upon him
for a split second and that some unfathomable emotion had
skyrocketed through the flashing emerald of her eyes. Was she
just a little bit relieved?

If she was frightened, she didn't give a single sign. Not a
single tremble was visible to the naked eye. With forehead still
shielded by a crooked arm, she surveyed their rickety-looking
vessel, from grayed sails to worm-gnawed bow to worm-
gnawed stern. Her gaze rested upon him once again, disdain
and annoyed indifference flicking through her eyes this time.
He waited, hands tense upon the tiller.

But as she remained scathingly silent, trying to sear his flesh
with her exuding contempt, his bitterness prompted him to goad
her into acknowledgment of his presence.

"Good morning, Mrs. Teile," he drawled.

Her vision was drawn immediately to him, her eyes blazing
despite her cool manner. "Taylor," she returned. He had never
heard his name spat with such disgust.

It was all that Blair had as a defense.

Craig, as always, seemed at home in his surroundings. Like
a chameleon, he easily wore new colors, and wore them well.
Negligently lounged against the bow while he held the tiller,
he appeared comfortable, too comfortable. He was barefoot,

bare-chested, and bare-legged in cutoffs, a striking specimen, the sun wreaking gold havoc with his tawny hair and bronze, superbly toned muscles. A glistening of sweat over his broad, hair-matted chest only enhanced the image of a handsome sportsman out for a leisurely sail. But she knew that his casual stance was as deceptive as his being. No matter how relaxed he appeared, Craig Taylor was a coiled cat, an explosive ready to discharge at any second.

Blair lowered her lashes to rip her gaze from his. Even now she found herself being hypnotized by his yellow fire eyes. She had seen his features tighten as she grated his name, but only for a fraction of a second. He now appeared as granite—hard, cold, implacable.

Having freed herself of his gaze, Blair focused on the water and the shoreline—land not too far distant. But the land was dismal looking; heavy foliage crawled all the way to the river's edge. The type of thick brush continually inhabited by snakes, insects, reptiles, and all creatures imaginable that slithered and crawled.

They were on a river; that was all she really gained from her perusal. What river or where she didn't have the faintest idea. She was sure they hadn't traveled terribly far—the landscape hadn't changed—the jungle had merely increased in density.

"Were you thinking of swimming, Mrs. Teile?" Craig inquired, his voice silky and polite and slightly arrogant. "I don't advise it. I believe I noticed a few crocodiles lounging on shore this morning, and"—he smiled at her dryly, flashing white teeth in an infuriating manner—"if you should avoid all the creatures, there's me. Among my other dubious talents, I do swim like a fish."

Blair glared at him in return, inwardly convincing herself that an attempt to pummel him into little pieces would not be the prudent thing to do. She was wishing with venom that the scorching sun would burn every inch of the skin he so unconsciously bared to it.

Stay cool, she warned herself. "Taylor," she said distinctly, "although the last weeks certainly do little to verify my point, I am not stupid."

"Glad to hear it."

His drawling amusement, irritatingly evident in the brilliant light of his yellow eyes, threatened to create a combustion within her. But she didn't explode. She managed to retain her air of scathing contempt and once more assess her surroundings.

"Well?" he inquired politely.

Blair managed a disinterested shrug. "I've heard of plans to raise the *Titanic,*" she said dryly, "but never the *African Queen.* Are you sure this thing isn't going to just sink with both of us aboard and ruin your scheme, whatever it is."

"Fear not, Mrs. Teile," he advised gravely, "this boat will not sink."

His calm, positive assurance drove the first chink into her armor. "Where are you taking me?" she demanded heatedly.

He met her angry question with cool indifference. "Out."

"Out where?"

He shrugged. "Sorry."

"How—" *Don't let me falter,* she prayed. "How long are you planning to keep me?"

"Since you don't seem to care for the accommodations," he responded, his body still at ease but his gaze piercing and alert, "I'll do my best to see it's as short a time as possible."

"Oh, and when will that be?"

"We'll both know when the time comes."

"So you are a mercenary!" Blair snapped contemptuously. "Working for someone else."

"Actually," he returned dryly—and Blair curled her lips into a grimly satisfied smile to see that she had struck a nerve of discord—"this particular assignment is in answer to a special request. A favor I wasn't quite allowed to refuse. But I can guarantee you, Blair, I would damned well rather be really working.''

"A terrorist," she scorned quietly.

"Whatever you wish," he told her with a tired shrug. "But at any rate, you're here for the duration. If you want, we can stare at each other out here for as long as you wish. Otherwise you can go back into the cabin and get yourself a cup of coffee. You do look as if you could use one."

Once again Blair forced herself to swallow back bile and dig her nails into her own palms to prevent herself from hurtling at him with an insane rage. He was looking exceptionally healthy—bathed, shaved, rested, and refreshed—while she was beginning to feel as if she had been dragged through the mud by a team of horses. Eyeing him with venomous acid, she turned her back on him and approached the hatch.

"Blair."

The uniquely authoritative velvet that was so often his voice stopped her in her tracks. She was too attuned to that voice not to halt. "What?" she demanded icily.

"I'd appreciate it if you would bring up a cup for me."

She started laughing, and then tried to stop the sound with the fear that she would grow hysterical. "You have to be bloody mad!" she charged him. "You've kidnapped me, I haven't the faintest idea of what is going on, and you're asking for coffee as if we were on a date."

"Nothing is going to happen to you," Craig grated firmly.

"Oh? And how do I know that? What is this? A political maneuver? A ransom attempt? What happens if no one pays up?" She was unaware of her own motion, but as her charges rose shrilly, she was advancing upon him. He rose to his full height as she approached him, abruptly reminding her as she came within inches of him that he was not only composed of pure steel and banded muscle, but that he towered over her, putting her at the grave disadvantage of straining her neck in her attempt to verbally accost him.

Panic and hysteria then began to grow despite all the mental assurances she had tried to give herself as she realized he was springing to pounce. Her urge to retreat came too late; he closed the distance between them with a single stride that didn't for a second deter the hand that propelled the tiller. His single-handed clamp on her shoulder was nonetheless expert and relentless. "I'm telling you," he snapped, "nothing is going to happen. You have to stay with me for a while, and that's it. Get used to it, accept it, and the time will pass much more quickly—and pleasantly."

"Get used to it?" Her fear was well hidden by incredulous fury. "Pretend we're out for a nice friendly sail through the jungle."

"Yes, if you like." There was suddenly a gleam in his eyes that she couldn't possibly misread. She had seen it before. "The company isn't half bad," he reminded her with low insinuation. "I know damned well that you don't think so—"

His speech was broken off as her hand connected with his cheek. She was a fool, but she didn't have time to think out her action. He had grossly added insult to injury, and her ravaged pride had struck with no dictation from the mind. She watched the imprint of her fingers with frozen fascination as it reddened across the bronze, painfully aware that his yellow gaze was rapidly changing to a flame gold.

His face lowered to within an inch of her; his clamp upon her shoulder constricted tightly. "I hit you last night, Blair. I had to," he rasped. "So I'll take that to even the score. But for your sake and mine, accept this. I swear that nothing is going to happen to you. Shortly your life will go on as normal. Now, I'm quite aware that you would like to beat me to a pulp with a two-by-four and then toss me overboard to the crocodiles, but you're not going to be able to do it. You will probably feel the vast temptation to slap me again, *but don't do it.* I can only turn the other cheek once."

"Let go of me!" Blair hissed, dangerously close to tears

and determined not to let him see the weakness. "I don't want you touching me."

Craig slowly relinquished his grip, a bitter grimace filling his features. "All right, princess," he drawled with insulting intonation on the third word. "I won't touch you. Unless you make me. So I suggest you try to live in peaceful coexistence."

Blair clenched her teeth and lowered her head. "How can I?" she demanded.

"Try," Craig replied mockingly. His fingers were suddenly around her wrist, not hurting her, but a vise that clearly announced the foolishness of her even dreaming of pitting her strength against his. "Try." His repeat of the word was a warning command.

"Let go of me, please!" Blair hissed. She had to get away from him, if only for a short respite. Pulled against the expanse of his chest, she realized that as friend or foe this enigma of a man was a dynamic force that couldn't be denied. The energy that pulsed within him was frightening. He was tireless, he was indomitable. He was the overwhelming power of rampant vitality.

Insatiable. Inhaling the scent of him that taunted her nostrils as she was drawn to him, it was impossible not to remember the night—just last night—the lover who could demand and satiate her into a blissful interlude while still craving more.

He wasn't releasing her. She couldn't see his deadly eyes because the top of her head was beneath his chin. She stared into his corded neck, into the chest below where every individual muscle could be identified.

"I asked you to trust me, Blair."

"I can't possibly trust you!" It was meant to be a retort but came out pathetically as a plea. "Tell me what's going on!"

"I can't! Get that through your thick skull—I can't!" His pressure on her wrist increased, and she wondered briefly how he hadn't once made the mistake of releasing the boat's tiller.

Because he needs only one hand to subdue me, she thought bitterly.

"Listen to me, Blair." She was suddenly jerked away from him so that she was forced to see his eyes. "Damn it, Blair! I want to do the best I can to make this easy for you! But we're in for a bit of roughing it, and damn you, woman, you're not going to make every minute on this boat a misery! Look around you! And, yes, look at this tub we're on! So help me God, you are going to put in. You can be agreeable, or I can cast the anchor down now, throw you over my shoulder like a sack of potatoes, and tie you up in the cabin. I don't want to hurt you. Believe that, and we'll get along just fine. Get this straight—cause me an overdose of trouble, and you will definitely regret it. Am I understood?"

Blair worked furiously at her wrist, to no avail. "Yes!" It was a desperate scream. "Yes, I've got it! I'm supposed to be an accomplice to my own kidnapping! Well, all right, Taylor, you've got it. You want coffee, I'll get your damned coffee!"

He released her abruptly, so quickly that Blair, still unaccustomed to the swaying boat and still faintly dizzy, her head pounding viciously, staggered backward. She regained her balance quickly, her strength derived from pure determination and will power. She was out of his reach, and wisely decided never to make the mistake of coming within it again. She had one advantage—Craig was trying his damnedest to get somewhere; therefore, he had to keep the boat going.

She paused at the hatchway. "Just don't ever sleep, Taylor," she warned menacingly as she lowered herself down the ladder. "Don't ever make the mistake of sleeping."

"That's my worry, isn't it?" he queried in her wake.

By the time she reached the galley she was shaking like a leaf. For some reason she did believe him. He didn't intend her harm. No one who really wanted to hurt apologized so sincerely while knocking you flat.

She was shaking because nothing changed her own reactions

to the man. Standing so near him, feeling the intensity of his eyes upon her, his breath rustling her hair, for countless moments all she had wanted to do was pretend the whole thing had been a nightmare and curl into his arms, arms that could be shockingly gentle, arms that could demand and swirl her into an abyss where nothing mattered except the erotic delights he created.

"I hate him," she whispered sharply, clenching her eyes closed. "I hate him, hate him, hate him. . . ."

She finally stopped her shaking, opened her eyes, and looked over the stove. Odd, she thought. Although rustic in appearance, the appliance seemed to be adequate and in good working order. It was fueled by gas, and a tiny flame hovered beneath an aluminum coffeepot.

Chalk one up for Craig Taylor. Among his "dubious" talents, he apparently had the capability of making decent coffee.

But he really couldn't be expecting her to run up the steps and cheerfully hand him a cup. They were not out for a pleasure cruise—she was his prisoner. Prisoners simply couldn't be expected to assist their jailers. Unless, of course, they were being granted a certain amount of freedom in return. Would he carry out his threat? she wondered. If she didn't toe the line as first mate to his captain, would she find herself bound in the cabin for the voyage?

Blair spent a little too much time pondering the problem. She suddenly realized that she had been hearing scampering up on the deck—sure movements, swift movements. There was a change in the feel of the sway.

Taylor had cast anchor and lowered the sails. And he was coming belowdecks.

Thoroughly annoyed with the interruption in her fumbling search, Blair continued to comb cabinets for cups. She knew when he was behind her; his presence permeated the small space of the galley section.

Dismayed with her panicked obedience, Blair refused to

glance his way. Willing her hands not to tremble, she poured coffee into two cups, knowing that he watched her, knowing that he was near. She turned and none too graciously pressed his cup into his hands. "Here."

He accepted the cup. "Sit down, Blair."

The only feasible course of action seemed to be acquiescence to his invitation—or command, whichever. Brushing past him, Blair took a seat at the round table, scooting far away to leave him plenty of room.

But he didn't sit immediately. He reached for a short-sleeve blue work shirt and shrugged into it, leaving it unbuttoned, then fit a hand into his pocket and tossed a pack of cigarettes and book of matches onto the table in front of her. He watched her speculatively, but said nothing and turned back to the galley section. Moments later he had produced a cast iron frying pan and procured a handful of brown eggs from a wire basket near the sink. Along with the eggs he cracked into the pan with a practiced hand, he threw in a thick slice of ham.

Blair drew a cigarette from the pack and lit it, noticing with dismay as the match trembled in her hand that she was still as nervous as a cat. He was being, in a strange way, courteous, she realized. If not courteous, at least concerned. He had known how very badly she needed that cigarette.

The aroma from the galley began to fill the cabin. Despite everything, Blair was aware of a voraciously growing hunger. Glad that she was to be fed, Blair took a covert look at her "host." In the unbuttoned shirt and cutoffs, moving about the galley with the innate precision that was his in all things, he was just too much the epitome of the male ideal. Her blood began to sizzle again with the pain of betrayal.

Craig set a plate of food before her, then procured a plate for himself. Placing utensils on the table, he sat down across from her and began to eat. "You haven't touched your coffee," he commented politely.

It was too easy to be drawn into his web. Blair determined

never to waver in the scorn she would show. "I was waiting for you," she told him with a biting bravado, as cool as he for all outward appearances as she smiled icily. "I thought I'd assure myself it contained no arsenic."

A look of intense annoyance flashed across his features. "That was silly, Blair."

She picked up her coffee cup, furious to find her fingers trembling. "How the hell would I know anything?" she flared.

His cup made a sharp, clattering return to the table. Craig had had it. He was doing his best to see to her creature comforts and safety and she was still acting as if he had grown horns and a tail overnight.

"All right, Blair, you don't know anything. So I'm going to fill you in." There was no anger in his voice; it was low, soft, excruciatingly silky, and deadly. He stood, his height wavering her resolves as he towered over her before lowering his torso down to hers, setting an arm behind her, the other on the table, creating a virtual prison without touching her. "I'm a member of an elite cult. We meet in the forest on Halloween night. I've gone through all this trouble so that we can use you in a ritual. I was all for having you drawn and quartered myself, or at least put to the rack, but, no, we decided to save you for bigger things. You would have made an absolutely lovely sacrifice dressed in white upon the high altar, but . . ." His confession, told with a serious deadpan that had Blair staring at him with an almost believing fascination, suddenly took a pause as he cast an insolent glance over her from the top of her head to the spot where she disappeared beneath the table. "I'm afraid they demand the virginal type for sacrificial maidens, and I could personally guarantee the high priests that you certainly couldn't be classified virgin material."

Blair sat stunned at first, hypnotized by the somber intensity of his absurd explanation. The last, however, sank in with sure, deliberate insult. There was no conscious thought to her action;

she simply responded with the spontaneity of rage and flicked the remainder of her coffee into his face.

Luckily it had cooled. Belatedly Blair thanked God for that small favor, sitting motionless, but regretting her impulse while cringing inside with the fear of reprisal.

There was none, unless eyes could be said to really wound. Craig was startled, definitely, and he stood as still as she for an explosive moment as the coffee dripped from his severe features. Then he grabbed his napkin, wiped his face slowly, and shot her that impaling glance. "Excuse me, will you?" His fingers lifted a side of the wet blue shirt from his chest. "I'll just grab another shirt."

Blair watched numbly as he walked to a cabinet in the far aft and extracted a similar shirt, a little more faded, and discarded the damp one to don the new. The man, Blair decided, was capable of tolerating a lot. But he did know what was going on; his nerves weren't shattered, he was striking exactly where it would hurt the worst.

He sauntered slowly back to the table, his facial expression unfathomable, his eyes firmly guarded. "I'll be happy to pour you another cup of coffee, Blair," he said with an edge of warning rasping his voice, "*if* you plan to drink it this time. It will be hot, and though I'm a patient man, I do tend to become irate when scalded."

Blair didn't answer him, but something in her expression must have given the assurance that she didn't have the innate maliciousness or nerve to purposely cause serious pain. He poured her a cup of fresh coffee and set it before her, watching her. Then he ran his fingers tensely through his hair before sitting opposite her a second time. "I'm sorry for what I said, but I don't like this situation any better than you do and that razor-edged tongue of yours is wearing on the nerves."

"What do you want me to do?" Blair demanded thickly. "Thank you for taking me along?"

"I asked you to trust me."

"You asked the impossible."

"You trusted me once."

Blair looked quickly to her plate and gave her concentration to her now very cold eggs. "Yes," she said lightly, trying to hide the tears that were forming behind her lids. "I made a very foolish mistake, didn't I? On top of your other tricks, you connived me into a confession scene where I bared not only my own life to you, but Ray Teile's."

"Damn it, Blair!" His fist connected with the table in an uncontrollable spurt of violence before he took a deep breath and started over. "Blair, all the time that we shared has nothing to do with this. You and I have nothing to do with this. Anything I asked or gave was real—"

"Oh?" Blair couldn't prevent the bitterly sarcastic interruption. "Seducing me wasn't part of the plan?"

She almost heard the grind of his teeth and his cynical reply made her desperately wish she had chosen to keep her mouth shut.

"It was the other way around, wasn't it? I distinctly remember *you* appearing in *my* tent. Although I will say that I'm perfectly willing to take up where we left off."

"Thank you, no," Blair denounced him with acid contempt. "That is, if I do have a choice. After all, I'm merely the victim, right?"

He laughed with no mirth, and the leonine eyes were keenly upon her. "Poor, ravaged victim, eh? Can't quite reconcile your own nature with the situation. Are you suggesting I rape you? It will be all right if Blair has no conscious choice?"

"No!" Blair gasped with horror, standing to viciously assault the table with her napkin. She had been ravenous; she now felt sick.

"Don't worry, my dear Mrs. Teile," he mocked her, lazily leaning his shoulders against the seat, "We haven't been at sea quite that long. Besides, I sincerely doubt that anything occurring between you and me could ever be classified as rape. I'd never have to use force, I promise.''

Blair glared at him for a split second, then turned from the table, certain that if she stayed any longer she would toss another cup of coffee into his face or do something even worse. She was equally certain that his reaction would not be so calm a second time.

''Where are you going?'' Craig demanded coolly.

She turned back to him and her gaze implied he had to be ridiculously stupid. ''Now, just where the hell could I go?'' she demanded in turn. ''Topside. I don't believe I'm compelled to carry on a conversation with you either.''

''Wait!'' he ordered in a stinging voice. Rather than trust her luck, Blair stood antagonistically still, wondering if and vaguely hoping that he was about to make another apology.

None was forthcoming. His eyes were imperious and hard as he reached for the wet shirt. ''We have a few things to get straight here.'' He stuffed the shirt into her hands. ''Our clothing supply is limited. You are laundry detail.''

''The hell I am!'' Blair denied in an adamant growl.

''The hell you aren't,'' he replied softly, eyes narrowing to their dangerous tilt. ''You're also going to cook and sail this tub along with me. We have a distance to go, my sweet, and you're going right along with me. There's nothing outside this boat, Mrs. Teile, not for a long, long way. We're surviving together out here, and you will be putting in your fair share.''

''You forget, Mr. Taylor, this sail was not my idea. And if you have problems to solve, you are just going to have to solve them yourself.''

''We'll see about that,'' he informed her, leaving no doubt in her mind that they certainly would. But for the moment he had little else to say. Brushing past her, he mounted the ladder to the deck.

Since he was on deck, Blair decided to stay below. She sat back down, glanced at the cigarette pack on the table, and hastily extracted one to light. She watched the smoke plume away in the cabin. Dusty gray curtains were pulled over the portholes, and with a flash of claustrophobia she yanked them open. She was just in time to catch a view of Craig's muscled calves and bare feet passing by fleetly as he moved busily across the deck weighing anchor.

She nervously smoked the cigarette down to the filter, aware that they were under sail again as the swaying of the cabin increased. The feeling wasn't uncomfortable though—she loved to sail. She and Ray had often spent their free time sailing the brilliant blue waters of the Chesapeake.

Ray! She thought of her husband with dismay. She had entrusted Craig with so many secrets.

But it had seemed so right at the time. She had purged herself of so much pain, relinquished the ghost she held so dear, found a new ecstasy that had shadowed the past into its proper perspective.

That was her fury, she knew. She should be frightened, she should be determined to escape her captor at any cost. But her humiliation was still taking precedence in her mind.

She was faced with the unhappy realization that Craig had indeed struck a bull's-eye. She hated him, didn't she? Despised and scorned him. She knew him to be a cunning and devious renegade. But she still wanted him, still wanted to feel his touch. His gaze, sensuous when lazily taunting, sensuous when honed by anger still held the power to send chills racing down her spine with the anticipation of excitement.

Blair sent her teeth down cruelly into her bottom lip. He would never know. She wasn't a witless animal, she was an intelligent human being capable of governing her physical actions with her mind. She would loathe Craig Taylor until this episode was over, and then she would happily see him behind bars, where he belonged.

Lions should be caged, she told herself.

Her mind continued to run in merry-go-round circles as she

desperately tried to figure out reasonably what was happening. He kept insisting that she trust him, but how could she possibly trust a man who had so carefully planned her abduction? Even now the memory of seeing the first shocking lights streak through the jungle had the power to cripple her over with new pain.

Who was he? her mind shrieked. And how dare he continue to behave as if she were at fault for not accepting this farce?

She sat until she thought her mind would drive her over the brink of sanity. Then she realized she had been sitting so long that her muscles were cramping. She stood, stretched, and flexed her muscles, grimacing ruefully. One thing was certain; she couldn't spend her days just sitting.

But pacing the confines of the cabin was not much better. Her naturally fastidious eyes kept reverting to the dishes left at the circular table, and although she kept telling herself there was no way she was going to cooperate in the least with Craig, she finally succumbed to the irresistible urge to straighten up. Stacking the plates and utensils in her arms, she moved into the galley with a sigh. He had been right on a point, and so had she. She had nowhere to go—and she was here as well as he. It appeared that she would eat again tonight in the cabin and just might be eating here for quite a while. Besides, a show of cooperation might put him off-guard. When the time came, she just might be able to get away if he believed himself secure in his control over her.

Blair dumped the dishes into the sink and began to raid the cabinets beneath it for soap. It was a strange-looking tub to be so well supplied, she thought again. Craig hadn't mentioned water conservation at all. The sailboat had to carry an impressive supply.

At the helm Craig stared unseeing at the mainsail, billowing ever so slightly in the slight breeze that carried them along at a poky four knots. But he didn't need speed at the moment; their voyage was moving along just as planned.

As he stared absently at the sail, he was busy silently berating himself. Why did he keep losing control? It was unlikely that even the most polite, courteous manner would sway Blair into renewed trust when he couldn't explain himself. But it was unnecessary for him to keep driving in the little stakes that were bringing her hostility upon him in full force.

Why was he doing it? He couldn't help it. Every time her chin rose with that scathing contempt, he couldn't control the primitive force that propelled him into reminding her that she had been his, completely his, intimately his.

He was in love with her, he reminded himself ruefully. Male instinct couldn't allow him to let her forget how she responded to his slightest touch.

The tiller suddenly jerked with the convulsive tightening of his hand. *Damn,* he hissed to himself. He was tempted to draw in the sails, weigh anchor, and run below to satisfy his charge, to take her forcefully on the cabin floor until she cried out the realization that she did want him, loved him no matter what, trusted him.

Easy, Taylor! his mind snapped. His eyes scanned the river. He did have a few problems, and he did need to solve them. They would be passing the village of Santa Maria Teresa before long, and the river would narrow. He wanted to make sure to pass by so that the villagers would notice nothing out of the ordinary. Hoisting a loose line around the tiller to hold the boat steady, he moved fleetly to the hatchway. "Blair!" he announced briskly. "Topside, I want to talk to you."

There was no reply, and Craig grimaced, a twitch of amusement pulling at his lips. He hadn't really expected the princess to come bounding obediently to the deck. Leaning down to the hatch, he was pleasantly surprised to hear the trickle of running water. He didn't kid himself into suspecting that she might be about to take him on trust. He was sure that her caged exile had just left her desperate for something to do, a way to pass the time.

"Blair," he called down sweetly, "could you please come up here? I'd hate like hell to have to cast anchor just to come to you." Though tauntingly pleasant, he made sure his voice implied that she too would hate for him to have to come to her.

Blair listened to the sound of his request with her teeth grating. She glanced around the galley, in order now, and dried her hands furiously on a piece of cloth she had found. Her mind wandered briefly. The boat gave her the same feeling that Craig's presence always had—something just didn't jell.

Their boat was definitely a rustic-looking tub, but on closer inspection it was a strange rustic. The drab coloring made one think of age and dirt, as did the chipping varnish and knotted wood. But there wasn't a piece of wood in the cabin that she had tested that wasn't hard and sturdy. And the galley was certainly well equipped. Cabinets opened by her questing hands had displayed a wide variety of canned goods and a small icebox had sported a nice array of meats. Wicker baskets like the one from which Craig had earlier procured the eggs rested in various places on the counter that was the separation of galley and cabin. In them were fruits, potatoes, beans, and rice.

None of it was particularly encouraging. It appeared that they were prepared for a long siege.

"Blair!" She heard Craig's snapping command once more and mimicked him with silent fury. The thought of ignoring his summons was tempting—she should give him every bit as much trouble as possible—but she wasn't terribly secure in her belief that he wasn't going to harm her. *He isn't going to harm me,* her mind persisted, *no matter what I do. Toward me he isn't a physically dangerous man.*

Like hell! He was the most physically dangerous man she had ever met.

That's not what I mean, another voice, shocked, replied. And none of it mattered anyway. She simply didn't have the nerve to find out.

"I'm coming!" she called back up the hatchway with vast irritation, squaring her shoulders in an attempt to build a wall of hostility. Warily she dropped the cloth and climbed the ladder.

"What?" she snapped icily, surprised and taken off-guard as she almost crashed into him. Skittering to one side, she narrowed her eyes upon him and repeated, "What?"

He cast a glance over his shoulder to the tiller. "Watch the helm, mate," he commanded briskly. Blair noticed then that he had affixed a sheet line to keep the tiller set at a dead-ahead direction.

"I'm not sailing your damned boat—" she began incredulously, but he cast her a glance with a single raised eyebrow that quelled her speech even before he disappeared into the hatch himself.

Muttering beneath her breath, Blair released the line and took the tiller into her hands. Wasn't he presuming a lot to be so sure that she knew what she was doing? Not that it took any expertise to follow a straight line at a slow pace on an almost calm river. But what if she took it into her mind to run them aground on the river bank? She glanced at the banks—distant at this wide part of the river. There was nothing welcoming to be seen. Dark foliage and dense underbrush.

With a sigh Blair cast her eyes to the mainsail billowing high and proud in the breeze. There wasn't much of a breeze at that, but at full sail the canvas, dingy and gray-looking as it was, held a certain mystique that captivated nevertheless. The sky was a clear, a soft blue without a cloud to mar it. If she closed her eyes, then opened them merely to the sail and the sky, she could be anywhere, languorously feeling the gentle touch of the breeze.

"Thanks." Craig cut into her thoughts briskly, slipping a hand over hers and retrieving the tiller. Blair was leaning against the captain's seat and immediately jumped up. The brief touch of his broad hand had filled her with an unnerving warmth, thoughts of those fingers coursing her body with tenderness and strength never out of her consciousness.

"Is that it?" she asked briskly.

"No, that's not it." He tossed a bundle of clothes into her hands and she saw that he had gone under to retrieve them with a purpose.

Blair stared at the clothing she had caught by reflex. It didn't take a genius to quickly fathom that the bundle consisted of peasant garb—a rough cotton skirt and blouse.

"I'd like you to wear that," Craig said blandly.

Blair tossed the clothing to his bare feet. She smiled nicely. "I'd rather not."

It seemed to be an endless time that they stared at each other, yellow eyes blazing into an emerald that coolly defied them. Beneath her façade Blair felt her nerves unwinding. What was the plan? If she were being held for ransom, surely she had to be returned in sound limb and health.

Craig smiled suddenly, a very engaging grin. "Okay, Blair, you don't want to wear the outfit? Suit yourself. I just thought you might be feeling a bit grubby. In case you haven't noticed, there's a shower in the head. I thought you might want to clean up a bit."

The idea of a shower was tremendously appealing, but she was suddenly sure she had gained a victory. He wanted her in the peasant garb, but she had been correct. His orders must proclaim that he couldn't touch her, and so he was stuck, wishing he could bodily shove her into the clothing.

"Thank you, Taylor," she acknowledged with an inclination of her head and lift of her brow. "Perhaps I will shower, but I will keep my own clothes."

Turning on her heels, she left him and retreated down the hatch. She had noticed the shower earlier, but it was a primitive thing, consisting of a spouted hose that hung on the wall and a curtain that followed a track against the bland tile that flanked the wood. She did feel dirty, and the feeling didn't help when desperately trying to keep calm. Apparently he planned to sail on awhile before casting anchor again. She would be wise to make use of the time while he was occupied.

Searching around the cupboards that lined the inner walls, Blair found not only a towel and soap, but an extra pair of jeans and a shirt that surely had to have been planted for her use—the jeans would have barely reached Craig's kneecaps. Chuckling softly, she went into the head with the new set of clothing. Craig had probably assumed she would wear the peasant garb just for a chance to wash what she had been wearing, she reasoned. "No dice, Taylor," she muttered smugly to herself, then frowned. There was no way to lock the door to the head. Well, she asked herself impatiently, what had she been expecting?

She paused for a second, listening, but heard nothing but the soft slap of water against the boat. With a shrug she decided Craig was definitely busy above board. Slipping behind the curtain, she fumbled for a few moments with the faucets and then managed to get the hose attachment working. The water was cold, but she didn't mind. It felt remarkably refreshing against the heat and seemed to have a marvelous effect on the spinning sensation that still riddled her head occasionally. How hard had he hit her? she wondered.

Her life had become a frustrating puzzle of heartache, fear, and betrayal. But her mind couldn't rest upon the few known facts continually. She would become an overloaded circuit and explode. She closed her eyes as the water cascaded over her, relishing the purely physical stimulation of the simple pleasure, a reprieve from the never-ending heat. The scent of the soap was fresh and clean; she began to feel as if she could once more do battle.

With a sigh Blair decided to turn the water off. Surely their tanks couldn't hold an indefinite amount of water, and she was loathe to lose the pleasure of bathing if they ran short. Taylor didn't seem concerned, but then maybe he knew for a fact that there were no crocodiles in the river they traveled.

A tiny, indiscernable sound suddenly pierced Blair's thoughts. Catching her breath as her heart fluttered, Blair held perfectly still, her hand on the curtain as she waited. And waited. But she didn't hear anything else and finally threw open the curtain with a bold flourish. She released her breath with a sigh of relief. There was no one with her in the tiny head. She reached for the sink where she had deposited her towel but discovered it missing. Her mind began to race double-time with doubt. She was sure she had brought the towel and her clothing in, hadn't she? Or had she left her things just outside on the tip of the bed, afraid that they would become soaked in the tiny quarters?

She began to chew her lip, deliberating for what seemed to be an eternity. But there wasn't a sound from the cabin, and she couldn't stand there all day.

It would be impossible for Craig to be in the cabin. Gingerly she opened the door, only to attempt to slam it back shut with furious dismay.

Craig was not only in the cabin; he was leaning casually and comfortably on the doorframe. A single movement with his arms blocked her attempt to slam the door, his yellow eyes assessing her with insolent indifference. As she stared back at him, her skin acquired the blood red shade of a boiled lobster. He stuffed her towel and the clothes into her hands. "Again, I suggest that you wear these, Blair," he said flatly. He smiled ever so slightly. "But it's your choice: these or nothing."

Twisting her jaw with rage, Blair began to fumble with the towel, dropping it in her attempt to cover herself from his eyes, eyes that fully assured her she was an absolute fool to ever believe a victory would be hers. He politely bent to pick up the towel for her and made matters worse by brushing her breasts with the thick texture of his hair. He saw the alarm in her face as he rose and slowly returned the towel, his head shaking slowly with vast mockery at her attempts to hide from him.

"Don't be absurd," he stated contemptuously. "There's not an inch of your body I'm not more familiar with than you are yourself."

Then he turned and left her, picked up a cigarette from the table, and moved away with indifference.

CHAPTER SEVEN

Craig lit his cigarette, wincing as he heard the head door slam in his wake. He reached into the small icebox, delved through the packets, and secured himself a beer. Kicking the door closed with an abrupt movement of his foot, he wrenched off the tab and dryly thanked Brad Shearer for the thought of packing him a supply of American beer. Taking a deep swig, he hoped to settle the jumbled chemistry that boiled inside him.

Both beer and cigarette in hand, he crawled up the ladder topside and walked to the bow to sit, casting his long legs over the edge of the boat. He had long ago moved toward shore to cast anchor and furl in the sails for a respite. He had come far enough. He wanted a little more time with his captive before moving any closer to inhabited areas. Later, in the night, he would move again and cover a little distance in the darkness.

Glancing at the anchor line as it bobbed in the water, he cursed himself miserably. He was a top man, known to be able to coerce people to his way of thinking with a minimum of pressure. He had to bear down on Blair; he had to make her realize that things would go his way. But his professionalism, long taken for granted, seemed to have deserted him. He couldn't stifle the taunts he continued to hurl at her.

And then he found himself thinking of her skin, of its satiny texture. The thought of skin led to that of curves, to breasts that came alive to his touch, to the way he could make her sigh with need when he stroked those luscious breasts with his tongue, circling the rose-hued nipples.

He groaned aloud with a sharp curse. *Taylor, man, what the hell has happened to you?* He always had a great gift for accepting reality, no matter how harsh. This should have been the chief's piece of cake. Reasons for the orders given him were classified, but it didn't take a terribly astute mind to know that a fear of guerrilla action was behind them. He could assume only that Blair couldn't be told anything, including his role in this fiasco, just in case something did go wrong, just in case she were to be captured by someone seeking information who was not averse to the usual methods used to assure its extraction.

Something was happening. If he had been told to move, there was a reason. And yet he was sure his slow crawl through the jungle to the coast was precautionary. He had been warned of guerrillas; he knew that guerrillas would still exist in a country still toddling like an infant to stand.

The chief had always been so sure that once they had moved out they would be doing nothing but playing for time. Obviously the chief did not know his old friend Huntington's daughter as well as he thought.

Damned princess out on this tub, he thought furiously. But the charge was completely out of line and he knew it. Blair was equipped with resources that went above and beyond the average woman. She would always be regal, aware of the pea beneath a hundred mattresses, but she would never complain.

His mind turned back to thoughts of facing her water-slicked, naked body and he cast his cigarette butt, burned low without his notice, out on the water with a vicious throw. He was getting to her, he knew it, but he was striking out, and she was tearing apart his very core simply by existing. One look at her and his body tensed with memory, his blood racing madly, his breath growing short and heavy.

Forget it, he warned himself. *She thinks you're a full-fledged demon.* The dregs of the earth, actually, had been her description. And it wouldn't be much better when she did know the truth. He wondered vaguely if she would begin to understand. Then he stood, impatient with himself, impatient with her. The sun was turning into a gleaming red sphere in the western sky. Dinner, another charming meal with his reluctant companion, seemed in order if he planned to hoist anchor later. It would be nice if she slept soundly for long hours.

Returning below, he found sound evidence that Blair had thoroughly ransacked the place looking for her own clothing in his absence. He allowed himself a grim smile. Obviously she had found nothing and frustrated herself to a satisfying fatigue. Clad in the native clothing, she rested on the bed, her jaw locked, seething as she stared at the planks above her.

Craig ignored her and turned his attention to the food. He was ravenous. It had been a long night and day for him, with the brunch he had prepared their only meal. He set a generous helping of rice on to boil and selected several of the thin native steaks, grimacing all the while. He wasn't much of a cook. He could think of a million restaurants he would like to be at right then.

His eyes turned covertly to Blair. She was obviously aware of his presence, but she had chosen to continue ignoring him. He clenched his jaw with tension. At the moment he was quite able to think of her as a pampered socialite. He would love to rip her out of the bed, give her a good boot in the rump, and insist that she help. She didn't have to be a Julia Child, she simply had to make their bland meals a bit more palatable. Nor was it a chauvinistic thought—merely a hungry one.

No, Taylor, he warned himself. He had long ago learned that patience was a virtue and that there were many more ways than one to skin a cat.

He watched the rice boil and set the meat on.

A few minutes later he had the meal, such as it was, prepared. He piled two plates with the food in the galley, collected flatware, and dumped the lot on the table with a loud clattering. "Dinner," he announced coolly, "is served." He turned from the table, went back into the galley, and began rummaging through compartments, happily discovering they had been stocked with a few wooden casks of wine. A local vintage, bitter and gritty, but anything would do. Removing the cork with more than necessary vengeance, he placed the cask and two cups on the table, then lit hungrily into his own food.

Blair was desperately wishing she could ignore his invitation, but she couldn't. The way out of this situation was not starvation. She had tossed away her food this morning, and was therefore ravenous now. It had been twenty-four hours since she had eaten.

He didn't glance up as she joined him at the table. Evidently he had decided that overtures toward her were a waste of time. She glanced at her plate. The rice was in starchy globs, but the meat was rare and appetizing looking. She cut off a square and bit into it, savoring the taste. Craig remained silent as she began to eat, his concentration on his own food. It was she who finally found the silence between them unbearable.

"I assume I'm to be sent back well fed and healthy," she said with a dry bravado she wasn't feeling. "My, my," she mused cattily, fingering the rough wooden cask of burgundy. "This outfit must really be on the financial rise."

"Sorry," he retorted, finishing his meal and pushing his plate to the side. "We didn't happen to have any Dom Pérignon on hand. But yes, you are to be returned in good condition." He lit a cigarette but made no move to pour the burgundy, nor did he offer her any. She reached across the table, asking with sweet sarcasm, "May I?"

"Please, help yourself. That is, if you're sure it won't offend your discriminating palate."

Blair smiled coolly, maintaining her saccharine demeanor. "Shall I pour you some?"

He shook his head slightly in mocking disbelief. "Please do. Will wonders never cease? You're actually offering to do something for me." He watched her as she poured the wine, his expression relaxed but assessive.

"Well," Blair murmured dryly, "I am supposed to trust you."

"That's right," he agreed, not batting an eye at her broad sarcasm.

"You're really just a nice guy."

"You got it."

"Well, then, Mr. Nice Guy," Blair said tartly, sipping the wine and grimacing at its acidic taste, "I hope you realize that the Hunger Crew is short people, and they're going to be in trouble."

"The Hunger Crew will not be in trouble," Craig informed her. "They'll shortly be receiving large quantities of something I'm afraid can be deemed far more important than even your precious presence—money."

Blair tried to hide her surprise with more sarcasm. "That's certainly big of you. You seem to cover all bases, don't you?"

A curious expression rippled almost instantly across his features and then was gone. "Yes," he said softly. "We are at the very least thorough. But I hate to disappoint you, Mrs. Teile. The donation was a personal gift from yours truly."

Blair wasn't quite able to stifle a gasp. Then he was wealthy, and certainly not out for a ransom. Unless, of course, he was lying. But she didn't think so; his education and experience seemed too vast. The information he gave her wasn't, however, particularly reassuring. If he wasn't after a ransom, the implications were grave. They could only be political.

"Then you are some type of a left-wing fanatic," she murmured.

He changed position with one of his lightning movements and leaned toward her, both elbows on the table, his head lowered conspiratorially. "No, Mrs. Teile," he said gravely. "I already told you—I practice black magic in the forest at night. With my forest friends. Some of us just happen to have money." He leaned back again with his expression tired rather than amused, quelling any biting comment she might have made in return. He picked up his cup of wine and rose with a curt "Excuse me," then strode to the ladder and climbed up the hatch, pausing on deck, his legs staunchly spread to counter the slight roll of the boat.

Blair finished eating quickly, glad that Craig's intent gaze wasn't still upon her as she voraciously cleaned her plate. Black magic! Pity that it wasn't the seventeenth century. She couldn't think of a scene she could possibly enjoy more than Craig Taylor tied to a stake with burning timber at his feet.

She glanced with rancor at the dishes left on the table and the pots and pans in the kitchen. So, he had just walked away, assuming that as of the morning he had acquired a dishwasher. Un-unh. Not on your life, buddy.

Blair stood and stretched, further irritated by the scratchy cloth that flowed around her body. Why the extra jeans if he was forcing her to wear this?

Everything was a question.

Feeling the confines of the cabin, she too climbed up to the deck. He didn't turn, but though she had risen silently, he had heard her. "What are you doing?" he demanded sharply.

"Seeking out a little fresh air at the bow," she responded tartly, adding with a feigned, very humble servility, "May I."

"Go."

She did, unaware that he did turn then as she picked up her skirt and moved lithely across the deck, pausing to balance by the mainmast before searching out privacy far aft and taking the same spot he had earlier to gaze out on the water.

Where the hell were they? she wondered listlessly, staring out into the darkness. A half moon provided a very faint glimmer of light, but it did little to illuminate the shoreline because the lights from the cabin were brighter, casting a haze upon all else. What would she see anyway? More jungle. She knew she was no longer near the Hunger Crew; she also knew she was still somewhere in Central America. But where? Would they ever come across a village where she might find help? It was unlikely. Craig was too thorough a person to afford her any such opportunity.

What would happen, she wondered idly, if she were to swim ashore? She was familiar with jungle, familiar enough to know it was dangerous. If she were to reach the land, which was a sound possibility from this proximity, could she make it to a small city or village? Her Spanish was excellent. Surely she could make herself understood.

But the darkness out there was overwhelming; it harbored all sorts of deadly night creatures. If she had light . . . *Wonderful,* she thought with an inner laugh. *I can just scamper back to the bow and politely request that Craig supply me with a flashlight for my flight.*

She gasped a scream, startled as his hand came down on her shoulder. ''No ideas, Blair,'' he cautioned softly, as if reading her mind. ''If you did swim in to shore, I'd be right after you, and as I told you earlier, I swim like a fish. If you reach land, I can run like a deer. I can also make it through the trees with the best of the chimps.''

''I'm impressed,'' Blair murmured, caustic but quiet as she shook his hand from her shoulder with a shrug. She glanced back at him to demand balefully, ''Tell me, Mr. Taylor, do you have any other talents on a par with the animal kingdom?''

There had been no cruelty on his face, no mockery, only a certain sadness that seemed to match her own. But now he suddenly laughed, his brows rising, and his tone taking on a strange tenderness, a tenderness she had known very well.

"I don't mean to brag," he said as he crouched beside her, his twinkling eyes reminding her how innuendos had once passed between them with comfortable ease, "but"—his voice lowered to a husky level—"there are certain things I can do just like a rabbit."

Blair sucked in air but didn't allow herself to move. She stared at him with all the disdain she could muster. She would have liked to hit him, but that would be foolish, and, dismayingly, that was only half of her reaction. Worse than that foolish urge, she would have liked to laugh. He stood as she stared, towering over her, reminding her of his vast length and how absurdly it fit against her smaller frame with aching perfection. Her temptation was to cling to his strength, to burrow into the protection of his broad chest, to hear him reassure her, tell her it was all a joke, a dream, to run to him for security.

Now, that was a laugh. He wasn't security; he was the enemy. And if she were ever to run anywhere, it would be away.

She rose with straight-backed grace. "Good night, Mr. Taylor," she told him flatly, brushing past him and returning to the bow to crawl back down to the cabin.

Craig watched her go, the proud tilt of her chin, the square line of her slender shoulders. Even in the dim light her hair flamed down her back with rich, dark, lustrous fire.

He clenched his hands into fists and stared into the night sky. For a moment there, just for a moment, he felt as if he had broken through. She had almost laughed at his impulsive teasing. Or had she? The desire to do him bodily harm had also gleamed in those vibrant eyes.

He heard her moving about the cabin and his teeth grated as he thought of the battle that would inevitably come this night. He couldn't keep her sedated forever. He played with the idea of spending his entire night above deck and leaving her alone, but discarded the notion almost immediately. It was going to be too long a trip for him to manage in total discomfort and with a complete lack of rest. There was also her to consider. She possessed a little too much bravado and courage. If she seriously considered an escape, she could easily hurt herself.

No, they would settle sleeping arrangements tonight, even if it did mean a battle. His teeth unlocked as he uttered an explosive, grating expletive to the night sky and stalked to the anchor line. Moments later they were moving into the current.

Blair once more ignored the mess that had been dinner as she returned to the cabin. Tired but restless she picked up her forgotten burgundy and sipped at it while she idly paced the few steps of the cabin. The acidic taste no longer bothered her; she hoped the alcohol would help still her whirling turmoil.

How long was this to go on? she wondered desperately. And who was Craig Taylor? Besides a warlock, she added with a spurt of wry humor. Unable to label her charismatic captor the renegade that he was, she began to rationalize, sliding back into a seat at the table and helping herself to another of his cigarettes. She finished her wine as she inhaled and expelled a fog of smoke, arguing with herself all along. There was a quality of goodness to Craig; there had to be. She simply couldn't equate the flesh-and-blood man she had come to know so well in the last three weeks with a cold-blooded assassin. And cruel lunatics didn't send money to charitable organizations in apology for stealing a pair of useful hands.

Was it at all possible to chip away at the rough edges of the man and convince him that his way of life was wrong? That he should let her go? She could promise to help him, she could intercede, swear not to bring charges against . . .

What a joke. He was not a man to be swerved from a course of action he had chosen to take. Whatever his principles were, he was a man who stuck to them indomitably.

Unless he could be made to see the error.

She started suddenly as she realized they were under way

again. Moving swiftly to the porthole over the table, she frowned, unable see a thing. Why was he moving at night?

Blair slid slowly back into the seat. What did it really matter? She wasn't going to make any escape attempts.

Bone weary and mentally and physically exhausted, she stood and dispiritedly moved back to the head. All she wanted to do right now was wash her face and crawl into bed.

Staring at her face in the cabinet mirror, she was idly surprised to see that she didn't look any different. Sighing softly, she opened the cabinet. She had been right. A hairbrush sat on the second shelf of the cabinet and Blair automatically threaded it through her hair. Setting it back and closing the cabinet, she sighed, feeling the never-ending round of questions springing up in her mind again. She didn't want to think anymore; the day had been filled with a gamut of emotions, all of them painful.

She wanted solace from the fear and betrayal, an escape from the fear, confusion, heartache, and quandary. She turned out the light in the head and returned to the cabin, crawling immediately into the bed and sinking her head into the pillow with relief. Actually she feared she wouldn't sleep; it had been late in the morning when she had woken, and a mind couldn't simply be turned off. But mental exhaustion was the most wearing type of tired there was. Even as she worried about sleeping, she slipped into a restless doze.

She had assumed she would awaken all through the night, but that wasn't the case. Her exhaustion took its toll. By the time Craig came back down to the cabin she was so soundly asleep that she didn't even twitch as he lay down beside her.

He had been given a night's reprieve, he thought wryly. What reprieve? She might have slept soundly, but his night was a misery. It wasn't difficult to rise long before she ever knew he was near.

* * *

They entered a test of willpower the following morning.
Craig attempted to be pleasant, but he was trying to prove a
point. She had to work with him.

And so, though he cooked and filled a plate for her at each
meal, he cleaned only what he needed to use. Irritated beneath
his calm façade, he tended to be clumsy. He broke several
plates, and then left them where they fell.

Eventually, he was sure, she would start to go crazy with
the mess and have to pick it up. But Blair, convinced the
breakage was done purposely to annoy her, just as stubbornly
skirted the broken stoneware. She ignored any of his remarks
and generally kept her distance. And yet, even keeping that
distance, with cutting, cynical remarks offered to Craig at any
chance given her, was a strain.

By nightfall, after a dinner consumed and the remains once
more left upon the table, Blair was once more exhausted, as if
she had spent the day sailing and Craig had spent it sunning
on the bow of the boat. When he went topside after dinner,
she lay down to doze, highly irritated that broken crockery lay
on the floor and a mess lay on the table, but determined to do
nothing about it.

And once again, sleep did come easily.

Sometime later she began to awaken to myriad sounds that
slowly filtered through her consciousness. She could hear voices
faintly, sometimes somber, sometimes rising in laughter. And
from very far off the light melody of a guitar.

Springing up in the bed, she pushed aside the material covering the porthole. They were passing a village, and the voices
were coming from the docks where late-night fishermen were
hauling in their catches. Lights from a town center blazed a

dull yellow, and in some café nearby, workers were sipping *cerveza* and listening to the haunting music of the guitar.

And the river was narrow here, very narrow. Surely she could call out to these people and receive some assistance.

Bolting from the bed, she raced to the hatchway, then stopped her headlong flight with caution. Climbing up the ladder quietly, she watched Craig. His eyes too were on the village as he held the tiller; he appeared deeply pensive. Bereft of shirt again, his golden-muscled physique gleamed in the eerie glow of light.

Blair bit down on her lip. She was going to have to flatten herself and crawl to the bow before shouting for help. Holding her breath carefully, she crept from the hatch and ducked, turning to attempt a slither to the bow.

She hadn't moved a foot before Craig's hand clamped down upon the small of her back, his fingers curling into the waistband of her skirt as he hauled her back to the tiller with him. Gasping for breath, Blair was able to expel a very weak "Help!" which, unfortunately couldn't be heard more than a yard from the boat. Translating her thought to Spanish, she tried again as he dragged her to his side, finally managing a slightly more substantial *"Ayudame! Ayud—"*

Navigation at this narrow section of the river was tricky, but Craig seemed to have it under perfect control single-handedly. He was quite effortlessly able to crush Blair to his side, pushing her mouth into his shoulder. She struggled against the iron band of his arm, but the action merely served as a Chinese torture—the more she twisted, the more tightly she was crushed.

"I can't let you do it, Blair," he said softly, his words a breath over her head. His grip on her eased somewhat. "No more calling out," he warned, catching sight of her eyes in the glow and seeking an agreement within them. He smiled at her, almost sadly again as they passed by the docks of the village and the late-night bustle that surrounded them. Friendly fishermen, stopping to watch them pass with idle interest, waved and hailed them.

Craig adjusted the arm that he had around Blair's body to lift her lower arm and hand by the elbow. "Un-unh," he warned, sensing a tension in her that meant another attempt for help. "Just wave good-bye to the nice people, Mrs. Teile."

Blair shut her mouth and watched helplessly as the village moved swiftly by them.

And then the glow that was the village began to fade. The fishermen in their boats and on the dock became minuscule, receding into the distance until she could only discern lights on the river. Even the breeze had seemed to pick up to accommodate Craig—mainsail, mizzen, and jib puffed out like night clouds, and the sailboat seemed to fly over the water.

"You can let go of me now," Blair commented tiredly. It was a pity she had ever gotten out of bed.

Craig didn't release her, but glancing up at his sharp profile, she realized that he wasn't looking at her; he probably hadn't even heard her. It was almost as if he had forgotten her. His eyes were keenly upon the sails.

"Hold the tiller," he commanded curtly, releasing her and springing to his feet. Blair glanced after him blankly, and the boat made a sudden sharp jerk. "Hold her steady!" Craig barked impatiently, crouching with instant coordination beneath the swaying boom. Feeling a rough wave suck at the boat a second time, Blair automatically grabbed the tiller tightly. She didn't like the role of first mate beneath a pirate captain, but she didn't much relish the thought of drowning either.

Craig quickly began to crank in the port sheet line, steadying the boom, then pulling in the mainsail. The craft immediately began to respond, rolling easily despite the increasing wind. Moments later the jib was furled, and their pace slowed to a more secure one, the boat keeling evenly starboard just slightly. In bare feet that seemed to hug the planks beneath them, Craig padded agilely back toward Blair and resumed control of the tiller.

"Go back to bed," he told Blair bluntly.

She stared at him silently for a moment, idly and dispiritedly wondering if he was aware of how very leonine he was capable of looking. His body had the grace of a great cat; his footsteps were as sure as the soft padding of the agile creatures. And now, so harshly alert, his eyes appeared more a true yellow-gold than ever. Night eyes, eyes that caught the slightest movement, eyes that ferreted into the soul.

Without a word Blair turned and carefully made her way down the ladder. The dinner plates she had ignored had crashed off the table and now lay in little pieces on the floor. Luckily Craig had picked up after himself in the galley. But combined with the previous shambles, the dinner plates made a true disaster area of the floor.

Feeling strangely disassociated from the situation, Blair bent to pick up the broken stoneware. Then she straightened. She wasn't going to clean up; she was a hostage, not the maid.

Tumbling back into the bed with a heavy depression weighing down upon her, she willed herself back to sleep.

Again she had no conception of how long she rested before being interrupted again, this time by the sense of movement nearby. She flicked her eyes open narrowly to see Craig, his expression hard as he viewed the destruction in the cabin. Apparently, though, he had no intention of dealing with the mess either. His displeasure evident, he turned abruptly to Blair, aware that she was awake despite the fact that she quickly closed her eyes tightly.

"You will pick this up in the morning," he said quietly.

She didn't respond, and he didn't feel it necessary to press his confident claim. Blair sensed each of his movements as he dimmed the cabin lights but refused to acknowledge that she was awake until she was forced to.

"Move over," he growled suddenly.

Her eyes flew wide open. *"What?"* It was a shriek, a disbelieving whisper.

"I said, move over," he repeated impatiently.

She didn't move over; she suddenly became very wide awake and leaped from the bed, facing him with hands on hips, feet firmly planted on the floor. "Oh, no!" she protested. "You are not sleeping in here with me." She meant to command with dignity, but her words were coming out as a plea. She was terribly aware that she was scared, and worse, she was more frightened of herself than she was of him. Despite all that had happened, she had kept trying to find excuses; she had still spent countless moments of the day admiring the man. "You promised," she charged him. "You said—"

"I think," Craig interrupted with a tired but firm voice, "that I promised I'd never force myself upon you, and don't worry, I have no intention of touching you." He stared back at the woman glaring at him, railing her scorn. Her eyes were sparkling like emeralds, as full of fire as her hair. Her form—the slender yet luscious form he had held with such tender wonder such a short time ago—was pulsating visibly with tension beneath the light cotton of her outfit. He had taken her underclothes earlier when he had stolen her jeans, and the rise and fall of full breasts—the peaks and darker hues of the nipples painfully visible—was scintillating despite his exhausted state. A hot sensation began to burn in his groin; his fraying nerves snapped and along with them, his temper.

"Listen, damn you," he grated sardonically, "I'd sooner bed with a porcupine at the moment. But I do have to sleep and I've done so beside you for two nights. And as you may or may not have noticed, I need room. I have no intention of trying to get my rest squeezed around the table. Nor do I feel like sleeping on the floor. So just get back in there on your own side."

"*I'll* curl around the table seat," Blair offered desperately, "or I can sleep on the floor." She was shocked she hadn't realized that he had lain beside her, but where had she thought he had been?

Arms crossed over his bare, imposing chest, Craig shook his

head. "Sorry, we're anchored too close to the shoreline. You don't trust me—I don't trust you. You may just decide you want to take a little swim and try to make the miles back to that village through the jungle. And honey, you are 'goods' to be delivered in prime condition. I don't want you attempting any night excursions."

"I won't run," Blair promised, sickly aware that she was pleading. "I'm bright enough to know the dangers. I give you my word—"

"Blair!" His interruption this time was very, very impatient although it was also evident that he was trying to remain reasonable. He paused for a moment, tiredly rubbing his fingers against his temple. "Under normal circumstances, I'd trust your word. Right now I can't. I'm too tired. Being next to you right now is my only guarantee that I could sense your slightest movement."

"I am not getting into that bed with you!" Blair shrilled adamantly, dismayed to find her voice rising hysterically.

All semblance of reason left his voice. "Listen, woman," he snapped harshly, "the body didn't change any overnight. It's the same one you were more than comfortable with about forty-eight hours ago. And the way I see it, you've got two choices. You can crawl in agreeably on your own side, or I can put you there and tie a rope to our ankles just to make sure you don't get restless during the night."

"You wouldn't!" Blair gasped.

"I'd rather not," Craig admitted, "but then again, I leave you the choice. Try me. I am dead on my feet and not particularly in the mood for a scuffle, but . . ."

He allowed his sentence to trail away with chilling warning. Blair hesitated, bewildered and dismayed for this stupidly unexpected turn of events. She wasn't particularly in a mood for a scuffle herself, especially one she knew she would lose.

She hesitated a moment too long. He took a first, menacing step toward her.

CHAPTER EIGHT

"Wait a minute!" Blair snapped haughtily, hands before her as if she could ward him off. "I'm crawling in on my own side—agreeably." She stretched out with far more cool than she was feeling and turned her back to him.

"Thank you," Craig clipped curtly.

"It's evident you know of my father," Blair murmured caustically. "Surely you can't imagine him to be a man to raise a complete fool!"

He didn't answer her, and of course she didn't see him wince. Craig thought his own position bad enough; he didn't envy Andrew Huntington trying to explain this mess to his firebrand daughter. But that would be Huntington's problem. At the moment, he had his own.

Craig padded across the cabin to a cabinet and withdrew an extra sheet. He ripped the one she was clutching from her and tossed her the fresh one before she could protest. "His and hers," he murmured briefly, then crawled into the bed himself and pulled his sheet high over his shoulders, wondering if he was shielding himself from the breeze filtering through the porthole or trying to contain his own demanding urges.

Minutes that were an eternity passed. Neither dared move; they were both acutely aware of the other, every breath, every nuance, every slight twitch of limb. The jungle seemed ridiculously still that night; not a rustle sounded from the shore. Even the lap of the water against the hull of the boat was soft. Two nights ago, Craig thought, just two nights ago he had held her, first in passion, then again, hours and a lifetime later, when she didn't know she had slipped into his arms.

But this was different. It was hell, and it was a hell he had sentenced them both to. But he couldn't do it differently. If and when he finally slept, it would be a sound sleep. If they slept apart ... He didn't think her in the least stupid, or a fool. She knew the dangers of her environs, but she was also desperate. He just couldn't take a chance, no matter how slim, that she might try to escape him, preferring a venomous predator to him.

Damn her!

She didn't find it in the least conceivable that he deserved her blind trust. Not that he had done much to warrant it, but he would never forget the hatred in her eyes when she had caught him flashing the communication in the clearing.

He sat up in the bed, disgusted with his inability to sleep. In forty-eight hours he had had less than three hours rest. He should be dead to the world.

He had slept in khakis on the hard ground, in the midst of shelling, catastrophe, and disaster. But for the life of him he couldn't sleep in this bed beside Blair. He had procured himself a sheet, but now he kicked it aside. It was hot, so damned hot. He was wearing only his cutoffs, but those cutoffs seemed to be strangling him, constricting him, pinching into his flesh.

He stood with something that sounded like a low growl and impatiently began to shed the offending pants. In the privacy of his own home, or tent, for that matter, he usually slept in the buff. He didn't have to go that far, but he'd be damned if he was going to spend the upcoming nights in stifled misery because of her.

"What *are* you doing?" she demanded stiffly from the darkness as his zipper rasped its way down.

"I'm taking my pants off," Craig snapped, surprised at the heat in his answer. "And if you don't like it, I'm sorry, but it's too damned bad." He had intended to leave his briefs on, but his misery sparked a flare of vengeance and they too dropped to the floor. His eyes were accustomed to the dim light, and although she was turned away from him, he knew she heard the sound and that she also knew what it was by the slight but telltale flinch that rippled through her form. *Damn her!* he thought for the zillionth time. Crawling back into bed, he leaned over and whispered, "Don't worry, Blair. If you roll over in the night, you aren't going to see anything you haven't seen before."

Blair didn't turn around. "That's true," she replied with a bland boredom, adding the final insult with a deep yawn.

More than ever he wanted to break her neck. He hadn't intended it, but the charged tension of the night had turned to a battle for control. And she was winning, or so Craig thought with his jaw clenching piano-wire tight.

Blair was not feeling any sense of triumph. He had been right—the facts might have changed overnight, but the body hadn't. All the animal magnetism was still blatantly there. Her flesh tingled with actual pain, as if the nerve endings had been cut and torn and left bleeding. He was at least a foot away, but she could feel him. Her body cried out for his. A heat rose from an involuntary core, a fire creeping into a system that knew delight and the epitome of pleasure lurked nearby. She could tell herself that she hated him, but her thoughts raged on, out of control with memory. Taut, bronzed skin, a rippling power-play of musculature. The sweet carnal ecstasy of the flesh his body had truly and thoroughly taught hers . . .

It had all been meaningless! she shouted silently to herself, drawing on that irrevocable fact for strength. From the beginning he had sought her out for who she was; he had befriended her to come close; he had made love to her to deceive her.

He had kidnapped her for his own secretive gain. She could not, would not, fall into his arms. She could not, would not, allow her imagination to stray to the magnificent, naked, male beauty so close beside her. Yet she couldn't help but spend the same hours of misery as he while they both lay motionless upon the bed. It was dawn, the pink streaks of morning casting their shadows through the cabin before she slept. And in sleep her mind had little control over her body As she unknowingly had before, she slowly but surely gravitated to his warm length.

That ended the sleep Craig had finally found. He hadn't moved, but she was fitted against him like a glove to a hand. Her hair, its fragrance soft and enticing, teased his nostrils as her head rested half next to and half on his shoulder. Her back was curved along his chest, her hips level with his. She too had discarded her sheet, and all that lay between them was the flimsy cotton barrier of the peasant cloth, no barrier at all against his feeling the satin feminine softness of her skin.

Craig lifted a hand almost helplessly in the near-dark stillness. It moved to the silken tangle of her hair. She shifted, and she fit to him even more smoothly as her body made a natural sensual adjustment. She would waken this time, he warned himself. But he was innocent. She had edged over to him. He took a deep breath and gave up the battle. His arms came around her and he held her as he gave in to the comfort, drifting in a no-man's-land between sleep and daydreams, exotic images spurred by scent and touch racing like a consuming blaze through his blood.

Blair didn't awake immediately. She was comfortable, and in a deep sleep. She began a slow, lazy stretch, and then halted. The limbs that moved with delicious leisure suddenly became

aware that they moved upon something hard but yielding, warm
. . . breathing.

Her eyes flew open and met a penetrating yellow stare. She
leaned up to find her hands planted in the tawny hair of his
chest, her body more than half reclined on his, a knee bent, a
slender leg cast over his. And as she became aware of her body
she also became aware of his, and a flash of crimson flushed
over her, beginning at the roots of her hair. His arousal was
against her like a burning brand.

"Take your hands off me!" Blair snapped in panic.

Craig lifted hands that were in no way touching her. He
smiled slowly with innocence and amusement, truly the helpless
victim.

"Damn!" Blair's outburst as she realized the inadvertent
aggressor was half seething growl and half wail. She leaped
from the bed, sputtering a stream of expletives that would have
done any seaman proud, leaving nothing aside in her efforts
to convince Craig of just what she did think of him.

"You left out a few," Craig reminded her calmly. Actually
he wasn't so calm. He was frustrated, and therefore irate, and
not nearly as blasé about his physical condition as he pretended.
"I think you forgot to tell me that I'm the dregs of the earth."

Blair stared at him for a single second of confusion, snapping
her mouth shut. Then she whirled about, stalking for the nearby
head where she could slam him out for a few moments of
privacy to regain her dignity and cool.

But she wasn't to make the door.

"Un-unh," Craig had bounded from the bed and his hand
firmly clamped her arm, spinning her about, evidently not in
the least concerned by his nudity. "I'd like to be a gentleman
and allow you in first, but—" He pushed her aside and brushed
on past her, pausing before closing the head door behind him.
"I think you'll agree that I'm the one in need of the shower.
That is, unless you have something else in mind to remedy my
situation?"

Blair finally did pick up part of the broken crockery. She did so to send a piece flying after him. He was far too quick. The door closed and the piece of plate hit the wooden door and fell harmlessly to the floor. Staring after it, Blair stamped a foot wrathfully, only to cut her bare sole upon another piece. Certain she would surely disintegrate with rage, she turned hobbling to the ladder and crawled topside to nurse her wounded foot—and pride.

It would have been common sense, she thought dryly as her temper cooled but her foot continued to smart, to pick up the broken glass last night. She had simply been too tired and discouraged and confused. The broken pottery had sliced a gash from her heel to the ball of her foot, and though she was sure the cut wasn't terribly deep, it continued to bleed despite her attempts to stop the flow. *Great,* she thought morosely. *Now if I do get some heaven-sent way to escape, I'll probably be limping with gangrene!* Cursing her own stupidity, she didn't notice as Craig joined her on the bow,

"What did you do?" he demanded sharply.

"Nothing," Blair snapped, glancing up at him from her Indianstyle perch. He was decently if not thoroughly clad in another pair of cutoffs. She noticed absently that the deep bronze of his skin showed no reaction yet to the blazing heat of the sun, even though he continually sailed nearly naked. She hadn't been out on deck nearly as much as he, yet she could feel her own nose beginning to redden and turn sore.

"Let me see your foot," he commanded, coming toward her.

"I don't want you touch—" Blair began, but her words caught in a gasp as he grasped her ankle despite her protests, leaving her scrambling for balance.

"You idiot!" he hissed, releasing her ankle and disappearing back down the hatch. She stared after him blankly, but he returned almost immediately, carrying a first-aid box. She stretched out a hand to take it from him, murmuring a grudging

"Thank you," but he ignored her, once more clutching her ankle and seating himself beside her.

"What is that?" she protested warily, wincing as he produced a bottle of clear liquid she assumed to be alcohol.

His eyes met hers momentarily, surprisingly filled with a sudden light of teasing amusement. "Chicken?" he inquired. "Come on now, Blair, take it like a man. If you do stupid things, you have to pay the price."

She didn't respond as he started to swab her foot; she proudly bit into her lip against the pain. But none was forthcoming. His cleanser wasn't alcohol.

"Peroxide," he explained as he saw her eyes fill with relief and confusion.

"Oh," she murmured, accepting his ministrations momentarily. Then her eyes began to blaze with a new growth of temper. "It wasn't my fault!" she hissed. "It was there, and I stepped on it."

"It wouldn't have been there if someone had thought to clean up the cabin while someone else was busy sailing this tub."

Blair smiled grimly. "Must have been the maid's day off."

"I see," Craig replied, nodding gravely as he took gauze out of the kit and a plastic bottle of nasty-looking red liquid.

"Merthiolate," he explained as he poured the red liquid on a piece of cotton. "And it will hurt."

Blair jerked involuntarily. He was right; it hurt like hell. She blinked back the stinging sensation in her eyes and her fingers dug into the planking.

"That's it," he murmured, his voice brisk but soothing. "I'll just wrap it up. Have you had a tetanus shot recently?"

"Of course," Blair replied absently, fascinated by his gentle bandaging of her foot. He released it finally. "You're going to be hobbling around for a while," he mused, "but I suppose worse things could have happened." He stood then, all previous anger vanished. His eyes were light as they gazed down into hers, seemingly from an incredible height. "I don't suppose you would make coffee?"

Blair lowered her head. She was sorely attempted to say, "Of course." But she couldn't. Even though it was easy to feel that he was truly concerned, that friendship and camaraderie could return between them with a simple word from her, she couldn't allow herself to forget that she had been taken here by force. *But I'm in love with him!* The painful thought flashed through her mind and she was unable to hide from that truth. But she had to hide it from him. She wasn't a naive fool to be brainwashed by her captor.

"No," she murmured. "You're right. I won't make coffee."

Did a shadow of disappointment flicker through the leonine eyes? If so, it was gone immediately. He shrugged indifferently. "Then do without."

Craig disappeared down the hatch and moments later she could smell coffee brewing—and she could also smell the tantalizing aroma of bacon. Curious, she hobbled back down the ladder. The cabin had been neatly rearranged; the broken stoneware was gone. Craig stood in the galley transferring food from the skillet to his plate.

Blair ignored him and moved back to the head. She closed the door behind her and brushed her teeth and hair and washed her face. When she returned to the cabin Craig was sitting comfortably eating; he acknowledged her presence with a slight nod, but said nothing. He finished his meal with apparent gusto, then pushed his plate aside and reached for a cigarette to smoke with his second cup of coffee.

The hell with him, she thought. He wasn't going to break her by refusing to cook for her. She didn't mind cooking for herself; she would simply wait until he went topside, then she would enjoy her meal leisurely. She passed through the cabin, determined to go topside herself until he left the cabin. Then she would change places. No problem.

But there was a problem. Not thinking, she paused to help

herself to a cigarette from his pack before climbing the ladder. The pack was pulled away just as her hand descended.

"Sorry, Mrs. Teile," Craig murmured politely. "My cigarettes."

Blair froze momentarily, then forced herself to shrug. "I'll live longer," she said dismissively before leaving him.

On deck she seethed.

She would have really loved a cigarette, and the denial was increasing the craving. She wasn't even much of a smoker, just a few cigarettes a day, but the one that was the most dear to her was that enjoyed with a second cup of coffee in the morning.

"So I'll quit," she grated aloud to herself.

Amazing how trivia could irritate beyond reason. But it did, and suddenly it was all-out war.

A cold war, a silent war, but a determined war. For three days Blair didn't speak a word to Craig. When he would finish in the galley, she would make her own meals. To prepare her own food she was forced to pick up after him, but she left the galley in a shambles so that he would have to do the same. On their third day out, he had offered her a change of clothes, telling her she could rot in her clothing or switch and wash. She didn't reply. She would do her own washing, but she would be damned if she would do his.

It was on their fourth morning out on the *River Tub,* as Blair had labeled the boat, not knowing its real name, if it did have one, when Blair heard voices from above. She had been wondering earlier why they hadn't been moving. Leaving her eggs sizzling in the frying pan, she limped on her still sore foot to the hatchway to listen.

Craig's voice sounded to her. Calling out in Spanish, he was hailing another vessel. *"Necesito un favor, amigo!"*

Blair couldn't see him, but she could well imagine his easy grin. The passing captain called back to Craig, and as Blair listened to the ensuing conversation, she was torn between laughter and a need to gather her wits. They had run aground! The indomitable Craig Taylor had actually managed to run aground! There had been high winds last night, therefore it hadn't been Craig's lack of sailing ability that had beached them, but still she loved it. Mr. Perfect making a mistake, falling prey to the laws of nature.

Now Blair realized that calling out when they had passed the village was a mistake. It had been ridiculous to imagine that she would have been heard or that the fishermen would have had the authority to do anything.

But the vessel Craig was asking for a tow had to be manned by a captain—a man of some prestige, a man who would be close enough to hear her fervent pleas, a man who could tell her where she was and steer her in the course of a fair-sized city.

They were already connecting tow lines; she could hear Craig moving about. Listening until his footsteps passed overhead, Blair scrambled to the ladder, forgetting about her foot and almost staggering as a bolt of pain shot through her. Taking a deep breath, she regained her balance and gingerly stuck her head out of the hatch.

She almost smiled. The boat towing them out of their suction was a large one, and several pot-bellied and mustachioed men were milling about the captain. Craig was busy at the helm, holding the tiller and guiding a line.

Blair crawled on out of the hatch and bolted past him as best she could limping. She scooted as far up on the bow as possible, attracting the captain's attention with a gasped, *"Ayudame! Ay, por favor!* Help me!"

"Qué pasa?" the captain queried back, not twenty feet from her.

She opened her mouth for an explanation, but Craig was upon her by then, dragging her back with a jerked, violent force. "Let go of me!" Blair hissed desperately, struggling against him as she quickly rasped loudly in Spanish, "I'm being kidnapped, I'm an American, I need to get to an embassy—"

The stabbing wrench of his arm against her midriff cut off her breath and Blair gasped against the pain. He wasn't playing with her now, she realized dully . . . *"Mi esposa!"* he shouted in Spanish, and she could hear the fury in his voice even as he apologized to the captain. *"Mi esposa,* she has gone *un poco loco* in *la cabeza, saben* . . ." His voice trailed away sadly; only she could feel the tension of his viselike grip upon her. "Get down in the hold, damn you!" he gritted through clenched teeth.

Blair gasped for air and stared up into his innocent features, stunned. How could he think he could get away with such a thing? Despite the pain of his hold she desperately struggled against him, shouting in Spanish. "This man is not my husband! He is a criminal, he is holding me against my will. . . ." Her voice simply ran out with a cry as Craig jerked her tightly again, his eyes denoting barely contained wrath.

It didn't matter, Blair thought brokenly. The men aboard the other vessel, captain included, were laughing. They were telling Craig he had asked for trouble when he had married a *norteamericana.*

"But a fine-looking one!" A particularly swarthy pot-belly called out. "I'd give you two cows and ten chickens for a single hour. Tell me, *amigo,* is she a fireball in bed?"

Craig's eyes turned down to her. His amusement still did not quell the fury. His arms came around her like bars, he drew her to his chest, the painful spike of his fingers a warning to her ribs as he spoke to the men over the top of her head. *"Sí, señores,"* he replied with a broad grin well feigned, *"mi esposa* is definitely a fireball. But she is not for sale, not even for a minute."

"Ah, a wild one!" the captain raucously replied, slapping his thigh with enjoyment. "But watch it, *amigo*—these redheads try to wear the pants in the household, especially these *norteameri-*

canas, sí? Put your foot down now, son, or you will find yourself in *mucho* trouble!''

Craig smiled over clenched teeth grimly and agreed with the men.

Blair thought she had previously known humiliation, but nothing like this. Nor had she ever believed Craig could hold her with such harsh, cold ruthlessness.

She was tiring from fighting him, but her instinct for survival warned her this might be her last chance. With all her might she dug an elbow into his ribs, granting herself the satisfaction of hearing him grunt now in pain.

But her satisfaction was short-lived. Since no local could possibly allow his wife to make a fool of him long, and still hold his head high, these men would expect Craig's treatment of her to be humiliating, even brutal.

He bent low and rasped in her ear. A stranger's voice. A dangerous, warning voice. ''Stop it, Blair. I really don't want to have to hurt you.''

''It's the *bambino!''* he called to their amused audience. ''They say women are worse at these times.''

It was apparent that every man aboard the fishing barge was a father. And all probably had wives who scolded around the roost. They were more than happy to give Craig complete empathy and advice.

''It is a crazy time,'' the captain called. ''But it will pass. *Felicidades!* May your child be a strong son.''

''Bambino!'' A shriek rent the air and Blair realized it was herself, shouting against all caution. It had simply been the final straw. ''I am not having any *bambino* and this man is not my hus—''

''Blair!'' She was sure her ribs would shortly disintegrate. ''I do not want to hurt you.''

She was simply too incensed to heed his growl; she was almost oblivious to the stifling pressure of his arms. ''I am not crazy,'' she shouted out in Spanish ''I'm not his wife, *damn it.* Don't you understand . . .''

''Mrs. Teile''—this time she couldn't help but be entirely aware of the growl of his voice—''I have warned you.''

Suddenly she was spinning around. She heard a loud crack and realized that Craig had slapped her face—with cold expertise, as usual. The pain was hardly a sting, and yet it was loud and staggering. Dazed, she found herself crushed into his arms, her mind unable to keep up with the whirlwind of her body. She was clamped fully to him, with a force that truly threatened to crush bone. A handful of terse fingers were threaded into her hair, drawing her head irrevocably back. It was a hold from which she could neither twist nor turn as he dragged her toward the hold. Stunned and shaken, helpless and infuriated at that very helplessness, Blair struggled against his bruising punishment to no avail. She was the hostage to be subdued.

It was the ultimate warning. He could do anything. His kindnesses to her were just that. She must learn to obey him.

It was also a hell of a show—one greeted with lavish applause, the entertainment clearly condoned by their audience.

Blair couldn't breathe. The strength seemed to be sapping from her body to his. She was mad enough to kill, she thought faintly, betrayed again in the worst way possible. But now, even now, her soul ransacked and robbed, she could not feel revulsion. As she stumbled along through the acrid taste of her salt tears and the blood of bruised lips, she wondered if it would matter if she could really hate him. He wasn't seeking any type of surrender, she thought, vaguely noticing the male aroma she had come to know so well, and just a while ago—love.

This was merely a well-executed and deliberate piece of showmanship, and just to make the show complete, he moved his crushing hand from the small of her back to bring it with firm possession in a slow slide over her breast, waist, and hip, and down to her thigh.

By the time he released her, she was trembling in desperate

spasms, half with rage and humiliation, and—God help her—
half with excitement. Even now he had the unique power to
stimulate her senses no matter what the circumstances.

Still, she was determined not to give herself away. Not that
that mattered either—the world was spinning, and even as she
attempted to stumble away from him, she collapsed against
him.

"Below, *mi esposa*," Craig whispered in low warning as he
half supported her, half shoved her toward the hatch. "One
more word out of your mouth, and I will sell you to that old
fisherman and I'll give him a damn cow and chicken to boot."

Instinctively she tried to wrench away from him, although
she had every intention of disappearing down the hatch. Unfortunately Craig didn't realize that. His arm came for hers once
again and a swift jerk brought her moving quickly. Too quickly.
She stumbled and her foot touched down hard on rough planking. The shriek that tore from her mouth was one of pure agony.
"Craig . . . my foot . . ." she gasped out.

Craig felt his entire body go stiff as he winced with her pain.
God, the last thing in the world he wanted to do was hurt her.
If she had only listened to him, damn it. Now he had caused
her to open the entire gash.

He was torn in two, speared by guilt, then further infuriated
that she had caused him such a terrible guilty feeling. Didn't
she know what the repercussions of her foolishness might have
been?

She was instantly in his arms, lifted effortlessly off both feet.
"*Un momentito, por favor*," he called to the tolerant fishing
captain. Supporting her over a shoulder, he brought her swiftly
down the ladder.

In the cabin they were hit with the foul smell of Blair's
burning eggs. Cursing beneath his breath, Craig paused a second
to shut the gas and move the skillet, then he carried her to the
bed, tension and anger tightening in his muscles, but his touch

still gentle as he lowered her down and captured her ankle to look at her foot.

"Damn you!" he murmured, his voice a cross between anger and tortured resignation. Blood was soaking through the gauze, and he bit imperceptibly into his lip before meeting her eyes. "You really are an idiot," he continued harshly to keep himself from pleading that she not force him to cause her pain again. It hurt him so much more. "What the hell did you think you were doing? You saw those men, you heard them. Do you really think you would have gotten to a city? You may have gotten somewhere eventually, but you would have been used by ten men ten times before . . ."

"Craig!" she cried out with misery.

His tone softened. "I am sorry I had to hurt you, Blair. Christ! Don't make me do this again. Stay here now, and stay off that foot! I mean it."

He did indeed mean it. She had seen that particular look in his eyes before. Twice, in fact. Both times had preceeded apologetic blows to her jaw.

He was awaiting a response from her, and she slowly nodded, miserably biting at her lip. He glanced back to her foot and his fingers touched the gauze as he assured himself the fresh bleeding had stopped.

And then they both suddenly became aware that the rough cloth skirt had bunched and risen high on Blair's thigh. A static tension rippled between them; her limb appeared so long, pale, and vulnerable—gracefully shaped and so inviting. And the hiking up of her skirt left so very little to the imagination.

Craig abruptly pulled her skirt back down and turned from her to head out of the cabin. "Stay right there until I come back," he commanded curtly.

Blair allowed her head to fall to the pillow. How was it possible to feel so many emotions within minutes? She had been so mad, she felt like a blazing torch, but just moments later, when he had responded so fleetly to her pain, she had felt an overwhelming urge to reach up and touch the tawny hair and tell him that she was all right with him near.

And again, even when he had held her in violence, she had felt that intense sensation of hot, stirring excitement.

God, what was the matter with her? she wondered, pressing her fingers against bruised lips. How could she be so foolish?

Because he wasn't innately a violent man; his power was that of mind more than body. Although dangerous, it was always clearly apparent to Blair that a gentleness toward her lurked beneath Craig's seeming roughness. A tenderness.

And then she was recalling his eyes, the lightness of his touch as he adjusted her skirt. And God, she could remember his touch of just a few nights ago, sometimes rough and always demanding, rough only when he had swept her to a passion to equal his own.

"Don't!" she whispered aloud to herself, "Don't!" She couldn't allow her mind to wander that way.

Cows and chickens! she reminded herself with a clench of the teeth. Think of the humiliation. Think of the anger.

The boat suddenly jarred. A long sucking sound issued through the cabin as the earth released its grip upon the hull. She could hear Craig calling thanks to the captain who had given them the tow. And then they were on their way.

She didn't have the strength or energy to disobey Craig and move. In time, she knew, he would come to her. She closed her eyes and fell into a restless sleep.

CHAPTER NINE

She must have slept a long while, because when she opened her eyes again, it was with the realization that though the boat was swaying, she wasn't moving forward. There was movement in the cabin, and as she focused sleep-fogged eyes, she saw Craig once more at work in the galley.

With that sixth sense of his, he knew she had wakened. He turned to her with a scowl. "I hope you realize you almost burned us up this morning."

Automatically smoothing her hair, Blair sat up in the bed. "Am I supposed to be sorry?"

"Yes!" he snapped, moving toward her with what at first appeared to be menace, but then she realized he was merely handing her a plate of something that looked like stew. "I value my hide, Mrs. Teile, and I assume that you value yours. Grow up a little. You aren't getting away from me, and it seems you're determined to kill one of us with your escape attempts."

Blair accepted the plate he handed her because she was ravenous. "Taylor, trying to get away from you has nothing to do with growing up. Someone neglected to tell you that kidnap victims were not necessarily cheerful and cooperative.''

"You could trust me," he said quietly.

It was tempting, so tempting that it hurt. "Sorry," she said coolly, turning her attention to her food.

He sighed and moved into the galley, then returned and sat across from her at the table. Suddenly feeling ridiculous and vulnerable sitting on the bed, Blair shifted to join him at the table.

"No," he ordered quickly, "you're not getting out of bed today. You do any more to that foot and we really will be in trouble."

"I can't just sit in a bed all day."

"Well, today you will," he told her firmly. Both fell silent as they finished eating, then Craig rose, took both plates, and put them in the sink. He returned to Blair's side and sat beside her, grasping her injured foot without a word. He unwound the bandages, cursed softly, and rose once more to return with the first-aid kit. Blair stiffened and dug her fingers into the bedding as he again cleaned and bound it.

"You will stay off it today," he repeated softly. Then he was rising and left her behind as he climbed the ladder topside.

Blair couldn't remember a longer day in her life. The sun had dropped low before Craig returned to the cabin, having cast anchor for the night. By that time Blair was thoroughly irritated and edgy.

She watched as he came directly to her. "How does it feel?" he inquired.

"Fine," she snapped shortly.

He shrugged and moved away. "I thought you might like to go up on deck for dinner," he murmured indifferently. "But . . ."

He seemed so capable of so easily dismissing her! Blair thought with a sudden fury. She swung both legs over the side of the bed and grasped the paneling for support.

"I can go topside," she insisted, then felt her fury drain as he looked at her with quelling eyes. "Really. All right, I was stupid this morning, but I'll be careful, I won't put any weight on it." He was silent and she suddenly found herself pleading, bargaining. "I'll cook dinner; I won't really have to move, I'll balance—"

"You have a deal, Mrs. Teile," Craig interrupted her.

She had a deal all right, but she hadn't counted on his hovering right next to her, determined to support her. Blair was amazed that she was eventually able to turn out a meal of well-seasoned pork and vegetables with his constant proximity.

"Stay here," he ordered her when two plates had been prepared. "I'll be back for you."

After taking their meals and another cask of the rather acidic burgundy topside, he did return, and she found herself being carried up the ladder. "After you sleep on that a night," he said huskily, setting her down and referring to her foot, "it will begin to heal. And then you can move around a little."

It was strangely peaceful on the river that night; the water moved in slow, hypnotic ripples. The breeze was faint, carrying the soft rustle of jungle foliage and the easy lap of the river. If she were just clothed differently, Blair thought as she glanced at Craig and he smiled, causing her heart to skip a beat, and if the sailboat were something other than this downtrodden tub, they could have been any couple out for the peace and beauty of the evening. Mr. and Mrs. Handsome America. The scene was mocking; Craig was a mockery, a man so secure in his masculinity that he afforded himself a vast sensitivity.

He lifted his cup of wine to her. "To a very pleasant meal, Mrs. Teile. Thanks."

Blair shrugged, unwilling to accept the compliment. "You seem to do all right yourself. You can cook."

"I can cook," he shrugged, "but not well."

A little pain tugged at Blair's heart as he grinned ruefully. Why? The question exploded in her mind. She had found a man who had effortlessly invaded her very soul; a man nothing less than incredible, and he was either a brilliant crook or a political fanatic.

"It surprises me that you're not a marvelous cook, Taylor," she murmured caustically. "After all, cooking is easily achieved by reading directions, and you seem to be adept at following instructions."

She felt his stiffening withdrawal and was pleased that she seemed to have struck a nerve.

"I do follow orders, Mrs. Teile," he said coolly.

"Whose orders?" Blair pounced immediately.

"We call him Chief," he said blandly.

"Very droll," Blair murmured acidly. "You're a waste, Taylor."

"Oh, really?" He picked up his burgundy and rolled it within the cup. "Would you care to explain that?"

"No," Blair rasped, picking up her own glass and draining the wine. Damn! Why had she let that slip? Because she was feeling reckless, the hours of solitude in the cabin below had left her . . . what? The time had left her craving his presence, his tenderness when he worried over the gash in her foot.

He was simply too right a man to be so wrong.

"I'd like to hear an explanation," Craig demanded, his cup connecting with the deck as he brought it sharply down beside him.

Explanation? If she tried, would he understand? Blair reached for the wine and refilled her cup. Keeping her hands from shaking through sheer will power, she once more drained her cup. Acidic or not, it had a marvelous effect. She couldn't feel her foot; she could ignore the tension that radiated from him. She could draw upon a false courage.

"You're a yes man, Taylor," she said with brash disdain. "You're a fool and I hate watching it. You're made of all the right stuff, but you're sending it in all the wrong directions." She paused for a second, realizing that her head was starting to reel but not caring as his hazel gaze narrowed to that sharp, piercing yellow that signified she had wandered into dangerous ground. She was adding fuel to a combustible furnace. "You are nothing more than a lackey. You have no mind of your own. If you're not after money, you're a terrorist, but you're not even the brains of the action. They found a prime subject with you, Taylor. You're just yes all the way, even if you disagree. You're sorry, you don't want to hit me, but they told you to get me away and so you did it. Yes, I'll keep a captive. Yes, yes, yes. Damn it, Taylor, you idiot, what you're doing is wrong! Can't you manage to think on your own? Christ, you obviously have brains somewhere, but evidently you sit on them!"

She had done it; she had ignited the spark. Suddenly their meals were forgotten and he was on his feet, dragging her up with a merciless grasp on both her upper arms. His facial muscles were stretched taut with a terrible tension.

"Watch it, Mrs. Teile," he hissed furiously. "I may be a yes man, but I've been given a free rein to deal with you, and right now, I can easily come up with a few ways to still that tongue of yours. I've done my best to be decent to you, *princess,*" he intoned contemptuously, "but you're pushing me too far."

A challenge rose to Blair's lips; she didn't believe he would dare do her physical damage. But she wisely swallowed her retort as she saw the implacable menace behind the gleaming narrowed eyes. She pressed her lips tightly together, torn between tears and anger because she didn't have the power to move or influence him. Swallowing convulsively, she stated, "I just hate to see it, Taylor."

"Hate to see what?" he charged, his fingers clamping even tighter into her flesh. "You have no idea of what I say yes to! I follow orders as you've ascertained, but I do so because I believe in what I'm doing. I believe in the men who issue the orders. If you granted me a single iota of trust, none of this would be necessary."

"I can't pretend I'm out for a leisurely sail—"

"You are out for a sail!"

"And I'm supposed to say it's all just fine," Blair continued derisively, "I can trust Taylor?"

He said nothing, his eyes glowing yellow fire.

Blair laughed. She had to keep laughing; she had to remain at a distance. She was too close to tears. They were alone in a private world out here, the sky above them, the water around them. Just them. And he was demanding so much of her . . . and she was beginning to feel it would not be as hard as she first thought to give.

"You have to be insane, Taylor," she snapped. "Totally insane. You're working for some lunatic and holding me a prisoner in a tub on some dead-zone river and saying 'trust me.' Yet you won't explain a thing. Where am I, Taylor? Why don't you tell me that for a start?"

"Where are you?" he exploded. "You're safe, you're with me."

Blair issued a bitter laugh and spoke without thinking. "A king cobra wouldn't be safe with you—"

"Why?" he cross-charged instantly, his steam billowing rather than decreasing. If she had slipped into a tangent, she had really pushed the button for him to continue it. There was no hiding from him here, and absolutely no thought that she had any control. He was determined in his relentless fashion of pursuit to drag everything out that was between them. She could read it in his searing, demanding, incredible eyes.

And Blair was left suddenly realizing that she was no match for him. It was like setting a cocker spaniel against a pit bull terrier. . . .

"Why?" he thundered again, shaking her. "Why can't you trust me? Have I ever harmed you? Don't tell me that I struck you, or that I dragged you on this boat! Answer that honestly. Have I ever harmed you? And answer this too while you're at it. Have I ever taken anything you weren't fully willing to give?''

Blair's head was spinning. Whereas the wine had once given her courage, it was now misting her mind. Held against him in his forceful grip, she felt overwhelmed by weakness. He was waiting for her answers; he would demand and demand and demand until she said something.

''Yes!'' she screamed. ''You have harmed me terribly. You are holding me against my will; you kidnapped me. But that wasn't bad enough—''

''Now we're at the crux of the matter,'' Craig declared coldly. ''Go on, Mrs. Teile. I'm breathless to hear the rest of this.''

''There is no rest,'' Blair denied too late.

''Oh, there is a rest, and if you're suddenly finding that the cat's got your rapier tongue, I'll finish for you. You're hating me because you did trust me. Because you came to me. And you opened yourself up to me. And now you think I've betrayed your trust, but you're wrong. And let's bear in mind—you came to my tent, I didn't drag you out of yours. And let's also be honest here. You asked for something; I merely gave in to you.''

''You really are loathsome!'' Blair raged furiously, interrupting him. More than at any time before in her life, she wanted to strike out and hurt, to cause a pain as violent as the one that lay inside her. A pain more gripping than most because it was caused by truth. But there was no question of her striking out, not even a slim chance that she could move. She couldn't even flex the muscles that his fingers clamped down upon; they were, in fact, growing numb.

''No,'' Craig retorted, his flow of words barely halted by her interruption. ''No, I am not loathsome, nor am I even remotely so to you. But if by loathsome and traitorous you refer to the fact that I did eagerly accept you and take all that you offered—love, beauty, trust—then I do plead guilty. I wanted you from the moment I saw you, and if you became mine, and realized that you were a passionate, desirable, sensual creature, more a woman than you ever knew, don't ask me to apologize. We were two human beings touching, Blair. You trusted me with the secrets of your past, with all that you are. I have never nor will I ever betray that trust, and if you don't know that yet, you will, if I have to spend every second left pounding it into your head, crushing it into your head.''

His grip on her arms relaxed, but before Blair could assimilate her momentary freedom, his fingers were threading through her hair as if he did indeed mean to crush his every word into her mind. But this touch, though spontaneous and rough, was not painful or cruel. He was like a man compelled, torn into as many pieces as she. His eyes glittered over hers only briefly, then his fingers tangled more thoroughly through her hair, holding her still, her neck arched, her parted lips opened to his conquest.

He didn't really need to hold her so forcefully, she dimly noted. She had no thought of resistance. She would rationalize later—and, God, how she would need that rationalization!—that it had been too much wine too quickly, that he had been too overwhelming, but for all the lies that she would later give herself, none would be so staunch as the truth.

She wanted him to kiss her, and it was so easy because his arms were so strong and she really didn't have a choice. But then that was a lie, too, because he certainly didn't force the response that she gave him. Not at first, at first she was just stunned, immobilized as his lips took hers with a bruising savagery, propelled by an urgent need. It was understandable that shock left her acquiescent, pliable, whimpering slightly as she was crushed to his onslaught, her arms slipping automatically, instinctively, around his neck. His demand was irresistible on every level, a hunger that created hunger, a fire that burned and consumed all that it came in contact with, and it was in contact with her. His fevered body seemed to meld hers to it, encroaching irrevocably, like the sparks that escaped a small fire and set the entire forest slowly, then rampantly ablaze.

No one forced Blair to ravage her fingers through his hair, to run them with raking, tantalizing pleasure across the breadth of his shoulders, down the length of his back. No one forced her to arch closer and closer against him, wallowing in the strength and heat. Nor could she hold anyone responsible but herself when her mouth opened fully to accept his hot, plundering tongue, to duel and play thirstily with her own, to wantonly seek every secret and crevice that was his.

Blank. She could later use that as an excuse. She had simply gone blank to everything except the sensations swimming sweetly in a body sensitized to his touch. After all, they took no courses not previously charted. Her body had become his willingly, his property, blossoming beneath his tutelage on not-so-long-ago nights that could never be recalled. When thought processes were stopped and responses were on instinct only. This was all that was right—being held in arms that were iron bands of security, the need to give in return flowing freely, naturally, from her, like the cascade that spewed and crashed from a waterfall with marvelous, earthly beauty.

It all just happened; she couldn't really blame herself, she couldn't blame him. *Two human beings touching,* he had said, but it was more than that. Very rarely did two human beings touch with such innate wisdom, bound by invisible ties that had no rationalization, needed no excuse, but existed pure and free, defying all else.

It just happened. The sun could not be prevented from rising, the earth from spinning. Some long-ago destiny had decreed that she should fit to Craig Taylor, perfectly attuned, a part of him. She was in no way restrained and his lips finally broke from hers to create a new, fiery trail as they sensuously massaged her throat and stroked the breasts that pressed high and firm against him, oblivious to the material of her blouse. She locked her fingers around his neck, holding him to her. Her teeth grazed his shoulder; she had drifted too far, she was willing to go on and on. . . . Her senses, shooting with a strident wildfire, demanded that she go on and on and follow that practiced route that he had led her upon before.

Craig knew that he should stop. He loved her so very much, but she was going to hate him all the more when she discovered that he was being a yes man to her own father and that his chief was Huntington's old friend George Merrill. But he couldn't reassure her now—he was held by a code of ethics and a belief in that code. There were reasons, sound reasons. Would she ever understand? Maybe she would at least forgive him—if he stopped now.

But he couldn't stop now. Not when her fingers wound through his hair, not when her lips clung to his, not when her nails grazed down the length of his spine, adding fuel to the eruption of chemistry between them.

He should let her go; he should give her every chance.

But thinking only gave him warning. He couldn't part from her even for an instant. Then she might start thinking . . .

He swept her into his arms, lips seeking hers even as he carried her down the ladder and to the bed, treading lightly as a cat so as not to break the binding spell. He lowered her with equal care, creating an exotic prison with his body as he worked upon the cotton blouse, lifting it over her shoulders with slow-moving fingers, his lips following the pattern of his hands, his tongue making quivering forays against her flesh as it was exposed. Sliding to kneel beside her and yet giving no quarter, he slowly slid her skirt down the length of her legs, once again tantalizing her flesh each inch of the way. All that could be heard in the cabin was the rustle of the fabric as it slipped from skin, that almost excruciatingly sensual sound. His lips touched her flesh and heartbeats began to hammer like the growing rumble of a storm.

Like the wind that accompanied the storm, their breathing rose. Then a moan broke through, a sound soft and sweet, piercing all others. Craig's lips left the tender creamy flesh of her upper thigh where his teeth had gently nibbled; his eyes sought hers.

They were glazed emeralds, murky with lost passion, deep with love. Sensuously lazy, seduced . . .

Craig was beyond feeling guilt.

She moved lithely from the bed to fold her arms around him, sending his strong frame shuddering as she planted tiny moist kisses over his throat and along his shoulders and she in turn now helped him to remove his clothing.

It was a slow process. Delectably slow . . .

Blair was released from rational cognizance. She did love Craig; she loved being with him in this maddening whirlpool, alone, oblivious to all else. There was no other experience on earth that could do this to her, but once plummeted into this swift-moving soul-shattering current, there was nothing to do but hold on.

In turn she kissed bronzed flesh, growing bolder and bolder with the deep guttural groans that sounded from his throat, echoing his quivering pleasure.

"Touch me, Blair," he murmured, a voice as deep and haunting as the golden orbs of his hypnotizing eyes. "Touch me. It's so good, babe. So good."

His clothing was gone; large, tender hands bore firmly down on her shoulders and together they sank down, entwined on the bed, soft femininity welcoming masculine strength. Golden eyes bored into Blair just before his lips sought hers and his knees wedged fully between her thighs. She jolted as his tongue plundered into her mouth just as his entry filled her entire being, taking her away in a wash of spiraling sensation as cleanly as a tidal wave.

The storm thundered on. Pelting, murderous winds, rains as gentle as flowers stretching through an eon of colors, cresting with a brilliant, shattering burst of pure white lightning to reach the sweet, satiating calm that always followed a storm.

But this calm couldn't last. The storm that obliviated reason was over, and in the wake came the pain of reason.

Blair first became aware of his breathing growing easy, of the damp, tawny hair on the chest where her cheek rested, of the raw, rugged profile facing their chipped ceiling, the texture of deeply bronzed skin, the long-fingered, powerful hands that draped casually around her shoulders in an intimate, possessive caress.

"Oh, God," she moaned with horror, pulling away, shaking.

His gaze riveted to her; he blinked. When they opened again a guarded look glazed his eyes. He was watching her very warily.

Blair tore her gaze from his and stumbled from the bed. She fumbled as she struggled back into her clothing, refusing to look his way again.

"Blair—" he began.

"Shut up, damn you!" she hissed.

"Blair, I didn't force—"

"Shut up! For God's sake, please, shut up!" she grated, grabbing his cutoffs with clamped jaw and hurling them upon his prone form. How could she have lost herself so easily? she wondered, flooded with shame and guilt. She was his hostage and she had fallen right into his arms. *Be serious, Blair!* she rudely admonished herself. She had done much, much more than simply fallen into his arms.

Craig didn't struggle with his pants, nor did he fumble. She felt him watching her as she dressed.

"I don't want to talk about this!" she snapped, quickly, firmly. "It didn't happen."

She was unprepared for his next move. Springing upon her with a mercurial pounce, he gripped her shoulders and wrenched her back into his arms. His touch was harsh, forceful. "It *did* happen, Blair."

"No!" she protested, uselessly flailing against his chest. "Don't touch me."

He could tell her something now, ease her agitation, still the guilt-ridden self-horror that sent her heart thundering anew. Yet anger was stirring in his own blood; he couldn't tell her anything. And she turned from him so easily, never, never to trust him again. And if he broke his word, his code of ethics, he broke himself and all that he was; he would then have nothing more to offer her, nothing more to give.

He didn't let her go, but he did change his touch. It had been severe; it became comforting. His arms encircled her, drawing her to him with tenderness, as if the woman he had held with wildfire had become a fragile porcelain doll. "Damn Huntington!" The whisper formed on his lips, yet it was just a breath of air, inaudible, a whistle that wafted softly through the tendrils of hair at the top of her head—deep, rich tendrils that glowed with unquenchable fire.

"I'm sorry, Blair," he said aloud, cradling her, listening as their heartbeats slowed. Thunderous beats and the sound and feel all but disappeared. "I wish you would trust me."

"Let go of me," Blair said tonelessly. She was able to think again, and, thinking, she knew she would be much better off completely away from him. Her heart and body hadn't the will to obey a humiliated mind.

"Blair—"

"Please, Craig," she said with great dignity, "let go of me. I—I don't want you touching me."

Craig released her, his face an implacable mask. Blair started to wander aimlessly away, but he halted her with a snapped, "Get off that foot!" She sank miserably into the seat surrounding the table, feeling curiously as if she had just viewed the end of a thunderstorm at sea.

Craig finally slipped back into his cutoffs and stalked to the far forward of the cabin. He stood straight beside the wall, his arms crossed over his chest. His voice was as devoid of emotion as hers. "You do want me touching you."

She cast aside the idea of making ridiculous denials. "Yes,

Craig, I want you, you goddamn well know it. But try to understand how I feel, and if anything between us ever was real, you'll honor what I'm saying. I do want you, but I don't want to want you. I don't want to be close to you. Don't you see, don't you understand? It's crazy, and I don't want to be crazy—''

"Blair!" He left his angry stance and moved quickly to her, one knee on the floor, the other bent with his elbow resting upon it. He took her hand, and she looked at him. "I do understand you, honey. Why do you think I said that I was sorry?''

Blair winced. "Please don't call me honey.''

He stiffened slightly; she knew that she had hurt him. The hurt wasn't intentional; it had to be.

"All right," Craig said softly, that underlying tone of steel slipping through. One by one his fingers moved until he had released her hand. It was slow agony for both of them, but they watched as if spellbound as his large tanned hand left her smaller, softer one.

"I won't touch you again," he said, his eyes rising to hers. "I will honor what you feel. But in return I want you to listen to me, and I want you to make a deal with me.''

"I can't make a deal with you," Blair said incredulously. But God, it was hard to deny him, hard to doubt the strength, the honor, and sincerity in hazel eyes that could gleam like yellow ice and then become a gold that was darker and deeper than the sun. She had to though. She had spent years studying psychology, behavior. She wasn't about to let herself become brainwashed, to be tricked into compliance.

Then what did she just do? she demanded of herself. That was different. It couldn't be denied. It wouldn't happen again; she wouldn't allow herself to get that close.

"I can't make any deals with you," she grated again.

"Bend, Blair," he suddenly warned, and there was a touch

of gravel to his voice. "The tree that won't bow to the wind is the one that is hurled over in the end."

An edge of panic swept through her. He was right; he held all the cards. He could really do anything that he wanted, and she was sitting here throwing out rules like the Queen Mother— a Queen Mother already fallen.

"All right, Taylor," she said, dismayed as the words slipped out a little too hastily. Taylor now? Who was she kidding? Certainly not herself. Not after the time they had just shared in a bed still warm from their exertions. "Let's hear this deal of yours."

"What would you say if I promised I would return you to Washington in no more than ten days time?"

Her eyes came to his again. Although he had released her, he was still haunched before her, so close that they were almost touching, so close that her mind screamed that he couldn't possibly be a renegade, not this man with his gentle strength, his passion, his tenderness.

"I would be pleased of course," she said primly. "But how would I know you were telling the truth?"

"I would give you my word," he said. The hard contours of his face were softened ever so slightly by the ghost of a challenging grin. Blair's eyes fell to her lap; she couldn't challenge the honesty she read in his eyes, but it was all so absurd, she was going to take the word of her kidnapper.

"Do you mean that?" she asked, drawing idle patterns over the weave of her skirt with nervous fingers.

"Yes."

She swallowed, wondering what her part of the deal would be, half frightened silly, half praying that it would be a demand on a personal level.

"In return," he supplied, leaving her little time to wonder, "you grant me a modicum of trust. No yelling out to anyone else we might happen to pass. If you have something to say, I'll listen. And you will listen to me."

Blair felt herself going very cold, very weak. She was relieved of course. Her fingers became perfectly still. A voice she tried to ignore demanded, *Are you so certain that you are relieved? Weren't you really hoping that he would demand you continue the relationship that you both know can exist, still exists?*

No! It would all boil down to the same thing; she would hate herself more than she already did if she allowed it to continue. She would hate him.

Unless . . . unless she could find out who Craig Taylor really was, what other crimes he had committed in pursuit of his strange ideals, if perhaps she couldn't help him, force himself to turn himself over to her father when he returned her, *if* he returned her . . .

"Is that all?" she demanded. She was determined to sound like an executive discussing a merger, but squeaked slightly nevertheless. The high, wavering note wasn't lost on Craig, and she could have kicked herself for even this slight admission of fear.

"That's all," he said slowly.

It appeared he wasn't going to move away, and Blair could no longer endure his being so close, picking up intuitively on her every thought. She stood, brushing past him quickly. "I guess we'd better clean up the deck," she said.

He shook his head. "I want you off that foot tonight. I'll get the plates." He hesitated a moment. "We'll be moving into the Caribbean shortly and I'll need you to help me sail. If you're careful for a few days, that gash will heal. Go to sleep now. It's been a long day."

Long day? It's been an eternity, she thought. "All right," she said briefly, lowering her eyes until he passed, assuming he would pick up and sail through part of the night as he so often did.

But he didn't. Reaching into the cupboard beside the table, he sprang some sort of a secret clasp and stretched his arm far to the back, extracting the jeans and shirts that had previously disappeared. A hidden compartment, Blair thought dryly, curious that he no longer cared that she was aware of its existence.

He tossed the bundle to her. "You can wear your own things from here on out," he said briefly. "Oh"—a twinkle set into his eyes—"the one set will need washing."

Blair lifted her chin a shade. "Fine, Mr. Taylor. But if you think this means I've agreed to become your laundress, you're mistaken."

He was grinning at her with good humor, and suddenly she couldn't ignore the undeniable bond that had formed between them. Before she realized it, she was opening her mouth, unable to control the impulse to tease him in return. "Men are all alike," she mocked with a feigned sigh, "give an inch and they think they can take a mile." She walked past him and crawled into the far corner of the bed. "You aren't that good, Mr. Taylor!"

His spontaneous laughter sent warm trickles of sensation trailing up her spine. He would never be offended; he knew just how good he was. . . .

He was suddenly leaning over her, but hovering a distance away, not touching her as he had promised. "I'm sorry, Mrs. Teile, perhaps if you were to give me another chance?"

"Get out of here, will you, please?" Blair responded, groaning with a good show of exasperation and pulling her sheet over her head.

Softly chuckling, Craig went topside.

Blair listened as he brought down the dirty tin dishes and cups and cleaned up in the galley. Her mind was spinning with plans to put into action, arguments that might force the man to turn his hand. The depth of her feelings shocked her; she was in love with him, so much so that she would mean every promise that she would give him.

"Blair"—he sat on the side of the bed, obviously aware that she was awake despite her tightly closed eyes—"I really would appreciate it if you would wash the clothes. I just don't have time, and I can't wear these pants forever. . . ." He let his voice trail away as he waited for a response. Blair refused to give him one.

He stood. "Okay, don't."

She kept her eyes closed as he moved away, which became difficult as curiosity almost made them fly open when she heard a faint cracking sound. But she didn't give in even when she felt his weight bear down on the bed beside her. He wouldn't touch her, she knew; he had given his word. Then what was he up to?

It wasn't until the middle of the night that she was to discover the answer. With the passage of time an odor that was definitely rank began to permeate the cabin.

It was so rank that it woke her up. And it was coming from the usually fastidious Craig. She sat up in the bed and stared at him, startled to find out that he too was awake, watching her with wide-open eyes.

And then she knew what the cracking noise had been. He had smeared eggs over one of his blue work shirts.

"All right, damn it!" she hissed. "I'll do your laundry. Just get rid of that stinking shirt!"

Laughing with the deep rumble that was always able to stir her blood, he rose and agreeably shed his shirt, walking forward to throw it topside where the night breeze would carry the dreadful odor away. "Thanks, Mrs. Teile," he promised, slipping back into the bed. "I promise to make it up to you someday."

Blair curled back into her corner. Could anything possibly be reconciled . . . one day?

CHAPTER TEN

They had called a strange truce, Craig decided a week later as he stood by the mainsail, watching the rugged coastline. Days ago they had moved into the Caribbean; the water they now sailed was salt. And if all would go as planned, Huntington would be meeting them off the coast of Belize in three days.

A strange truce indeed, he thought. They were getting along like a pair of roommates tossed together by lot, stepping carefully around each other, being so cool and polite it was almost disgusting. But they were surviving together. Even their sleepless nights had eased. They had both accepted the fact that by morning they would gravitate together—and they both ignored the fact that it occurred. That type of touching he was allowed, Craig thought wryly. He wondered if she, like himself, was grateful for those spare moments of comfort when all else was denied.

She was, to an extent, trusting him. They had made a nice split in the duties of day-to-day life; Blair was even proving herself to be the competent sailor he had known her to be from the dossiers he had read about her. Actually, he assumed, she wasn't out so much to help him as she was to stay busy. She had always been an active woman, full of that vital energy that had made her so invaluable to the Hunger Crew.

A slight beading of perspiration broke out across his forehead despite the cool breeze drifting down from the distant mountains. If something went wrong, if the top brass had been off in their estimations about whatever it was that was going wrong, Huntington would not make the rendezvous on time. Then what was he was going to do, Craig asked himself dryly. He had cornered himself; he had promised Blair.

Craig sighed, thinking how the peaceful scene of the mountains and sea clashed with the turmoil of his thoughts. Blair, who had shouted all those accusations at him completely contrary to the facts, would never know how her words had affected him. In his work he gave orders, harsh orders, strict orders, orders he expected to be carried out.

But he also took orders. One, two, three. Directions followed. He wasn't as blind as Blair imagined, not usually, but sometimes, as now, he disagreed with directives. He never feigned subservience; he didn't give a damn about getting ahead of the other fellow. He did, as he had told Blair, believe in his cause, if not always its means. Years and experience had taught him that his cause, though not perfect, was the best to be found in this far from perfect world.

Except that he was getting tired. He had given fifteen years of his life, and although he didn't begrudge a day of it he was discovering a need in himself that hadn't existed in his youth and hadn't fully formed until he had met Blair. He had sensed it before, standing as he was now, watching the sun's descent in a splendid, peaceful glow behind mountains in the west.

Face it, buddy, he warned himself with a dry, rueful laugh. *You're getting old. You want a hearth to come home to, children to carry on the ego trip of leaving something behind for perpetuity.* No, it was more than that. He needed a wife, and not just any wife, but a woman with a mind, soul, and courage, a certain woman with flame-tipped hair and eyes to rival a valley of evergreens.

"You're a fool, Taylor." He was startled to find himself talking aloud. *A senile fool,* he thought, *talking to yourself like that.* Senile or whatever, he was a fool. He wanted desperately what he couldn't have but could have taken. Even now he could barge below and drag her into his arms until he drew from her the eager submission that must surely come.

No, he couldn't, and he damned well knew it. She had challenged him on a level that was stronger than the physical, stronger than any force.

He turned to glance out seaward and a frown puzzled into his brow. Not minutes ago the sky had been clear, a strange yellow-blue with the setting of the sun. Now it was gray with more than encroaching darkness. A storm was brewing, and from the looks of it, it was going to be one big gale.

He had been going to move on after dinner, not that he was in a big hurry, but night sailing kept him away from Blair during the hours that they both seemed most vulnerable. Yet now he knew he must move toward land and seek whatever shelter the coastline might offer. Even as he moved toward the line to crank in the anchor, he could feel the breeze switch subtly, building in force.

Left at half mast, the mainsail began to fill. Craig watched as the fickle weather changed before his eyes. He was annoyed rather than alarmed. He knew that despite appearances he was on a vessel sounder than most. They would ride out the storm well; it just meant that the next half hour would be a busy one.

"Blair!" he called sharply down the hatch. "Up on deck."

Apparently she had noticed the abrupt change in weather as he had. She appeared immediately in the hatch, eyes bright and alert, a guard carefully set over the fear that lurked in their depths.

"I need you," Craig said with an easy tone designed to dispel her nervousness. ''Grab the tiller.'' Momentarily forgetting his promise, he set a hand upon her shoulder to point out the coastline. A natural harbor of clean white beach lurked ahead beneath the shadow of a long dormant volcanic mountain. ''We're heading in there,'' he informed her briefly. ''I don't think we can run aground if we just shelter between those outstretching arms of land.''

Blair nodded with a little swallow and grabbed the tiller. With the anchor weighed, Craig set to trimming the sails. Blair scanned her direction, then allowed her eyes to revert to Craig. It was impossible not to marvel at his coordination. He moved lithely across the deck with a quick, sure step, the strength that belied that lightness apparent as he cranked in sails with biceps bulging. In motion he was such a pleasure to watch, a body and will perfectly attuned.

He caught her eyes upon him and smiled encouragement. Blair quickly turned her eyes back to the coast. The rain was beginning to fall in a mist, a portent of what was to come. Uneasily she cast her eyes back to the east from whence the storm was brewing. She was an adequate sailor, but she had always preferred fair weather to foul. And in this tub . . . an involuntary shiver riddled through her.

It was raining in earnest by the time she reached the cove, sheltered between the two natural land barriers. She could feel the suction of the waves pulling at the hull, but it was easier to wait out the storm in this harbor. Craig cast anchor, then set to work furling and covering the sails. He glanced at Blair, hunched and miserable at her seat, her hands still upon the tiller.

''Go below!'' he shouted. ''You're going to catch pneumonia up here!''

Even above the whistle of the wind that was working its way up to a rage, Craig's voice was a clear whiplash. A command. But Blair shook her head. She was loathe to go below without him. She was drenched; rain dripped into her eyes, down the neck of her shirt. She couldn't possibly get any wetter than she was already.

"Go on!" he repeated, exasperated, halting his action with the main crank as he stared at her with hands on his hips.

She shook her head. "I'll wait for you."

Cursing beneath his breath, Craig turned his attention back to the crank, only to find that the sheet line had tangled. His expletives growing louder and more annoyed, he glanced back to her. "All right, if you must stay up here, come be helpful. Watch the line."

Blair scurried to him, careful of her footing as the deck rose and fell beneath her feet as if it had taken on life and the boat itself had become some huge monster that breathed deeply and laboriously in huge swells. She grasped the crank, almost falling upon it, vaguely wondering again that Craig could keep such effortless balance even now.

He held on to the mainmast as he sought out the problem, his sinewed strength a seemingly implacable power against the pelting rain and ravaging wind that hissed and shrieked around him. Huddled miserably by the crank, Blair felt her fingers turning numb, and yet he appeared to find it all no more than irritating.

He shouted something at her that she didn't hear. Narrowing her eyes against the sodden moisture that was blinding her, she yelled back, "What?"

Then to her horror she realized that the crank was spinning madly, and that she hadn't the strength to make it stop. Craig pounced back to her side, shoving her away as he caught the crank and line, slowly bringing both under control. Still it was loose. Something knotted somewhere. The boom was reeling starboard and port, out like the massive arm of an inebriated giant. "Get down!" Craig hissed to her, finally finding the tangle and bringing tension back to the crank.

But he was just a fraction too late. Just as the tension caught, the boom took its last swing and caught Craig neatly at the base of his skull.

He went down without a sound.

It had been like a horror picture to Blair, a scene in which slow motion had been used for full effect. She had been powerless to do a thing. Now the boom was steady, but Craig lay immobile, his complexion ashen, the arm he had thrown up to shield her draped limply over her legs.

She sat still in stunned stupefaction for only seconds. Then she secured the crank and knelt beside him, desperately praying that he was alive. She found a pulse. Was it faint or was it just that nothing could feel strong against the fury of the elements?

"Oh, God, Taylor," she groaned feverishly, blinking against the downpour. She had to get him down to the cabin, but his weight was tremendous. "Taylor!" She sent up the anguished cry, praying that he would open his eyes, that it would be a joke. . . .

But it wasn't a joke. His rugged profile was perfectly still beneath the onslaught of drenching rain and screaming wind. His flesh was growing so terribly cold.

What if he had a fracture, a concussion? Blair knew under normal circumstances that she shouldn't be moving him, but she had to move him. The boards beneath her feet were sodden. The boat was heaving even within the harbor of the cove.

"Help me, God," she prayed aloud, grabbing Craig's arms at the shoulders and taking a deep breath. What if he were dead. God, no! He couldn't be dead. She couldn't even consider it. He would be all right. She had to get him down below. "Oh, dear God, please help me." Her prayer was lost to the wind. If there was a deity present, it was Neptune, and the god of the sea was angered. Her pleas seemed to go unheeded.

Then suddenly she was able to budge him. Straining with everything that was in her, Blair found herself able to drag him. It was tedious going. Blair clenched her jaw with the effort, panting and halting every few inches, finally growing immune to the deluge of the rain. Every muscle in her body pained her until she found that the battle of straining against Craig's dead weight was totally exhausting her. She stopped periodically to wipe rain and plastered hair from her face, but each time she continued again, coming closer and closer to the hatch.

Once there she was faced with a new problem—how to get him down.

She couldn't lower him; she would definitely drop him. With tears of perplexity starting to form in her eyes, she knew she had to move fast. Her strength would only hold out so long in the driving rain.

Finally she crawled onto the ladder herself and once again began to drag him. He would still fall; she wouldn't be able to support his weight once she had pulled the balance of his form in, but she would be prepared and buffer the fall for them both.

Heaving and half sobbing and half grunting, Blair pulled him after her down the ladder. With her feet firmly on the floor, she gathered her forces for a final, drastic tug, bracing herself as best she could. Craig's weight came through the hatch, sending them both sprawling to the rough planking, sodden heaps piled atop each other. They landed with Blair partially sitting, Craig's head caught upon her lap.

Struggling up, Blair cupped her hands beneath Craig's head and began to slip her legs from beneath it. It was then, gasping for every breath, limbs still shaking with exertion, that she glanced into his face. And saw his eyes. Open. Staring at her. Seeming to pierce her soul with a strange light that was both knowing and curious.

For seconds Blair stared at him incredulously while her shaking and chattering became that of rage. "You bastard!" she hissed, dropping his head like a hot potato and eliciting a wince and an "Ouch!" from him. "You were faking, you son of a—"

"Hold it! Hold it!" Craig protested, lifting a hand in defense, fully aware that she would find a new source of energy with which to tear his hair out if she gathered any more steam. "I wasn't faking anything! I just opened my eyes this second and saw your face, and if you please wouldn't yell, I have one hell of a splitting headache."

Blair clamped her lips tight with uncertainty and pushed a straying tendril of bedraggled hair from her face. She saw him wince again and knew that he was in pain. "Can you move, do you think?" she asked cautiously. "I barely got you down here. I don't think I can get you to the bed."

He nodded, skin stretching tight across his features with another wince, and started to rise. Just then, though, another swell hit and lifted the boat, sending him sprawling again. "Wait!" Blair cried as he immediately set forth on a new attempt to rise. Ducking her frame beneath his shoulder, she supported him, managing to sloppily walk him to the bed before the next swell hit, but then losing her balance and falling flatly on top of him. His arms immediately came around her, a protective, reflex action despite his own infirmity.

And for a moment Blair was happy to be there in his arms, against his warmth, cradled by his security as the sea howled around them and the waves played havoc with the boat. She would gladly leave it all to him, trust in him, give herself over to his unwavering strength and shelter out the storm in his arms.

But she couldn't, not now, she told herself harshly. She had to come up with a little strength of her own. Gently extracting herself, she peered back into his face. "I have to get something for your head," she murmured, balancing back off the bed and holding on to the wall as she made her way to the galley. Grabbing a sponge, she flooded it with fresh water and swayed back to the bed, willing herself to think. *If he has a concussion, he shouldn't be allowed to sleep.*

Maneuvering him into the bed, Blair again met yellow eyes that were staring at her with a curious mixture of humor, affection, and pain. He had to be all right, she thought fleetingly, his eyes were too keen and bright for anything to be seriously wrong, or so she desperately hoped.

Straddling over him, she very gently lifted his head and set the cool wet sponge beneath it. She started when a hand, surprisingly strong, vised around her wrist. Once again she met his eyes.

"I'm all right, Blair," he said gruffly. With his own fingers he began to test his lower scalp. "Nothing irrevocable," he said, trying to grin. "Get the first-aid kit," he instructed her.

Although he had used it on her several times, Blair had no idea where he kept it. "Where is it?"

He pointed weakly in the direction of the cabinets by the table. Staggering, but growing more accustomed to the constant rough motion of the boat, Blair hurried to do as directed.

She found it in the cabinet closest to the floor, but as she reached for the box, her hand brushed a latch in the back. A second door sprang open.

Revealing a gun. A nine millimeter.

Stunned, Blair stared at the lethal metal, her heart pounding. Why was she so surprised? she wondered. She knew him to be a criminal; criminals carried guns. God, how she hated guns.

But she couldn't relate the weapon to the man. She couldn't believe that the prone figure behind her had ever meant her any harm. At every stage of the game he had been there to shelter and protect her, to care for her.

She slammed the secret latch and hurried back to the bed with the first-aid kit. Craig pulled himself to an elbow as she returned, and grasped the box from her fingers, lifting the lid himself.

"Would you lie back down?" Blair demanded irritably. "I can get what you want—"

He already had his fingers around a large plastic capsule. It snapped beneath his grasp and a strong scent of ammonia filled the area, making Blair avert her head with a gag. Apparently, though, it just worked the trick for Craig. Whatever faculties he had been lacking were restored. He pulled himself to a full sitting position and burrowed back through the box again. Finding a container of pills, he dropped two into his hand, dry-swallowed them, shrugged, and reached for another two. That completed, he tiredly dropped his head back to the pillow, adjusting the sponge beneath his neck. His eyes lit upon Blair again. "Thank you."

"For what?" she demanded, disturbed by the stare that seemed to fathom all the secrets of her soul.

"For saving me," he said briefly.

Turning away, Blair bit her lip. Not really. It had been her fault that the crank had slipped, that the boom had fallen. "You could have left me and tried to escape when the weather cleared."

Blair shrugged indifferently, determined he not read the depths of her feelings. "I just want to make it through the storm, Taylor. If I'm going to escape—or be returned, as you promise—I'd just as soon be alive at the time."

He raised a brow, but allowed the subject to drop. His next statement took her completely by surprise.

"Get your clothes off."

Blair instantly froze to rigidity. "Really, Taylor—"

"At the moment," he snapped, "I can truthfully promise that I'm not after your delectable body. You're drenched. You're drenching the bed. The rational thing to do is warm up. There are blankets in the back—"

"I know where the blankets are," she interrupted sharply, rising to tread her drunken sea stagger to the far aft once more. By the cabinets she paused hesitantly, then turned her back and shed her clothes, shrugging into a blanket cocoon before returning with a second for Craig.

He stared up at her, his lion's eyes glimmering a true gold. "I'm drenched myself, you know," he informed her.

He was clad only in his usual sailing cutoffs, but they certainly were soaked

"So?" Blair murmured awkwardly.

"So," he said impatiently, "I need some help."

Exhaling a long sigh of exasperation, Blair shimmied to the foot of the bed, trying desperately to keep her own blanket around herself while the boat pitched and heaved. She tugged at the legs of his pants while also trying to keep her eyes lowered. It was a miserable process. She felt the warmth of his body, each instinctive reaction of his flesh as her fingers brushed it. "You really better have a headache," she grated harshly as he raised his hips to allow her to pull his pants from beneath him. Despite the circumstances Blair could feel blood rushing hotly to her face. He might have claimed that he wasn't after her body, but he hadn't told *his* body that was the case.

With his cutoffs freed from his body, Blair tossed them to the floor and dumped his blanket over him unceremoniously. His response was a soft chuckle, which she ignored.

"What now?" she queried briskly.

A half grin which he attempted to squelch slipped onto his features, and he lowered his lids over teasing eyes, holding back an answer to the wide-open but innocent question. "See if you can get one of the casks of wine back here," he said simply.

"Wine?" Blair protested. "You should have something hot."

"Granted," he agreed, "but you can't even boil water with the boat keeling like this. Just get the wine and we'll try to get some sleep."

"Sleep?" Blair echoed unbelievingly. "How could we sleep with this cyclone going on. Besides, you might have a concussion. You shouldn't sleep."

"This isn't a cyclone. It will pass within the hour. And I haven't got a concussion. Just a terrible headache. Now, would you just do as I say?"

"How do you know you haven't got a concussion?"

"Because I've had one before, and it was much worse than this. Now, please? If I can sleep off the pain and the pills, I'll be just fine."

"You shouldn't drink with pills," Blair said firmly.

"Oh, Lord, woman!" His voice suddenly thundered impatiently. "I just want a cup of wine. I'm not going out on a beer bust with the boys! I've managed pretty damn well the past thirty-eight years without your help, Mrs. Teile. I know what I'm doing!"

"All right!" Blair hissed, this time wavering her way forward. She was able to secure the primitive cask of wine from the galley with no difficulty, but on her return trip the boat took a severe port keel and in grasping for the paneled wall for balance, she succeeded in losing her blanket. Muttering her staunch opinion of the entire situation, Blair grabbed her blanket and secured it around herself, floundering the last few steps back to the bed with irritation and impatience.

Craig had managed to prop up his pillow and he watched her return, unable to hide the amusement in his eyes. She tried so hard to maintain her air of propriety, he thought somewhat wistfully. And yet it was all such a waste on her part. Years from now, with his eyes closed, he would be able to conjure up the image of her naked body, every curve, every plane, every silken inch of tantalizing flesh.

"Laugh at me, Taylor," she snapped warningly, "and I can promise you won't get another bit of assistance from me."

"I'm not laughing!" he protested.

Blair began to fumble with the cork on top of the wooden cask, but she hadn't the force in her fingers to work it loose quickly. Craig watched her efforts for a second, then grabbed the wine from her. It was Blair's turn to watch, mentally noting with both unease and a shiver that was nothing less than sexual, the power that lay in his hands. Twisting the cork out only high enough to pinch, Craig grabbed it between two fingers and it gave immediately.

Oblivious to her confused survey, he glanced up and smiled. "You forgot the cups."

"Taylor!"

"But that's all right," he murmured hastily, his eyes still full of teasing amusement. "We can share." He took a swig from the cask and handed it to her.

Blair glanced at it distastefully for a second and then accepted it. But as soon as she brought the cask to her lips, the sea heaved again and the wine spilled over her face, down her neck, and disappeared in trickles down the valley of her breasts, just barely visible over her clutch on the blanket.

Groaning with exasperation, Blair started to hand the wine back to Craig, only to pause with dismay as she saw his eyes. All mocking amusement was gone; they were very dark, very intent. His entire expression was tense.

She knew that look, and just the look sent little shivers racing down her spine, shivers that turned to heat, back to shivers.

She was unaware of the anguished panic that appeared in her own wide eyes at the mere cast of his—until he blinked, and a slow, easy smile once more filtered across his jaw.

"Sorry, darling," he teased, "not tonight—I've got a headache."

"Oh, will you shut up!" Blair snapped, furious to find that she was blushing from the roots of her hair to her toes.

"Ouch!" he winced. "Yes, yes, I'll hush up! Just don't shout." He took the wine from her and swallowed a long drink, still wincing. He handed it back to her. Adjusting himself so that the pillow and his head upon it were propped against the planking, he reached an arm around her and pulled her head against his shoulder, silencing her protests before they could begin. "Don't go getting panicky there on me again, princess. When I say headache, honey, I do mean headache. I'm just trying to get into a position so that we can get some rest. Sip some of that stuff and try to sleep.''

She would never sleep. The boat was still heaving too violently. But as they passed the wine back and forth, she did find herself growing drowsy. ''You're lucky I don't get seasick,'' she muttered as the minutes passed and the rocking continued at a constant level along with the howls and the shrieks of the wind.

''Yes,'' he returned dryly. ''I'm lucky. So lucky,'' he added with a sad bitterness. ''I must have tripped into a whole field of four-leaf clovers.''

Blair fell silent. The patter of the rain was actually becoming lulling. Within the warm cocoon of blanket and supporting shoulder, she did fall asleep.

Very early in the morning it was over. The almost dead stillness of the boat woke Blair. Glancing around quickly, she saw that Craig was gone, already up and out on the deck. Scrambling out of her blanket, she reached into the cabinet that had become hers and withdrew her dry set of jeans and shirt. Hurrying into her clothing, she raced into the head, splashed water on her face and brushed her teeth, then hastened up the ladder.

Craig was standing by the mainmast, one hand against it, one on his hip. Sinewed legs steady and staunch, he stared out on a horizon that was vastly beautiful in the wake of the storm. The not too distant beach shimmered as if composed of a million white crystals; the mountains rose in the background in a brilliant panorama of green. The sea itself was calm and clear, barely rippling, the sky an artist's blush of radiant pinks and golds. Watching Craig in the proud, indomitable stance that was part of the man—the lion surveying his domain, for, clearly, the entire world was his domain—Blair felt a pain stab her chest as if her heart had truly constricted. It was impossible to believe that evil lurked beneath such a courageous façade. If only . . .

"Good morning, Mrs. Teile," he called, flashing her an engaging smile. His voice was deep, low velvet. "It is a beautiful morning, you know."

Blair lifted a skeptical brow, but couldn't resist a return smile—and a measure of concern. He looked as fit as an Olympic trainee, but surely even he couldn't be totally immune to that type of blow to the head. "Yes, it is a beautiful morning," she agreed, watching him quizzically. "And you look rather spry yourself. How do you feel?"

He grimaced. "Rotten. I have a headache that won't quit." But that was all the admission she was going to get from him. He chuckled softly. "Our 'tub' did ride out the storm quite nicely, don't you think?"

"Yes," she agreed again ruefully. "The tub did manage quite nicely." She paused for a second with a frown. "What is this boat's real name anyway? Or doesn't it have one."

"Yeah," Craig replied, going silent for a few seconds afterward with his lips twisting ironically. "This tub is *La Princesa.*"

"Oh," Blair murmured, fully aware that "the princess" was also his term for her. "Well," she said briskly, "in a storm I guess she is a princess."

"Ummmm . . . yes, she is," Craig murmured cryptically. He hopped down from the main to stand beside her. "How about some coffee? And some breakfast? We did miss dinner."

"Yes, we did," Blair returned dryly. "But you do seem mobile. You could have had breakfast started."

"I got caught up looking at the sunrise," he admitted with a grin. "And I want to check the sheet lines and sails before we get under way. We're getting closer to your ten days you know."

"Okay." Blair involuntarily took a step back from him,

aware that her heart began to pound harder with his mere proximity. "I'll get breakfast started."

"Hey," he called after her retreating form. "When the coffee is brewed, run me up a couple of those pills, would you? My head is still pounding like all hell."

Blair barely nodded as she disappeared into the cabin. Her mind was in a quandary. With each passing day, it became more impossible to believe that—if Craig stuck to his word— whatever he was after would be granted him and she would return home. He would escape, of that she was sure, and she would never see him again. Perhaps she would read in the paper one day that his group of political fanatics had been rounded up and he had been captured. Or killed . . .

And she would never be the same. She would have lost part of herself, a part she had given him that she could never retrieve.

The coffee finished brewing as she tortured herself with her thoughts. Sighing, she poured a cup for Craig and walked aft to the cabinet to procure the pills he wanted for his headache.

Once again her fingers brushed against the panel that was the false rear of the cabinet.

And her eyes fell upon the gun.

For a few seconds she felt herself shake. She closed her eyes tightly and swallowed convulsively.

She had long ago accepted Ray's death, but she would never forget his assassination as long as she lived. A firearm, any firearm could conjure up the picture of that day—the sharp report, the beautiful, caring smile fading from Ray's face, the bright red blood that seeped from his navy suit in clashing contrast, spattering to fleck his golden hair, her own scream, echoing and echoing endlessly as a secret service man cast his body over hers, saving her from other bullets, from herself as she hysterically tried to get to her husband, dead before she even became fully aware he had been hit.

Tears welled into her eyes, but she willed them away. Convulsively she reached for the gun. She knew guns. Her father had taught her to shoot in ranges starting from her tenth birthday. She could aim at a fly a hundred yards away and hit it. Hunched on the balls of her feet in a squat, she felt the cold metal of the butt, slipping her fingers around it.

And then she sensed Craig's presence.

It was her chance; a chance to demand to know where they were going, why she was being held, who he was. A chance to reverse roles, to take *him* hostage, to turn him over to the authorities before he went further in his life of violence.

He stood ten feet away from her, hands on hips, yellow eyes gleaming without a hint of fear. Slowly she pointed the muzzle in his direction.

"That is loaded, you know, Blair," he said flatly.

She nodded, her throat suddenly gone thick, her tongue too heavy to voice all her questions.

He started walking toward her. She finally managed to speak.

"Taylor, I can shoot this thing," she warned. "I'm an expert marksman."

"I know," he said calmly, pausing right before her. "I also know that you're not going to shoot me."

Blair clicked off the safety. "Don't count on it, Taylor," she rasped. Her hand was steady, her aim sure. He moved toward her. "Don't," she warned, and for an instant his eyes flickered with a strange light and utter disbelief. He'd come as close as she could ever imagine this man coming to showing shock. Then, just as suddenly, his eyes, his entire expression, showed nothing.

A silence stretched between them; neither one moved, neither even breathed. There was only the slight rocking of the boat, the sound of the waves lapping against the hull, the call of birds flying above the open sea. Flying free, Blair thought. The gun weighed heavy in her hand, the yellow glow of Craig's eyes, luminous in the cabin's darkness, boring relentlessly into her.

And then she was shaking like a leaf. And Craig was reaching down to take the gun from fingers that had gone cold and limp. With the safety back on, he returned the gun to its niche and reached for Blair, who was now hunched over, head bowed in despair and defeat.

He pulled her into his arms and she didn't protest. The tears she had tried to hold on to fell freely, silently, in torrents down her cheeks.

Lifting her like a child, he carried her to the bed and soothed her, lifting tendrils of hair from her face and smoothing them back as he cradled her in his lap. Then suddenly she gathered strength again, and feverishly pummeled his chest. "Damn you, Taylor," she cried in a scream and wail, aware that she was pitting such feeble force against him that he wasn't even protesting. "You're a goddamn criminal and I couldn't do it. I couldn't do it. . . ." Her voice trailed away with her energy and her hands fell limply against his chest.

"Blair," he murmured consolingly, "you couldn't do it because you know I'm no danger to you. You know that I would never hurt you. You couldn't do it because you know that I love you, because you love me."

She couldn't still her shaking; she could only dimly accept his words. She knew why she couldn't ever have shot him; it would be a horrendous replay of the past, seeing this man that she loved with all her heart, blood gushing from him, washing away his life. And then she was voicing her thoughts out loud, burrowing to him for the strength he had given her from the start.

"Oh, Craig, it was so awful, so awful, he was standing one moment, laughing, waving, so vital, so alive. And then he was down, the life leaving his eyes, the blood, oh, God, there was so much blood. . . ."

Craig let her talk on and on, feeling her pain, desperately wishing he could absorb it for her. He had seen the results of war and terrorism, and his only comfort was that in some instances he had been able to prevent possible carnage. But as he loved her, he could never imagine the pain of losing her. He could well imagine what the devastation had been for her to view the demise of the man she had adored.

And so he continued to hold her, uttering soothing words, cradling her with tenderness rather than passion, until she had it all out. Until the sun rose high in the sky, until he could feel her exhausted body relax against his.

Still they sat silent. Finally her eyes rose to meet his. Emerald and brilliant with the liquid glaze of her tears, they also carried a touching concern.

"Your head, Craig. I'm sorry, I forgot all about it."

He smiled softly. "That's okay, so did I. It's all right now."

"Really?"

"Really." It was true. Somewhere along the line the nagging pain had subdued to a slight throb, and now he felt only the slightest soreness at the base of his head. He twisted his head to prove that all was well to both her and himself. "Really," he repeated. "Much better."

She sighed suddenly, a jagged sigh, her emerald eyes still upon him, beseeching him with a weary depth. "Craig . . ." she began weakly, raising a slender, trembling finger to brush his stubble-rough cheek. "Please, Craig, turn yourself in. Don't you see? I don't . . . I can't . . . You're so good! Turn yourself in. I won't press charges. Whatever you've done, we can straighten it out. I'll help you."

Craig was staring down at her, a very soft, very tender smile curling the edges of the lips set in the square steel jaw. The hazel of his eyes was neither cold nor yellow. But deep, a dark golden color—poignant, wistful.

He forgot—or if he didn't completely forget, he pushed aside—the sure notion that she would one day charge him like a proud eagle for stringing her along, for allowing her to make such a plea. All he saw at the moment was the depth of her caring, and the moment was precious to him. He would sell his soul to allow it to continue. He wanted to stretch it out; he craved to hear the words spoken from her lips that she would never say again.

"Why, Blair?" he demanded hoarsely. "Why would you do this for me?"

"Because I—I—" She was floundering, her voice was catching, choking. And then she became certain. "Because I do love you." The words slipped out with a simple dignity— a sweet yearning whisper on the air.

Craig's arms tightened around her. "I love you, Blair," he murmured huskily, his lips trembling against her hair.

"Please—" she protested, pulling from him and finding the strength to stand and move away from him.

"I love you, Craig, but I'm not about to become a partner to this, whatever it is."

"I told you I would return you to Washington to your father," Craig said, his eyes narrowing and hardening, his tone becoming guarded. "Do you doubt my word?"

"No," she said softly. "I believe you intend to keep your word."

He laughed suddenly, a dry, bitter chuckle. "You want me to turn myself in?"

"Yes," Blair whispered.

"But you don't know all that I've done," he reminded her.

Blair fixed her gaze on the coffeepot, now grown ice cold.

"I can't believe that anything you've done can be that bad. They say that a hypnotized man will not obey an order, even in a trance, if that order is against his moral instincts. I believe you're like that, Craig. Misguided, but moral beneath it. If you turn now, you can go back. Maybe you'll never be able to do so again, maybe the time will come when it will be too late."

Craig had to catch himself, catch himself hard.

He heard someone laughing, distant, outside himself. But it was he himself. He was sure Blair must think he was cracking up. Was he hysterical? About to laugh until he cried? That was how he was feeling. It was so ironic. So pathetically, damned ironic.

He squelched the laughter that was bubbling up inside of him. He might as well agree; he was definitely going to see Huntington. And maybe, just maybe, in the few days remaining them, he might store up more sweet memories to take with him and cherish.

"All right, Blair," he said gravely. "I'll turn myself in to your father."

Blair stared into his eyes, fascinated by the brown stars that streaked against the lime, creating the illusions of yellow and gold. She was astounded that he had capitulated so easily. It couldn't be real.

"Do you mean that?"

"Yes, of course," he said impatiently. "I don't think you can accuse me of being a liar."

No, strangely, she couldn't accuse him of being a liar. When he made a promise, he stuck to it.

"I have a question for you." He interrupted her thoughts quietly.

"Yes?" She felt a little numb, as if a trophy had just been thrown onto her lap and she wasn't quite sure what she had won.

"What happens then?" Craig knew he shouldn't be pushing the charade. He was twisting a knife wound deeper and deeper before his victim was even aware of the first plunge. But as soon as this ordeal was over she was probably going to hang him anyway. Throwing all caution to the wind, he decided to take it all the way, and the hell with eventual consequences.

"You and I. Us. What happens then?" He was looking at her blandly, demanding an answer.

"W-well," Blair stuttered. "I—I don't know exactly. It's going to depend. I don't know what you've done, who you've been involved with. There is a good possibility that you will have to serve some time in prison."

"Are you going to wait for me?"

There was no hedging around with Craig Taylor; he asked his questions bluntly, questions that left her fumbling for answers, frightened, unsure, praying she had the strength she now tried to convey to him.

"Yes." She didn't really need to fumble for an answer. She loved him, and she had borne hard times before for love. Yet even the sweet love of the past was nothing compared to this all-consuming emotion. She could stand up to anything, she believed. He was putting himself in her hands, trusting her, promising her. The least she could do was promise in return to be there, through whatever, when the chips were down and he needed her. "Yes," she repeated, believing firmly in his love considering the enormous step he was willing to take for her. "Yes, I will wait."

"What if your father disapproves? He isn't going to be happy about his daughter and a criminal." Lord, Craig wondered, what was the matter with him? But he wanted the answers now, and it really didn't matter if he allowed the devil to niggle him on to have the next few days with Blair. He had, as the saying went, already cooked his goose. Charbroiled, as a matter of fact.

"Andrew Huntington doesn't control me," she answered serenely.

Now, that one was really worth a good laugh, Craig thought dryly, but he contained himself. His devil was in complete control. "Think about it, Blair," he warned, stalking toward her with his cat's tread. "Think about where you've come from, where you've been. Your family, your circle of friends. I'll be an ex-con. Will you be able to handle that?"

"Craig," she said firmly, and the woman who had broken with the thought of spilling his blood was gone, replaced by the fighter, the assured, cultured Blair who knew her own mind, who had won beyond doubt what he had thought to be a nonexistent heart. "I have never worried about what was.

The important thing is that you're willing to start over. My father is my family; he loves me, he will accept you. He is also a man to judge a person for what he is, not what he was. And my true friends will be your friends. Yes, if you mean what you say, I can handle anything.''

In a way Craig felt like kicking himself; he was humbled by her steady declaration, humbled by the beauty of the inner woman. But then again, he knew he would have changed nothing to hear her words.

He reached for her, large hands, powerful hands, hands that could break wood and brick, trembling. His fingers touched her hair, followed the delicate contours of her face. ''Blair . . .'' he whispered.

Then she caught his hand and stopped him.

''No, Craig, please . . .'' she beseeched him, and there was once more a hint of tears in her eyes.

''I thought you loved me.''

''I do love you.'' She held the hand that had touched her with such reverence with both her own. ''But I'm still afraid of what's going on. We need to get to a large city fast; I'll put through a call to Washington.''

Craig pulled his hand away impatiently. ''I said I'd turn myself in to your father when I returned you. That's still a few days away, two and a half to be precise.''

At first Blair was merely puzzled, then she felt the dark cloud of doubt and dread spreading through her. Was this just another clever ploy? A ruse for Craig to entertain himself while time inexorably passed?

''What difference does it make?'' she demanded sharply. ''If you've made the decision to turn yourself in, why not do it now?''

Craig didn't answer right away. He moved into the galley and dumped the pot of cold coffee down the drain and set about making another. Once it was set upon the flame, he turned back to her, a man with a decision made. Smiling slightly, he traced a calloused finger delicately down her cheek, making no effort to come nearer. "Blair," he said with a deathly quiet that both pricked her skin and convinced her immediately of his sincerity, "it's imperative to your safety and perhaps that of others that we not move toward inhabited land until we reach Belize. I swear to you that when we get there I will go to your father with you. You have to accept that for now. There's nothing else I can tell you, nothing else that I can do."

Blair stared at him for several seconds, but she knew that was all she was going to get. She knew the closed and determined set of his hard features. Her eyes fell first. "I guess there's not much I can do myself then, is there?" she asked softly.

"No, not too much," Craig replied. "But you can keep on trusting me."

Blair shook her head slightly, as if still considering the notion of trusting at all as sheer lunacy. "I guess I am trusting you."

"You can do one more thing," Craig suggested.

"What's that?"

"Tell me that you love me again."

"I love you, Craig," she whispered, then admitted, "but I'm not happy about this, not at all. We should be hurrying in."

"We can't." He reached out to take her into his arms but she went rigid against him. "Craig, please."

He released her immediately, but not with anger. His eyes held a deep and strange regret. "I think I understand," he murmured. She trusted him, but she couldn't control the doubt planted in her mind by the fact that she had been kidnapped by him. She wanted to see him turn himself in, which would be the end. Charade—which hadn't been his fault at the beginning—all over. But he couldn't be sorry. He had come to find out what love was, what it entailed, the joy, the pain. He would never regret that the intensity of his emotion had been returned, even if only for a brief, shining moment between them.

"Why don't you make breakfast, or is it lunch, now," he

suggested, that deep sadness and resignation in his voice coming through despite his smile.

Blair nodded; Craig disappeared up the ladder.

It was a remarkably undramatic end to the very special time when two people had just declared their love.

But it was the way it had to be.

Blair turned her attention to the task of feeding them both. Would everything really turn out all right? she wondered. She wanted so desperately for it to be so. So desperately that she didn't dare allow her mind to whirl away and question all that happened, all that had been said.

She would stand by him, she would be there, she would wait forever and a day.

But there was something else wrong; she could sense it. At times there had been an almost satanic twinkle to Craig's eyes, but then, at other times, they had been hard, self-mocking, haunted. . . .

She bit into her lip as she worked, worried, but feeling a strange jubilation. She was in love, and the man she loved had said that he loved her in return. And she believed him. She didn't question his sincerity.

CHAPTER ELEVEN

Topside Craig lit a cigarette moodily and stared out at the perfect, clean calm of the sea.

She was definitely going to be ready to kill him when she knew the truth.

But he did love her; God, did he love her, and in loving he was discovering all sorts of new facets to his own personality. But had it been so terribly wrong to need to hear things in return. To grab whatever chance he had?

Somewhere along the line he had to convince her that the loving was true. It wouldn't be easy, but she did love him. And wasn't forgiving a part of loving?

She was going to be mad. *Understated, Taylor,* he told himself with a wince. She was going to be more than mad. Furious. Sizzling.

The question was, would she ever simmer down enough to care whether she loved him or not?

Today and tomorrow—that was all that he had left. By midmorning of the third day hence he would be meeting Huntington at the dock in Belize . . . unless something went wrong, which it wouldn't

He glanced around the peaceful cove where they had found refuge. They could stay here today, he thought. Despite the storm and the morning he had run aground, he was ahead of schedule. The wind, if nothing else, had been with him.

"Breakfast!"

He glanced up from the position he had often taken by the mainsail to see Blair smiling up at him. Smiling in return, he hopped back to the deck and followed her down the ladder.

"Brunch." He corrected her with a smile as they sat down together to ham and eggs.

"Brunch," she agreed with a half smile.

He watched the little furrow in her brow as she pensively sipped her cup of coffee.

"Tell me about it," he suddenly commanded.

"About what?" she asked, glancing at him guiltily.

"Whatever it is you're thinking," he told her with a broad grin. "First you're smiling like a sly cat, then you're frowning as if just asked the meaning of X squared equals Z minus four."

"I was worrying," Blair admitted, and her frown deepened as she gazed reflectively upon his handsome features. His hair was long, creeping over the collar of his perpetual blue work shirt. Come to think of it, it was odd that he had started shaving so meticulously since he had first arrived at the Hunger Crew compound. That first day he had worn a stubble, as if he didn't care. He hadn't shaved yet today, but he had every other day of their voyage, and today he had been busy calming her.

She shrugged mentally. So what if he had come a little grubby looking. Habits did go with environment. And if he had come from the brush . . . where had he come from?

"What are you worrying about?"

"What? Oh!" Blair dismissed her ponderings on his personal habits and went silent, wondering how to voice her misgivings. She gave up a roundabout approach and asked bluntly, "Craig, how serious is this going to be? I mean, considering that I'm not going to press kidnapping charges.''

He was as silent as she for several minutes and a feeling of dread slipped back over her. ''Backing out already, huh?'' he finally asked wiping his mouth with a brush of his napkin and tossing it to his quickly cleaned plate.

''That's not at all what I said,'' she reproached him huskily. ''I want to know what we're going to be going through. I think I have that right.''

''You're asking me if I'm a petty thief, a murderer, or just your run-of-the-mill terrorist?''

''Yes, that's exactly what I'm asking,'' Blair said, reaching nervously for a cigarette but keeping her eyes on his.

He took a long sip of his coffee, the mask that guarded his emotions and thoughts so well making his face hard and cold. He set his cup back down on the table, cradling it with his massive hands, and sighed. ''Petty thief, no. Kidnapper, you answer that one. Murderer, well, I was in a war, so I can't guarantee it, but as far as I know I've never taken a human life. Run-of-the-mill terrorist, not run-of-the-mill I hope, and not a terrorist. My prison term should not be a lengthy one.''

He clicked off his answers as if he were reading an invoice, his tone vaguely resentful. He watched her as he spoke, then rose abruptly and moved toward the ladder, leaving her sitting stunned in his wake. She snapped her mouth shut, seething. Here she was, trying to help the man, and he bit into her like a caged rat when she asked for the particulars. A man who supposedly loved her.

The same thing, but running along a different track, seemed to be on his mind. ''I thought you loved me,'' he suddenly snapped.

''I do!'' Blair exclaimed, feeling her temper bristle at the sound of his voice. ''At least I thought I did,'' she continued coldly.

''Damn it!'' Craig started back for her, visibly annoyed.

"Two and a half days, Blair, and then you will have all your answers. Can't you give me that much? There must be a million topics of discussion, but your mind is on one track only."

"That's understandable, don't you think?"

He shook his head fervently. "No. We're heading into trouble, and today we have a calm sea."

Trembling slightly as she felt him bend beside her, Blair picked up her coffee cup and swallowed a sip of the hot liquid. But his eyes were on her, they seared through her, they commanded that she turn to him.

"What do you want from me?" she whispered nervously.

"I want today," he stated blandly. He took the coffee cup from her hands and set it on the table, then drew her up into an embrace.

"No—" Blair began, but she didn't get anywhere. He claimed her with an all-encompassing kiss, crushing her to him, winding his fingers into her hair with a demanding urgency. "Craig—" she protested breathlessly as he broke away, showering the top of her head, her cheeks, her neck, with butterfly kisses. "Craig . . ." Her voice trailed away. It was senseless to give him vocal denial when she melded to him, her arms sliding around his neck, her fingers light and soft against its nape. She started to talk again, whispering against his cheek, savoring his scent that was clean and natural, that of the air and of the sea. "There's so much to be worked out yet," she told him, scrambling desperately for reason as he continued an all-out assault on her senses, finding the hollow of her throat with hot lips even as she spoke. "I mean . . . I want to see you turn yourself in; I want to know what we'll be up against." She was talking all right, but her words were making little sense, not when they were uttered brokenly and interspersed with the soft moans he was eliciting. His tongue had found her earlobe, and along with the effect of the moist warmth of his breath she was reeling under the impact on her flesh, a touch that surely tingled through her like mercury, until she felt like hot wax, waiting to be molded to his form.

"Blair," he groaned with a hungry need, his fingers spanning the back of her head and neck, holding her near. "I want to make love to you. Now. I need you."

She was filled with poignant memories of a night when she had been the one with the need, a desperate need; she had come to him and he had fulfilled and forever changed her, reassured her, held her. Buried all the fears and hauntings of her past with tenderness and care. He had treated her so carefully, so selflessly. . . .

But this was insane; she was still his hostage.

But could she deny him? She was losing the will to fight, her physical responses overwhelming her. She tried to think, but all her reasons to protest were becoming hazy; she couldn't articulate them.

"God, babe, do I need you," Craig was murmuring, his voice alone inflaming her. His hands moved along her back, large hands, strong hands, rough hands . . . tender, gentle hands that commanded and seduced. His fingers molded her spine, curved over her buttocks, arched her ever closer. She felt his need, a special need, just for her, and her reaction was instant, an answer of sensual adjustment that was just as special and timeless, allowing no room for thought. "Craig . . ." she murmured again, desperately trying to remember her arguments against this offer of loving that was so beautiful.

"Blair," he whispered huskily in return, "we have now. The future is always so risky. We don't know what our tomorrows will bring. We could be apart for such a long, long time."

Damn! he thought with an inward groan. What was he doing? What the hell possessed him to lie like this? The answer was actually easy. She possessed him, totally, irrevocably. And maybe his deceitful appeal would be forgiven. Maybe she would love him enough, need him enough, understand that he had loved her so much he was going crazy with fear, grabbing desperately for what he could take, remember, cherish.

"Craig . . ." Was she protesting again or calling his name in love? He didn't know, but she was in his arms, soft, pliant, steaming, sensual. He didn't wait to hear another protest; he took her lips again and his hands began to course her body urgently, covering the rich swells of her breasts, the slender, shapely indentation of her waist, the seductive curves of her hips. His fingers crept beneath her shirt, touching silken skin and reveling in that touch, feeling the ripple of stirring desire in its quiver. Blair moaned softly, and Craig felt as if he were whirling at fever pitch, his mind spinning with the feminine beauty of her. He heard the strange quaking of a rumbling thunder, and that thunder was him, groaning with wave upon wave of molten yearning.

She broke away from him and an agony ripped through his loins. He stared at her, golden eyes both begging and commanding that she return.

She smiled softly, and he understood. Her hand, so fragile and soft as it touched upon his, was nevertheless firm.

She led him to the bed.

Later Blair would wonder what had possessed her. But the things he had said were so poignantly true. She had learned the sad lesson that you could never count on a tomorrow.

And she had her hands on the present. She had simply lost all desire to try to ignore what couldn't be denied. With her back to Craig, she slipped out of her clothing.

"Turn to me."

She heard his husky whisper and obeyed. He, too, had shed his clothes in his quiet, catlike way. For moments they merely watched each other, taking time to appreciate the beauty of the one they loved.

Let my eyes adore this altar where I will worship, Craig thought fleetingly, wondering at his turn of whimsy. He had changed in so many ways, there were simply things in him which she alone could bring to surface. She captured the passion of his soul.

But also of the body. His eyes might be reveling, but his fingers had to touch, slowly assess by feel all that he saw. He felt his blood begin to steam, his heart pound as he watched her body respond to the provocative strokes of his fingers, her nipples peaking high, her breasts quivering with the rise and fall of her breathing.

Her hands reached out to touch him in return, his muscles constricting beneath them, heat and passion tightening them to coils.

Both trembled as they stood there practicing a restraint, their kisses slow, deep, languorous, growing erotically sensuous as they tasted the salt of each other's flesh. Then Blair arched into him, her breasts, like pebble-tipped silk, searing his flesh as she lowered herself to plant exotic kisses along his hips.

It was more than he could take. Reverence erupted into raging passion; restraint was lost to the whirlpool that spun within his head. Cradled in his arms, she was his before her back fell upon the downy cushion that was their high-seas bed. In time he would learn temperance, were they to have time. He had lain beside her too many nights, held her too many nights, longed for her for too many hours. Knowing that she was as keenly attuned to him as he was to her was all the invitation he needed. Slender thighs parted to his onslaught and he found a moist feminine heat that passionately welcomed his demand.

"You are wildfire . . ." he whispered to her, his eyes golden and deeply gleaming as he stared into her eyes, always demanding that nothing be held back, that they boldly enjoy all that they created. His hands moved to cradle the hips that undulated beneath him. "Wildfire," he whispered in a husk that filled her ear with new sensations as their bodies swept into their own storm. "Wonderful, beautiful, fire."

Time stood still; life stood still. For Blair no other power on earth could ever so thoroughly sweep her away. There was nothing but him, the feel, the sight, the touch, the scent, the sensation. Being so filled with him, separate but one, intoxicated but astute, rhythmically flying higher and higher, needing, anticipating. They reached together the sweet wonder of ecstasy, then thrilled in that miraculous moment when sweet ecstasy crept up in a thrust of thunder that was nothing less than soul-shattering.

And when the storm had abated and the thunder had dimmed, Blair didn't turn from him. It was just as sweet, just as beautiful to bask beside him in wondrous contentment, still touching with gentle awe, her hand relaxed upon his chest, her fingers twirling with intimate comfort into the tawny bristle of hair on his damp chest.

His arm was around her, his eyes met hers. They both started to smile.

But just then they heard a new sound of thunder.

Locked in their private, all-exclusive world, it had taken countless moments for either to recognize the sound, but now it was almost upon them. Shifting abruptly, Craig moved the cloth from the porthole and stared rigidly out to the sea.

"Get up," he told her woodenly.

Blair stared at him in confusion, astounded by his abrupt change of demeanor, vaguely realizing she should be recognizing the sound that had created it, but still too groggy in the lazy aftermath of her love to think with coherent speed.

Craig had stiffened as if he had been frozen solid from the feet up. He was more astounded than Blair, although he knew exactly what was happening. He was still stunned and dismayed.

Blair watched as a gamut of pained twitches flashed across Craig's features. Then any visible emotion vanished. Even as he spoke to her, repeating a curt "Get up," he was on his feet, calmly slipping into his shorts and shirt. The hardness was back in the face, the chilling guard that was indomitable when set in place.

Blair jumped from the bed, the sure knowledge that something was wrong ripping apart her recent contentment. The change in Craig's features struck her like a blow after his endearments.

He was dressed and heading for the ladder while she was still struggling into her jeans. Finally yanking up the zipper, she followed closely behind him.

"What is it?" she began, her perplexity joined by a cold dread. Suddenly she didn't know Craig Taylor; she didn't know him at all. It was impossible that the emotionless icicle before her could be the man who had held her with such warmth just moments before.

"Don't you know?" Gold ice lit upon her momentarily. "Your freedom, Mrs. Teile. That which you so dearly crave."

And then she did know. Of course. The sound had been that of a boat approaching. A sleek cabin cruiser, she discovered as she followed him up the ladder, sporting the name U.S.S. *Wind.* Aboard it she could see a handful of marines spread across the forty-foot port.

Rescue. Somehow, someone had come to rescue her.

"Craig," she said, her tone wavering. "Don't panic. Things haven't changed. Don't try to get away; they'll kill you. I'll tell them that you were turning yourself in, we'll still get to my father—"

"Don't worry," he interrupted her tonelessly, "I'm not going to do a thing."

Blair looked at him, her eyes searching his desperately, seeking, beseeching, begging for an answer that would explain his cold, reserved calm. Again she thought that she didn't know him. He was a stranger. She had just given herself to a man who was totally indifferent to her, who had left her bed and become a hostile tyrant.

"Ahoy there!"

The cabin cruiser had pulled alongside their boat and cut its motor. The two boats almost bumped, and a rope was thrown to secure them.

For a brief second Blair thought Craig meant to shield himself behind her, to use her as a foil.

But he wasn't grabbing her—he was brushing by her. He was taking the tossed line, his expression, himself, completely closed to her, as if they were barely acquainted.

And then she realized that one of the marines wasn't a marine at all. He was her father, and he was hopping from the cruiser to the tub. Smiling.

"Taylor!" Huntington said, pumping Craig's hand briefly as his eyes searched out his daughter. Then he saw her, and his arms, trembling, reached out to her. "Blair, oh, my dear God, Blair!"

She had frozen. Simply frozen. Her limbs felt like lead, as useless as the mind that fumbled with the message her eyes were giving it. She blinked in her numbness, wondering if she was seeing things.

But she wasn't seeing things. Her father was standing before her; he had addressed Craig by name.

Her jumbled thoughts suddenly hit upon the point that her father was shaking and reaching for her. "Dad!" she cried, flying across the deck to throw herself into his arms. He held her, touching her hair, molding his fingers around her face, hugging her. Blair felt his age at that moment, the weakness of a loving parent, ravaged by worry and concern.

But he obviously knew Craig.

She stepped back, her eyes narrowing. "What the hell is going on here?" her eyes accused her father, darting from his face to Craig's impassive one. She tried to control herself, to keep her tone light, to remind herself that her father was old, riddled by the concerns of a nation. Her voice rose anyway. She began to shake with anger, the anger of one who has made an idiot of herself and only slowly, stupidly, begins to realize it, an idiot who believed she should give all to a man about to change his colors for love of her.

''What the hell is going on here?'' she repeated in a shrill voice.

Craig stood implacably straight, crossing his arms over his chest as he kept his eyes hard on Huntington. Obviously *he* didn't intend to answer any questions. He intended Huntington to have that job; his look portrayed a mildly interested observer, nothing more, as he waited expectantly to see how the old man was going to handle it.

Blair turned her own eyes, snapping with fury, to her father. ''Dad?''

''It's a long story, Blair, classified until this morning at nine A.M. Taylor here works for the government—''

''I see,'' Blair interrupted coldly, not seeing anything at all, but knowing that she was going numb all over again with a terrible chill. Her thoughts ran through her mind like quicksilver, jumbled and incoherent. She should be grateful. She had never been with a terrorist; her father was here now, she was safe, had been all along. It was all over.

But oddly, she wasn't grateful. In the bed below, the sheets would still carry the moist warmth of their bodies, and Craig had certainly never needed redemption. Nor was he a terrorist. He was some type of agent, stringing her along, entertaining himself—oh, Lord, how he had strung her along! How gullible she had been. He must have spent half his days doubled over in secret laughter.

''An intelligence agent,'' she snapped sarcastically.

''Craig is a diplomat, Blair,'' Huntington told his daughter with a frown. ''Special Services.''

''A *diplomat*. My, my,'' she drawled, her eyes boring into his. ''Is this the newest in U.S. diplomacy? Knocking out innocent victims and kidnapping them on rat-trap boats?''

Tension seemed to permeate the entire cove. Huntington glanced helplessly to Craig, who shrugged, then back to Blair. ''Taylor was under my direct orders. None of this could be explained because the entire set-up was classified. Taylor never knew exactly why he was holding you.''

"Your orders!" Blair gasped. Her own father had ordered her abducted.

"Blair," Huntington sighed sheepishly, "I told you this would be a long and confusing story. We have a long trek home. Hours of flying once we reach Belize. I can explain over a few stiff drinks. If you're ready, we have half a corps standing by."

"Oh, I'm ready," Blair said grimly.

"Taylor?" Huntington queried. "I can have someone else bring in *La Princesa*—''

"Thank you, sir, no," Craig said blandly. "You're early." Damn! Was he early.

"Things were solved this morning," Huntington said. "I couldn't wait, and I knew I could locate you along the coast. You understand . . . I'm afraid I couldn't wait."

"Yes, I understand," Craig said stiffly. "But I have a few things on the boat and a few things I have to tie up in Belize before flying back."

"All right," Huntington agreed. "Blair? Would you like to get anything?"

"No," she said coolly. She looked at Craig, her face as hard and as implacable as his. "There isn't a single thing on the boat I ever want to see again." She swept past her father and Craig and accepted the proffered hand of assistance from a young marine with a dazzling smile. Her father caught Blair's hand right before she could hop from boat to boat. "I'll be just a second. I owe Taylor a quick briefing. He didn't want any part of this."

Blair noticed then that Craig had already disappeared back down to the cabin. Andrew Huntington, surprisingly agile for a man his age, turned to follow.

Blair halted on the deck of *La Princesa*, standing ramrod straight as she waited in a silent rage. She was the one who deserved the explanation, and her father was worrying about Craig! She wondered sickly just what type of "orders" her father had given, and what part Craig's "orders" had played in his ardent lovemaking.

Huntington reappeared. "Let's go, daughter," he murmured, about to slip an arm around her shoulder.

"Wait a minute, Dad," Blair said. "I have something to tell Taylor myself."

She turned from her father and crawled down the ladder to the cabin, walking directly to the devil-eyed man who stood as straight as she, arms crossed over his chest, a faint light of wariness in his expression as he waited for her to speak.

"So you're a diplomat—" she hissed scathingly.

"Blair," he interrupted, and for the slightest fraction of a second she thought he might try to plead with her, to tell her he had reasons for not trusting her when he begged trust for himself. To tell her that his love was real, not an amusement to pass the time.

No, that wasn't going to happen, and she wasn't going to play the little naive fool any longer. There had been something between them, yes, and he was capable of kindness, yes, but when she thought of all the things he had told her . . .

Before he could speak her hand careened across his face with anger-driven vehemence, creating a sharp, resounding slap in the tense air between them. "Take that to jail with you, my poor, dear Mr. Taylor," she said sweetly, spinning on her heels to leave him. He wouldn't dare retaliate now; her father was just on the deck.

He didn't retaliate, but he didn't let her go. His arm snaked out, his fingers biting into her wrist, spinning her back around. She was fully aware from the expression he wore that if he had chosen to retaliate, he wouldn't give a damn who was just deckside.

"Listen, princess, I'm beginning to understand what this whole thing was about," he said harshly. "Why it was all necessary to begin with—everything. But you can't listen. You make a judgment in that warped little mind of yours, and that's it. You still don't know—''

''I know,'' Blair interrupted furiously, ''that you could have given me some hint as to the truth, but oh, no, we had to talk about radical cults and criminals willing to turn themselves in.''

''I *couldn't* have told you anything, Blair. Everything was classified. I didn't even know why—''

''You knew damned well you worked for my father. You let me sit there like an idiot, trying to save you, reform you, making love to you . . . oh, Lord! You must have almost choked to death on the laughter!''

''Damn it, Blair, I had to—''

''Go to hell, Taylor,'' Blair snapped. God, she was close to tears. She had to get out. She wrenched her arm from his grasp. ''If you'll excuse me,'' she drawled with the last iota of cool dignity she knew she would be able to summon, ''I'd like to go find out why I was knocked out, dragged around, and imprisoned—on orders from my own father.''

Blair eluded the hand that rose to stop her a second time and scrambled up the ladder. She was breathless when she rejoined her father, and shaking like a leaf. ''Let's go,'' she begged quickly, closing her eyes for a second of steadying balance. But she couldn't close out her last image of Craig—welts from her fingers stark against the bronze planes of his lean face, his eyes aflame with that golden yellow as he vised fingers around her arm and spoke with such intensity.

Again she accepted the arm of a marine and stepped aboard the cruiser to stay. Huntington wearily followed.

''Don't take it out on Taylor,'' Huntington told her, beseechingly holding his only child's hand as the cruiser cut its lines. He could only pray that she would eventually understand. ''Taylor didn't want any part of the job. I demanded him. He's the best we've got. He's spent years with the worst, in the Middle East, Londonderry . . .''

"Dad," Blair murmured, fighting her tears and just barely managing to hold them in. She was furious with her father, but he was her father. She adored him; she wouldn't hurt him for the world. He was going to give her an explanation, and it had best be a good one. She couldn't help but think—but, no matter what, he would still be her father, a good man, a gentle man, a man devoting his life to the concerns of others. "Dad," she repeated, swallowing her last vestiges of outward emotion, "I'd rather not talk here." She inclined her head to the friendly marines on board, and the captain coming toward them.

Huntington's hand squeezed his daughter's. He loved her; he was proud of her. Despite the hell her past weeks must have been, she was determined to maintain a mask of calm before the others.

Blair managed to muster up a smile even as Craig's scent lingered on her skin. And her seeming indifference masked the bleeding misery and humiliation inside her.

They were a long, long way from home and privacy. The Caribbean to Belize, Belize to Texas. And Texas to D.C.

Damn, did she need that mask.

INTERLUDE

Craig Taylor sat belowdecks as the hum of the larger boat roared, then dimmed, finally fading to stillness. His fingers reached automatically for his cigarette pack; he lit one, and exhaled shakily.

Blair had had a few surprises that day, but she would never guess that the cruelest surprise had been his.

Never, never in his wildest imagination had he thought Huntington might search them out along the coastline.

At least, he thought wryly, he now knew why he had been ordered to kidnap his "princess." The fact that it all made perfect sense, however, was doing little to ease the turmoil in his mind.

And then there was the question of the woman herself. Was she ever going to understand that it all made sense? If so, it might take a long, long time. She wasn't the type of woman who tolerated being duped.

Perhaps she would eventually comprehend why he couldn't possibly break his word of silence. With the "classified" rigamarole lifted, Huntington could make her understand how very precarious the situation had been.

Yes, the situation could be explained. Huntington would be in the clear. He was her father. She would forgive the father she loved. *But what about me?* Craig wondered with a wince. Admittedly he had looped his own noose; he had even known what he was doing every step of the way. He had simply wanted her so badly at times, he had been unable to prevent himself from playing along with anything that she wanted to think.

And then he had certainly gotten a little carried away with the bit about his being incarcerated for a substantial time. But he had truly cherished every minute that she had lovingly tried to reform him; he just hadn't been able to stop.

Her slap was still stinging his cheek; he was fully and ruefully aware of just exactly what she thought of him.

Craig wondered vaguely how much of what happened Huntington would hear about. Probably very little, but he didn't really care. He was in love with Blair, and if Huntington were to ask him, he would tell him so.

Craig moved desultorily up the ladder and weighed the anchor. It was time to give the boat full throttle with her high-speed motor. No one would be looking for him anymore. The job was over. He wanted to bring *La Princesa* in; he wanted to get back to Washington. Back to work. The work he did best, right in the heart of things. Walking the fine line between hell and high water.

Damn! He couldn't shake the vision of his hostage. His princess. Her scent still seemed to be all around him, her vibrance just around the corner. She was a ghost of delicate strength, pride, loyalty, and determination. A beautiful ghost, unfading, showing no pity for his loneliness and pain.

He raced the boat across the water as if he could outrun the wind, outrun the images that spun in his mind. *It's over, Taylor,* he repeated endlessly. But he couldn't accept that.

He hugged the coastline now as he sped along, no longer

concerned with the scattered habitations he would pass. White-tipped foam rose and spewed around him; salt breezes stung his face. But still he couldn't shut out memory. He couldn't shut out love.

Even her voice seemed to haunt him, a melody that rang ceaselessly, that whispered in silk along with the breeze.

I love you, Craig.

Suddenly he cut the motor, and *La Princesa* came to a slow drift over the light waves. Craig was laughing, laughing to the breeze, laughing at himself.

"You're supposed to believe that the patient and persistent will persevere, Taylor," he told himself.

Dusk was falling. With his high-speed navy motor in use, he was just a few hours from the dock in Belize.

He could afford the time to take a break.

Walking with a springing step to the ladder, he crawled to the cabin, rummaged through the icebox, and found himself a beer.

Flipping the top, he raised it to himself.

"To you, Taylor," he saluted himself, "and to patience and persistence winning out!"

He turned to the bed, stared upon the still rumpled sheets. "And to you, princess," he whispered. "Okay, let's face it. I messed up a bit. I led you on. I had to. Think about it, you'll understand. But honey, they've pitted me against some of the most unreasonable fanatics of our time. Do you really think one little slap is going to put an end to the pursuit of C. Taylor, USA?

"Not on your life, babe."

She was going to need time to simmer down. Whoever it was who decreed redheads should have flaming tempers was probably right on the button. But she was hardly the spoiled socialite he had expected. She would reason; she would under-stand all that Huntington would have to tell her.

Of course there wasn't an explanation for his inventing a

fear of a long jail term that might keep them apart, just to get her into bed.

That she would have to forgive.

But she had forgiven her father on faith already.

Because she loved her father.

And she loves me, Craig assured himself grimly.

He finished his beer.

That night he turned in *La Princesa*. He slept soundly in an air-conditioned hotel room in the coastal tourist town.

The mattress was firm yet plush, the bedding soft and warm. And still his first waking thought was that he would rather be sleeping in the cabin of that rat-trap boat; the only softness and warmth he craved were what belonged to a certain auburn-haired spitfire.

Two days later he was in D.C., taking the hall that led to the chief's office in long strides. His mind was made up.

Lorna Patterson, the chief's longtime secretary, gave him a welcoming smile at his approach. "Taylor!" she began in enthusiastic greeting. "You're back!"

But he was past her desk already. Craig never stood on ceremony, but Lorna was stunned nevertheless. She was not a beautiful woman; she had acknowledged that long ago, But one of the qualities that had endeared Craig to staff and coworkers alike was a simple ability to sense human frailty and sensitively bolster neglected egos. He never passed through without a compliment for Lorna. He would notice a change in her hair, a new dress; without dishonest flattery, he was capable of making her feel like she was beautiful—and she loved him for it.

But today he was distracted. He barely waved in acknowledgment of her gasped "He is in," and was able to send her only a ghost of his usual encouraging smile.

Lorna heard the chief's "Taylor! I've been waiting for you. We've got trouble with the new policy in—"

"Hold it," was Craig Taylor's firm reply. "I've got to talk to you. I want to request a trans—"

The door closed firmly. Lorna heard no more.

Thirty minutes later both Craig and the chief emerged, neither man looking particularly happy.

"How long do I have?" Craig asked.

"A week," the chief replied apologetically.

Craig contemplated his superior for several moments. "And then that is it," he said with a quiet force that was indisputable.

"And then that's it," the chief agreed. He still looked unhappy. He opened his mouth as if to speak, then shut it, which surprised Lorna because the chief was never at a loss for words. Nine out of ten times he roared like a bull. She was almost shocked speechless herself when he opened his mouth a second time and voiced a soft "Thank you, Craig."

Emotions rippled across Craig's usually unfathomable features. Tension, pain, regret. Resignation, fortitude. Then he forced a dry smile that didn't touch the misery in his uniquely compelling eyes.

"Sure, Chief, compromise, as you say."

"It will be set when you return, Taylor. I guarantee it."

The chief returned to his office. Craig appeared momentarily lost. Then he became aware of Lorna watching him with an empathy despite her complete lack of understanding of the situation.

Craig smiled. She knew it was an abstract smile, but she was glad nevertheless. He perched upon her desk corner.

"So how's it going, Lorna?"

"Fine," she replied. "It's going just like usual." She proceeded to fill him in on the latest in the office, but though he kept smiling, she realized he wasn't listening; he was merely being polite. What a man, she thought, tough as nails but innately gallant. The stuff of legends. A pirate, a modern day Robin Hood, a sinner, a saint. She wasn't in his league, but she was his friend for life.

"Taylor," she continued, then hesitated. He never discussed anything personal, but he seemed so down. "Can I help you in any way? If you've a problem, I'll gladly listen."

His smile became real for the first time; he ruffled her hair gently. "Thanks, Lorna, but you can't help." Grimacing, he stood and started away from her desk. "Compromise," he muttered. At the door he suddenly swung back to her. "Maybe you can help, Lorna. Tell me, do women believe in compromise?"

Lorna frowned, startled. Craig could have his pick of women. He had been seen with some of the great beauties of the world. He had never, to her knowledge, taken an affair seriously. It was impossible to believe he might be having a problem with a *woman*.

"Why, ah, of course women believe in compromise!" she assured him.

"Yes, I guess they might," he agreed, but he didn't appear any less down. He smiled again absently and waved as he left. "I wonder if they believe in compromise when they'd rather strangle you in the first place," she thought she heard him murmur.

Minutes later Craig stared idly at Capitol Hill.

First it was classified, now it was compromise.

He wanted his life back! his mind screamed. If he compromised, everything might be too late.

And yet he couldn't just turn his back. Ethics, his own ethics, kept standing in his way.

He fought a long, hard mental battle as he stood there, oblivious to the fact that it was late spring, and that late spring in Washington was beautiful. Cherry blossoms were in splendid abundance; the sky was a crystal blue. The air carried a delightful nip.

Just once he wished he could turn his back. Not care.

But he couldn't.

Again, it would be less than himself that he offered to her.

A week.

In a week he had to convince her to forgive him. And then to compromise.

It would never happen. Because he would be gone then . . . and he knew how she felt. He would never forget how she had broken when holding his gun. In truth, she would rather have him be a convict than see him leave for a danger zone.

His fists clenched tightly by his side. She was his! He had to have her, would have her.

He had only one choice, and that was to make her realize just how fully she was his before he left. And that was a bit of a sticky problem. If he knocked on Huntington's door, she would merely slam it in his face. There was a chance. Merrill's party. Surely she would be there.

And he would use every trick he knew to make damn sure *she* knew she belonged to him—body, heart, and soul—before he left.

Compromise or compromised? he wondered dryly.

This was one battle of diplomacy he was going to win, even if the means weren't particularly diplomatic.

CHAPTER TWELVE

"I still don't understand," Blair said grimly. She was finally home alone with her father in his Washington town house, staring at the rise of Capitol Hill through the picture window. Her fingers were tensely curled around the long stem of a martini glass. "You knew the guerrillas were planning to attack the Hunger Crew, but you just let them stay there in danger because the tip on the attack was classified?" Her question was thick with stunned disbelief.

"Blair"—Andrew Huntington took a very long sip of his own martini and paced before the window—"we had a man in with the guerrillas undercover. His had been a long and delicate assignment—drawing their trust. If any of the information he discovered leaked, they would have caught him immediately. His life would have been the forfeit—"

"But the Hunger Crew!" Blair interrupted. "You were willing to let them be killed?" She simply couldn't believe that her father would allow such a thing, or even be involved with powers that would offer up a sacrifice of such dedicated humanity.

Huntington winced at his daughter's tone. "You don't understand," he told her softly. "The members of the Hunger Crew were not in danger—just you. The only reason the guerrillas planned to attack was to abduct you. To hold you for ransom—support for their operation, guns, equipment, rations. They didn't give a damn about the Hunger Crew. I couldn't just call you home. They would have hit before you walked two steps off the compound, and the repercussions might have been tragic. If, just if, you would have merrily flown on out, they might have tortured our agent to death, and retaliated against us by staging a massacre on either a friendly civilian population, or on the very people you're worrying about protecting—the Hunger Crew."

"But I would have understood," Blair interjected softly.

"Would you have?" Her father shook his head with a dry smile. "Blair, if you would have had the slightest inkling of danger, you would have thought that I, as your father, was conning just to save you. And I know you. You would have wanted to stick by your friends." He waved a hand in the air before she could utter a protest. "But then there would have been the fact that your friends were in no danger. With you out of the picture, they were left in peace. The guerrillas had no point in attacking without their prize for ransom. And that's one of the main reasons your removal from the picture by us had to look real. The guerrillas had to believe that another terrorist group had beaten them to the punch."

"Okay, Dad," Blair said with a sigh, "I understand now why all this information was classified. I understand that your man might have been killed if his tips had leaked. I understand that my disappearance by pseudo-abduction was necessary to prevent catastrophe before it could happen. I understand why you sent . . . Taylor''—she spat out his name—''to watch me and then get me out when you knew it was definitely crucial.

But why all that time on the boat? Why couldn't he just explain it all to me once we were out.''

"Taylor couldn't have told you anything because he didn't know anything,'' Huntington said slowly. "And he was under my direct orders not to breathe a word to you about our government being involved.''

"But why?'' Blair demanded.

"Several reasons,'' Huntington said, rubbing his temple with one hand as he weighed his answer. "Blair, I really wasn't running this show. My orders came from higher up; no matter what I was thinking or feeling, I had to handle things as I would have with anyone else involved. I couldn't act as your father. You couldn't be told anything because''—his voice trembled slightly—"because you weren't really out of danger until the afternoon we picked you up. That's why you were on *La Princesa*. She looks like a dump, but she is, of course, one of our military vessels. We couldn't send in a plane or a chopper; we couldn't do anything obvious. You had to get out slow and safe. We knew the first point of clear harbor would be Belize.''

Blair was shaking her head with a rueful smile. "Dad, the time involved is not the point I'm trying to get across. I knew we were following the coast when we left the river behind, although I didn't really know exactly where I was. What I'm getting at is why keep me in the dark once I was out of the compound? Why didn't Taylor just tell me he worked for you, and that all he was doing was trying to get me to you?''

Huntington was silent for so long that Blair almost prodded him. But she didn't. She suddenly realized that his face was contorted with pain, that he trembled as with palsy. "Dad,'' she said nervously, "are you all right?''

He nodded and put up a hand when she would have come to him. A second later he spoke, his voice rasping. "I told you, Blair. I could make no allowances for the fact that you were my daughter. My orders were classified. If something had gone wrong, if the guerrillas had gotten hold of you, we couldn't take the chance that you would tell them anything.''

"But I wouldn't have told them anything—'' Blair began, stopping as she saw her father wince and feeling a chill crawl down her back with a grasp of understanding even before he spoke.

"Blair, the expression is often used as a joke, but it isn't a joke at all. They have ways to make you talk. If you had been taken, they would have eventually found out everything you knew. As it stood, all you could have said was that you had already been kidnapped. And in the event that you were captured, there was still more at stake. The welfare of the Hunger Crew, our agent, any number of random, innocent villagers.''

It was funny, Blair thought. There had been times when Craig first took her that she had been frightened. But now, with it all over, she felt a cold rising of gut-chilling panic. What might have happened to her under the wing of a true fanatical terrorist suddenly became visible to her mind.

"What about Taylor?'' she rasped. "If I were taken, he would have been too.''

"Taylor would have never been made to break,'' her father explained softly.

"Oh, come on, Dad! Granted, you sent me the next best thing to James Bond, but even I know they have truth serums—''

"Taylor would have never given them information,'' Huntington repeated with soft but firm assurance, refusing to meet his daughter's eyes.

Blair clamped her lips together. She didn't need a further explanation. She understood. Within Craig's ranks certain things were merely accepted. If other lives were at stake, you forfeited your own.

She swallowed the remainder of her martini in one gulp, then walked to the attractive portable bar that stood beside the gray suede sofa and poured herself a second drink, forgetting all about her customary olive. But alcohol couldn't numb the as yet unaccepted, gut-wrenching agony she was feeling.

"We had to keep everything classified until the guerrilla terrorists could be rounded up, which occurred the day before I came for you. We had arranged to meet at a certain secluded harbor in Belize, but once I was given the all clear, well, I couldn't wait to see you." Huntington began pacing the length of the picture window again as Blair silently absorbed his words. "Our man with the guerrillas," he told her, "led them right into Central American forces when they attempted a sabotage. With the main wing broken, it will only be a matter of time before any scattered dissidents give up."

Blair was still silent, and her father finally quit his pacing to sit beside her on the sofa. He took her hand until she looked into his eyes.

"Blair, I never wanted you to be harmed in any way by my work. I'm sorry, so sorry."

"Oh, Dad," Blair murmured, drawn from her brooding by the sorrow and tension in his worn features. Half-spilling what remained of her drink, she cast her arms around his neck and hugged him to her. "It's okay, Dad, it's over." She felt herself stiffen suddenly. "They were after you, Dad, weren't they? You were the main target. I was just a means to an end."

Blair could feel her father's shrug beneath her arms. "It is all over, Blair," he replied vaguely. Then he pulled away from her and smiled. "You know, honey, if it had been completely my decision, I would have had Taylor keep you in the dark anyway. You would have figured that out and tried to get me. If you knew he would have never really harmed you, you would have driven him absolutely nuts with escape attempts!"

"Dad! You could have trusted me!" Blair protested.

Huntington shrugged again. "It really doesn't matter. I don't make up classified listings."

"And you wouldn't break them, even for me, would you?" Blair asked softly.

It took Huntington a long time to answer, but when he did, his eyes didn't waver from hers. "No, Blair." He released a sigh, and Blair saw how very tired he was and how much fright and tension he had lived with for her. "I am a servant of the country," he said with quiet, unassuming dignity, "and though I'll admit ethics are sometimes confused, I don't confuse mine. You're my only child, Blair, and I'd happily die for you. Don't look at me like that, almost any parent would say the same and I'm still hoping that one day you'll know that for a fact, but I do not break government seals."

Blair touched his cheek gently with love and pride. "I understand, Dad, and I love you for all that you are."

"Everything that was had to be," he responded gruffly, "but I did bulldoze my way into calling the majority of the shots. I demanded Taylor. I've watched him for years, and I know he's the best."

Blair lowered her eyes and moved away from her father, taking his place pacing before the picture window. "Taylor," she mused dryly. "Yes, Taylor. Well, whatever the circumstance, you would have never needed to worry about me managing to get away from that man. I don't think a Sherman tank could escape him."

"Blair," Huntington queried, sounding a little strangled. "Were you ever hurt?"

Yes, Dad, Blair thought fleetingly, *you'll never know how I was hurt.* "No," she said aloud, adding with a reassuring grimace, "not really." The thought of the blow to her jaw that had sent her to blackness couldn't be felt as the hint of a memory in the morning. "But I was frightened silly at times. Oh, Dad," she muttered impatiently, "what are we doing in Central America anyway? Never mind!" She held up a hand before he could speak. "I don't want to hear 'classified!' "

Huntington grimaced as he looked into his daughter's eyes. She was trying to be light for his sake, but there was still anger deep within the emerald green, a frustrated anger. She was handling things as he had known she eventually would—with a dry acceptance. She had grasped all the complications of the situation, and he had also known, she had easily understood his position and how others had been concerned.

And it was over. She was home safe.

He kissed her cheek. "I'm not going to say 'classified.' Your question is a debate in itself. I can answer only that I've been with the State Department for almost forty years. I've seen mistakes; I've disagreed with policy many times. But in my job I serve the officials that have been elected by the majority of the people. Those are the rules of the game." He stopped, grimacing sheepishly. "Am I forgiven?"

Blair kissed her father's cheek. "There is nothing to forgive, Dad. I'm grateful that I'm alive, well, and here with you." An unwelcome stab of pain made her wince inadvertently. She was grateful; she was glad to be with this parent she so adored and admired. But she was also lonely. Although it had been less than two months since she had first set eyes on Craig, he had come to be the center of her life, whether in love, passion, hate, or anger. She could no longer go to bed and know that he would crawl in beside her later.

And even when she had decreed that he not touch her, he had been there. She had slept ridiculously soundly. She had crept into his arms, to strength, to security, by morning.

The man made a fool of you, she reminded herself.

As if reading his daughter's mind, Huntington said softly, "You need to forgive Taylor, too, Blair. He wanted no part of this, you know. He was furious when we sent him out. He felt like he was going on baby-sitting duty."

Great, Blair thought dryly. Taylor had wanted no part of her . . . well, he had certainly exacted his revenge. The humiliation of falling for his ridiculous lines was galling, the more so with hindsight. *Oh, God, what an idiot I was!* A real idiot, because even now she still wanted him, still loved him.

No, she told herself firmly. It was good that she had been nothing more than a "princess" to take down a peg to him. She was relieved that she needn't worry that he might really love her. Because she couldn't take it again. She could no longer handle the thought that those she loved were in danger. She was going to have to forget Craig because as it was she would spend her days worrying.

Blair suddenly realized that her father was watching her with both concern and amusement. Loathe to have him perform any more mind reading, she indignantly snapped, "What kind of diplomat is that man anyway? What happened to the staid, cordial types?"

Huntington listened to his daughter's questions, sure there was more to them than met the eye. She was a responsible woman; she wouldn't resent a man for having done his duty. He hesitated, answering slowly because of his perception, and also because there was no real explanation or title for Craig Taylor's expertise. "Taylor is ... well, he is a diplomat. He specializes in touchy situations."

"Danger, you mean."

Huntington shrugged. "He's a good man," he said softly.

Oh, he's good all right, Blair reflected dryly. "Yeah," she murmured aloud, dismayed at the pain given away with the tone of her single word. She forced a smile and held her empty glass up to her father. "Pour me another, will you, Dad? I think I deserve to get a little tipsy."

Tipsy, hah! She wanted to knock herself out. She wanted to forget, if for only the release of a few hours, all that happened. She wanted to make herself stop thinking about Craig. She wanted to ease the agony of wanting him.

"Sure, sweetheart," Huntington agreed, hopping to his feet and refilling both glasses. He remembered her olive. He handed back her glass and reached into an onyx cigarette box, taking one for himself while offering one to Blair.

"No, thanks, Dad," she said, adding wryly. "Haven't you noticed? I quit."

Huntington's brows rose. Although she hadn't smoked much, all her attempts to give up the habit in the past had been futile. "Oh? How did you manage that?"

Blair shrugged, then ordered her lips to curl into a small smile. "Oh, I just took it into my head, I guess." A wide yawn suddenly escaped her and she glanced at her father apologetically. "I think I'll take this up with me for a long hot bath," she murmured, inclining her head toward her drink. "Then bed. Changing time zones has gotten me off kilter!" Impulsively she hugged her father again, smiling her assurance of love and understanding as she released him.

" 'Night," she murmured, striding for the stairs and the upper level and the bedroom her father had always insisted upon keeping ready for her at any time. She paused halfway as he called a soft "Blair!"

"Yes, Dad?"

"Please don't be angry with Taylor. He *is* a good man."

She offered him the ghost of a smile. "I doubt whether he would really care if I was angry or not. We'll probably never meet again, but you're right, Dad, he is a good man. Tremendous. You should use him for all your abductions. His title should be changed to Taylor the Hun."

Huntington sternly held back a chuckle. "A tyrant, huh?" he queried, not expecting or wanting an answer. "Forgive him anyway. Like I told you, he really wanted no part of this."

No, of course not, Blair thought sourly. Poor Taylor, rugged man of action deprived of the danger he thrived upon to babysit a do-gooding rich man's widow. No, spoiled little princess. Get his terms correct here, she mocked herself. She had fallen into his hands so easily! What entertainment she must have provided—his due with ironic vengeance for being stuck with the job!

God, he had waltzed her down a primrose path, and she hadn't balked a single step!

And the pity of it was that now, even now, if he walked into the room with his lies of love on his lips, she would trip down the steps to be in his arms. No. She wanted no part of that deceitful adventure seeker.

But did she want to sleep! To still her rampant thoughts, to stop her heart from tearing to shreds, split between anger and fear, and then relief and then the need that overrode it all—love.

Huntington watched his daughter, knowing something was wrong. Then he lowered his eyelids to hide a discovery he had found in her delicate features. Something was wrong, but it was a good wrong, a right wrong if such a thing existed. She was feeling, really feeling something for a man for the first time since her husband's death. She would never react so otherwise. Her father had seen her often enough before this escapade—always polite to dates and escorts but always distant. Never really touched.

"Blair?"

"Sorry, Dad, my mind was wandering. What?"

"Please, don't be bitter."

"I'm not, Dad."

"I mean against Taylor. I think he was finally given an assignment he couldn't quite handle."

"What difference does it make?" Blair asked, trying to tone down her impatience. "He'll be flying off somewhere else soon, I imagine."

"He also spends a lot of time in Washington."

"*I* won't be here that long."

"What do you mean?" Huntington queried sharply, wincing as he did so. She wasn't his little girl any longer, hadn't been for some time.

"Dad," she said firmly in return, smiling a little at the autocratic tone he had used. She knew it well. A parent never liked to believe a child had really grown up. "I still owe the Hunger Crew three months. I'm going to finish my time."

Huntington frowned. "Blair, we still haven't totally cleared this situation. It will be weeks before—"

"Whoa," Blair laughed. "I'm not heading back tomorrow." A ghost of mischief lit into her eyes. "I guess I owe you three months too. How's that for a deal?"

Huntington grinned ruefully. "I guess it's fair." She had changed, he thought with a hint of sadness. Somewhere along the line, in the jungle or in the boat, something had changed her. She had always been mature, but now the haunted self-doubt she had carried after Ray Teile's death was totally erased.

"There's a shindig for George Merrill this week—you know him, my old crony from S.S. A birthday party. Your old man needs a date. Will you humor the poor guy and come along with him?"

"Humor him?" Blair chuckled affectionately. "Of course I'll come with you. I'll have the most dashing escort at the ball."

Huntington smiled serenely at his daughter. He was manipulating her life again, but what the hell, he was her father and he wasn't getting any younger. If he didn't push things along a bit, he might never live to be a grandfather.

The years had made him a profound reader of human nature, and at this particular time, he was sure he was reading between the lines correctly.

Blair continued up the stairs, oblivious to the deviousness of her father's smile. She halted one more time. "Dad! What about the crew? They must be worried sick by now. Do you have any buttons I could push to get a quick message through? I—"

"They aren't worried." her father interrupted. "They know almost everything you do by now."

"Oh? Oh, of course," she answered her own query. "Brad Shearer is one of your diplomats, too, isn't he?" She had been foolish not to catch on from the beginning. The Hunger Crew would normally be lucky to attract one such "hulk," as Kate termed Craig and Brad, in a year. Two in a month? She really had been blind.

"No," Andrew Huntington informed her innocently. "Brad isn't a diplomat."

"He isn't?"

"No. Brad Shearer is regular army intelligence."

"Oh, of course," Blair murmured. "Just regular army intelligence."

She finished her third martini before she reached her hot bath.

Andrew Huntington sat before his picture window and propped his feet upon his coffee table, sighing happily in his moment of leisure. He could have been angry—wasn't a father supposed to be angry if he believed his daughter had been compromised? He wasn't angry. He felt as smug as a Cheshire cat. It appeared as if something good just might come of a bad situation. If only he could believe that more often. . . .

Blair spent her days keeping busy. There were old friends to see in Washington, the Smithsonian to prowl endlessly, and the parks and Georgetown shops when she was in the mood for idle walking. She tailored her days around her father's free hours to be with him as much as possible.

But everything she did, every place she went was busy. She tried to be moving every minute. Then on Friday morning, the day of Merrill's party, she forced herself to stop and make a long assessment of what she was doing. She finally admitted that her breakneck scheduling was all created to douse the terrible feeling of loneliness that held her in its grip.

She wanted to hate Craig. He had made a grade-A fool of her. The terrorist bit had been bad enough, but the jail sentence was the killer. And he had known that she loved him! Oh, Lord, how she cringed with the memory of telling him so now.

Directions, she thought bitterly. Orders. Orders had sent him to her in the first place, orders to befriend her, to watch her, to take her away, to hold her.

He had elaborated on his orders, but then why not? Why not have a little fun with a captive princess. He was definitely a man, with man-sized appetites. Why not appease them with a partner all too willing to capitulate?

Her face grew scarlet with her thoughts, then a twist of pain jackknifed through her, leaving her short of breath, weak.

She had fallen so deeply in love with him that she would have waited forever, endured anything. But none of it had been real. From the very beginning Craig Taylor had felt nothing; he had only been following orders.

She would make sure that she never saw him again. So in a crowd of people she was still lonely, far more lonely than she had ever felt as a captive on a boat with only one other living person to see.

She had loved that person, and that made all the difference. Friend, lover, stranger, betrayer, she loved him all the same. But somehow she would get over it. She would have to. Mr. Craig Taylor, she was sure, was already off again, back to the work he loved. Released from his baby-sitting duty. Off to risk his foolish hide again.

Anyway, she told herself morosely, she didn't need another man to worry about. She didn't want another man to worry about. Craig Taylor walked into explosive situations with his eyes wide open. No, never again. She had lost Ray, and memory of that pain was enough to convince her she couldn't bear the thought of living with and loving a man who she knew for a fact put his life on the line every day.

"What difference does it make?" she asked herself irritably. "The man is done being amused by me. He's off playing cloak-and-dagger somewhere else."

With bittersweet poignancy she knew it was best that he was out of her life.

She shivered. Thinking about loneliness made her understand

her father better, and her empathy became great. He spent his days worrying about a nation, but when it came to his private life, all that he had was her.

She did love him so much; he was such a good person, such a dedicated, loyal man.

Like Craig.

Hah!

Get Craig out of your mind!

Think about Dad, she told herself firmly. Tonight she was going with him to the Merrills'. And despite her mood she was going to make him happy and proud. *And I am going to slow down!* she told herself.

With that firm resolve in mind, she spent the day at home, catching up on all the luxuries of civilization she had ignored for so long. She manicured and pedicured, conditioned her hair, and even tried a newly advertised mud facial.

"I could have done this in the damn jungle," she told her ridiculous-looking reflection. Would Craig think her a little "princess" if he were to see her now?

She shrugged with a little wince as she washed off the "mud" and started to dress for the night. She was wearing a floor length green velvet dress with long, fitted sleeves, an empire bodice, and a skirt that flowed elegantly with her movements—her father's favorite. She had to agree that it was probably her most flattering gown—the green complemented her hair and drew out the color of her eyes.

After all her days in the jungle and then on the boat, it felt odd to dress up. As if her real life had been in the jungle and on that boat and this gown merely a costume for a play.

She barely recognized herself when she finished. She had piled her hair high on her head and secured it with a small tiara that had belonged to her mother.

"There you are, Taylor," she muttered to the mirror. "A real princess." A laugh started to sound deep in her throat and she closed her eyes tightly against her reflection. *You're growing bitter, Blair,* she warned herself. *You know you're not a princess; you know that you are responsible, mature, caring . . .*

Being happy with yourself is what counts.

No, her heart raged silently, it counted more when dreams, feelings, and thoughts were shared.

She opened her eyes and stared blankly at the mirror. Then she coerced her lips into a cheerful smile and went down the stairs to meet her father.

The capital's beautiful people were out. The massive ball-room in the Hilton was glittering with chandeliers, crystal, fine vases of exotic flowers, and of course, people.

It was a mixed crowd. Merrill had been in Washington as long as her father and the guests were a mixture from all walks of political life. Senators, congressmen, cabinet members— even the president was supposed to be in attendance, which meant an additional host of working security.

Blair knew a good number of people in the crowd—old, hard-core politicians and civil servants like her father. But there were also a lot of new faces. She had been gone for almost two years and elected officials changed with the mercy and whim of the people. A good thing, she thought, thinking of her conversation with her father. The people did have their say.

Although she was still too involved with her inner battle to be honestly excited about the evening, Blair put her best foot forward for her father's sake. She greeted old acquaintances while escorted by his proud and protective arm, a bright smile on her face, and graciously accepted new introductions. She gave George Merrill—heavier set but just as worn and dignified as her father—a hug and a kiss and sincere good wishes for many more happy birthdays to come. He kissed her soundly in return, watching her peculiarly, and Blair realized that this was one man who was always in on "classified," who knew she had just returned from a nerve-racking escapade, who knew . . .

Chief! The word shrilled in her mind and she belatedly realized how stupid she had been. Merrill was always referred to as "the Chief." He could be none other than the chief Craig had mentioned in his far-fetched tale.

Of course. Why hadn't she realized? Merrill was Craig's boss. And since, according to her father, Craig was Merrill's number-one man, it stood to reason that he would be at the party if he were in the country.

He was.

She wasn't sure what alerted her to his presence. Perhaps she heard his voice, low-timbred, quiet, assured. Maybe it was the very scent of him, crisp, unique, ingrained upon her senses—a subconscious trigger to a torrent of memories.

Maybe it was just a sixth sense. Or a combination of everything. But she was suddenly sure beyond a doubt that he was near her, long before Merrill hailed him and summoned him to their group.

"Craig, glad to see you made it, boy!" George Merrill called enthusiastically. Craig, who had been in conversation with an attractive blonde, excused himself and turned to Blair's group, addressing his boss, but watching Blair, his yellow-streaked gaze portraying a taunting amusement that belied the gravity of his expression.

"Wouldn't have missed it for the world, sir," Craig said cordially, shaking his superior's hand and adding, "Many happy returns of the day." He turned to Andrew Huntington and inclined his head. "Sir, nice to see you."

"Good to see you, Taylor," Huntington said cheerfully, offering a handshake.

"Blair . . ." Craig acknowledged her, and before she knew it, he had taken her hand and brought it to his lips, a perfect example of charming protocol.

"Mr. Taylor," she said coolly, fighting to keep her tone level and her response equally calm and light for "protocol." It was difficult. She had seemed to lose control of the natural act of breathing when he had neared, and the flesh on the hand he kissed seemed to burn, as if it had been seared with a brand.

"It's a pleasure to see you," Craig said, refusing to release her hand.

Even for protocol she couldn't return that statement. It wasn't a pleasure, or if it was, it was a pleasure that was mixed cruelly with pure torture. She forced a dry smile that was the working of facial muscles and nothing more. "It's a surprise to see you, Mr. Taylor," she said. "I would have thought you off on another diplomatic mission by now."

Did a flicker of pain pass through his eyes? No, she must have imagined it. He was quirking a cynical brow toward the chief. "My last mission was hazardous. I needed a little relaxation tonight."

Blair flicked her lashes with annoyance but held her composure as her father and Merrill both made attempts to hide their reactions. *She* had been Craig's main hazard, as things worked out.

Blair decided it was time to opt out of the small gathering and find someone else, anyone she knew, and join any conversation that didn't include Craig. "Excuse me—" she began.

"Excuse us," Craig interrupted, securing a steady hold at her waist. "I hear a waltz, Mr. Huntington, and I'd like to steal your date if I may."

"You two go right ahead," Andrew Huntington dismissed them benignly. "The chief here and I can rehash old—let me correct that—*ancient* times all night."

"Dad—" Blair protested, shooting him desperate pleas with her eyes which he appeared not to notice. She didn't get any further. Craig was leading her to the dance floor, and, short of throwing herself on the floor, she had little choice but to follow, or rather, be dragged along. Even if she were to throw herself on the floor, she thought with fleeting resentment, he would probably pick her up, apologize to the crowd around them with his casual diplomacy, and calmly proceed.

"You have a hell of a lot of nerve!" Blair hissed as he swirled her into his arms on the dance floor. "I would have thought you would have realized I don't wish to see you, speak to you, or be anywhere near you ever again!'' *What a liar I am,* she thought, clenching her teeth and shutting her eyes as her cheek grazed the rough texture of his tuxedo. He was already overwhelming her, making her senses swim with his magnetic touch, guiding her in the centuries-old waltz with a strong and firm command. *And he's different tonight,* she thought poignantly. In his ragged bush attire he had been shabby yet ruggedly appealing; in a tuxedo he was still every bit the rogue, but, damn, what a dashing renegade. His physique was such that the custom-tailored tuxedo hugged the lean muscles of his tall body, emphasizing broad shoulders and trim hips that surely made every female in the place shiver with a touch of longing. Rather than detracting from the raw masculinity no outfit would ever hide, the ruffles of his rich cream-colored shirt merely stood to complement the swashbuckling look of the adventurer.

Blair became so immersed in her musings about his appearance that she almost missed his words.

''I do have a hell of a lot of nerve,'' he replied blandly, shifting his hold slightly so that she was forced to lift her eyes and meet his. The yellow-gold stars in them sparkled with amusement. And danger. And determination. Blair's fingers convulsively clutched into the fabric on his shoulders. ''I want to talk to you,'' he told her firmly.

''I don't want to talk to you!'' she responded instantly. Her voice wavered slightly because she did want to talk to him, but she was still furious and confused, and what good could possibly come of it? She knew that he didn't really care for her; it had all been orders. And if, just if, he did care, it meant only pain.

A grim smile crept forbiddingly into Craig's features, drawing his lips to a tight line. ''Too bad, princess,'' he said with a shrug, ''because you are going to talk to me whether you want to or not.''

Blair had seen the scene in a dozen movies, and she had

never expected to be the ingenue caught in the suave, smooth movement, but she was. Craig spun and swirled her cleanly across the floor before she could catch her breath, and then out the terrace doors.

He kept going until he found a secluded bench and his last guiding pressure on her elbow sent her plopping onto it. He released her and put his hands into his pockets, but he blocked any escape route by planting a polished shoe beside her and enclosing her with his body.

Blair glanced from his shoe to his eyes, hers blazing an angry, shocking emerald. "Okay, Taylor," she hissed, having wisely judged her chances of eluding him as nil. "You want to talk, talk."

"Nice party, isn't it?" he drawled with a mockingly raised brow.

"It was," she snapped. "Is that it? May I go back?"

"No, that's not it," he growled, fire replacing the amusement in his gaze. "You told me that you loved me, Blair." He laughed with no mirth. "You even promised to wait out a jail term. What happened? You were willing to reform a terrorist, but you can't love a government man? What's the matter? You can't play philanthropist this way? It's not self-sacrificing enough?"

"What?" Blair screeched, astounded by the attack. She started to rise, but his hand fell to her shoulder. She shook it off as she sat again, her fury spouting over like steam from a teakettle, mincing her flow of words.

"You're crazy, Taylor. I couldn't care less that you work for the government; I'm delighted for you. Oh, no, Mr. Taylor, you play James Bond all you like, until you get yourself killed one day, and I'll even send flowers. What you are isn't even worth discussing. I've known what you are all along— a yes man—it doesn't matter to whom! I despise you, Taylor, because you made a fool out of me. You used me; you deceived me—"

"Just hold on a minute!" Craig roared in interruption, leaning an elbow on a knee and bringing the bold contours of his face to hers, nose to nose. "I couldn't tell you the truth, Blair, and you damned well know it!"

"Because you're a yes man!" she flared, not sure she was reasonable herself but tense with warring emotions and afraid to take the chance, the risky chance, that anything could ever exist between them. "Okay, you were working for my father. But still you could have reassured me, hinted at what you were. Instead you strung me along, let me behave like an idiot! Oh, you must have been vastly amused."

"I was never amused, Blair, I was—"

"Following orders!" she screeched, trying to keep her teeth from chattering. She was wound up like a broken watch unable to stop until she had spun herself out. "Did it ever occur to you that your orders might be wrong! Or are you so mesmerized by reading the damn directions that you don't exercise judgment anymore, or have an opinion, or the will to act—"

Craig was like a time bomb that finally went off. "Yes!" he roared, and the heat of his anger seemed to singe her face. "Yes, Mrs. Teile, I do sometimes disagree with directives. But yes, Mrs. Teile, I work for the government, and *yes* my superiors do make mistakes. The system is imperfect. But I've been around a lot, Mrs. Teile. An awful lot. Enough to know that although imperfect I'll take what we've got. I make my opinions known, Mrs. Teile, and when my subordinates come to me, I listen to their opinions. But I'm in my position because I have the experience to deal with the decisions I have to make. Your father and Merrill are where they are because they learned what they were doing the hard way. And you'll have to admit, *princess*, that this time they carried it all off well, damned well. No one was even scratched when an international fiasco could have blown up in our faces."

For a moment Blair was silent, aware that he was reasonable, rational, and fiercely right. She couldn't bring herself to say so. He had called her princess again with that scathing tone; he had decreed that she should love him still while giving no hint of the depth, or even the reality, of his own feelings.

They were so close, their breaths mingling as they stared at each other, that she wanted nothing more than to forget the deceit of the past and the fear of the future and bring her lips that one inch closer to meet explosively with his. *No,* she begged herself, *please, no, don't let him take you again.*

"Taylor," she clipped, "what you did to me wasn't necessary. You let me think I was in the hands of a terrorist and then—" She choked off, unable to remind him that he had held her willingly in his arms, so in love was she that she would give herself to her captor. "Never mind! Just leave me alone and go on to your next assignment, James Bond. I don't want to be around when you say yes once too often."

Craig continued his close scrutiny of her, but suddenly the anger flashed out of his eyes. They were sparked again by the sizzling gold fire of amusement.

"You are still in love with me," he said, and if she didn't know him better, she would have thought his cynical tone was touched by awe.

"I'm not!"

"You were; you told me so."

"I was infatuated," Blair said, protesting as she felt the furious thumping of her heart and praying her denial would be strong enough to keep herself from being read by his searing, leonine eyes. "I fell in and out of love equally quickly, Mr. Taylor. A sexual attraction," she said coolly, giving him a bitter, dry smile. "I'm sure I was just one of many for you."

"Really?" Craig no longer seemed angry at all, merely fascinated by the conversation. He drew away from her and rested an elbow on his bent knee. He grinned with a secret mirth. "Go on, Mrs. Teile," he urged her. "I've never had my character analyzed by a psychologist before."

Unnerved by his sudden turnaround and certain that he

mocked her, Blair batted her lashes while she struggled for a suitable reply. "You don't need a psychologist to tell you your behavior was purposely deceitful, Taylor."

"Yes, ma'am," Craig said, the dancing fire in his eyes belying his humble tone.

He was mocking her again, Blair thought furiously. "You're a lying con artist. I don't care what government you work for!" she charged him.

"Yes, ma'am," Craig repeated. He grin broadened, a devil-may-care, enticing mask of amusement. He was sure now, sure for both of them, sure about the rest of their lives. And yet he couldn't make offers yet, no promises. He had to go. Leave tomorrow. All he could do tonight was take and pray and talk. And for the first time in his life, he feared not coming back. He wanted so much, so badly. A shiver hit him. He wanted a life with his princess, the woman who stared at him now, outraged by his behavior. She truly was a princess tonight, an American princess, breathtakingly regal in the empire velvet, her breasts heaving slightly, intoxicatingly, with her agitation. Her fine features were as light and lovely as crystal. But unlike crystal, they were strong and vibrant, characterized by the power of the mind he loved so dearly that lurked behind them. *Forget tomorrow, win her tonight, make her wait . . . take tonight.*

"I don't love you, Taylor. I don't give a damn about you. I never did. Can't you get that through your thick, uncrackable skull?" she demanded.

"Oh, yes, ma'am!" Craig rejoined with a start. He had to cajole her from anger before anything else. "Only because you're right, my love."

"I'm not your love," Blair snapped, "and I no longer care to allow you to amuse yourself at my expense. I—"

"Then don't amuse me," Craig commanded, his voice growing tense while a wistful, nonmocking smile appeared on his features.

"What?" Blair murmured, riddled with new confusion.

"Don't amuse me," Craig repeated softly, his head lowering once more toward hers. "Thrill me," he directed, "tease me, torment me . . . kiss me." His voice was a rasp of velvet caressing her as the warmth of his breath caressed her cheeks. His eyes held hers as if by magnetic power, as if she were drowning in compelling golden suns, pulled by the force of gravity, unable to look away. She seemed paralyzed as his lips descended ever closer to hers; her body was cold, as if frozen to immobility. Then his lips finally touched hers and the cold was dispelled as liquid fire seeped through her. His kiss was a brush of lightness, a slow savoring as his tongue moved to outline her mouth, tasting the nectar as might a wine connoisseur before giving vent to indulging in a fine bouquet.

Blair was startled, stunned, simply too astounded to protest at first, taken as easily as a deer frozen by oncoming lights. Then she had no chance to weigh choice, to raise the objections she knew made so much sense, the denial that would save her so much pain and self-reproach later.

His warmth permeating through her held her to his will as surely as the trembling cold that had besieged her. His touch brought her to that plane where there was no time or space, no need for conscious thought. It was their world, the one she came to only in his arms, the cloud where all that mattered was sweet sensation and nothing could be wrong because it was right to yield to him. The only course was to be with him, to bask in the comfortable and yet wildly erotic, blood-racing, tantalizing security of his possessive presence.

His lips came down harder on hers, moving slowly, sensuously. His hands came to her chin, tilting it to adjust her face to his languorous assault. Blair shivered as his tongue grazed along her teeth, and her lips parted to his, moist and warm, issuing unspoken surrender and invitation. She was barely aware next that she was standing, her arms curling around his neck with urgent need, her body arched to his with exquisite torment as the kiss became deep and driving, electrifying and consuming. Time indeed had no meaning; Blair heard nothing but the rustle of velvet, felt nothing but the rugged play of his muscles beneath her touch, knew no scent on the night air except that of crisp and clean masculine essence.

"They must be out on the terrace."

The pleasant drawl of her father's voice drew Blair slowly but surely back to the present time—and space. And back to the humiliating realization that he had done it to her again—seduced her against her common sense.

Her hands fell from his shoulders and she jerked away. "Damn you, Taylor," she hissed, aware that her father and George Merrill were stepping out onto the terrace. Her words came in a vehemently irate whisper. "Don't do that again! I told you, I want nothing more to do with you! Go kill yourself and leave me in peace!"

She was quaking, she knew, torn into pieces. Still, within the gamut of emotions that raged inside her, not the least of which was heartache for what could never really be, she fought a fierce battle for momentary composure and won.

"Hi, Dad," she waved cheerfully, shaking off the arm that Craig brought to her elbow, ignoring the seething anger in his eyes and moving quickly past him before she could hear his sharp reply. Blair rushed straight to Andrew Huntington and hooked her hand through his elbow. "Craig and I just came out for a little air, but you know, it's getting chilly out here."

"Good." Merrill laughed boomingly as Huntington viewed his daughter through narrowed eyes. "They're about to light my cake—it was rude of them to find so many candles, huh, Andrew?—and I wanted you two there."

''Wonderful!'' Blair enthused, a falsely bright smile in place. ''Let's go in.''

''Yes, let's,'' Craig said sardonically from behind her. He was able to catch her arm and detain her before the group passed into the ballroom.

''I'm not through with you yet,'' he hissed quickly into her ear, drawing a new spasm of shivers from her.

She unobtrusively wrenched away and hurried inside, sticking close to Merrill and her father. *You are through with me!* she thought, pain outweighing anger with the finality of what she must do. *Because I won't be taking any more chances of running into you again.*

It was a good resolve. A firm resolve. She felt as if she were amputating a part of her body, but she meant it.

But it was also true that when Craig said he wasn't through with her, he wasn't through with her.

Sixty-odd candles on Merrill's cake had just been blown out when Blair once more felt Craig behind her. He gripped her elbow with a certain nonchalance that clearly indicated he assumed her his private property, but he didn't address her. He spoke to her father. ''Mr. Huntington, the chief wishes to meet with you privately after the festivities have died down.'' His voice lowered although his tone remained casual. ''The president has arrived, sir, and something crucial has come up. I'll be more than happy to see Blair home for you.''

''Oh. Fine,'' Andrew agreed before Blair could get her mouth open. He smiled at Craig, unaware or not caring that Blair was clearly wishing she could tape her own father's mouth shut at the moment. What was he doing to her? she wondered desperately. Throwing her straight to the lions? And then she understood. Of course, he was throwing her to this particular jungle cat. He believed that she was in love with him; he would do everything in his power to throw them together. He was her father; he would give her the world if he could.

''Dad,'' Blair said, trying to stand her ground without making a scene. "I'll wait for you. I came with you, I don't mind if I wander around a bit—"

"Thanks, sweetheart," her father said dismissively, "but that's silly. You two go on ahead. Oh"—a little twinkle in his eyes made a fine mesh of the grooves surrounding them—"I won't wait up for you."

"Dad—" Blair half-wailed, but he had moved away already; he didn't understand. He thought her merely angry, and that she and Craig could talk things out. And of course she was angry. But anger wasn't the problem. It was difficult to retain a hurt anger if that emotion was directed at someone loved. Loving encompassed so many things. Among them, forgiving—and she was already forgiving Craig. With a little bit of humor she could almost admit that Craig had been a clever manipulator and that she really couldn't blame him for the stories he had woven under the circumstances.

But she couldn't afford to laugh, just as she couldn't afford to love. Her father just didn't understand the deep-rooted fear she lived with.

"Even if he were obliging, Blair, I wouldn't let you hide behind your father."

Startled from her thoughts by the very man who spawned them, Blair made a subtle attempt to wrest her elbow from his grip. He wasn't letting go.

"Taylor," she enunciated with a low growl. "I can get a cab. I don't want you to take me home—"

"Fine," he snapped back, "because I'm not taking you home."

Her elbow jerked; she was being propelled toward the ballroom doors.

She could have done something. But her options were limited to making some type of scene, and she hated to be conspicuous or create scenes. And then again, there was the possibility that it would have gained her nothing anyway.

She did nothing; she attempted nothing. She clamped her

lips together and accepted his assistance into his silver-gray Porsche that the valet produced at the hotel entrance.

All right, Taylor, she thought dispiritedly. *We'll talk tonight. We'll have tonight. I'll even admit anything that you want.*

But it can't change the future.

CHAPTER THIRTEEN

Blair had assumed he would take her to his apartment, and she had also assumed that his apartment would be close to Capitol Hill. But as she sat stone-faced and silent beside him as he drove, her listless resignation gave rise to curiosity.

He was heading for the Beltway, and once on the Beltway, he headed south. She watched uneasily as they circled D.C., well aware that they would shortly be reaching Virginia.

She finally broke her silence. "Where are you taking me?" she demanded acidly. "I hope you know that it's *kidnapping* if you take me over a state line against my will."

He gave her a swift, unappreciative glance. "We're going to my home."

Blair dryly raised a brow. "I don't believe you live this far out."

He shrugged. "I have a town house near Merrill. But it's not my home."

They both fell silent again and Blair began to grow more uneasy as they passed the Alexandria exits. Just when she was about to protest in earnest, he pulled off the Interstate. They followed a dark and lonely road as seconds ticked by, then drew into a drive that led to an attractive, unpretentious, split-level ranch house that was lit as if awaiting their appearance.

Blair tried to open her own door, but she couldn't handle the unusual upward-swinging Porsche door. Craig came around to help her instantly, impatient with her efforts to avoid his courtesies.

"You're acting like a sulky kid, Blair," he said caustically, helping her from the car despite her desire to avoid him.

"Excuse me," she drawled sarcastically. "I'll try to act like a sulky adult."

He dropped her arm with an oath of annoyance and walked up a path bordered by a handsome rock garden. Twisting his key in the lock, he pushed the door open and turned back to her. "Mrs. Teile?"

Blair swept by him into a large, airy living room, pleasantly paneled in white oak, a fireplace of natural granite offsetting the light tone of the wood. A modular sofa sat before the fire, an inviting fur rug covering the floor space between them. A stereo was to the left of the room, a small portable bar to the right.

It was a masculine but comfortable room, and Blair was suddenly sure why he had brought her here. His town house, she was sure, would be cold and austere—lifeless.

This was what he called home. She could tell by the rows of record albums filling the stereo cabinets that he was a music buff, by the bookshelves that filled the wall opposite the fire that he was an ardent reader. All the handsome knick-knacks that graced hardwood end tables and various shelves gave credence to his love of travel and other cultures, other places. . . .

"Okay, Taylor," she said briskly, aware that she was falling in love with the house that proclaimed the man, that she would love to comb through the books, through the albums, that she could be perfectly content curling into a corner of the immense couch with a book as snow fell and a fire blazed, that it was just such a place as she too would love to call home. "We're here. Did you want to talk? Or did you just want to go to bed? If so, just say it. You don't have to waste time with any clever schemes. I'll go to bed with you."

"Stop it, Blair!" he hissed behind her, his hands rough and angry as he took her wrap. "That isn't the way you talk and it isn't the way you are. Sit down and get comfortable. Take your shoes off if you like. You're not going anywhere for a while."

Blair stared at him a moment, then shrugged and kicked off her heels, never once losing a challenging eye contact with him. "Okay, Taylor, my shoes are off and I'm not going anywhere."

Aggravated annoyance hardened his craggy features. "Will you please quit calling me Taylor? And sit. You look like a caged lion."

"Princess, Tay—Craig," she corrected herself obligingly, "not a lion."

"Will you sit, damn it!" he grated.

Shrugging again with the casual indifference she had determined to wear as her shield against his onslaught, Blair sat, curling her feet beneath her on the huge sofa. She watched as Craig shed his jacket and opened his tie. He expertly stoked up a fire, holding a silence. Satisfied with his efforts at the fireplace, Craig rose, dusted off his hands absently, and walked over to the portable bar. "What would you like to drink?"

"I don't want a drink."

"I think you should have a drink. You tend to be a little more honest with your tongue loosened."

Blair sighed and shrugged once more. "Martini, with an olive."

A moment later he brought the drinks to the sofa, handed her one, and sat beside her, uncomfortably close. The angle in which he perched left his left hand resting on the sofa close enough to touch her neck. His knee brushed her thigh. "Want a cigarette?" he offered.

"No, thanks. I quit, remember?" she said acidly.

He raised a brow. "Well, I was good for your health if nothing else," he muttered dryly. "All right, let's get past the petty stuff. I'm sorry I deceived you, although it was necessary to a certain point. I never intended that you should feel I was making a fool of you. I knew you would be furious, but I was scared myself. I wanted you, Blair, and for that brief span of time, I knew I had you. I probably would have said anything to feel you in my arms. Can you understand that? Maybe not," he answered himself a little bitterly. "I might not have understood myself three months ago. But I am in love with you, Blair, and I've discovered myself capable of all sorts of things because I love you."

He had stopped speaking, and Blair found herself helplessly staring at him. Her chemistry seemed to have come alive within her body; she was shaky, as if composed of molten liquid. He did love her; he really did love her. She had longed to believe it, and yet feared it. It would have been so much easier if she had never seen him.

He was waiting; she was supposed to say something, but if she opened her mouth, he would know that he had become her world, and then he would persist, and it would be terrible, because he wasn't the type of man you could ever hope to change. And anyway, why would you try to change what you loved? And could you still be loved in return if you tied a noose around a man's neck? If you took his lifelong work and forced him to make a choice? Surely it would all be a disaster. But if he persisted with his life, she wouldn't be able to handle it, she would die a little every time he left; she would become a shrew, a witch, a basket case.

"I think I will take a cigarette," she said nervously.

He shook his head, commenting briefly. "Not if you've really managed to quit. And a cigarette isn't going to help you. You have to face this sooner or later. I love you, Blair, and I believe that you love me. I want to hear you talk, I want to know if you forgive me, I want to hear you say that you love me.''

''I forgive you; I love you,'' she said woodenly, well aware that she was about to cry. It had been easier to love a criminal, a criminal could reform, could atone, and live. Sweet Jesus, all she wanted him to do was live!

His golden lion gaze never left her. She was convinced more than ever that there was something extra to his vision, that he really had the power to sear through to the soul, rob the heart with his eyes. His brow began to furrow now; his fingers tensed against his glass and the rear of the sofa. Her tone had perplexed him.

''When are you leaving again?'' she asked bluntly so that he could no longer be perplexed.

The question was a bull's-eye. His jaw tightened, making the cast of his chin hard and impenetrable. He blinked before answering. ''Tomorrow.''

''Oh.''

''That's it?'' He suddenly sounded furious. ''Just 'oh?' ''

''What did you expect me to say?'' Blair snapped back. ''All right, please don't go!''

''I have to—''

''So what did you bring it up for?'' Blair demanded. ''I knew nothing I had to say would matter, so why bother? You have to go, go. But Christ, Craig, don't ask me to wait for the pieces to be flown back in a box. I can't, I just can't, I can't!''

''Blair, wait a minute! You never listen! I have to go tomorrow, but it will be the last time and . . .''

''No!'' She set her drink upon an end table and sprang to her feet, moving about the room with agitation and a fear she would dissolve into helpless tears. *Don't do this to me, Taylor,* she wailed silently. *Oh, don't, please don't.* ''Craig, you have to go tomorrow; next time it will be the same. Just one more time, on and on until it's just all over and—'' A vision of Ray, bleeding on the asphalt, compassionate eyes closed to the world forever suddenly blinded her to all else. She was so weak she could barely stand, so furious she couldn't possibly fall.

"Blair, damn it! People are killed in traffic accidents every day! You can be mugged walking down the street. There are no goddamn guarantees in life. But I mean what I say. No, I can't forget all that I've been; I can't just turn my back no matter how much I do love you. There is no one else to fill in for me on this assignment on such short notice. But soon there will be." He was on his feet, too, trying to force her attention, her understanding. She wouldn't stand still. She was pacing the fur rug before the fire like an exquisitely beautiful, but caged cat. Craig tried to remain in front of her to read her features, but she just kept moving. Finally he issued a thunderous oath and grabbed her upper arms, shaking her slightly, "Damn it, Blair! I love you, you love me. Doesn't that count for anything? Doesn't it mean something? I'm willing to change. Can't you compromise? Can't you have a little faith? Love me enough to give me a chance?"

He shook her for so long that she gave up the effort to fight him and allowed her head to fall back so that she was staring into his eyes. They were touched by the fire; they were alive with seething emotion. They sizzled, they burned, they held her. There was a fierce tension to his grip upon her arms; it was static, it was harsh, but it was charged with an electricity that was impossible to ignore or deny, and suddenly nothing mattered except the moment. "Taylor," she muttered, her voice a bitter shell that just escaped a sob, "I do love you." Fear, panic, pain, and anger suddenly erupted into a desire so overwhelming that the past was nonexistent, the future a haze in timelessness. Blair lowered her head and whispered, "And I want you."

If possible, his grip upon her tightened even more. She was drawn against him, pressed flat to feel the tremendous pounding of his heart, the wealth of flesh, muscle, and sinew that corded like tensed wire within his frame. She could feel his breath, harsh and raspy, riding across her temple.

''Now?'' he demanded with a curt bluntness that bordered upon cruelty.

But she couldn't help herself. She nodded.

When they had made love previously, whether he had been gently cajoling her or teaching new delights, he had been almost excruciatingly thorough and exquisitely, torturously slow, driving her half mad before making her his.

But tonight there was something different to him—a hint of violence, a thread of voracious danger. She had never known his own hunger to control him, yet now it did. His fingers threaded through her hair as he clasped her to him, sending the pins flying across the room heedlessly. Blair clamped hard on her jaw with the pain, but said nothing. She met the fever in his eyes, the onslaught of his lips as they devoured hers, the thrust of his tongue that was simultaneous with that of his grinding hips.

A second later she was sinking to the rug with him. Her clothing was roughly and quickly dismissed. She should have cried out against the strange violence. But she couldn't because she was meeting it with a wild urgency of her own, an obliviousness to everything but him and the need to be with him this one last time. She never did lose eye contact with him as they sat upon the rug discarding the last of their garments; she reveled in the devil's fire that blazed in his eyes His hands were upon her shoulders and he was pushing her down, pausing as he hovered over her, his length already pressed hard against her, his need a tantalizing power that pulsed a driving heat, a sweet promise, a strange threat, an intrigue that compelled discovery . . .

And still his eyes carried that firelight. They asked a mocking question; they offered an out. They seemed to laugh a bitterness that neither of them would ever accept that out.

Blair had her answer. She finally closed her eyes; she arched to him and for a single moment of soft tenderness traced the grim curve of his lips with her tongue. And then she was imprisoned, caught, held as his teeth took a grip of her lower lip, forceful, then sensuously light and grazing, holding, controlling all the same. And then he was looking at her again; his voice was rough velvet, it was a whisper, it was thunder, it permeated all that was conscious.

"You will wait for me."

Again she found herself nodding. Anything. She would agree to anything at the moment. "Craig, please . . ."

Her slender body reached beneath his in a high arch, his hands coursed her body to his hips. Still he watched her, waiting for her touch. And then he was alive inside her, a tempest, a possession that was total, complete. Something in her understood, but it was a vague understanding, to be truly fathomed at a later date. It was a branding of sorts, he never intended that she forget this night, that she forget just how complete and total his possession was.

She would never, could never, forget. She would always remember the fire shooting high in the grate, orange flames reflecting the broad, damp shoulders of the man she loved. Fire, always, in his eyes, seeming to ebb only with that in the grate, far into the predawn hours of a mist-hazed morning.

God, he consisted of incredible energy. In life, in love, he was incredible. Surely more than mortal.

But he wasn't more than mortal, Blair finally forced herself to accept. In all those hours of clinging to him, of greedily capitulating to all his demands, hoarding all that she could take in turn, she hadn't forced herself to think at all. She had known that was the way it would be from the beginning. She had also known the reckoning would have to come.

The fire was dying, the spring air was cool. She should have been cold, but she wasn't. Burrowed next to Craig, cushioned by the fur rug, sheltered by a haphazard leg and arm that held her with casual, comfortable intimacy, she was warm. Exhausted, spent, pleasantly aching—but warm.

She attempted to glance at Craig's profile, but her hair was caught beneath his shoulder. Still she was sure that he slept. Had she slept at all? She really wasn't sure. The night had been something like a Roman feast—fabulous, course after course. Such gluttony could only bring exhaustion.

She finally managed to shift enough to see his face. Yes, he slept. She tasted salt and realized that tears slipped silently from her eyes. He was mortal. The breath that heaved his power-hewn chest could cease; the blood that coursed that vital, relentless energy could spill. The heart that pounded courage, loyalty, and love could stop. Incredible, yes, it was all incredible. All that was warm, living, vital could turn to dust with one bit of metal and explosive powder. A bullet . . . such a little thing to bring down such an indomitable creation.

Why am I doing this to myself? she asked. Because she loved him so, because she loved the way his hair fell over his forehead as he slept, the way his limp fingers touched her, possessive even in his sleep.

She swallowed; she was shaking.

He did love her; she knew that. He meant all that he promised. But she also knew what happened to responsible, dependable people. The chief would even mean to let him go. But Craig Taylor was his number-one man. A new emergency would always be popping up.

Knowing that she would leave him, she felt half dead already. And she was either too old, too mature, or too world-weary to believe in forcing choices, especially when they really had so little control.

She should go now before they could talk again. Before he pushed, and they went round and round in circles. *Don't be an idiot,* she chastised herself. One didn't just slip away with Craig. It was a bear rug, she noted idly. Had she seen that when she came in? It didn't really matter. What did matter was that she would never make it past the wide, stone hearth before he awoke and grabbed her back.

And what would she do then anyway? There sure as hell wasn't going to be a Yellow Cab waiting just outside the door. She glanced once more at the rugged planes of his face that were so beautiful to her. She still tasted salt upon her lips. How to con a con artist. Her only chance was to get him into a shower. And then she would have to steal his car. He was on assignment, she reminded herself. He had to be somewhere at some time.

Well, if the damned government wanted him badly enough, they'd just have to come and get him. After all, they were taking him from her, and she had already given them so much. *I just can't give everything,* she thought, biting her lip to hold her tears back.

She closed her eyes and drifted into an uneasy sleep, her calculations complete, her mind resigned to all she must do.

She wasn't prepared for the intentness of his gaze when she woke again. He was leaning upon an elbow, watching her, and the naked love unguarded in his eyes caused her breath to catch. *Dear God,* she prayed in fleeting silence, *keep him safe, keep him safe . . .*

"I love you, Blair," he stated simply. She knew it; it had been said already. But it could never be said too much.

She tried to smile. The effort wasn't particularly successful, but it seemed enough for him.

"Will you wait?"

"Yes," she lied baldly, never blinking. She traced his profile with a shaky finger and forced a grin. "Tomorrow has become today. Shouldn't we get moving?"

"Blair, we need to talk. I wouldn't trade the night for anything. I'm sorry, but not really sorry. But we still need to talk—"

"There's nothing to be sorry for," Blair interrupted him ruefully, her voice lowering to a husky whisper. "I wouldn't trade the night—it meant as much to me as it did to you." She cleared her throat and produced a more believable smile. "We can talk on our way back in. Why don't you hop in the shower and if you point me toward the kitchen, I'll make coffee."

He was silent for a second, then he kissed her very gently, as it he were tenderly apologetic toward lips still puffed from the bruising they had willfully accepted during the night. "Okay," he finally agreed, rising and pausing just a second before helping her up. Her hair looked so beautiful tangled and spread over the rug, her hair and her slender form, delightfully curved and soft . . .

He reached a hand down to help her up, wincing over her head as he gave in to the temptation to draw her naked form to his once more. God, did he hate to leave.

"Kitchen is this way," he mumbled, releasing her with reluctance and indicating the direction. "Coffee will have to be black—I haven't any milk here. Of course, you could shower with me . . ."

"No," Blair protested, unconscious of her nakedness but poignantly aware of his as she moved swiftly for the kitchen. "It's your last job. I'm sure they'll come here if you don't show up there nice and early." She didn't wait for his reaction; she moved into the kitchen.

Seconds later she heard the water and rushed back into the living room. She paused for a minute by the fire. Perhaps she should wait, hear what he had to say as they drove back together.

No, she couldn't do it. She couldn't listen to pipe dreams, begin to believe, make promises. She had already lied in essence.

Her clothing was scattered all over the floor; she didn't dare take the time to fool around with dressing. Finding a closet door, she wrenched it open and found just what she needed—

a trench coat. It fell almost to her feet, and the arms flapped ludicrously, but that didn't matter. All she needed was covering.

Next, the keys. She prayed that they were in his trouser pocket. They were. Simple. Easy. Except that her fingers also clasped a small box, and even in her desperation she couldn't help but unlatch the box with trembling fingers.

A diamond solitaire stared up at her, brilliant even in the misty light of early morning. A sob caught in her throat, but she had always known deep inside her that he meant marriage. She closed her eyes, fighting a spasm of shivers. She couldn't be a widow again.

Biting down into her lips until she tasted blood, she snapped the velvet box closed and replaced it in the trousers. Actually it was harder to drop the trousers than it had been to shut the box. Cruel to be kind, she told herself bitterly. He would understand when she left that it was over, that there was no future, that he needn't believe that he could change the color of his stripes.

The water was still running, but she didn't have long. Blair opened the front door as silently as possible and headed for the Porsche. Of all things, the upward swinging door once more gave her trouble. Why couldn't he drive a normal car? she wondered dispiritedly. The best laid plans of mice and men . . . He wasn't an average man. She had also known that from the very beginning.

The door finally gave. The Porsche floored instantly into action. She had no trouble retracing the roads they had traveled the previous night. Within fifteen minutes she was back on the Washington Beltway. It was spring, a beautiful spring. Crisp, clean.

She had never been colder in her life. More numb.

Craig heard the whirr of his car's motor even in the shower. Not bothering to turn off the faucets, he sped from the enclosure, pausing only a fraction of a second to loop the ends of a towel tightly over his hips. He reached the drive just as the car jerked and accelerated into a dust-twirling screech and pelted down the road.

He knew instantly that she wouldn't be looking back.

He stood silently in the chill morning for a moment, watching as the silver car became a tiny speck. "I'll be damned," he muttered finally, brooding motionlessly despite the sting of the chill against his bare damp flesh. He was furious, but also touched by a dry admiration. She hadn't made a single mistake; she had coerced him, manipulated him perfectly. She had lied with the sweetest of smiles.

And as she had expected, he understood her message.

Tensing his jaw, he moved back into the house. He picked up the phone and touched a single digit; a pre-set number. "Taylor here," he said tonelessly. "I need a pickup."

He set the phone down and began to dress. He stuffed all necessary papers into the pockets of a short ski jacket, noticing without a blink that his trench coat was gone.

At least she hadn't lit out stark naked, he thought with a certain jealous relief. He almost smiled, wondering how Huntington was going to react when Blair walked in like a flasher.

He had a feeling Huntington wouldn't even lift a dignified brow. Huntington was on his side. Well, maybe not on his side, but Huntington loved his daughter above all else. If Huntington had his way, Craig believed, he would be gift-wrapped right now. One C. Taylor, tied up in bows.

He was glad Huntington didn't have complete control. Blair was right about one thing; he couldn't handle it that way. He did have to be his own man; he had to make his own choices. It would have been nice if she would have believed in him.

He had a little time left after packing. He picked up the clothing scattered around his living room, then sat down and stared at the ashes of the fire, unable to stop the memories of how rampantly it had burned through the night.

He found the small tiara that highlighted the coiled piles of her hair the night before. Twisting it in his hands, he felt his lips curl into a grim lock of determination. He shook his head half tenderly, half fiercely.

"It's not over, princess," he murmured. "Not by a long shot. I will be back."

He heard the car coming for him and carefully placed the tiara on the fur before the ashes of the fire. Walking to the door, he glanced back to the room once more.

"I will be back," he repeated softly aloud. "And princess, you won't be able to find a place in heaven or earth to hide."

It was with a trace of dry amusement that he closed his door. Little witch. Stole his damned car. She was surely going to pay for that one. Another one for the boys in S.S. if the story ever got out. Taylor bested by a slip of a girl.

Taylor, he decided wryly of himself, had been bested by a slip of a girl.

A woman.

His princess.

CHAPTER FOURTEEN

Andrew Huntington was every bit as cool about his daughter's appearance as Craig had expected.

Blair was a bit ruffled. She had forgotten all about her father until she was unlatching the door and entering his living room.

But he didn't say a word. He didn't even blink. He said a brisk good-morning and mentioned that there was coffee in the kitchen. He brushed her forehead with a kiss and promised to be home early for dinner before leaving in his customary quiet suit and tie, as if she were clad in everyday leisurewear.

As a father, Blair decided with drained relief and gratification, he was definitely an A-plus with gold stars.

Alone in the house, Blair poured herself a cup of coffee and climbed the steps to her room, intending to shower. But she didn't, not right away. Although memory carried the sting of torture, she wanted to remember. She wanted to hoard the night; she couldn't bear the thought of immediately washing away the scent that was Taylor, which still clung to her skin.

Blair stayed in the town house for three days straight, functioning, walking, talking, breathing, sitting quietly with her father at night, playing chess, sometimes merely reading with him in his study while he worked.

She didn't cry. She was empty. At night she would stare long at her ceiling, and no matter how she tried to convince herself that she had taken the only course possible, she would be unable to prevent herself from plaguing her mind with ifs.

But Craig was gone. She had firmly slammed a door in his face. It was now really unlikely that she would see him again, at least not for years, and then they would meet as strangers at some casual function; their love would be a distant thing of youth and passion, something they might both smile over with a futile poignancy.

If he lived that long.

She didn't want to know if and when Craig made a mistake and paid the highest price his country could ask.

And she didn't want to know where he had gone—no one would tell her anyway, she was sure—and she didn't want to know when he would be back. Not at first anyway.

On the fourth day after his departure she forced herself to meet a few friends from nearby Johns Hopkins for lunch. During the meal she was urged to accept a post in research under a well-known psychologist.

Explaining that it would have to be temporary, Blair accepted. She was going crazy with little to do but care for the town house and her eternally busy father. And all her free hours were plagued by images of Craig and all that she had determined that she had to throw away.

Still, time passed slowly. Her research was tedious, her contact for the project was limited to rats. She had never been overly fond of lab work, and she had already spent years studying the behavior of the little rodents, also chimps, rhesus monkeys, and so forth.

She longed to return to the Hunger Crew. Miles and miles away. A place where she had once found solace because she had been so needed that her life had consisted solely of constant, rewarding work. But she had made her father a promise, and neither was she a witless idiot. She had to sit tight and wait.

Craig's car had disappeared from the town house garage the day she had brought it home.

She had known it would, quietly and efficiently. Nothing was ever said to her by her father or Merrill, who joined them occasionally for dinner. She wondered sometimes if she wished Craig would make another surprise appearance, and she admitted that a part of her prayed such a thing would happen. There were times when she desperately wished she could get a message to Craig. She had composed its contents in her head a million times. *I can't marry you, I can't wait for you, but oh, God, other than that, I'd take anything, give anything just to see you, just to hold you close occasionally.*

No, the clean split had been right. Craig never appeared, and Merrill never once mentioned his number-one man.

Nor did Andrew Huntington ever bring up the name.

It was a day in late June when Andrew Huntington returned home from work to seek out his daughter with both a certain pain and a happy relief. He was going to miss her terribly, but he knew that she needed to go. Her delicate face had been growing more and more pale and gaunt; although she always maintained a cheerful demeanor for him, he knew that she was lonely and miserable.

And it wasn't in his power to reassure her. Only Craig could do that, and only when the time came. He hadn't known what had passed between the two; he could only believe that Craig did love his daughter and that the man was attempting to set things straight. But although he was a perpetual optimist, Andrew Huntington had long ago learned that false promises and guarantees were far more painful than silence and truth.

And he couldn't promise her Craig's return.

But he could give her an all-clear to return to Central America. The relief and happiness in her haunted eyes at his announcement helped relieve the pain in his heart that she would be leaving him again.

She was an adult, he knew. He couldn't hang on; he couldn't live her life.

"I'll make arrangements to get you back in a week or so, okay?" he inquired, forcing a cheerful smile.

"Wonderful," Blair murmured. "Thanks, Dad."

They dined out that night, danced, then played chess until two A.M. They were lucky, Huntington finally admitted to himself. Love wasn't limited by the miles, but by the heart. And no father in the world could be more blessed, or more proud.

Blair announced her resignation the following morning, and then tried to set to work as usual. She was even able to feel a bit more amiable toward her rats. She felt like one of the tiny rodents—caged. Would the miles help to break the barriers of the caged constriction that was her heart? Surely. Time, she told herself, time and distance—the healers of wounds.

She was surprised and puzzled when the friendly doctor she assisted announced that she had an emergency phone call.

And then she felt as if the constriction around her heart had become a boa that squeezed and squeezed. She felt faint, a blackness spinning before her eyes, an illness gripping her stomach. Her body felt like liquid. It was rubber; it wouldn't function.

Craig. Something had happened. Someone had decided to let her know.

She could barely get the receiver to her ear; she had to struggle and swallow several times before rasping out a simple hello.

Relief overwhelmed her at first, making her, if possible, even weaker. Perhaps she did black out for a single second. She had to swallow again before issuing a stunned "Kate!" and asking her friend to slow down and repeat what she had said so far.

"I'm here, Blair, in Washington, and I need you! We only have a few hours. Brad is being shipped back out, and, oh, can you get here right away? It has to be you, Blair. I'm going to just be a wreck when it's over. Perhaps we can go back together ourselves. What do you think? Oh, please, Blair—''

"Kate!" Blair finally managed to whip her shaking thoughts and weak-kneed relief and confused surprise together. "I'm here! I'll help with whatever you need, but calm down. Brad *who* is being shipped where? What's going on?''

She could hear Kate breathing deeply, trying to collect herself. "Brad, Blair, you remember him. He was with us when you disappeared. Brad Shearer. Oh, Blair, I am sorry. I should be asking how you are, except that I know everything is fine.''

"I am fine, Kate," Blair assured her with a dry tug at her insides. "Go on."

"I'm marrying him, Blair. Oh, God, I've never been so happy in my life! But you have to stand up for me. In two hours. We have so little time.''

Why was she surprised? Blair wondered. She had known Kate for years; she had known that when her friend did fall in love it would be impetuous, but hook, line, and sinker all the way.

"Kate," she said cautiously. "You do know what Brad does for a living, don't you?''

"Well, of course I do!" Kate exclaimed reproachfully. "Blair, I'm marrying him today. Why?''

"I—" Blair hesitated. She had no right to instill her own fears upon her friend, no right to ruin the blissful happiness. "I—I'm sorry, I guess I was just worrying for you.''

Kate was silent for a moment with empathy; she knew Blair was thinking of Ray. Or was she? Perhaps it was Craig that Blair feared for now. "Blair," she said, suddenly quiet and serious. "How are you doing? Are you and Craig seeing each other now that all this is over? Did you know who he was all along?''

"No, I didn't," Blair said briefly, "and no, I'm not involved with him." She tried an off-hand chuckle. "You know me, I go for the shy retiring type . . ." She paused for a second, unable to resist the question. "Kate, is Brad planning on quitting?"

Kate replied with a dry chuckle. "Brad is army, Blair. You don't just quit the army."

"No," Blair murmured, "I suppose not." She stood with the receiver still in her hand. "Tell me where you are, Kate. I'll be right there. We're holding up a wedding."

Within an hour she had been excused by her easy-going supervisor and drove the short distance back to D.C. from the Maryland research institute. She stood witness to Kate's wedding along with a friend of Brad's, then shared a glass of champagne with the newlyweds, promising Kate discreetly that she would return when the few remaining hours the pair had together were over.

For all her bravado, Blair knew, that would be when Kate needed her.

Wandering the streets aimlessly to fill her own time, Blair decided to call her father and tell him the good news. She wasn't surprised to have to wait for quite a while before he came to the phone, and in that time she thought of his work. He had kept her sheltered for so many years. Of course she hadn't lived with him, except sporadically, for years. She had been with the crew, before that with Ray, before that in college.

She closed her eyes tightly for a moment. Her escapade had really drawn them close. Then she heard his voice, gentle as always when he spoke to her. She told him about the wedding, and that she would be out late, keeping Kate company. They chatted for a moment, then Blair found herself pensively silent, recalling what Kate had told her right before the service.

"I know there's danger, Blair, but it doesn't matter. I would rather have my time with Brad, whatever it is, than any guarantees for a lifetime. I know I haven't been on the losing end as you have, Blair"—she had smiled with rueful sadness—"but

I love Brad. And think about it. Yes, you lost Ray, but even for that pain, would you have given up all that the two of you did have?''

"Blair, are you there?''

Blair suddenly snapped back to the present at the sound of her father's query. "Yes, Dad, I'm here. I—uh, nothing, Dad. See you in the morning.'' She hung up the receiver, dismayed to find herself shaking. She had wanted to ask about Craig— and then she hadn't been able to. No, she couldn't question her father. She couldn't allow him to know how she worried.

She glanced at the phone again. She could discreetly ask Merrill. She bit her lip, then decided to do so, only to be disappointed when a feminine voice told her Merrill was out of the office.

"May I take a message?'' the girl asked politely.

"No . . . no . . . I guess not—''

"Is this Blair?'' the girl suddenly inquired.

Startled, Blair frowned and hesitated. "Yes, this is Blair Teile.'' She paused again, baffled. "Who is this?''

"Lorna. Lorna Patterson. We've met at several occasions.'' Lorna didn't mention that they had just met briefly at the chief's party, that she had watched Blair that night, that she deciphered Craig's problem.

"Oh, Lorna, yes! How are you?'' Blair asked, remembering the pleasant, quiet woman. Her tone was polite and sincere, but inwardly she was wincing. She felt as if she suddenly announced herself to the world, and, ridiculously, she hadn't wanted her call known.

"Very good, thank you.'' There was a silence for a second. "Would you like George to return your call?''

"Ah, no, that won't be necessary,'' Blair murmured. She shouldn't have called in the first place. "I'll catch him later.''

"Blair?''

"Yes?'' Curiously there had been a hesitance in Lorna's

voice, and now, again, there was a silence. Then suddenly Lorna rushed into speech.

"This is none of my business, I know. But I don't know where Craig Taylor is, and I don't know when he'll be back, but"—again there was a slight hesitance and another rush of words, as if they had to come out quickly or not at all—"but I do know that he loves you very much, and he's trying, he's really trying."

It was Blair's turn for a stunned silence. She was sure Craig never confided in people, and that Lorna's statement had been intuitive. She also knew that the woman must care very much to have spoken as blindly as she did.

Blair finally spoke. "Thank you," she said softly. She returned the receiver to the hook of the pay phone and sagged against the glass booth. *But that's not the problem, Lorna, I do believe that he loves me.*

That was smart, Blair, real smart, she chastised herself as she left the phone booth. She was now more plagued by misery than ever.

Tiring of walking the streets, she decided to drive around and kill the remaining two hours before the time would arrive when she had promised Kate to return. Without really knowing on a conscious level what she was doing, she found herself approaching Arlington. Once there, she was walking the velvet grass to the ridiculously simple plaque that announced unpretentiously the remains that were once the wonderfully complex Ray Teile.

What is the matter with me? she wondered. *What am I doing here, dwelling on the past?* She wasn't intentionally being morose.

No, she wasn't. She curled her legs beneath her and sat on the grass. Kate had been right; no matter how bad the outcome had been, she couldn't begrudge the beauty of her time with Ray. She was a far better person for having known him, for having loved him. It was all sweet memory; it would always be with her. But it was faint and dim; her mind and memory had been overwhelmed by another man. Strangely she knew that Ray would be pleased, that he would understand.

"But I still don't think I can do it again, Ray," she whispered aloud, and then ruefully smiled to herself despite the mist of tears that veiled her. *Wonderful. I'm cracking up. I'm talking to a headstone.*

But she wasn't talking to the headstone, she was talking to the memory of a wonderful friend; she was searching for an answer from his always judicial viewpoint.

"Maybe it doesn't matter, Ray. Maybe he'll believe that I never want to see him again and leave me alone."

That, she finally decided with a painful tug of the heart, was the case. She glanced at her watch. It was time to return to Kate. And she would smile and be light; she would keep Kate from worrying, she would keep her from the misery that belonged to a bride of just hours who would spend her first night sleeping alone.

She was cheerful when she met Kate. If nothing else, the women could return to join the crew together. They could support each other; they could move back into the spare, rough way of life that was so important to others and themselves.

Three days later, the women were saying good-bye to Andrew Huntington and boarding a special transport plane. Kate said an affectionate and bright good-bye to Huntington, then discreetly disappeared into the plane, leaving Blair alone.

She clung tightly to her father. "I love you, Dad."

He ruffled her hair, so like that of the wife he had lost long ago but never ceased to mourn, and hugged her close. "I love you, Blair." He held her a little away to smile into her eyes. "I'm going to miss you, sweetheart."

"I'm going to miss you, Dad."

He pulled her back into his embrace again and they held

tight for a minute. Then Huntington sighed softly. "Be happy, Blair. That's what I want more for you than anything in the world."

"I am happy," she protested.

With a sad little smile he shook his head. "You're afraid to be happy," he said sagely, then took a deep breath. "I don't like to meddle, Blair, so I've never said anything. But I know you're pining for Taylor. I'm going to give you a word of advice—and warning. He never gives up. I think he loves you, and I think you should enter into honest negotiation."

"Dad!" Blair exclaimed. "I can't enter into anything! I have no idea of where the man is. And besides"—she bit her lip— "I'm not terribly sure he's going to love me anymore. I think I made my decision rather clear. It's unlikely we'll cross paths again." She paused for a minute. "Dad, do you know where he is? Do you know if . . . if he's okay."

Huntington looked acutely uncomfortable for a moment. "Taylor is fine," he said cryptically. Then, unhappily meeting the puzzle in his daughter's eyes he added, "He's back in Washington. He came in yesterday morning."

Why she should be stunned and agonized by the news, she didn't know. She had done all she could to purposely assure them both that he would never call again.

But he should have called, he should have tried to see her. If only to let her know he was alive.

Don't be ridiculous. What was the matter with her? She did want him, she didn't want him. But in this case, absence had made the heart go crazy. And she couldn't forget the things Kate had made her accept. If you love someone, time—any amount of time—with that person was important.

"Oh," she said aloud to her father. "Well, I'm glad to hear that he returned."

"Blair—"

"Please, Dad," she protested, fighting back an absurd urge to cry over milk long ago intentionally spilled. "Kiss me good-bye, Dad," she said, managing a rueful smile. "I've got to go."

He brushed her forehead tenderly. "Things will work out, Blair, they have a way of doing so."

"Yes," She couldn't leave him worrying, and she managed a truly brilliant smile. "Things do work out. Now, you take care of yourself, okay?" The typical daughter, she straightened a perfectly straight collar for him.

"I will," her father promised. "Go on before that plane leaves without you."

Grimacing, Blair waved and moved away. She stopped just before the ramp, unable to prevent herself from asking a final question. "Dad . . . did Craig know I'd be leaving today?"

Huntington wasn't much of a liar. His face gave him away even before his simple, "Yes."

Blair grimaced, hiding the hurt. She began to mount the ramp backward. "I'll drop you a line as soon as we get there!" she called cheerfully. "Of course, you know how long our mail takes!"

He grimaced in return and waved, and then Blair was seated in the transport plane, next to Kate. She no longer had to keep smiling, but she did. She was afraid if she let her mask crack, it would be all over.

Craig knew she would be gone and he hadn't bothered to try to get to her. Well, that had been what she wanted. She hated people who said no to be encouraged into saying yes. And that wasn't what she meant.

But I would have seen you again, she mouthed miserably to herself. For what? Another parting? How stupid. They were neither one a masochist.

But it hurt to believe his feeling for her was fading. Had, perhaps, already faded completely. Because her father was right. If Craig really wanted something, he went after it until he got it.

"Oh, Blair!" Kate suddenly gasped.

Blair glanced to her friend; Kate's face was going chalky white. Her nails were gripping into the serviceable fabric of the armrests.

Blair had forgotten about Kate's terror of flying. It was always worse at first, when the jets raced down the strip, shuddering for power to rise into the vastness of the sky.

"Close your eyes, Kate," Blair advised, glad to keep herself occupied trying to ease her friend's mind. She began to make crazy, ludicrous comments, designed to make Kate laugh. She eventually succeeded. Her psychology training did sometimes pay off. Once in the air, she ordered her friend a large scotch. Kate would be okay until landing

Some psychologist, though! she told herself with disgust. *I know the whys of the human mind; I know a million patterns of thinking, of feeling.*

But I can never use a damn thing I know to help myself! Logic is just fine, beautiful. But it doesn't do a damn thing to help the hurting.

INTERLUDE

Craig hadn't planned on running into Huntington at the airport. His time was tight. If he missed his flight, there wouldn't be another one for days—and he couldn't wait days.

He was dressed similarly to that day almost five months ago when he had first been sent after his princess.

Only now he was eager; he moved on his own. He was finally a free man. Or as free as a man of conscience and responsibility would ever be.

He literally ran into Huntington. Collided would be a better description.

And he was stunned by the depth of anger in the eyes of the usually cool and guarded administrator.

"Huntington!"

"Taylor."

They eyed each other for a moment. It was Craig who broke the silence. "Did Blair catch the first plane out?"

"She did." A heavy silence reigned again, then Huntington

puffed out his cheeks with indignity. "You knew she was leaving?"

"Yes, sir, I did—"

"Then would you mind telling me just why you've decided to come rushing out here? You had plenty of time . . ."

"Sir—"

"I would like to know just what your intentions are!"

Craig couldn't prevent a rueful smile. "Very honorable, I assure you. I keep trying to marry Blair, but she keeps giving me trouble. I couldn't call her until my own future was set."

Huntington raised quizzical brows. "And?"

"Sorry," Craig replied with a look of guileless regret, "the information is classified." A grin slowly filtered its way across his features and Huntington couldn't prevent his own rueful grin in return. Huntington had been aware, of course, that Craig had requested a transfer. The brass, however, had been a bit concerned. Craig was known for being intelligent and quick as a whip, but he was also known for making his opinions starkly evident. There had been fear in high places that he might make his astute observations a little too apparent.

"I can tell you this," Craig continued, pleased that Huntington had taken his statement with such good grace. "They seem to have decided I might just be right for the tact department— if I've reached a point of settling down. I must have mellowed."

Huntington laughed out loud. "Congratulations!"

Craig shrugged. "I still have to reason with your daughter. Any advice?"

Huntington grimaced; his lips continued to twitch. "Yes, I guess I do have some. Employ any means. And quit chattering here with me. That second transport is supposed to leave right behind the first."

Taylor stuck out his hand. Huntington accepted it.

"Good luck, Taylor."

But Craig was already moving down the concourse, his duffel bag tossed over his shoulder. "I want to know about that wedding!'' Huntington called after his retreating form. ''I'm her father, you know. If I'm losing her, I might as well get to give her away!''

Huntington watched the tall, dominating figure of the man he was sure would shortly be his son-in-law slowly disappear from view. It was a long time that he stood there. Craig's tawny head was visible high above all others.

''Taylor,'' Huntington murmured to himself, shaking his head a bit as if he didn't quite believe the turn of events. Then he was smiling again. After all, he had chosen the man himself. He scowled after his smile. ''I'll bet I don't make the damn wedding,'' he muttered to himself, shaking his head once more as he slowly returned to his car.

On second thought, maybe it would be best if he didn't make the wedding.

He was a father, and no matter how cool and up-to-date he was capable of being, he wanted the pair married quickly.

The two of them were powerful characters. Headstrong, determined, a remarkable match.

Huntington wanted a grandchild, but it would nice if the birth would be conventional, with both parents sharing a name. And it was hard to forget the picture of his blushing daughter arriving home in nothing but an oversized trench coat.

CHAPTER FIFTEEN

The lines to the soup cauldron were growing very short, Blair noted at the end of her second day back as she ladled out her final tin cup for the evening. The sturdy peasants, proud and tenacious, were getting back on their feet. With human perseverance they were putting the terror and upheaval of the fighting that had ravaged their land and the natural disasters that plagued it behind them.

She was glad to be back. Very glad. At the end of a long day here, she was tired, but also filled with a certain satisfaction. She enjoyed seeing the victory of the people, the triumph as they rose on the wings of willpower like a phoenix from ashes to become strong again.

The crew would be moving on shortly.

"Señora! Señora!"

Blair wiped a shirt sleeve across her damp brow and squinted against the glare of the dying sun to glance across the compound. Miguelito, whom she had not seen in the soup line, was racing to her pell-mell on sturdy bare brown feet. She smiled as he stopped breathlessly before her.

"Miguelito! *Como estas?*"

"*Muy bien, señora!*" he said proudly, shuffling his feet and sheepishly dropping his eyes to the ground. He raised them again, a shy smile on his lips. His hands were locked together behind in back, but suddenly he pulled an arm forward— producing a slightly wilted purple orchid, "Welcome, back, *señora,* we have missed you, *mucho!*"

Having uttered his words, his shyness overwhelmed him and he raced back across the compound toward the village.

"Thank you, Miguelito! *Muchas gracias!*" she called after him, gently fingering the petals of the dying flower. There were definitely rewards in life, even if the rewards didn't dispel the terrible loneliness she had thought would dissipate, but instead grew stronger with the passage of time.

"Blair!"

She glanced up to see a frazzled Kate calling to her. "Coming to the stream?" Kate asked.

"Wild horses couldn't keep me from it!" Blair laughed.

Minutes later the women were walking along the jungle path together. "You know," Kate confided with emotion, "I've been so wrapped up with myself since I've seen you, that I've neglected to tell you how worried we were! Doc and I were both in a raw panic. We raised a stink you wouldn't believe. Brad," she admitted huskily, hesitating just an instant at the sound of her new husband's name, "was the only one able to keep us calm. And he did it without ever admitting a thing! I should have known though, right from the start, that it was a safety move. The story appeared in so few papers! And considering who you are . . ." Kate's voice trailed away uneasily, and then she produced a rueful grimace. "Actually I had another thought myself."

"Oh?" Blair queried. They had reached the stream and she could see and hear the cascade of the waterfall as she stripped off her sweat-soaked clothing. Washington in spring, with its cherry blossoms and cool air, already seemed a lifetime away. "What was your thought?"

"I thought you had run off with Craig."

"Kate!" Blair gasped, her face flushing hotly and the gnawing pain that continually chewed upon her heart flaring to violent action "Don't be silly!" she stuttered. "I barely knew him then."

She paused, aware of how ridiculous her statement sounded. Kate, she was sure, had been aware of just how well she had known Craig. Blair allowed her hair to fall over her face as she feigned intense preoccupation with the zipper of her boot. "Kate, you know I would never have done anything like that— just disappeared without some type of an explanation. And I'd never do anything like that to Doc! I wouldn't leave him short."

Kate was already splashing into the water. "I kind of knew that," she said, sighing with blissfully closed eyes as the stream enveloped her with coolness. "You're the most thoughtful and responsible person I know. It was just that in this case I thought you might have lost all sense of reason. I mean, I could have completely lost my head—"

"Kate!" Blair protested. "What a thing for a newlywed to come out with! What about Brad, Mrs. Shearer? You are married, remember?" she added dryly.

Kate opened an eye, unperturbed by her friend's pursed-lip scolding. "I'm married, not blind!" She sighed suddenly. "Very married, and I love Brad with all my heart and I miss him like crazy! But don't try to tell me Craig isn't an incredible man."

I'd never try to tell anyone that, Blair thought with a rush of pain. Aloud she murmured dryly, "Incredible."

"And just think," Kate continued, soaking her hair in the water, then opening her eyes wide, "you had him pegged from the very beginning. He was a dangerous man. A spy!" She shivered deliciously. "Thank goodness he's on our side!"

"He's not a spy," Blair protested, for what reason she didn't know, except that it was bad enough knowing she would spend her life worrying over any incident the U.S. became involved in without giving Craig that particular title. "He's a diplomat," she explained weakly.

Kate arched a dubious brow. "You forget who you're talking to," she murmured dryly, then smiled. "Oh, well, I can imagine he can be very diplomatic!" She chuckled diabolically, then winced and shivered. "Are you coming in or what? Believe it or not, I'm freezing!"

"Yeah," Blair muttered, casting both boots aside and shimmying from her clothing to plunge into the water. When she emerged to the surface, she saw that Kate really was freezing. Goose pimples were fighting with her freckles for supremacy on her skin. "Get out of here!" Blair ordered with a chuckle. "I want to swim around a bit and you'll be an icicle by then!"

Blue lips trembling a hundred miles an hour, Kate stubbornly shook her head. "I don't like leaving you."

"Kate, the place is all clear now!" Blair informed her firmly. "Believe me," she added dryly. "I would have never been allowed back if this area wasn't safe."

"Okay," Kate finally agreed, knowing Andrew Huntington and certain that Blair's comment was not without wisdom. "I won't make you insist a second time!" Her teeth still chattering audibly, Kate emerged in a streak from the water and burrowed into her towel, then hastily jerked into her fresh clothing. Shaking her head slightly at Blair's resistance to the chill water, she called gratefully, "I'm on my way back. See you later."

After Kate disappeared through the trees, Blair began to regret having told her friend to leave. She wasn't frightened in the stream, but being there alone she was plagued by memories. She could almost hear the haunting echo of her own laughter on the air, a haunting echo of a night when she had loved happily and shamelessly beneath the waterfall, as uninhibited as Eve with her Adam. Despite the chill of the water her body flashed with heat and she swam furiously to dispel it, finally perching beneath the waterfall to catch its jolting spray upon her face.

Nothing helped. It was as if the essence of Craig Taylor were somehow forever captured in the private world of the stream.

No, it was more than that. His essence was forever captured within her heart . . . and within a body that could not help but ache with memories of a passion that knew no equal.

Blair was totally unaware that she was being observed. A branch rustled lightly from the shore, but to her it was no more than the natural rustle of the early evening.

But, in truth, more than a haunting essence of Craig Taylor hovered near the stream that night. The man was there himself, in the flesh, undaunted now by the fact that he watched her with pure male appreciation, delighting in the tanned cream of her skin, the firm slope of silky breasts, the graceful movements that turned her supple frame to a picture of glittering beauty.

He smiled as he observed her, completely relaxed. He made no effort to talk to her, but neither did he turn away until she rose with naked splendor from the water, moving with the innate sensuality that always drove him a little nuts. She dressed in khaki-green fatigues and started down the path to the trees.

"Employ any means, huh, Huntington?" he murmured to himself. "That, old man, is exactly what I intend to do."

He turned from the stream then; he had a few preparations to make before he carried out his plans for the night.

Dinner for the Hunger Crew was a lighthearted affair that evening. The day before their return Blair and Kate had purchased a number of "gourmet" canned goods and Huntington had sent the workers a case of a very fine vintage burgundy. Everyone knew that Blair had been whisked away for her own safety, although no one but Kate knew that she had been as much in the dark as they while it was all going on. The conversation inevitably turned to the excitement of her disappearance. Blair hedged all questions the best she could, making no reference to her time aboard *La Princesa* in the jungle rivers.

"Well, you know," Dr. Hardy admitted, "it didn't go so badly when Brad was still with us." He smiled with affection and apology as Kate winced a little. "It won't be forever," he mumbled, tousling his crew worker's hair. The fire was dying slowly while they all sat around in a tight little circle, friends as those sharing such a situation could only be. He glanced back to Blair after Kate smiled in return. "But, boy, did we miss you and Taylor! I sure do wish you could have brought that man back with you. I'll never be able to replace him." The doctor sighed heavily. "As I said, thanks to Brad we were all right for a while. He kept us calm, and he kept us working. But then when he was shipped out, and Kate followed, we really wound up in a hole." The doctor sniffed with great indignity. "They sent us an insipid little do-gooder. Wanted to change the world without chipping a fingernail."

Blair and Kate both laughed at Tom's uncharacteristic disgust. "What happened to him?" Blair asked.

"Hightailed it out of here in two days! Said he wasn't in shape for our kind of manual labor." He tossed a twig onto the embers of the fire and the crackle joined the murmur of grunted agreement from the others. "Yup," Doc said slowly, nodding his grizzled head, "sure am glad to have you back, Blair, and you, too, Kate. Of course"—he smiled conspiratorially to Blair—"Kate was really on an illegal leave. But since it was to become an honest woman, I can only applaud! Pity I can't get that Taylor back here."

Blair smiled through clenched teeth. "Pity," she agreed.

Moments later yawns started to become audible within the group. As if on cue they all scrambled to stiffening legs and rose, sheepishly grinning at one another.

"Boy," Kate said with good-natured disgust. "We are a pack of live wires! Nine o'clock and we're dragging our tails!"

"Bet it wasn't like that in Washington!" Dolly teased.

"I don't know," Kate said mournfully, "I wasn't there long enough. Just enough time to get married and get to see my husband of three hours fly away!" She smiled. "At least here I feel like sleeping!"

Both Blair and Dolly chuckled sympathetically. "How about you, honey?" Dolly quizzed Blair. "Lots of late nights and excitement, huh?"

"Ummm . . . sure," Blair responded, hoping Dolly was unaware that her smile was as dry as a desert. Well, she had had lots of late nights. They weren't due to excitement though, but to a lack of ability to fall asleep, like Kate. But unlike Kate she wasn't sure that being back was going to help her. She was probably going to lie awake, wondering just how long it would be before she could press her memories of Craig into a far and mist-enshrouded corner of her mind. "Good night!" she said cheerfully to both Dolly and Kate, waving as they split and moved toward their respective tents. Kate, she decided, might worry, but Kate was an eternal optimist. She would dream of Brad, but her dreams would be good, they would be plans for a future sure to come.

Blair lit her kerosene lamp and pulled on a white cotton gown. She curled into her cot and plumped her pillow thoroughly while convincing herself, halfway at least, that she was exhausted and that sleep would come as soon as she hit the pillow.

But she didn't sleep. Her mind went immediately to Craig. Or did it? she wondered. Could your mind turn to where it always was in some measure? She clenched her teeth tightly with self-disgust. So much time had passed. Still her every waking moment was filled with thoughts of Craig. She could function, think, and work, but no matter what she was doing, he was always there, in the back of her thoughts.

It had been almost three months since she had seen him last.

Since she had driven from his house, determined that it be forever. *Okay, Madame Psychologist,* she mocked herself, *why do we continue to plague ourselves against all reason? I know this is best, I know it, I know it, I know it . . .*

Then why did it hurt her so badly to know that Craig had been in Washington and hadn't called her? She had told him no and he had accepted. And if he had called her, he would have received only another no. Because she didn't have Kate's strength, she couldn't be his wife and allow him to leave, she couldn't live on faith.

With a muffled and impatient oath she turned off her lantern and buried her face in her pillow, groaning aloud with disgust. She had thought that the jungle would bring her to an acceptance of reality, but instead her memories seemed to multiply. She could sense Craig at the stream, hear echoes of his laughter by the orange glow of the dying campfire. It was unfair, she thought with resentment, that after suffering her crazy tortured mind all day she couldn't just turn it off like the lamp and seek a modicum of peace.

She plumped her pillow again and shifted position. *Maybe,* she told herself, *just maybe I go over and over all this because I have a slight suspicion that I might be wrong.*

No. A voice cut in vehemently. She thought of the debilitating fear that had swept over her when she believed the emergency phone call from Kate had been about Craig. She thought of the way her heart had ceased to pound, how she had lost her breath, how the world had gone black. No, Kate could do it because Kate hadn't been through it before. And Brad was not quite in the same position as Craig. Brad would also eventually rise to a position where he would use his strategic reasoning from the vantage point of a desk.

But I would see Craig, Blair thought, finally making the positive admission. *Not steadily. And I still don't think I could ever marry him. I wouldn't want to know when he was coming or going.*

How ridiculous, she chastised herself. Neither of them could ever abide such a relationship. Which put her back to square one. Or did it? Oh, God, if she loved him enough, maybe she could bear anything, learn to control the fear.

Except that I'll probably not see him again. It's been three months. He didn't try to call me. He's probably already involved with someone new.

Suddenly she was angry. Here she was, three months after their parting and thousands of miles away, still pining for a glimpse of him. And he might very probably be in the arms of another woman at the very moment.

She simply wasn't going to do it anymore, she simply wasn't. *I will get over him,* she promised herself, and then she mentally repeated the words over and over again, as if she were counting sheep. Allowing her mind to shout was the only way to protect herself from the terrible, gut-wrenching pain of a picture of him being even touched by another.

Anger somewhat eased pain. And when she repeated the sentence long enough, she did eventually sleep. Physical exhaustion and the jet lag that was still catching up with her both took a toll and she found the release she sought.

Her anger was her first emotion as she began to wake in what seemed just seconds after she had finally fallen asleep. Who would disturb her? she wondered furiously, after all she had gone through to sleep. Her eyes opened, desperately trying to focus, and then she blinked furiously. There was a movement in her tent, a whispered rustling of sound, which was what had woken her. She opened her mouth to demand to know who was there, when a hand clamped firmly over it.

Now her eyes flew wide open with alarm and she began to struggle in a pure panic. "Will you please stop struggling!" a voice hissed. "I'll tell you, woman, sometimes I think you are more trouble than you're worth."

Blair froze for a second in stark amazement. She knew the voice, she knew the clean scent that seemed to wash over her,

she knew the strength and the comfort of the arms that held
her.

But it was impossible!

Before she could struggle again or attempt to talk, she was
lifted effortlessly from her cot and carried smoothly from her
tent. By the dim light of the dying compound fire she looked
up incredulously to see the angled profile of the man who
carried her swiftly by the other canvas tents and straight to the
pathway to the stream.

Impossible or not, her senses had not betrayed her. It was
Craig. A Craig not looking down to her, but walking with
purpose, his strides long and sure, his face set, the expression
unyielding and determined.

She started to struggle again, but the action was futile. She
was no more bother than a fly to him. What was he doing here?
she wondered desperately. Was something wrong again? What
was it this time? She would not be kept in the dark again; she
would not be manhandled like so much meat merely because
she was an assignment.

But, oh, it was torture. She was stunned, she was furious,
but she was glad of the feel of his arms, glad of the sight of
his relentlessly determined features. *Damn it, no,* she told herself. She was just getting over him. She needed the anger, Lord,
how she needed the anger, because she wanted to curl into his
arms and yet she must demand that he let her go.

But her thoughts didn't matter because her struggles were
futile. Her angry demands were nothing more than mumbled
gibberish that was barely audible even to her own ears since
he was able to carry her easily with one large hand still spanning
her mouth.

He didn't stop until they reached the stream, and once there
he still didn't release her, but sat carefully, still cradling her
in his arms, although he did remove the hand over her mouth.

"What the hell are you doing?" she demanded heatedly,
fighting the part of her that cried it didn't matter; it was simply

a miracle that should be taken as such. The hands that struggled against him wanted nothing more than to touch him, to devour him, to drink their fill of him with touch.

"That, princess, is a foolish question. I'm abducting you."

"Why? What happened?" Blair demanded sharply. She pushed furiously against his chest and received frustration for her answers. "Will you let go of me! Whose orders are you under now?"

"Whoa, please!" he chuckled, squeezing her more tightly. The moonbeams from the water were reflected in his eyes, making them appear more devilishly golden than ever, literally gleaming with satyric amusement. "Let's go back a step. Now, I can abduct you, or make a citizen's arrest for grand theft auto! I'll take abduction, I think. For grand theft auto, they could lock you up for years, and I'm not a patient man. Or perhaps I was, but my patience has been greatly strained lately. Not that I'm forgetting about the grand theft auto! Oh, my dear, you are going to pay for that one. I was snickered at! Actually snickered at! You entertained an entire department. A top agent, and my own car disappears under my nose! Oh, well, we'll get back to that. What were your questions? Let's see. Why? Why am I abducting you, that is. Because I want to. What happened? Nothing that I know of. I think there was a 'Will you let go of me?' in there. No. Never. And let me see, what was the last? Ah! Whose orders am I on? My own. Completely my own."

"What? Oh, Taylor! You scared me half to death. Of all the damn nerve . . ."

"Yes, ma'am. Of all the nerve. I told you I was full of nerve."

She must be going crazy, Blair decided, or else she was hallucinating. Maybe jungle fever had sneaked up upon her. She couldn't believe he was here, couldn't believe she was touching him. And she was terrified that she would forget everything in a minute and meld deliriously into his heat with no further explanation demanded, as if he were indeed an incredibly sweet dream.

"Then what are you doing here?" she snapped acidly. "You must have gotten directions wrong somewhere along the line. This spot on the globe is pretty quiet now. No wars, no volatile diplomatic problems to settle."

"Well, now, honey, I wouldn't say that. You're the most volatile problem I've come across in a long, long career," Craig drawled gravely, securing both her hands with one of his to free the other to tenderly trace the curve of her cheek. "You always seemed so insulted that I'd kidnapped you on orders," he explained softly. "I decided I had best come and kidnap you again, entirely on my own. I didn't read a single directive. Oh, but I will do my best to see that you stay in very good condition. I intend to make your welfare my highest priority."

"You're a crazy man, Taylor," Blair hissed.

"You always did have a wise mouth for a hostage," he admonished serenely, smiling down into her face as his fingers continued to roam its contours, reading the delicate lines by touch. "But then," he added huskily, "I suppose you know you can push the line almost as far as you like. You know damned well that I'm the hostage—I was captured for life in this very spot."

"Taylor," Blair murmured warily, afraid to trust what she was seeing, what she was hearing and feeling. He hadn't bothered to pick up a phone in Washington, but suddenly he was here. She forced herself to fight the urge to lean more closely against him. She had to have a guarantee that he was real, and not just an illusion induced by longing. And if he was real, she had to make some sense of all the gibberish he was talking. "You're crazy," she accused him again, torn between a desire to escape and run as far as she could and to hold on to whatever he had to give.

"Really, Blair," he said with mock annoyance, "you're

going to have to stop pegging me in categories when we're married. Husbands deserve respect. I can't allow you to run around accusing me of insanity all of the time.''

"Married?" Blair queried faintly, stalling for time. She had seen the diamond. She had known he would demand all. Nothing less. "I can't marry you, Taylor," she said harshly, "and you know it."

"You have to marry me," he corrected. "They still frown heavily upon . . . shall we say, living in sin, in diplomatic circles. I mean, suppose we meet the queen one day? How would I introduce you? I don't think I could look the lady in the eye and say, 'Meet Blair, my roommate and lover.' No, better not to struggle with the problem. Marriage is far more simple. Same name, et cetera. Besides, I'm a very possessive captor, and a bit of a romantic at heart. I like the idea of the vows. 'Love, honor, and cherish till death do us part.' It has a certain ring, don't you think.''

"Craig—"

"You are the most contrary person I have met, princess. You insist upon arguing with me when I can feel you shiver.'' His finger touched upon her lip, stilling any comment she might try to make. Then that finger slowly drew a line around her lips, nudging them apart to touch the moistness inside and retrace them.

"Craig," she protested miserably, "you know that I love you, you know that . . .'' She let that trail away. Yes, he knew she wanted him, but she wouldn't voice it aloud. There was still too much unsolvable between them. Unless he understood her terms, unless she could understand what he was really doing there, appearing out of the night like a cat to claim his prey. "But—"

He wasn't a man in a mood to hear buts. "Lord, Blair," he muttered harshly, "it's been three months." Before she could utter another word his mouth descended over hers with that same commanding harshness, a reminder that her need should have been as great as his own. He became persuasive only when her stunned stillness became a wealth of reciprocated warmth and sensual demand. Only when her muffled protests became moans, whimpered capitulations to all that was between them that couldn't be denied by logic or reason. Blair sought to move before she drowned in the sensations, before he swept her away without reason or thought. But his teeth caught her lower lip, holding her still. No matter. She had to give in to her own desires if only for the moment. She had wanted him so desperately. Admittedly she had been willing to give all for just such a chance. It was a long time before the kiss ended; held or freed, her lips couldn't part because of the erotic movement from his, nor could she stop her wildly sensitized fingertips from touching and touching again the thick hair that curled over his collar, the shoulder blades that were rippling with vibrant life beneath her caress. He was real; he wasn't a dream. No dream could possibly feel so enticing and delicious.

But it was an almost unendurable reality, because she couldn't bear the possibility of it ending. She finally managed to pull herself away, no longer thinking it possible to deny the shattering impact he could create at will upon her body, yet still determined that they come to an understanding.

"Craig," she gasped, aware that he did not release her at her whim, but simply because they both needed to draw breath, "you know that it can't be marriage."

"It will be marriage," he informed her, the stern cast of voice and eyes reminding her with quiet civility that he was a dangerous, authoritative man. She could be sure the aura of power he created was a guarantee that any order he gave in his work was carried out to a perfect T. But she didn't work for Craig Taylor.

"We've been through this!" she exclaimed irritably, wondering how it was possible to be touching someone and feeling as if she were clay to be molded while still wishing she could regain control and bat sense into his head. "Dear God, you idiot. Ray stumbled into a bad situation accidentally. You don't even walk into situations like that blindly; you run into them purposefully."

"Your faith," he told her chillingly, "is overwhelming. I was never suicidal, Mrs. Teile, merely well trained, and if I do say so myself, highly intelligent." For a moment his anger overwhelmed him. He had so much to say, so much to tell her. And above all that, he simply wanted her so desperately. It had been a long three months for him; he hadn't even thought of seeking the company of another woman. Three months in which he had learned to pray fervent prayers every night, just to get back to her, just to hold her, possesses her, love her, lose himself in her sheer, passionate beauty again.

"Craig," she was objecting, her voice faltering, but her determination coming through. "You never go on simple business trips. They are always classified missions. And someday something isn't going to go right diplomatically, something will become explosive, literally, with you there."

Blair stopped speaking suddenly, because of all things he seemed to have lost his anger and was laughing. His eyes were riddled with tender amusement. He knew the outcome of their discussion no matter what she had to say. But perversely he was once again willing to corner her, to force her hand.

"What is so funny now, Taylor?" she snapped, her frazzled nerves reaching a point of their own combustion. "I told you once I don't care to create your amusement for you."

"And what was my answer?" he chuckled, undaunted by her anger. She had a temper, but he could deal with that. "Something profound, I'm sure. Something like, 'Don't amuse me, then.' Love me, babe. Make me quiver, make me shake," he added huskily. "Burn me up, princess. Wildfire. It's so easy for you to create." His voice went low, intense. The laughter was gone as quickly as the anger. He was simply relentlessly determined. His hands became erratically entangled in the white cotton gown, growing more clumsy as the warmth of her firm silken breasts fell fully to his touch. He muttered a fierce "Oh, hell!" as he struggled with the tiny buttons. "Throw this damn thing away after tonight, will you?" he suggested.

"Taylor!" Blair grabbed feebly at the gown that was leaving her body despite her frenzied efforts to remain clothed. "Will you stop? You can't do this to me! You can't even bother to let me know when you come back alive. Then you show up when I've got my life in order!" She felt the roughness of his palms massaging her breasts as fabric left them, coursing her nipples to erect peaks on contact. "You can't do this to me!" she repeated, her fingers clawing into the fabric of his shirt with a torn tension.

"I'm doing it, aren't I?" he queried with satanically raised brows. He met her eyes for a second and then smiled as a quick jerk stole the gown entirely from her form. "No one's orders," he assured her with teasing consolation. "I shall always be able to say with a clear conscience that I seduced my wife purely on my own!" He half-set, half-pushed Blair aside and made quick work shedding his own attire while she looked on, unable to drop her eyes, unable to deny to herself that a bolt of desire as strong as lightning rippled through her simply at the sight of his splendid, muscled body.

Too late she stuttered out her confused protests. "Taylor, this isn't what you call a seduction. This is a—"

He was quick at stripping. Before she could finish her accusation, he had tossed his briefs aside, swung her into his arms, and heaved her into the water, managing to be at her side as she emerged sputtering.

"Hush up!" he charged her, pulling her back into his arms where his water-slick body crushed to hers, drawing a gasp of instant pleasure. "Lord," he groaned, complaining into the curve of her neck. "I'm marrying a shrew. Oh, well, some things can't be helped."

"You hush up!" Blair groaned. "And pay attention." It was difficult to concentrate with the vital warmth of his body seeping into hers, seeming to spark electric life to her flesh, her blood, her being. "I'm not marrying a spy."

"That's right," Craig agreed amicably, nibbling at her ear and unperturbedly running his lips down the length of her neck to graze her shoulder.

"All right," she panted, fighting for the reason that was fast becoming lost to her. "Call yourself whatever you like. I'm not marrying a Special Services diplomat!"

"That's right," he repeated, his voice growing deeper and more husky still as his lips continued their erotic movement without hesitation, spreading moist fire over the firm slope of her breasts, fastening with provocative motion over a nipple that was already hard and erect, tantalized to his pleasure by his touch. He stood back then, his hands fondling her breasts, his eyes upon them, his grip half crushing as if his hands really wallowed in silk. "God, babe, it's been so long . . ." Then his lips were on her again; he had been hungry too long, he desired a feast.

"Oh, stop!" Blair gasped. "No, don't stop . . ." she wailed in consternation. "You're too good at this diplomacy," she charged breathlessly, digging her fingers into his hair and almost crying out with want of him.

His words, spoken with bare coherence as he continued to mouth the flesh of her breasts, her throat, her shoulders, her arms with his lips, nipping, nuzzling gently, were still quellingly firm. "Tell me that you love me, Blair. Tell me that you want me, tell me that you will always be mine."

Tears formed in her eyes. They were partially of joy, partially of need, partially of the sorrow to come. His hands moved in the water beneath their waists. His fingers brushed along her upper thighs, hypnotizing her to sobs as they taunted ever closer to the center of her delirious heat and need.

"I love you," she murmured with a catch, arching against him. Why not vocalize the evident? "And I want you." Strong fingers coursed into her and she gasped, then she was sighing her pleasure, saying all that she had been trying to deny to herself. "I will always be yours, I will always be waiting, I want you so badly, I'll be anything you want, anywhere you want."

His lips came back to hers, but he didn't crush them. He was mumbling with as much gentle tenderness as he could summon while feeling he had really gone crazy with his urgency, raging out of control, and with the sweet, wonderful gratification of her words. "I'm a very good diplomat, darling, and I'll need to be, because, ahhhhhh . . ."

He forgot his train of thought as her hands, coursing his back, trailed a core of obliterating fire with nails grazing down the small of his back to his buttocks.

"Because what?" Blair persisted, suddenly struck by his words.

"What?" he asked distractedly, entrapped and fascinated as his tongue flicked against a pulse beating rampantly along her collarbone. "Oh, Lord, you do taste delicious."

"Craig!" Blair groaned in beseechment. "Because what? What are you talking about?"

He forced himself to meet her eyes, but he couldn't release her. She had given so much to say all that she had; she had loved him enough to accept her own terror and accept him for what he was—or what she thought he was. He couldn't tease any longer, he had to reassure her.

"I'm glad your Spanish is so profficient, my love. Because I'm not a spy or a diplomat of any kind any longer. I'm now the newest U.S. ambassador assigned to the embassy in Madrid. No more cloak-and-dagger, Blair, no more one last times. I'll never be leaving you again."

She was stunned speechless for several seconds. Then her lips began to tremble, "Oh, Craig! Really?"

"Really," he guaranteed her with a solemn smile. Then he was surprised to see her eyes take on a glimmer he was coming to recognize all too well. The famous Huntington temper.

"Damn you, Taylor!" she hissed. "You made me go through all that misery when you could have just told me straight off the bat! You could have told me first, you could have called me in Washington . . ."

"I wasn't set until that day in Washington!" he protested. "The final papers had to be signed, and after you refused to trust me—going so far as to steal my car to make your point!— I wasn't going to tell you a damn thing until it was positive, present fact! And besides, I like to hear how much you love me. It's good for my ego. Now, princess"—he jerked her back and took her into his arms and continued hoarsely—"it's been long. Three long months. Do you think we could hold off any further serious discussion for a while?"

Blair's anger faded and a smile slipped slowly but radiantly across her features. She stared at him for several seconds, absorbing all his words and suddenly thinking that all the gold in Fort Knox couldn't possibly rival the incredible power of his gaze. "*You* stopped," she said simply.

"Pardon?" he murmured. "What are you talking about now?"

She slid more snugly into his arms, arching against him, relishing the need she felt within the magnetic strength of his body. "*You* stopped," she repeated. "I'm absolutely certain that I told you just minutes ago *not* to stop. . . .

"Oh. Ohhhhh . . ." Craig returned, drowning his words as he kissed her mouth fully.

His arms around her almost crushed her in their embrace, but Blair loved the feeling of being enveloped by him, touching flesh against flesh from head to toe. He was right; it had been an excruciatingly long time.

Still they broke again in the waist-high water. Craig reached out a hand to tilt Blair's chin. His knuckles grazed tenderly against her cheek as he smiled. His thumb, rough, calloused, but ever gentle, very slowly traced the outline of her lips, the curve of her throat.

Then his fingers wound into her damp hair and he drew her to him, now planting kisses that were all fever from her forehead to her chin and all along the graceful arch of her neck. His tongue, warm and moist, drew circles along her earlobe as he uttered incomprehensible whispers that created a new wave of shivery delight.

Tears formed in Blair's eyes as she pressed her lips to his shoulder, her teeth taunting him in return. She had never thought that he could really be hers for a lifetime . . . that they might actually have a lifetime . . . that she could thrill to his touch again and again, finding that sweet, delirious abandon.

He seemed to be finding every sensitized, erogenous zone on her, and yet was persistent to find more. She was exploring the breadth of his back with tantalizing fingers, tasting the salt of his corded neck, when suddenly he sank into the stream, kissing her navel just at the point where the water lapped below it. Blair became certain that she would soon slip beneath the surface with dizzying desire. But ever sensitive to the messages of her body, Craig scooped her high in his arms and carried her to a distant point on the shore, one sheltered by the branches of a heavy tree, yet allowing the advantage of a lustrous vision of a full, benign moon. Blair vaguely noted that Craig had prepared for just this inevitable end to their conversation. A blanket was spread upon the sand-encrusted grass and a duffel bag was crammed against the trunk of the tree.

"Confident bastard, aren't you?" she whispered with a smile.

"I always set out to fully accomplish my missions, ma'am," he replied.

Blair started to chuckle, but her laughter died in her throat, becoming an escaped moan of uncontrollable need as he laid her down and settled over her, his frame warm and slick, powerful and demanding as it form-fit within the invitation of soft, parted thighs.

"I love you, Blair," he said tersely, his face dark and taut with his passion, his eyes the fire gold she knew so well.

She formed the reply, but neither heard it. It didn't matter; they both knew the words that sang between them with unspoken harmony. They had both denied want for so long, and so effectively tormented each other with seductive, loving preliminaries, that the moment of fusing together was so sweetly good that it was a little bit like dying. Excitement seemed to explode like a blast furnace, shooting into the moonlit sky and becoming a burst of stars that shattered the heavens like white light. They moved together, loved together, flew together, both wanting the exotic, whirling, pounding rhythm. Thrusting deeper and deeper until it consumed, to go on forever; both wanting to reach the peak of ultimate, infinite ecstasy; both knowing that they were forever forged together in the wonder of physical and mental sharing that was uniquely theirs.

Blair thought she would pass out at the burst of ecstasy that was physically hers as Craig brought them to the explosive climax. Maybe she did pass out. It would be excusable. He had taught her that such heights existed. It was only natural that she wallow in the physical sensations as a pupil who had learned well the lesson and was then long denied the experience.

"Thank you," she murmured, her whisper falling against Craig's ear as he remained with his length against hers, wondering if he would understand what she meant.

He raised his head and smiled at her tenderly; the smile told her he understood completely. "Not at all, princess," he teased lovingly. "We yes men love to be obliging."

Blair sniffed and smiled. "Taunt heard and rejected."

"Good, Blair," Craig said seriously. "Because I don't want you getting any ideas. I always did think I was better at giving orders than receiving them. Be prepared for what you're really getting. If you think you do have a yes man on your hands, you're going to be in trouble. I can be awfully opinionated and demanding."

Blair chuckled and brushed the damp hair back from his

forehead. "Tell me about it!" she moaned, her mocking tone
less than respectful.

He raised a brow at her. "Don't get cocky, there, princess!"
he warned. "I still owe you one for that car episode. Damn,
Blair, that was embarrassing! You're lucky the guys in S.S.
didn't discover that I'd lost my car, and that I'd been hood-
winked by a woman."

"Poor baby, they might have snickered louder. How did you
explain it?"

"I didn't," Craig admitted dryly. "I said I'd loaned my car
to a friend and then I gave the driver a good glare just to make
sure he believed my story."

"Oh," Blair murmured, quite certain one of his glares would
do the trick. A slight frown creased her brow. "Craig, I do
want us both to be prepared. Are you absolutely sure about
what you're doing? If you give up your work because of me,
I really am afraid that you'll get bored and wind up resenting
me, and then hating me, and then—"

"Blair!" He shushed her with a quick kiss and smiled ruefully as he adjusted his position and reached for the duffel bag.
"If we're going to keep talking, we might as well enjoy some
champagne brought just for the occasion. It isn't chilled just
right," he apologized, rummaging until he produced two plastic
glasses, put them into her hands, and fiddled with the cork
while she looked on with amused wonder. The cork popped
with a sharp bang. "The vintage, however, is excellent!"

Blair laughed softly through her frown as Craig poured them
each a bubbling portion. A powerful, dangerous man he might
be, but he was right about himself. He was a bit of a romantic
and she loved it. "To us," she murmured, striking her glass
to his, and taking a sip with her eyes glued to his over the rim
of the glass. "But, Craig—"

"To answer your question," he stated firmly, "trust me.
You did so once under much more difficult circumstances if
you'll recall. I know what I want out of life, and it all involves

you. I think I've spent half my life waiting for you to come along. But now I've put in my share of the rough side of the coin, and I'm glad I did. I'm ready to settle down. I began to feel the cravings for a home and stability when we met. Then I was afraid you'd never forgive me, except that I believed you loved me, and I trusted you enough to believe you'd understand all that I had done. I requested the transfer the moment I got back; it just took time. Actually''—he gave her a sheepish glance—''my new line of work is dependent on you. They were afraid I was a little too brash to be subtle, but Merrill knew I was after you, and, well, he had confidence, so he convinced the powers that be that you would keep me in line!''

Blair quirked a brow, unable to stifle laughter. ''I'm going to keep you in line? Marvelous!'' She sobered suddenly ''Oh, Craig, I started regretting walking out on you almost as soon as I did it! I was half dead without you anyway! And then with Kate and Brad getting married. Did you know about that?''

Craig nodded. ''I heard. Grapevine, you know. I'm happy for them. Two very nice people. And I'm grateful to them if they helped convince you that love could be stronger than fear.'' He took a long sip of his champagne. ''You know,'' he mused, his eyes beginning to twinkle, ''I knew I was coming for you no matter what you had said or done, but . . .'' He smiled. ''When Lorna told me that you had called Merrill, I was more determined than ever. I just wanted to wait until I had all my cards in my hand.''

Blair lowered her eyes and blushed. She should have known Lorna would mention her call to Craig. She didn't resent the interference, no more than she had resented being assured that Craig did love her, even when she had been sure it could all come to nothing.

''I had a bit of a run-in with your father too,'' Craig informed her dryly.

''Really?''

''He wanted to know my intentions.''

"Oh, no!" Blair chuckled.

"Your father is no laughing matter, young lady," Craig admonished her. "And I'll have you know this second abduction attempt was basically his idea, although he might not know it."

"Dad told you to ... to ... to ..."

"Seduce you? No. But he did imply that you were stubborn, and that I should 'employ any means' to get you legally wed. I don't think he liked the idea of your walking in with nothing on but a trench coat."

Blair smiled and once more lowered her eyes. "Dad is pretty great," she murmured. "He never batted an eye."

"I didn't think he would. Well—" he refilled the champagne glasses. "How do you think you'll like being an ambassador's wife?"

"I'll love it, Craig!" Blair vowed. He was never going to be happy without challenge, but she knew he was ready for his new challenge—a new source of power. The spoken word. "I'll love anything that you share with me," she promised. "I want to work with you."

"Good. We won't be able to fail. We'll be indomitable."

Blair shaded her eyes with a sweep of her lashes, hiding a secret grin. She was fully convinced he was indomitable all by himself. But she wasn't about to tell him so. Why spoil him?

"Now," he instructed, "hurry up and finish your champagne."

"Why?" Blair queried. "What is our hurry?"

"Okay," Craig said with an amiable grin, ignoring her question. "Don't finish your champagne. I can douse you with it and judge its merits along with the delectable taste of your flesh."

"Craig!" Blair tightly grasped her glass in protest, trying not to laugh. It was ridiculous. They were both sitting as naked as jaybirds in the middle of a jungle, sipping champagne, perfectly comfortable. "You didn't answer my question!" she exclaimed.

"We need some sleep," he told her blandly, "and I'm not quite ready to sleep." A single brow jiggled insinuatively. "Though I do have some ideas about what to do in the meantime . . . Since we're getting married in the morning I want to have you chastely returned to your tent before the padre shows up."

"In the morning!" Blair suddenly thought of the Hunger Crew. "Oh, Craig, we can't get married tomorrow. I still owe the crew time."

"My dear Mrs. Morgan Huntington Teile soon to be Taylor!" Craig feigned gross exasperation. "You forget you are dealing with a highly trained government mind. I have taken all that into consideration. I am on leave now. We don't make the move to Spain until January. That gives us plenty of time to finish out your two years together."

"You know," Blair said slowly, her love and appreciation sparkling her eyes to an emerald deeper than the sea. "I think I might really like that governmental mind of yours, my love. Not only are you going to make me the happiest woman in the world, you're going to make Dr. Hardy the happiest man!"

"Un-unh," Craig disagreed gravely "I'm going to be the happiest man." He shrugged. "Your father is going to be a little tiffed about not making the wedding, but he'll get over it." Craig paused, his brows furrowing together into a scowl as he noticed Blair ignoring him and rummaging through the duffel bag. "What are you doing now?"

"Looking for more champagne!" she laughed. "And oh, yes, Dad will be tiffed, but he will get over it." She threw her arms around Craig and met his eyes with heavy, sensual, half-closed lids. "I need that champagne. If we're going to have a champagne fight going here, I want plenty of my own ammunition!" It wasn't at all ridiculous to be sitting by the moonlit jungle stream stark naked sipping champagne.

It was beautiful and exotic. Craig to her would always be a man of the jungle, sleek and powerful as its predatory cats, as agile and superb as the wonders of nature that surrounded them.

He tipped her face to his. "As they seem fond of saying, princess, employ any means . . ."

She was lost again in the yellow-gold of compelling eyes as they descended over hers.

EPILOGUE

The letter on George Merrill's desk was marked Personal and was accompanied by a small package. With knit brows and a growing smile of suspicion, he first ripped open the letter with a quick gesture of thumb and forefinger. His smile turned to a broad grin when he saw that the message had been written on interoffice stationery.

MEMO
From: Taylor
To: G.M.

Thought you might like to know that the royal wedding took place Monday morning. Princess became Mrs. Craig Taylor at ten A.M. our time, a relief because we can dispense with the Morgan, Huntington, and Teile. Says she is looking forward to Spain. I think the Spanish will like our American royalty.

Have two days honeymooning in Mexico City so won't

waste time writing. (Dr. Hardy got generous. Forty-eight hours, then we have to be back.)

C.T.

P.S. Enclosed turquoise earrings are for Lorna with love from Blair and myself. (Did you think it was for you? Really, Chief, turquoise won't do much for your eyes.)

The return didn't catch up to Craig and Blair for almost two months, since the Hunger Crew had left the village behind to move inland and bring relief to a few of the major cities.

MEMO
From: G.M.
To: Taylor

Craig!

My heartiest congratulations. Missed the royal wedding, but will be there with bells on for the royal reception Huntington is planning in December.

Speaking of Huntington, beware! The man shocked us all with a temper tantrum when he heard wedding took place without him present. Then he laughed for two days straight. Read Blair's letter over and over, grinning like a coon. Word of warning—watch your step with your father-in-law.

Give the princess my love. (And best wishes and thanks from Lorna.) Long life and happiness to you both.

The Chief

Another letter marked Personal appeared on the chief's desk a few days after Thanksgiving. George Merrill smiled before opening it.

MEMO
From: Taylor
To: G.M.

   Sir,

   This should catch you, with any luck, a week or so
before our arrival home. Am looking forward to seeing
you before leaving for Spain, and want you to check your
schedule now for a small party by princess and myself
on Christmas Eve. The occasion is CLASSIFIED, but
I'll clue you into the surprise since it's in respect to
warnings regarding Andrew Huntington. Don't worry, I
can handle the man. We plan to announce that a royal
birth will take place early next summer. Think that will
keep him smiling?

                                        Taylor

ROMANCE FROM JANELLE TAYLOR

ANYTHING FOR LOVE   (0-8217-4992-7, $5.99)

DESTINY MINE   (0-8217-5185-9, $5.99)

CHASE THE WIND   (0-8217-4740-1, $5.99)

MIDNIGHT SECRETS   (0-8217-5280-4, $5.99)

MOONBEAMS AND MAGIC   (0-8217-0184-4, $5.99)

SWEET SAVAGE HEART   (0-8217-5276-6, $5.99)

ROMANCE FROM FERN MICHAELS

DEAR EMILY   (0-8217-4952-8, $5.99)

WISH LIST   (0-8217-5228-6, $6.99)

AND IN HARDCOVER:

VEGAS RICH   (1-57566-057-1, $25.00)